Behind THE Camera

CHELSEA CURTO

To those of you who have been with me since the very beginning.
Thank you for sticking around.

*(And to the girlies who love to hear **good girl**, but also love to say **good boy**. This one is for you.)*

CONTENT WARNINGS

While this book contains lots of laughter and tender moments, there are some other elements that might be triggering to some readers.

First and foremost, this is a book with explicit sexual content. The scenes are detailed and graphic, and there are multiple of them. If open door romance isn't your jam, I highly suggest you don't read any further.

This story also revolves around a single dad. There is no other woman drama (he has full custody and she's not in the picture at all), but please be aware his daughter stems from a one night stand. There's a brief conversation about that night between our main characters, but he hasn't been with anyone since his daughter's birth.

Additionally, his daughter has had a lot of nannies. The number is high because it's fiction. I really wanted to drive home how much of a struggle it's been for him to find someone who genuinely cares about his daughter. He's the one who lets them go...they don't leave because of him!

Full list of trigger warnings:

-explicit sexual themes including multiple descriptive intimate moments between two consenting adults and words that might be considered degrading (briefly mentioned)
-explicit language
-mention of divorce (brief, one scene)
-parental abandonment (brief, one scene)
-a concussion from a football injury (mentioned with light details)

As always, my DMs are always open on Instagram (@authorchelseacurto) if you have any other questions or concerns about possible content warnings.

Take care of yourselves, friends.

CHARACTER CATCH UP

While Behind the Camera is a stand alone novel, it does mention characters from the first two books in the series, **Camera Chemistry** and **Caught on Camera**. I wanted to give a quick catch up in case you haven't read book one and two so you don't feel lost.

In **Camera Chemistry**, Aiden (Maven's dad) and Maggie meet at a strangers photo shoot and have a one night stand. They end up falling for each other and live happily ever after.

In **Caught on Camera**, Lacey and Shawn (Dallas's coach) stumble into a fake dating relationship after a kiss cam kiss at his football game goes viral. They also fall for each other and live happily ever after.

Maven and Dallas are mentioned briefly in the first two books, but have almost no interaction until the start of Behind the Camera.

As always, my DMs are always open on Instagram (@authorchelseacurto) if you have any other questions.

ONE

DALLAS

"I THINK I MIGHT BE FUCKED."

Shawn Holmes, the head coach of the D.C. Titans and one of the best football players of all time, barely glances up from the whiteboard he's studying at his desk. I stand in the doorway of his office and wait for him to acknowledge me. After three long minutes, he finally lifts his head.

"If you didn't kill anyone, steal anything, or say something derogatory or offensive, it's salvageable." He caps a purple dry erase marker and gives me his full attention. "What did you do Lansfield?"

"Come on, Coach." I sit in the chair across from him and hold my daughter, June, on my lap. At four, she hates sitting still, so I bounce my knee up and down to keep her smiling. We already had one meltdown today, and I'd like to get through this afternoon without another. "You know I'd never get myself in trouble."

"Debatable. I think you might give me the biggest headache out of everyone on the team. Don't think I forgot about the time you gave my wife your jersey to wear to a game," he says.

"*Technically* you weren't dating Lacey at the time, so *techni-*

1

cally I didn't break any rules." I grin when he rolls his eyes. "It was years ago. You sleep next to her every night, and your PDA at the Super Bowl made more headlines than our win. Don't tell me you're still pissed about it."

"I'm probably going to be pissed about it forever."

"Wow," I whisper in June's ear, loud enough for him to hear me. "Mr. Shawn doesn't know how to take a joke, June Bug. The old man really needs to lighten up."

"You have five seconds to tell me what's going on, or I'm kicking you out."

"I need a nanny."

"You have a nanny."

"I *had* a nanny," I say.

"What happened to Tonya?"

"Gone."

"Alicia?" he asks.

"Fired."

"Brittany?"

"How the hell do you remember all of their names? I can barely keep track, and they worked for me. Brittany is sailing off into the sunset, but that one isn't my fault. She's following her boyfriend out west for his new job."

"You've had so many nannies, I can mention any woman's name, and chances are it's probably someone you've hired," Shawn says. "What does your lack of childcare have to do with me?"

Because I need help, I think.

A lot of fucking help.

I never thought I'd be a thirty-year-old Super Bowl champion with a four-year-old daughter, but here we are.

I guess that's the thing about life: it's fucking unpredictable.

I went from buying bottles of vodka to warming up bottles of milk.

Late nights at the club and enjoying the VIP section with my teammates turned into me sitting in a rocking chair with a newborn, trying to get her to fall asleep.

My credit card purchases changed from new TVs and a top-of-the-line grill to baby gates and pacifiers.

It's been a learning curve. A painstaking process with mistakes and fuck ups and ten million lessons in humility and empathy.

But there's also been a lot of good.

I never dreamed of having children or being a dad. I was the fun uncle; the one who spoiled the shit out of his niece and always gave her back to her mom at the end of the day.

I never thought I could care about something more than I cared about football—sports have always been the center of my life, and there was no way anything was going to top the game I loved.

Then June came along.

When I look at her dark eyes and brown hair that matches mine, I realize I didn't have a clue what true love was until I held her in my arms for the very first time.

I feel immense joy every second I'm with her. My heart is full, and I know that despite all the ups and downs, everything worked out exactly how it was supposed to. She's the most important person in the world to me, and no one else will ever come close.

I'm just overwhelmed. Fucking exhausted and guilty that I'm feeling this way.

No one tells you how hard it is to be a parent, and no one tells you how hard it is to be a single parent.

I'm dropping the ball on being a dad, a teammate, and a human.

I can do better—I *need* to do better—but I can't do it alone.

I scrub a hand over my face and wonder how many of my problems I should unload on Shawn.

When he first joined the Titans, he implemented weekly player-coach conferences as a way to check in on us individually. We usually use the time to talk about areas of improvement on the field and analyze game film.

Occasionally they turn into a makeshift therapy session, and I think we might be heading that way today.

"The season starts in a few weeks. My parents are leaving on a six-month cruise around the world. My sister can't get any time off from work to come up and visit until Christmas, and I don't know how I'm going to manage playing football while also raising June by myself. Maybe you should move me to the practice squad," I say. "Hell, maybe I should just retire."

Shawn leans forward with a deep frown on his face. "Start from the beginning."

"I've been through seventy-one nannies in four years," I say, and if it wasn't so pathetic, I'd laugh. "No one has stuck around for longer than a couple of days."

"*Seventy-one*? How is that even possible? You're not an asshole to them, are you?"

"Asshole," June repeats, and I cover her ears.

"Let's keep the locker room talk PG," I say. "She repeats everything, and the last thing I need on my list of failures as a father is her cursing like a sailor before she can tie her shoes."

"Sorry. That's my fault," Shawn says with a sheepish grin. "Why are you having such a problem with the nannies?"

"They, uh, all want to sleep with me or befriend me so I can introduce them to the other guys on the team. One literally told me she was only there because she heard I might have a piercing on—" I clear my throat. "You get the idea."

"Do you?"

"Dang, Coach. Buy a man dinner first before asking about his Prince Albert piercing. I don't, by the way. I'm piercing-free."

"That's something I never thought I'd learn about you."

"I'm full of surprises," I say with a smile, and he rolls his eyes.

"So these women you hire are there for you, not for your kid?"

"Exactly. June isn't a priority to them. All they care about is getting close to an athlete or finding a way to weasel their way into this lifestyle. It's the same thing, every single time. They have a resume with lots of experience, and they pretend to care about my daughter in the initial interview. I hire them. A week passes, then they start asking questions about tickets and locker room access and how much money I make, and that's when I let them go. I'm a kicker, for Christ's sake. I'm on the field for five minutes a game if I'm lucky. If this is what it's like for me, I can't imagine what QBs deal with."

"You must be fantastic in bed."

"I mean, maybe? I don't know." I move my hands away from June's ears and shrug. "I haven't been with anyone since JB was born, and before that, there was only one woman, one time, since I entered the league."

"You're not serious," he deadpans.

"I'm dead serious. Football—and now my daughter—are my priorities. I'm not interested in a random hookup. I had a couple in college when the stakes weren't so high, but that lifestyle isn't for me."

"We don't need to get into a conversation about your..." Shawn trails off, and his eyes flick to June. "Can she spell?"

"She's barely mastered the whole alphabet. Pretty sure she's not entering the National Spelling Bee anytime soon."

"Right. We don't need to talk about your s-e-x life. I don't want my ears to bleed, and I feel bad for you."

"Lack of s-e-x life. My right hand wants nothing to do with me anymore."

"Thanks for that visual, Lansfield. I need to wash my eyes out with soap now. Okay. Let's figure out a solution. When do you need someone to watch June? On game days? During the week?"

"Game days I have covered. She goes to the nursery when I'm in the stadium. It's all the other times that have me stressed out. I don't want her to have to sit on the sidelines and watch practice every afternoon. She should be playing with dolls and coloring books, not kicking tees."

"Let me do some digging," he says. "I'll see if anyone has any connections. Are there any personality traits to avoid? Certain kinds of people you want to stay away from?"

"Someone who doesn't want to sleep with me is literally the only criteria."

"Great. That's going to eliminate ninety-nine percent of the eligible population. This won't be difficult at all."

I smirk and wink at him. "I think Mr. Shawn likes me, June Bug."

"Alright. You're done here." He gestures to the door. "I have something else I need to get to."

"During our scheduled conference time? You're making me feel like a middle child."

"This isn't our scheduled time. That's tomorrow. It's always on Thursdays, and today is Wednesday."

"Oh." I frown. "Shoot. I guess I got my days mixed up. Sorry. I'm only getting a few hours of sleep a night."

Shawn's face softens in understanding, and he pinches the bridge of his nose. "I'm sorry for giving you crap. This is important, and I'm being a di—jerk. Give me a few days to try and see what I can do on my end, okay? Let's postpone our meeting tomorrow. Go home after practice, and we'll get together next week. Hopefully I'll have some answers by then."

"Thanks, Coach." I reach across the table to shake his hand. "I appreciate you."

"Thanks, Coach," June repeats, and I laugh, standing up and setting her on the floor.

"Ready to head home, JB?" I ask.

She nods and wraps her fingers around my thumb, waving to Shawn. "Bye, Mr. Shawn," she says, and he cracks a smile.

"Bye, June. Thank you for coming to visit today. You be good for your dad, okay? He's doing a really good job, even if he doesn't feel like he is all the time."

"That's the nicest thing you've ever said to me." I grab June's pink backpack and sling it over my shoulder. "See you at practice tomorrow."

"Chin up, Lansfield. We'll get through this," Shawn says, and he gives me an encouraging nod.

June and I leave his office and head down the hall to the player's parking garage. I sigh and throw up an offering, a prayer, a fucking smoke signal to the universe, hoping I find the help I desperately need soon.

TWO

MAVEN

I'VE BEEN COMING to UPS Field for years. I'm usually sitting up in the stands with my dad and his girlfriend, Maggie, as we watch his best friend and my godfather, Shawn, coach the Titans from the sidelines.

It's different today.

I walk down the tunnel as a member of the team. A recent addition to the organization and experiencing the stadium in new light with Shawn by my side.

Players pass us in their practice gear as they head to the athletic trainers' offices for stretching and an ice bath. Someone from the ticket sales department stops Shawn for a quick autograph on a framed photo from the Super Bowl being given to a loyal season ticket holder who's been around for thirty years.

We're still weeks away from the season starting, but it's busy and hectic. There are dozens of people who need to be in dozens of places, and I love seeing things from this side.

"I know it could be classified as nepotism, but thank you for getting me this job, Shawn," I say to him as we come around a corner. "Dad was *pissed* at me for deciding not to finish college, but I don't know what I want to do with my life yet. Why waste all that time and money when I'm still undecided about my future?"

"I got you an interview as an in-game photographer, not a throne to a European country, Mae. And you got yourself hired." Shawn chuckles and nudges me with his elbow. "Don't worry about your dad. He'll come around. There's nothing wrong with not getting your degree, and there's a different route for everyone to get to their final destination. This is just a stop along the way for you."

"You're getting wiser with age. How's fifty treating you?"

"Look who's talking, smart ass. Twenty-two years old and a legal adult who can drink. When the hell did you grow up?" he asks as we stop near the locker room. "This is all happening too fast, and I hate it."

"It all happened too fast for me, too. One minute, I'm a Division I athlete with my future charted out for me, and the next I'm tearing my ACL and losing my scholarship." I adjust the bag on my shoulder and wince under the weight of the new Nikon Z9 camera my dad bought me. "Maybe this change will be good for me. I love photography, and now I have a chance to figure out who I might be away from cleats and a ball."

"Only to take photos of guys wearing cleats and throwing a ball. I can't promise working here will open other doors for you long term, but you deserve a shot to find success. To find yourself too."

"Thanks." I loop my arm around his waist and hug him tight. "You've always been my favorite honorary uncle and godfather."

"I'm your only honorary uncle and godfather, you little shit," he says into the top of my head. "Johnathan, the lead photographer, is going to meet you in the admin offices, and you'll be with him the rest of the day. Do you know where the elevators are?"

"I'll figure it out. Thanks for the pep talk, Shawn."

"You're going to do great. And if any of my guys give you a hard time, let me know. I'll handle them."

"Don't worry. I'm going to stay out of everyone's hair." I frown when I pull away from his embrace and see his eyebrows wrinkled together. "Are you okay? You seem a little off today."

"I'm fine. Just dealing with some personal stuff with my players. Football is a lot more fun when all I have to do is coach instead of put out fires and find childcare, but it's part of the job. Helping my team solve problems off the field allows them to play better on the field."

"That's why they pay you the big bucks. Anything I can help with?"

"Definitely not. Have a good weekend, Mae. I'll see you on Monday for the team photo. Stay out of trouble," he says.

I wave goodbye and turn toward the elevators that will take me up to the admin offices on the fourth floor. Anticipation zips up my spine as I pass the photos on the tunnel walls. Pivotal moments in Titans history are captured on film and hung with pride. I've passed them a hundred times when I walked through these halls as a fan, but it feels extra special to take a second and study them today.

I see the picture of their first Super Bowl win a few years ago in Las Vegas and the elation on the players' faces as they huddle around the Vince Lombardi trophy. Next to it is a smaller image from a team event at the D.C. Food Bank on Thanksgiving last year. Two dozen Titans players are in their community engagement shirts and interacting with people as they scoop stuffing and hand out turkeys.

My favorite photo is the one of Shawn dressed up like Santa Claus and sitting in the back of a sleigh in the middle of UPS Field. He's surrounded by Christmas trees with twinkling lights, and there is a sack of presents by his side.

Anticipation makes way for excitement knowing my images

might be up there soon. A game-winning touchdown or an undefeated season forever immortalized by the very camera hanging from my shoulder. Scrimmages and home games with seventy thousand fans roaring in the crowd.

I'm doing this.

And I'm going to do it damn well.

My phone buzzes in my pocket, and I pull it out, continuing on my way toward the elevators up ahead. I smile when I read a text from my friend and old college teammate, Isabella, inviting me to grab dinner and drinks with her tonight to celebrate my first day on the job.

I fire off a quick response, distracted by the list of choices she gives me. My attention is on picking between margaritas or a wine bar, not where I'm walking, and I run straight into something.

A tall, sturdy, warm something.

I stumble. My phone goes flying. My bag slides off my shoulder and falls to the floor, and I nearly go tumbling backward. A hand wraps around my wrist, keeping me on two feet and not my ass, and whoever it is must be strong as hell.

I blink and try to get my bearings. When I steady myself, I find Dallas Lansfield, the Titans kicker, blinking right back at me.

"Maven?"

He's wearing a backwards hat. The sleeves of his sweatshirt are pushed up to his elbows and show off sun-kissed skin and forearms with thick veins. My gaze bounces to his sharp cheekbones and wide, dark brown eyes.

I haven't seen him up close in a couple of years, and he's more intimidating than I remember. Broad shoulders. Biceps straining against the cotton of his hoodie. Messy brown hair with pieces that sneak out from under the cap on his head. A dazzling smile and dimples on both of his cheeks. At six-foot-two with long arms and even longer legs, he's tall enough that I have to tilt my chin back to meet his gaze.

He still has the same deep, rumbly voice. The same southern twang, drawing out the vowels in my name like he wants to hold them to his chest like a secret before he lets them go. The same curve of his mouth and the flicker of mischief in his eyes.

Hell.

He looks good.

"That's me," I say, and my voice is two octaves higher than normal.

I'm flustered and thrown off balance, and I add an awkward wave to seal the deal of being an absolute loser in front of a guy who's been voted America's favorite athlete.

"What are you doing here?" He unwraps his fingers from my wrist and bends down to pluck my phone and bag off the floor. "Are you visiting Shawn?"

"I actually got a job as a team photographer. I'm now a proud member of the Titans organization."

"No way. Congratulations. I didn't know you were into photography."

"It's always been a hobby of mine, and after dropping out of college, I—" I bite the inside of my cheek and swallow down the story he doesn't want to hear. "Sorry. I'm rambling. Yes, I'm interested in photography."

"Awesome. Guess that means I'll see you around the stadium instead of in the stands. It's way more fun down here, and it'll be good to have some new faces on the sidelines." His grin stretches wider, and there's no way there's not a line of women fawning over him at every fan meet and greet. "It's been a couple years since I've seen you, hasn't it?"

"Yeah. It feels like you fell off the face of the earth," I say. "How is everything?"

"Daddy." There's a girl at his side tugging on his athletic shorts. She's so small, I didn't notice her before. "She's pretty."

"Oh, gosh. Sorry," I say. "I didn't mean to—"

"No, you didn't. I'm just—"

"I should—"

"Pretty," she says again, interrupting us. "Pretty, Daddy. Say hi?"

Dallas scoops the little girl in his arms and holds her against his hip. "Sure, June Bug. Maven, this is my daughter, June. We're working on speaking in full sentences, so to translate for my babbling spawn, she thinks you're pretty, and she wants to say hi."

My eyes dart between them.

She's the spitting image of him, a carbon copy down to the way her nose turns up at the end and the dimple on her left cheek. Even her eyes twinkle the same way, flecks of gold mixed in with the brown, and I don't know what to say.

Dallas and I aren't friends; we're more like friend-adjacent, cordial in passing when we see each other at games or team events but never close enough to know he has a *daughter*. He's done a good job of keeping her out of the spotlight.

My gaze bounces to his left hand to see if there's a ring there, but all I find is a smudge of pink nail polish chipping on his middle finger.

"I didn't know you were married," is the first thing my brain decides to come up with, and I cringe. "Sorry. Wow. That was incredibly invasive."

"I'm not," he answers. "It's just June and me."

"Oh. *Oh.* Right." I nod, and I turn my attention to the girl in his arms. Her cheek rests on his shoulder, and she watches me. "Hi, June. It's nice to meet you. You have a very pretty name."

June giggles and buries her face in Dallas's sweatshirt. I

glance up at him, afraid I might have said something wrong, but he gives me a reassuring smile.

"She can be shy. Besides the guys on the team and her nannies, she doesn't meet a lot of new people," he explains, then he frowns. A line of wrinkles forms across his forehead, and suddenly he looks years older. "That makes it seem like I never let her leave the house. I do, clearly. I'm just protective over who is in her life, and now I'm talking your ear off, aren't I?"

"Not at all. I understand why you're protective of her. Not that I fully understand; I don't have a kid or anything. There's nothing *wrong* with having a kid, I'm just—" I laugh. "This is going well, isn't it?"

His frown melts away, and he grins. Two dimples again, and a tint of color on his cheeks. "I don't know about you, but this is the most fun I've had all day."

"That means you have low expectations for fun." I check my watch and gesture to the elevators behind him. "I should get going. My orientation starts soon."

"Good luck today. I'm sorry for knocking you over."

"Don't worry about it. I wasn't paying attention. I'm the guilty party here."

"Call it even by saying hi at the preseason game in a couple weeks?" Dallas asks. "We can't let this be our only interaction this year. That would be tragic."

"I will. I promise. It can only go up from here." I give him and June a wave and start down the tunnel. My shoulder grazes his arm as I pass, and I get a whiff of his cologne; wood and spice. Vanilla. The faint trace of coffee beans. "Have a good practice."

"See you around, Maven. Don't be a stranger."

I all but dive headfirst into the elevator. I let the doors shut before I take a deep breath and sort through the last five minutes.

Holy *shit*.

Dallas is a *dad*.

A *girl dad*, and she's the cutest kid I've ever seen.

I bite my bottom lip and hit the button for the fourth floor, grinning to myself as the elevator lurches up.

This season just got a lot more fun.

THREE
DALLAS

"CAN someone please tell me why we're at a restaurant that serves chicken fingers and chocolate milk to children in sippy cups when we could be at the strip club?" Maverick Miller, captain of the D.C. Stars hockey team and one of my best friends, leans back in his chair and groans. "I'm miserable."

"Because taking her to the strip club would be child endangerment." I shoot him a look and hand June a coloring book. She grins at me from her booster seat, and when she grabs an orange crayon to color in the house I drew for her, I take the opportunity to flip Maverick off. "I'm sorry this is so difficult for you."

"It's fine. I'll survive." He grabs his drink off the table and swirls the Old Fashioned around. "Maybe next time we could pick somewhere that doesn't have eighteen dipping sauces on the menu."

"I don't think there are enough dipping sauces, if we're being honest."

"Okay, Georgia Peach. You know I love June Bug, but you couldn't find a sitter? Some college kid looking for money?" he asks.

"Nope. No sitters, unless you're offering," I say.

"I have my hands full with the kids at the rink doing my summer skating camp. You could always bring JB by one day, if you want. I'll teach her the hockey basics, and she'll be hitting slap shots by the end of the afternoon. Way better than tossing a football around. You run for like, eight seconds."

"Says the guy who only skates for forty-five seconds. I'm going to keep my daughter on dry land for the time being. Preferably somewhere she can't break a leg or lose a tooth."

Maverick grins. "I've never lost a tooth."

"That's a shame, because I've never met someone as cocky as you. It would humble you a bit. Bring you back to mortal attractiveness instead of whatever god-like fantasy you have of yourself in your head."

He laughs. "Good one, Dal. The invitation is there, if you ever want to bring her by. Even if it's just an afternoon you need off. My teammates would love to hang out with her." His eyes flick across the table to Reid Duncan, our other best friend, and he shakes his head. "Are you going to join the conversation or stare at your phone all night?"

Reid pushes his thick-framed glasses up his nose. He's ignoring us—his attention has been on his screen for the last twenty minutes. June stole six French fries off his plate, and he didn't notice. Now he looks pissed we're distracting him.

"You know my phone is my job," he draws out. "I literally cannot make money unless I'm using it."

"You do social media for the Titans," Maverick argues. "Not insider trading. What the hell do you need to post at eight on a Wednesday night during the off season?"

"Anything to keep our fans engaged," Reid grumbles. "My boss has been up my ass lately."

"Ass," June repeats, and I sigh, defeated.

"Watch it," I tell Reid. "Her hearing is sharp, and she's probably going to be expelled from school next year for calling someone an inappropriate name she heard us use."

"Maybe they deserve it," Maverick says. "We have to teach her to stand up for herself."

I'm still not sure how we stumbled into a companionship that's stretched for more than half a decade. We're from different backgrounds with different personalities, yet somehow, we work.

They're my best friends. The guys who jumped in to help when I brought home a newborn baby from the hospital and didn't ask any questions. We watched videos on changing diapers together. They learned how to swaddle an infant, and they were there when June took her first steps.

She's just as much theirs as she is mine, and I don't think I would've made it to this point without them by my side.

"Yeah, maybe. But I don't want to be pulled into a principal's office and get lectured on how my kid is dropping four letter curse words before she can spell her own name." I turn my attention to Reid. "Do you need help with social media?"

"I'm out of ideas for fresh, new content. Everything is overused at this point," he explains.

"What about a player takeover?" Maverick suggests. "A day in the life thing. Or have fans send in questions and let the players answer them. Someone commented on our TikTok the other day and asked which of our teammates we'd let our sister date, and it was hysterical. Our social media girl turned it into a whole video."

"That's actually really smart," I agree.

Reid grabs a napkin from the stack in the center of the table. He pulls an honest to god pen out from behind his ear and starts jotting down notes. "Brilliant, Mav. What else do you have?"

"Nothing, but Dallas can be the first installment." Maverick gives me a smug grin. "He's thoughtful, and I'm sure he'd *love* to help out his friend."

"Absolutely not."

"Come on," Reid says. "I'll monitor the questions and only ask the appropriate ones. Please? Everyone loves you. You have that southern charm, and Cosmo voted you the hottest NFL player. We could use that to our advantage."

"There's a hottest NFL player award? And they picked *me*?" I stare at him.

"They love your dimples," Reid adds, and he bursts out laughing. "And there was a comment about how you flip your hair when you take off your helmet."

"I do not flip my hair." I narrow my eyes. "You're messing with me."

"Our handsome boy." Maverick pinches my cheek, and I bat him away. "First up, a Cosmo article. Next, People's *Sexiest Man Alive*. We need to start a campaign."

"Y'all are full of it."

"Come on, Dal," Reid says. "It would be fun. People love stuff like this, and our posts with players always score more engagement."

I pinch the bridge of my nose. "Fine. But leave June Bug out of it."

Reid pumps his fist in the air. "*Yes*. Thanks, Dal. You're the best."

"I don't know why you're so secretive about your life." Maverick spears a bite of mac and cheese on his fork and hands it to June. "You're the All-American guy. You come from a small town and work hard. You have the world's cutest daughter, and you're a Super Bowl champion. The personal ad practically writes itself. What is there to hide?"

"I don't want a personal ad, and I don't want to invite people into the conversation about my life." I shrug and finish off my beer. "Interviewing me seems like a lot of fuss for a video on the internet."

"I'm not only interviewing you," Reid says. "I'm going to do this with everyone on the team. You won't have to share your deepest, darkest secret. Just your favorite dessert."

"Ice cream!" June says, and we all laugh.

"Ice cream is the best." Maverick lifts her from her booster seat with one tattooed arm and pulls her into his lap. "What do you say, JB? Should Daddy help out Uncle Reid?"

"Please don't call me Daddy," I say.

"Nah. I'm definitely going to call you Daddy every chance I get."

"Yes." June nods and claps, obviously elated by the attention. "Daddy help."

"You heard the girl." Maverick tosses her in the air and catches her. "You're required to do it now."

"Fine. Come up with some questions, Reid, and I'll answer them after practice one day."

"Thanks, man." He clasps my shoulder and smiles. "You're the best."

I stand up and take June from Maverick, bouncing her against my hip. "I should get going. I'm meeting with Shawn tomorrow before practice to see if he's had any luck in finding me a nanny."

"You're still looking?" Maverick asks. "This has to be a new record."

"You're telling me. Maybe number seventy-two will be lucky."

"Hang in there." Reid gives me a sympathetic look. "The right person is going to come along soon."

"Love that optimism, but I'm not getting my hopes up." I kiss the top of June's head and hold her close to my chest. "Say bye to Uncle Mav and Uncle Reid, JB."

"Bye bye." She waves to the guys then buries her face in my shirt. It's past her bedtime, and I know she'll be asleep the second I get her in her car seat. "Love you."

"We love you more, June Bug." Maverick grins, and he turns his attention to me. "We love you too, Dal. We're here if you need us."

"Thanks, y'all. I appreciate you."

I slip out of the restaurant, grateful when the sticky July air hits my face.

Tomorrow, I think.

Tomorrow something good is going to come my way.

It fucking has to.

FOUR

DALLAS

"I'M REALLY HOPING you have some good news for me." I sit in the chair across from Shawn after dropping June off at the stadium nursery and put my elbows on my knees. "Or I might actually cry."

Shawn winces. "Define good."

I groan. "How is this so difficult?"

"I'm sorry, Dal. I'm still looking. Lacey has some babysitter recommendations from people around her office, but no one is old enough to stay overnight while you're out of town. What about bringing June on the road with us?"

"And, what? Start a daddy daycare with all the free time I have between film review, traveling, practices and switching time zones? No way. I'm not letting her development suffer because of me."

"I admire how committed you are to her," Shawn says. "It says a lot about your character."

"Are we just going to wait for someone to bust through the door?" I laugh and shake my head. "Shit like that doesn't happen in real life, Coach, and unless we figure this out before the season starts, I think it'll be best for me to take a spot on the inactive roster."

"I'm not—"

The door to Shawn's office flies open. Someone tumbles inside, a flurry of limbs and blonde hair and irritated sighs.

"Holy shit," I whisper. "Did I just speak something into existence? Am I a prophet?"

Maven Wood walks into the room. She drops her bags at her feet—there are five of them that I can count—and groans.

"I am so pissed off," she says. "Why can't anything go my way?"

Shawn's eyes bounce to me, and he mouths *sorry*. I wave him off, unbothered. It feels good to know I'm not the only one who doesn't have my shit together.

"Mae. I'm a little busy right now," Shawn says. "Can you come back later?"

Maven turns her head and spots me for the first time. Her mouth pops open, and her eyes turn into wide blue saucers. She blushes, and my lips twitch in amusement.

"Hey. We're really not good at this whole running into each other thing," I say.

"Shit," she curses. "I'm so sorry. This is so unprofessional. I didn't mean to disturb anyone."

"It's fine." I rub my thumb across my jaw and try to hide my smile. "I'm having an existential crisis myself. Want to stay? We can compare stories and see who has it worse. It could be fun."

"Are you sure?" Maven asks. "I don't want to interrupt anything important."

"You're not. Trust me."

"What are you worried about?" She accepts my invitation and plops into the seat next to me. Her thigh knocks against mine as she gets settled, and I pull my leg away to give her more room. "Which cleats to wear at practice? Which hair flip of yours is best?"

I don't bother to cover up my grin. "You saw that article?"

"I think all of America saw that article. They picked a really nice photo of you. Your football pants look exceptionally white."

"Thanks, Maven. You really know how to make someone feel special."

"If it's not the hair flips, what's got you down in the dumps?"

"It's my daughter, June. With the season starting soon, I need someone to watch her, and we're coming up short on options."

Maven shifts in the chair and stares at me, and I fidget under her attention. It's different from how Shawn was looking at me. Her gaze is softer. More understanding. Like she's the kind of person who would go to the ends of the earth to try and find a solution to my problems, even though she probably doesn't have any answers.

"This might be obvious, but why not hire a babysitter?" she asks.

"They keep trying to sleep with me," I say, embarrassed, and Maven lets out a cackling laugh. It echoes around us and explodes in the center of my chest like a firework. "What's so funny?"

"You think highly of yourself. Who says they want to sleep with you?"

"They were in my bed."

"Maybe they were tired."

"They were *naked* in my bed."

"Oh." She hides the edges of her smile with a cough into her fist. "You think they'd try to be a little less obvious. Walking around in a towel or sunbathing topless are way more conspicuous than just jumping under your sheets."

"No subtlety, whatsoever, and zero points for creativity." I gesture to her bags in a heap on the floor. "What's your crisis?

Anything we can help with? Is it how much shit you're carrying around?"

"I am carrying around a lot of shit, aren't I? Don't worry about me. This is your time, and I'm overstepping. I should get going."

"Stay." I reach out and touch her elbow before pulling my fingers away and sitting on my hands. "Really. It's fine. There's no solution to my problem yet, so we might as well use this time to help out someone else."

Maven looks at me, and her eyes search my face. I'm not sure what she's looking for, but I hope she finds it.

"Are you sure?" she asks.

"I'm positive. I need a good deed for the day, and this can be it."

"My roommate moved out to live with her boyfriend, which means my rent is going to double when our lease renews next month. I've tried to find a studio apartment, but with the semester starting soon, everything is already snatched up. My job with the Titans pays well, but I'm going to need more income if I want to have a roof over my head."

"I'll pay your rent," Shawn says. "Problem solved."

"I appreciate the offer, Shawn, but I want to do this on my own." Maven sighs and rubs her forehead. "I'll figure it out."

"If it means you're not going to be eating dinner, Mae, I'm going to help you pay your rent," he argues, and it feels like I'm interrupting something. A family conversation I'm not sure I should be present for.

"I can do it," she says, and there's a fierceness in her tone that wasn't there before. "I've thought about doing private coaching sessions with local athletes for some extra money, but I need to figure out the logistics."

"Coaching?" I ask, interested. "What do you play?"

"Played," Maven says softly, and her pride is gone. Her shoulders hunch forward with the word. It's barely noticeable, but I can see the shift in her demeanor. The corners of her mouth turn down, and she folds in on herself. "Soccer."

"No shit. I practiced kicking with some of the soccer girls in college. They were awesome."

"I haven't thought it all the way through yet, but I could make good money. I'd have to figure out a schedule, and I couldn't work on Sundays because of the Titans games. The occasional Monday and Thursday night would be out, too." Her eyebrows knit together, and she sighs. "Never mind. It would never work. I need a new plan. How much are they charging for organ harvesting?"

"I'll pay you seven thousand dollars a month to watch June," I blurt out, and she gapes at me. "And you wouldn't have to lose any vital organs."

"What?" Maven asks.

"*What*?" Shawn repeats, and my stomach drops to the floor.

I think I might have just asked for my ass to be kicked, and I hold my hands up in innocence. There aren't any ulterior motives underlying the proposal besides me being *really fucking desperate*, but I doubt he sees it that way.

"I need a nanny. You need money," I explain to her, and I'm really pulling things out of my ass. "If seven thousand dollars doesn't work, name the price that will, and I'll give it to you."

The room is so quiet, I swear I can hear the guys in the locker room down the hall putting on their practice gear. I'm not breathing, and I'm afraid to even move.

"Will you give us a second, Maven?" Shawn asks, and his eyes are locked on mine.

Maven jumps up and retreats from the office. "Sure," she says, and she shuts the door behind her.

"What the *fuck* is wrong with you?" Shawn seethes when she's gone, and I grimace. "Did you listen to a word of that long

PowerPoint presentation I put together at the start of training camp about players having a relationship with a member of the team? Do I need to remind you that it's not allowed and a fireable offense? I've already had to do that shit once. Do *not* put me in this position again, Dallas."

Something in me snaps.

All the frustration I've been holding on to, all the hours of being so fucking tired from working so fucking hard boil to the surface, and I see red.

"For fuck's sake, I don't want to sleep with her," I say sharply. "And we're not in a relationship, so no one is getting fired. If we're being honest with each other, I'm two seconds away from walking out that door and hanging up my jersey for good because my daughter is my top fucking priority. If you know of anyone else who would pass a background check and be more focused on June's well-being instead of becoming a wife or girl-friend of an athlete, I'm all ears. Hell, if the person just avoids trying to grab my dick when I'm in the shower that would be a huge win."

I take a deep breath, and guilt hits me.

I shouldn't have let all that slip out. I should've squashed it down like I do with everything else. Compartmentalized it and kept it to myself. I'm usually more in check with my emotions and an expert at biting my tongue.

I'm ready to offer an apology for my behavior when Shawn sighs.

"You don't even know her and you want to hire her?" he asks.

I don't know how to explain to him that I've felt a pull toward Maven since the moment she sat down next to me. The more she talked, the more I relaxed. The weight I've been carrying for months seemed to lessen when she smiled at me. Her questions seemed like she cared to know the answer and cared to know *me*.

That's never happened before.

"I do know her, and I want to hire her because she's nice. Because my gut tells me I can trust her. Because she'll be at the stadium on game days and understands how my schedule works. Because when she met June the other day in the tunnel, she talked to her and not me." I say. "Because I can't take feeling like a failure for much longer, and we both know this is the solution I've been looking for."

"I'm going to tell you this one time," Shawn says, and I lean forward to hear him. "If you touch her. If you hurt her. If you do *anything* to make her feel uncomfortable, I will rip your balls from your body and hang them from the goalpost."

"God, no. I wouldn't. I won't. This isn't—I'm not interested in a relationship. In anything with anyone. All I want is an extra set of hands. Not on my dick, I mean. In the kitchen. Or with folding laundry. That's it."

"Good." A muscle in Shawn's jaw ticks. "I don't care how much we're paying you or how good your right foot is. Do something you shouldn't, and I will end you."

"I promise. It's strictly professional. Business partners, if you will."

"Don't make me regret this." He sighs again and leans back in his chair. "You can stop listening, Mae, and come back in."

The door opens, and she almost falls back inside. I squash down the smile that creeps across my mouth as I watch her run her fingers through her blonde hair then fix the collar of her team issued polo shirt.

"I wasn't listening. I was checking to make sure the door can hold my weight. Good news; it can," Maven says. Her gaze bounces to me, and my cheeks turn red as her lips stretch into a slow and lazy grin. "You were pretty adamant with that *god, no*, Lansfield. I don't think you answered fast enough."

The tips of my ears are going to burn off. "Sorry. I didn't know I had an audience. Does the nanny thing interest you? It's totally cool if not. I thought I'd offer since it sounds like we could both use some help."

"It definitely does, but everyone needs to calm down. I'm not going to try and grab your dick while you're in the shower. No offense, of course. I'm sure you have a very grabbable dick, I'm just—"

"Jesus Christ." Shawn stands up. "Enough."

"Here." I grab a Post-it and scribble down my address before he can change his mind. "Come by on Sunday around noon. You can spend some time with June. I'll ask you some questions, and we can make sure this is the right fit."

"Sounds good." Maven takes the note from me, and her fingers brush against mine. A jolt of electricity runs up my arm when she pulls away and looks me up and down. "See you on Sunday, Lansfield."

She picks her bags up off the floor. I keep my eyes on my sneakers as she leaves the room. Watching her walk away doesn't seem like it would be filed under *strictly professional.*

When the door closes, I peek at Shawn.

"You're on thin ice," he warns.

Relief spreads through me like a wildfire for the first time in months. "Lighten up, Coach. What could go wrong?"

FIVE

MAVEN

MY PHONE BUZZES when I'm on the Metro. A text from a number I don't recognize comes through, and I slide the screen open.

UNKNOWN NUMBER:

> Hey. Let me know when you're a block away, and I'll meet you out front.

> Are you driving or taking the Metro?

> It's Dallas, btw. I got your number from Shawn. Not a stalker, I promise.

I laugh and type out a quick reply.

ME

> Dallas "God no" Lansfield? How can I be sure this isn't a stalker in disguise? I'm going to need some proof.

UNKNOWN NUMBER:

> Attachment: 1 image

The picture takes a second to download, but once it does, a

photo of Dallas and June pops up. They're both sticking out their tongues, and there are little wrinkles around Dallas's eyes that make it look like he snapped it mid-laugh.

It's a little blurry. A little off center and a little hard to make out thanks to the sun beams cutting across the lens of the camera, but it's also kind of perfect. It's in the moment. Taken by him, for me, and I don't know why, but it makes me smile.

UNKNOWN NUMBER:

Better?

ME

The best. How much did it cost you to get my number?

UNKNOWN NUMBER:

A thirty-minute lecture and four toes off my left foot.

Good thing I kick with my right. Worth it, though.

ME

The sacrifices we have to make. I'm on the Metro and getting off at the next stop, so I'm probably five minutes away.

UNKNOWN NUMBER:

Now that I think about it, how can I be so sure this is really Maven Wood and not someone fucking with me? If I'm going to show you mine, you're going to have to show me yours.

I lift my phone and mimic their poses, my tongue out and my face cast in the shadow of artificial subway lighting. I ignore the look from the woman sitting next to me and fire it off to him.

My phone buzzes again seconds later.

UNKNOWN NUMBER:

You're wearing clothes, which is better than a lot of the other people that have come for an interview. We're off to a good start.

ME

I'm not sure a guy has ever said that to me before.

Do I get a medal for showing up clothed?

UNKNOWN NUMBER:

A medal. And a gold star.

ME

I love positive reinforcement.

I save his number and stand up, holding the handrails as the train comes to a stop. I dodge someone with a backpack and hightail it up the escalator, grateful for fresh air when I'm back above ground.

"Maven!"

I turn around and see Dallas heading toward me with June perched on his shoulders. His white T-shirt stretches across his chest, and his dark athletic shorts hit the top of his knee. June tries to knock the bill of his hat with her small hands as he jogs across the street with a smile on his face.

"Hey," I say, a little breathless. I figured I'd have a minute or two before I saw him, but he's here. Two feet in front of me and meeting me at the subway station so I don't have to walk alone, looking obscenely good. "I thought we were meeting at your place."

"Figured we'd come here so we can show you which route we like to take. It's good to see you."

His grin pulls wider when he gives me a one-armed hug and tugs me close. He smells exactly like he did the other day when I ran into him at the stadium, like coffee and vanilla and the hint of wood mixed in the cotton of his shirt.

It feels like coming home after a long day as he presses me to his chest, and I melt into his embrace for the quickest of seconds before I pull away and look up at his daughter. She's watching me, and her crooked pigtails blow in the breeze.

"Hi, June," I say softly.

"June Bug, you remember Maven, right?" Dallas slides her from his shoulders and onto his hip. "We met her at the stadium the other day."

"Pretty," June says, and she grins. "I remember."

"Good." Dallas's brown eyes flick down to the hem of my green dress, and he clears his throat. "Let's go. Important things await."

With long legs and an easy stride, Dallas is a giant who covers twice the distance I do as we head down the sidewalk. I try to keep up with him, but soon we're separated by throngs of people, and a wall of pedestrians and tourists keeps us half a block apart.

When he turns around and can't find me, there's a flash of panic on his face until our eyes meet. His shoulders relax. He slows his pace and falls in step beside me when I catch up, letting me dictate our speed.

"Sorry," I say. "That's going to happen a lot. My legs might be strong, but they're short."

"Don't apologize. I should've been more aware of my surroundings. That's my fault."

"Now we're even after I ran into you in the tunnel." Our arms brush as I sidestep a melting ice cream cone, and a drop of chocolate gets on my white sneakers. "I haven't spent a lot of time on this side of town. It's nice."

"There's a lot going on. Plenty of restaurants and parks, and

June and I go to the playground around the corner. Do you have a car?" he asks.

"I do. I wasn't sure what the parking situation was going to be like, so I decided to take the Metro." We stop at an intersection, and I shield my eyes to look up at him. "June uses a car seat, right?"

"She does. I'll order one for you so y'all can go out if you want." Dallas touches my elbow when the crosswalk changes to let me know he's moving. "I have parking at my apartment. There are plenty of visitors' spots."

"Cool. I'll drive next time." I bite my bottom lip when I realize what I've said. "Sorry. I didn't mean to assume there's going to be a next time."

"Assume away, Maven. There's definitely going to be a next time." Dallas's grin morphs into something different. It's teasing, just like the one I remember him having years ago. There's no strain behind the flash of his eyes or anxiousness in the little brackets of wrinkles around his mouth. It's light. Fun. *Beautiful.* "Talk to me about food."

"That's a broad topic. I eat it. What else do you want to know?"

"What are your favorite cuisines? There are tons of options around here."

"Anything, really. Thai. Italian. Cookies."

"Do we classify cookies as a cuisine?" he asks.

"I don't see why not."

"Good to know." He points across the street to a building with a red and white checkered awning. There's a line down the sidewalk, and I count three dozen people queueing up and waiting to go inside. "That's the place to go for the best cookies in the city. Mama Rose's Bakery. It's been around since the seventies, and she still comes in every morning to roll out dough."

"Do you get to skip the line?" I ask. "One flash of your smile and everyone lets you jump ahead of them? Do they drop to their knees and call you *Our Savior*?"

Dallas laughs, and both of his dimples pop. His shoulders shake, and he drops his head back like I just said the funniest thing in the world. June claps her hands together and laughs too, matching her dad's enthusiasm.

I can't help but stare at them. I look longer than I should, longer than should be allowed, and when his gaze meets mine and locks in place, my stomach flutters with a hundred butterflies.

Heat works up my spine and spreads over my shoulders under his attention. I've had boys stare at me before; the guys in college I hung out with and the occasional boyfriend.

But it's never been like *this*, a man with something dark and liquid-hot behind his eyes. With intent and purpose. Pleasure ripples through me, and I bite my bottom lip. His attention flicks to my mouth, a blip in time where he looks hungry, *starved*, before his face is wiped clean.

"No," he smirks. "I wait in line just like everyone else. No one drops to their knees, and they don't roll out the red carpet for me. Mama Rose does slip me an extra cookie or two when no one is looking, though, but that's our little secret."

"There's that special treatment." I smile and he smiles back. "Are we close to your place?"

"Yeah." Dallas points to the tall residential building half a block away. "Just up there. Courtyard Gardens. Main entrance is on this street, and the parking garage underneath the building has elevator access to all floors. There's an alleyway in the back, but avoid it if you can. The side door likes to get stuck, and then you're trapped in the stairwell with nowhere to go."

"Sounds like there's a story there."

"There is. It involves pizza, too much whiskey, and an idiot best friend. He's a hazard to my health. It was embarrassing to have to explain to the firefighters who came and rescued us that we were two professional athletes and the alcohol dwindled our intelligence level; we aren't that stupid in real life."

"I would've liked to see that. How long until you were rescued?" I ask.

"Maverick got through sixty-four rounds of 'Ninety-Nine Bottles of Beer' on the Wall by the time they finally opened the door. I can't think of a worse song to have to listen to when you have nowhere to go."

I imagine Dallas sitting in a corner. A pizza box open in his lap and a string of cheese hanging from his mouth. It makes me burst out laughing.

"I hope there are pictures."

"There are. Get me hammered and you might see them one day," he says.

"New life goal unlocked."

"We were such idiots. That was before June was born, obviously. I'd have a panic attack if that happened now."

Dallas holds the door to his apartment building open for me, and I slide inside. He sets June down on the lobby floor, and she takes off running toward a security guard who gives her a high five.

"She has a lot of energy," I say.

"Tons," he says. "She hates to sit still and loves to be outside. The swings at the park are her favorite, and an hour of physical activity usually tires her out."

"Is she allergic to anything? Bees? Ants? Peanut butter?"

"Nope. She's a healthy kid and an excellent eater who sleeps through the night. Potty trained, too, but if it's been a while, you might need to ask her if she needs to go."

"Wow." I watch June accept a sticker from the man behind

the reception desk. She unpeels it and puts it on her shirt, waving her arms in delight. "She seems so easy."

"She is. I'm very lucky."

"Lucky, yeah. But that's also a testament to your parenting." I tilt my chin to look up at him, and his cheeks are pink. "You've done a good job, Dallas."

"Thanks, Maven. I appreciate it. I figured I'd show you my place then ask you a couple of questions. This isn't going to be formal or anything. June Bug," he calls out. "Let's take Maven to the apartment."

"Okay." June sprints ahead of us to the elevator and pushes the up arrow. "It's nice, May-van." She frowns. "That's a hard name."

"It is a hard name," I agree. "You can call me Mae Mae if you want. That's what my dad used to call me when I was your age."

"Mae Mae," June repeats. "I like it."

We file into the elevator, and June presses the button for the top floor. Music plays softly over the speakers, but neither Dallas or I try to fill the silence. It's obvious he's anxious; he keeps tapping his foot. He pulls at the sleeve of his shirt, and I hear him let out a huff of air.

I get it. I'm nervous, too, because I *need* this job.

If I don't get it, there's no way I'll be able to afford my rent.

I'll have to pack up my stuff and move back in with my dad and his girlfriend who can barely keep their hands off each other. I shudder at the thought of sharing a wall with them.

"You okay?" Dallas asks. "Not a fan of jazz music?"

"No, I—well, I haven't listened to enough jazz music to form an opinion on it, but I'm leaning toward tolerable? I'm fine. It's nothing. No big deal."

He lifts an eyebrow and crosses his arms over his chest. "Now you have to tell me."

"It's embarrassing. Not something I should share with the world."

He smiles, and his dimple cuts deep into his cheek. "Not helping your case, Maven. I think we need to enact an honesty policy right now. If we're going to be around each other, we need to be able to share things. All the things, even if it's something we might not want to hear. Spill."

"Spill!" June repeats, and she's so cute, I cave.

I groan and cover my face with my hands. "Fine. I'm thinking about how you're clearly nervous, but I'm nervous, too. I really want—really *need*—this job. If not, I'm going to have to move back in with my dad and hear him and his girlfriend engaging in... activities. I'm really hoping to make a good impression. My sanity and ear drums depend on it."

Dallas laughs and bumps my shoulder with his arm. "I think I'm required to hire you now. What kind of person would I be if I just let your ears bleed?"

"You're such a Good Samaritan."

"I sure am." Warm, thick fingers curl around my wrists and bring my hands down. I blink, and the elevator doors open. "It's time to stop hiding, though. We're here."

SIX

DALLAS

MAVEN GLANCES up at me from under a fan of long, dark eyelashes. There are freckles across her nose and her eyes are bright blue, like the ocean I'd jump in during the summertime when I was a kid without any worries.

She's beautiful, in that natural sort of way I've always found attractive. A green dress with thin straps that makes her skin look tan. Blonde hair with a pretty white ribbon tied through it. A sense of humor and a genuine smile.

She's exactly who I'd go for if I allowed myself to go for anyone.

"Twenty-sixth floor, number three," I say, breaking the silence. I let go of Maven's wrist and take June's hand to help her step out of the elevator. Maven follows us down the hall, and I stop outside the door to my apartment. "There are only four tenants up here, one on each side of the building. My best friend, Maverick, lives on the opposite side."

"Is this the same Maverick from StairGate?" she asks, and I laugh.

"It is. He's a right-winger for the D.C. Stars and lives in number one if you ever need him."

"A hockey player. This is starting to make sense now. Is he nice?"

"Nicest guy you'll ever meet. He'll give you the shirt off his back, but he's also full of himself. He could use someone to take him down a peg or two."

I pull out my keys and unlock the door. Maven gasps when she steps into the foyer.

"No way," she whispers. "I've always wondered what penthouse apartments looked like."

"Shawn lives somewhere nice, doesn't he?"

"He's out in the suburbs now, and where he was before wasn't nearly as big as this. How many bedrooms are there?"

"Four." I head for the kitchen and drop my keys on the counter. I hear her footsteps behind me, and I'm taking it as a good sign she hasn't run away. "Do you want a tour?"

"Sure. Do I need supplies for the journey? Water and food in case I get lost? You don't even know my emergency contact."

"She's got more jokes." I laugh and pat June's head, letting her run toward the playroom down the hall. "I have binoculars somewhere. You can use them to see me from across the living room."

Maven's smile splits into a grin. "I'm glad you can take it and dish it back out, Lansfield. That's going to make this so much more fun. Show me around. I'm sure I'm going to have a couple other one-liners up my sleeve."

"I'd be disappointed if you didn't. Trust me; for the boy from Georgia who grew up in a two-bedroom house and had to share a room with his sister until he was sixteen, this still blows my mind a little."

I lead her to the playroom first where June is busy with her Barbies. Instead of giving the pink walls and the toys in messy piles a quick glance then asking what's next, Maven walks to my daughter and sits down. Her dress fans out on the ground, and she reaches for a doll.

"Which one is your favorite?" she asks June.

June holds up a doll with brown hair and a gold dress. "This one."

"Mine, too. Her outfit is gorgeous. I think I still have some of my old Barbies in storage somewhere. Do you want to see the ones I played with when I was younger?"

"You like Barbies?" June's eyes widen, and she scoots closer to Maven. "Which ones?"

"I like all of them. For my sixth birthday, my dad took me to the toy store and let me pick out anything I wanted, no matter how big it was. I found a Barbie Jeep and rolled out of there in the driver's seat with ten new Barbies by my side. I used to cut their hair and give them makeovers, too."

"Wow," June says, and I don't think she's blinked in two minutes.

"Maybe we can convince your dad to get you a Jeep. We could drive it down the hall. It's wide enough to be a freeway."

"Whoa, okay, slow down. Three minutes together and y'all are already joining forces? I think I might be in trouble." I lean against the doorframe and watch them. A wave of affection ebbs towards me the longer I stare, and something pulls tight in my chest like a string. I don't remember the last time someone showed an interest in the things June liked, and I feel bad pulling Maven away from her. "JB?"

She's too busy handing Maven a plastic hairbrush to glance up at me. "Yes, Daddy?"

"I'm going to show Maven the rest of the apartment, okay?"

"Can she stay for dinner?" June asks. "Please?"

"She might be very busy. Maybe we can plan another day," I say.

"I'm not busy," Maven says. "And I love dinner, believe it or not."

"Are you sure?"

"Positive." She stands up and smooths her palms over her dress. My eyes follow her hands as they run over her thighs before I blink and pull my gaze away. "I'll be back soon, June. Then you can show me your other toys."

We head down the hall, but Maven stops and stares at the framed photos hanging on the wall. She taps the picture of me with confetti stuck to my uniform and helmet, and she smiles.

"This was after you kicked that game-winning extra point at the Super Bowl a couple of years ago, isn't it?" she asks.

"Yeah. First ring of mine, and definitely the sweetest."

It's my turn to smile at the memory. I can still remember the thrill that ran through me when my foot connected with the football. The elation I felt when it soared over the goalpost and of being scooped into my teammates' arms after. It's one of the best moments of my career, and when I think about walking away from the sport, I know I'd miss those experiences the most.

Maven looks up at me. "Are you okay?"

"I'm good. Just reminiscing."

"They look like they were very good days. I'd reminisce on them, too."

"Sometimes I forget how lucky I am." I gesture her down the hall and open a door on our right. "This is the guest room, and there's a bathroom attached. Feel free to leave some clothes in the dresser if you want. No one else uses this space."

"You don't have people that come and stay with you? Family or friends?"

"Most of my friends are local. My sister visits occasionally, but she's not going to be here anytime soon."

She nods and glances out the window. "Talk about an incredible view."

"If you think that's nice, wait until you see the balcony. It wraps around half the apartment."

"Of course it does. Is that where you go to contemplate your existence and try to find the meaning of life?"

Her smile is teasing, and I like it. I like that she's giving me shit, and I like that she's not afraid to be herself around me.

There have been so many times when a woman changes who she is when she finds out who I am, and everything feels so fake. Forced and off-putting.

Not with Maven, though.

She speaks her mind and says what she's thinking without holding back.

It's new and different, and I like it.

"When I can't sleep, I'll go out there for some fresh air. I like the quiet," I explain. "Which is funny, because my job is the furthest thing from quiet. It's easy to get caught up in the frenzy of it all—the media. Press conferences. National news and internet fame. Social media followers who want to know what I'm doing every second of every day. It's overwhelming sometimes, and it's nice to slow down. To appreciate the small stuff. Like how traffic in this city is the fucking worst, but at two in the morning, I could stare at the empty roads for hours."

"It's your secret spot," Maven says. "The place you go when you want to settle and calm your mind. The place where you can be yourself without anyone else watching."

"Huh. I never thought of it that way." I rub my jaw and give her a slow nod. "But I think you're right."

"It's important to have a place like that."

"Yeah? Where's yours?"

Her hands twist together, and for a second, she's deep in thought. "It was the soccer field. I haven't found a replacement yet. Maybe one day I will."

There's more to that story, but I'm not going to pry. I know firsthand about keeping personal things personal, and I let her have the moment of quiet contemplation.

"I'd love to show you the balcony," I find myself saying, and she lifts her chin.

Her smile is soft and slow, and it lights up her whole face. There are wrinkles on her nose. There's a gleam in her eye, and she looks happy.

I'd like to make her smile like that again.

"I'd love to see it. Lead the way, Lansfield," she says, and I do.

We head back to the living room. I grab June's baby monitor from the table next to the couch and open the double glass doors that lead outside. Maven laughs as she steps onto the balcony. She holds her arms out at her sides and twirls around in a small circle.

"What do you think?" I ask.

"I love it. Best view in the city." Maven walks over to the ledge and leans over. "If I squint, I think I can see my apartment building."

"It's better at night." I walk across the terrace and stand next to her. The breeze picks up her hair and blows it across my face. She wrestles with it, a couple of blonde strands getting caught in her earrings, and she laughs. "Are you trying to suffocate me?"

"Not before you add me to your will. I saw that coffee maker of yours—I'd murder for it." She holds a handful of hair at the base of her neck. "Sorry. I didn't anticipate being on top of a weather tower or anything."

"You're forgiven. Can I ask you a couple of questions?"

"Here comes the scary part." She spins and presses her back against the glass partition. Her attention shifts to me, and she takes a deep breath. "Hit me."

"You have a car, so I'm assuming you have a valid driver's license, right?"

"I do. The expiration date is seven years from now."

"Good. And your car has functional seatbelts and airbags?"

"Yes? I mean, I'm not a mechanic, but I haven't been told otherwise. It's driveable, and I haven't been in any accidents, so they should be fine."

My lips turn up. "Checking all the boxes so far. Any criminal offenses?"

"No." She pauses and rubs her lips together. "Well. That's a lie."

Shit.

"What, uh, did you do?" I ask.

I reason with myself, a quick decision made in my head.

If it's murder, she's out. If it's something stupid like vandalism, well, I could work with that.

It's not like she's going to graffiti my kid.

"You're familiar with clothing stores, right? How some places have those big, metal, circular racks?"

"Yes," I say slowly, and I'm not sure where this is going. *Jesus Christ.* Did she shoplift? "What about them?"

"When I was younger, my dad and I were shopping. We were at Ross, and there was this candy necklace I really wanted. He wouldn't let me have it and told me we were eating dinner soon. I could have it *next* time, but not now. Well, I didn't like that answer. When he was in the dressing room, I made a run for it. I stole the necklace and hid in one of those racks. My dad couldn't find me. They put the store on lockdown. Called the police. Searched high and low, only to find me eating the necklace ten minutes later. He was *livid.* I was in so much trouble."

I stare at her for a beat and try to figure out if she's fucking with me. When she blinks at me with innocent eyes, I burst out laughing.

"Stop," I wheeze, and I clutch my side. "You're joking."

"Nope. True story. I think they might have a WANTED poster of my four-year-old face still hanging in the store."

"What was your thought process? You took the necklace, and you thought he wouldn't notice you were missing? Were you just going to drive his Volvo out of the parking lot to freedom?"

She gasps. "How did you know it was a Volvo?"

"What middle aged white guy *didn't* have a Volvo in the nineties and early two thousands, you klepto?"

"I was a child, Dallas." Maven levels me with a look that's anything but serious, and she gives my chest a gentle shove. "I didn't know what I was doing. I saw what I wanted, and I took it."

"So you're not a felon, but you're definitely not innocent, either. Noted. I think I can let that slide." I grin and draw a check in the air. "You're passing with flying colors, Maven."

"The bar is keeping my clothes on, Dallas, not finding a solution to world peace."

I choke on my laugh. "You're doing that well, too."

"All these compliments are going to go to my head if you're not careful."

"Okay. Enough tooting your horn. Let's talk about serious shit. Do you know CPR? What about how to operate an AED?"

"I'm comfortable with both. My college coach made sure we were familiar in case we needed it at practice. I wish everyone could say the same."

"Agreed. Besides your job with the Titans, do you have any other scheduling conflicts? Something part time? A small business?"

"No. I'm available whenever you need me, and I'm happy to be here as much or as little as you want. I live about twenty-five minutes away with traffic during rush hour, though. If you need me to be somewhere quickly, it might take me a second to get there."

"I feel ya. Getting to the stadium is a chore; I leave an hour before practice and I barely make it there on time. Let's talk about game days. When we play on the road on Sundays, we typically fly out Friday afternoon or very early Saturday morning, and we don't get home until late Sunday night. When we play at home, the team requires us to stay in a hotel room the night before games," I explain.

"Wait, what? Even when you're playing fifteen miles up the road?"

"Yup. They claim it's to keep us free from distractions, but I think it's because they don't want anyone getting out of hand and showing up to games inebriated or out of control. It's a pain in the ass, but that rule isn't going to change anytime soon."

"Wow. I had no idea. So I'd be here on weekend nights, basically."

"Yeah. And on Sundays when we have a home game, you can bring June to UPS Field with you and drop her off in the nursery. I'll pick her up after, then you'll be free."

"Got it. I'm sure you have a routine with her, and I'll follow that routine as best as I can. Naps. When she eats and when she goes to bed. I'd never do anything with her outside the house you didn't approve first," Maven says.

"Skydiving is allowed," I say. "She really likes to jump out of planes."

"Cool. I thought I'd take her to an archery range. Or maybe do some bullfighting or ax throwing. We could also walk barefoot on glass. Nothing builds character like cutting your foot open on broken bottles."

"Have you ever considered a career in early education? Who needs addition and subtraction when you can teach kids how to fire a bow and arrow like they're in *The Hunger Games*?"

"Survival of the fittest. She'll be fine," she says.

"What questions do you have for me?" I ask.

"Talk to me about June. Is there anything you want me to focus on with her? Things we should or shouldn't do?"

"She's the best kid in the world, and I hate that she has to come to the stadium with me every day. I'd love it if she could spend her time in museums. Art galleries. The park for more than twenty minutes on our way to practice. She deserves to have her own childhood."

"I'll come up with some fun things we can do together. What about around the house? Running errands? Cooking? Cleaning?"

"Don't worry about cleaning—I have someone who comes once a week to mop and dust. Everything else helps, though. Being one person but having the responsibility of two... it's a lot," I admit. "I know how privileged I am to have the job I have. I make good money. We have a roof over our heads, and we never have to worry about where our next meal is going to come from. Sometimes I'm not sure I'm allowed to complain."

"Money or not, you can still be exhausted and overworked, Dallas," she says gently. "Tell me about your nights with her."

"We usually get home from practice around five. It's a rush to make dinner, give her a bath, change into pajamas and have a little bit of playtime before I'm reading her a bedtime story and turning the lights out around seven-thirty. When she falls asleep, I still have things to do. I catch up on team emails and messages from my agent. I shower and have groceries delivered so I can get food going for the next day. By then, it's late. I don't go to sleep until after midnight. June wakes up around six, and then we're at it again."

It feels safe to tell Maven the things because I don't see any judgment on her face. I see understanding and the recognition that I'm *trying*, even if I'm coming up short half the time.

"Hey." She bumps my shoulder, and I look down at her. "I

got you, okay? I know you've been doing this by yourself for a while now, and you're so *good* at it, Dallas. June loves you, and you're present in her life. That's the most important thing in the world. But you don't have to do it alone anymore. I'd love to help you, if you'll let me."

I suck down a lungful of air. "When can you start?"

"Are you saying I got the job even though no one else applied and I'm your only choice?" Maven asks.

"That's exactly what I'm saying."

She lunges for me. Her arms wrap around my neck before I can blink, and she buries her face in my shirt. I stand there for a minute, frozen.

It's been so long since I've had a real hug by someone other than my daughter, and I forgot how nice it is.

"Thank you," she says. "This means a lot. I won't let you down."

"I know you won't. We're going to make a good team."

"Should we check on June?" Maven asks into my chest, and I nod, a little disoriented and a little confused. She's warm and soft and I feel like I've been tipped off balance. "And eat some dinner?"

"Yeah. We can go over schedules for the next few weeks after we eat. I'll show you her nighttime routine for when I'm away, too. There's a lot of bedtime reading, and if you don't do voices with the characters, she'll make you do it again."

"Oh, I can't wait. I've been training my whole life to perform a dramatic reading of children's books."

"You're going to fit right in here," I say.

Her fingers drag across my stomach when she pulls away and heads for the door. My brain short circuits when she looks at me over her shoulder and tosses me a smile. She disappears with the swish of her dress, leaving me to panic.

I've made a big fucking mistake.

I lied when I talked to Shawn.

A lot of things *can* go wrong.

Staring at Maven's ass as she walks away is at the top of that list, and I wonder if I should just hurl myself off the balcony now.

SEVEN

MAVEN

"I THINK some celebrations are in order."

I look up from my computer and find Dallas standing in front of me, a beer extended my way. "It's late, and I should get going so you can have some time alone. You've been going nonstop since this morning."

"I'd like it if you stayed. June's asleep, and it would be nice to have some company," he says.

"And what are we celebrating?"

"Your first week with us. Your first day taking pictures of the team while we're on the field. Lots of things."

"When you put it that way, I guess I have to stay." I accept the drink and smile. "Am I allowed to drink on the job, though?"

"I won't tell the boss. Cheers, Maven."

We knock the bottles together. I take a long sip and sigh as I swallow. "Today was such a good day."

"How was the scrimmage?" Dallas asks. "You looked like you were having fun."

"Fun doesn't even begin to describe it. I think I blacked out because I was so freaking excited. I know I wasn't the one playing, obviously, but it felt like I was right in the middle of the huddles and the drives down the field. You don't get that kind of experience when you're in the stands, and I feel lucky this is my job."

He lifts his chin toward my computer. "Can I see the pictures you took?"

"You can, but they're probably not very good. I'm still getting the hang of things with my new camera."

"Do you always doubt yourself?" He props his elbow on the edge of the island and stares at me with a serious gaze. "You did it in Shawn's office, too."

My mouth pops open, and I blush. I didn't realize he had been paying attention to me. "No. Yes? I don't know, to be honest. Photography has always been a hobby of mine, but doing it on an almost professional level is outside my comfort zone. I'm remembering what it's like to not be good at something right away, and I hate feeling behind."

Dallas hums. He sets down his beer and reaches for the laptop. His long fingers tap the plastic case as he watches me. "May I?"

I set my beer next to his and wring my hands together. Nervous energy hums through me, and I nod, a little reluctant. "As long as you don't judge me for any underexposed images or poor composition."

"I don't know what any of those words mean, Maven. Regardless of how the photos look to you, I'm going to think they're masterpieces."

I huff out a laugh and gesture for him to go ahead. "Fine. Enjoy."

He's quiet as he flicks through the snapshots of the team I took earlier this morning. Hundreds of pictures fly across the screen until he stops on one of him and Jett, the starting quarterback.

I captured them doing some affectionate trash talking as

they walked to opposite ends of the field during a water break to catch some relief from the late July sun. Their arms are slung around each other and their foreheads are almost pressed together, some private conversation happening between them.

It's my favorite picture of the day.

I couldn't help myself from snapping away when I saw the dimples on Dallas's cheeks. The pure joy in the glint of his eyes and the hook of a smile on his mouth. It's like his stress melts away when he steps on a football field.

It's where he comes alive.

"This one is great," he finally says. "Jett was telling me his fourteen-year-old brother could beat me in a fight, and I agreed with him."

"Is his brother also six-foot-two? If not, I'd put my money on you."

"He's close, believe it or not. And two hundred and fifteen pounds. He'd break me like a stick. If the NFL didn't have such strict draft eligibility rules, I'd be begging Shawn to throw every penny at him so he could join our defensive line when he graduates high school." Dallas chuckles, and his knee knocks against mine. "These pictures are incredible, Maven. I like that you don't only get the action shot, but what comes after it, too."

"That's what I love about sports photography." I scoot closer to the counter and lean forward, invading his space. "There's a story. We get a beginning, a middle, and an end. Like this one." I click on an image of Dallas. It's taken from the side, just as he's kicked a field goal. I zoomed in, close enough where you can see his eyes tracking the ball. The way he sticks the tip of his tongue out of his mouth in concentration, and the bead of sweat rolling down his cheek. "If I showed this to anyone, they'd be able to tell exactly what's happening."

"They'd know I just kicked a sixty-one-yard field goal and got out of running laps with the rest of the team after our scrimmage. Guess I haven't lost my touch."

"Cocky, I see." I turn to look at him. We're so close, I can feel the heat on his arms from hours spent outside. I can smell his shampoo and the lingering traces of the spices he used to cook dinner. "I'm glad you like them."

"They're fantastic. You should be proud of yourself. I don't see any under composition or exposure images."

I laugh. "Close. I'm excited to shoot an actual game. That'll be my chance to see how much I've learned."

"Tons, I bet. How did June do today when y'all got home from the stadium?"

"She was great. We're past the crying phase when you leave, I think. We went to the park, and after her nap, we spent the rest of the time before you got home on the couch watching *Frozen*."

Dallas groans. "Sorry. I should've warned you that's her favorite movie. She watches it every day, and singing along is required."

"I figured that out on Thursday after watching it for the fourth day in a row."

"If you want the television to mysteriously stop working for an afternoon so you can get a break from the singing snowman, let me know. I'll unplug it before I leave tomorrow."

"No way." I prop my feet up on the foot rest of his stool and lean an inch closer to him. "We had a blast, and I already can't wait to watch it again."

"Famous last words. I'll come back in two months and see if you're still saying that."

"In two months, we'll be deep into the season. Are you ready to get back into the swing of things? You strike me as a guy who likes routine."

"What makes you say that?"

"Everything in the apartment is organized. Bins for toys are labeled. You have a color-coded calendar on the wall by the refrigerator, and over the past few seasons, I've noticed your pregame warm up is always exactly the same," I say.

"Keeping an eye on me, Maven?" he teases, and the dimple on his right cheek pops, sharp enough to cut glass.

"I guess I am. You're so busy taking care of a tiny human, and it makes me wonder who's taking care of you."

Dallas pauses, and he fills the silence with a long sip from his beer. "I do like routine," he says, and his voice is lower than before. Rough and ragged, and pulled from deep in his chest. "I like it a lot more now that I'm responsible for another human."

"Is that your biggest fear? Responsibility and being the one in charge?"

"No. I love responsibility—it's why I like being captain so much. I'm afraid of failure, though. I'm constantly worried about having someone else rely on me, and I'm afraid if one little thing shifts out of balance, everything else will be ruined." He lifts his chin, and our eyes meet. "What's your biggest fear?"

"We're getting deep, aren't we?"

"We could go back to talking about singing snowmen. I know every lyric to every song, and it's much lighter than this adult bullshit."

"How often do you talk about this adult bullshit, though?"

"Never," he says.

"That's what I thought. Maybe it's good to get it out." I consider his question for a minute before answering. "I'm afraid I'll never be good enough. That I missed out on the opportunity to be the best version of myself, and everything else is just going to be second best. I'm still trying to figure out who the hell I am. For so long, my entire world was a singular thing—soccer. I lived it. I breathed it. Everything revolved around *that*. Now that that thing has been taken from me, I'm having an identity crisis. And, within that crisis, there's this constant fear that no matter what I do, I'll never be as good as the old Maven."

"You're young, and change can be good. I'm so different from who I was at twenty-two, and I'm glad for that. Younger Dallas wouldn't stand a chance at being a father and keeping another human healthy and alive, but we're hanging in there okay." There's another pause. He runs his hand through his hair and tugs on the longer pieces near his ears. He turns thoughtful and quiet when he says, "For the record, I like the new Maven. She's kicking ass. She's kind and she's thoughtful, and she's definitely *more* than enough. Even if she can't see it for herself just yet."

"Wow." I blow out a breath, suddenly warm all over. "Seems like we're both trying to figure this whole life thing out."

"I think I'm going to be trying to figure it out for a long time. And I think that's okay." Dallas adjusts his position on his stool and taps his fingers on his beer bottle. "Will you tell me about soccer? When did you start? Why did you stop?"

EIGHT

MAVEN

IT'S a story I dread sharing.

There's resentment in the memory and anger when I think about how different things would be if the freak accident didn't happen. I try to avoid talking about it. I bat away questions when asked why I no longer play.

With Dallas next to me, though, I feel like I can be honest. We've only spent seven days together, and he's already shown me bits and pieces of himself. The messy parts and the moments of weakness he's tried to hide, but I've caught glimpses of them.

Like when he pressed the heels of his hands into his eyes last night when June had a meltdown, screaming on her back in the middle of the living room and refusing to be held or soothed. I remember the exhaustion on his face when he got home tonight after the team's debrief post scrimmage, his body aching and his mind tired.

I don't know how he does it, but I admire the hell out of him for accomplishing it all.

His knee against mine is a steady pillar. The thick line of his thigh is the courage I need to roll my shoulders back and talk.

"My dad signed me up for a recreational soccer league when

I was four, and I never looked back. I was obsessed. Totally infatuated. I did other sports too, like swimming and cross country, but I kept coming back to soccer," I say.

"You played in college, right?"

"I did. I was on an athletic scholarship. I had dreams of making a team in the National Women's Soccer League then earning a spot on the World Cup team. The universe had other plans for me, and here we are."

"An injury," he says, and I nod.

I touch my necklace and pull the chain from side to side. The gold piece of jewelry with an M dangling from the chain is a gift from Shawn on my sixteenth birthday, and I always find myself reaching for it when I'm nervous or on edge. "My junior year. A mistimed tackle caused my leg to shatter in two places. My knee, in particular, was the most fucked up."

Dallas winces. He squeezes my shoulder before letting go. "Shit. That's devastating, Maven. How fucking painful."

"It was excruciating, but the aftermath was even worse. I did my rehab. I followed the doctor's orders. The tendons and ligaments repaired themselves, but they weren't as strong as before. I was warned that if I tried to play at that high of a level again, I'd risk another injury. I was so defeated the first time, and I couldn't imagine going through it again. I haven't stepped on a field since."

I rub my right knee as I talk. There's always a phantom ache in my leg, a shitty reminder I'll never be the athlete I once was.

My brain accepted the change in my life two years ago without skipping a beat, ready to move on and excited to find the next thing that would define me. My heart has been slower. Reluctant to catch up and holding on to something from the past.

I keep waiting, like maybe soon I'll wake up and be who I was before.

It hasn't happened yet. And every day I stay the same, that mediocre girl who's flailing through life, trying to find the direction she wants to go and lay down some roots, I lose a little more hope.

"I'll tell you a story about this college football player," Dallas says. "A running back set to be a star in the NFL with a lucrative contract on the horizon. First game of freshman year, he tore his ACL on a freak play. He slipped on the field. Didn't even get hit, and his season was over. He came back sophomore year and played, but it was like he was afraid. He didn't take the risks he used to. His body didn't move the same way. He was always a half step behind when he used to be two steps ahead."

"That's sad." There's a pang in my chest, all too familiar. "What happened to him?"

Dallas stands up. He walks across the living room and grabs something off the bookshelf in the corner. When he makes his way back to the kitchen, he tosses me a small velvet box. I open the hinges and see a Super Bowl ring, a hundred diamonds sparkling under the ceiling lights.

"He adjusted," he says, and his voice is thick with emotion. I whip my head up and stare at him, confused.

"I thought you were always a kicker," I say softly and I run my finger over the engravings on the ring. "You're so small. Smaller than the other running backs in the league, I mean. Compared to the general population you're a giant."

"Don't kick my ego when I'm down, Maven." He smiles, but it's strained. "I figured out how to keep doing the thing I love and be the best to ever do it. It looks a little different from how it used to, but I'm still out there. I've failed a lot of times, and it's why I'm so fucking terrified of it. I know how it feels when you're in the trenches of hell, and I know how awful it is when you feel like nothing can go right. But let me tell you something; *you* are not a failure. If you never play soccer again, then you never play again. It doesn't make you any less than the woman you'd be if you went pro. Am I any less because I kick the ball instead of run it?"

"No," I whisper, and it's the truth. I spent more time today watching him than anyone else, awed by his poise and the strength of his leg. "You're not."

"And neither are you. You can hang on to that pain of the past, of what you used to be, or you can recognize that sometimes life doesn't go the way you want it to. You find a new way to get what you want. Football was the love of my life, and I refused to give it up. So I found a loophole. A workaround. If soccer is what you want to do, you'll find a way. And if you don't, that's okay, too."

"I'm not sure life advice was in the job description when I started working for you, but thank you. Thank you for listening to me, and for sharing your story, too."

Dallas opens his arms and welcomes me into a hug. I practically leap into his embrace. He wraps me up tight, and I rest my cheek against his chest. "You're going to be alright. I can already tell you work so hard at things, Maven. If your heart's in it, it's yours."

"You sound like my therapist," I say into his shirt. "Or like you're trying to hit on me."

His laugh is a deep rumble. "I have to admit I'm out of practice and have no idea how to hit on anyone, so if that's the way it came across, I'm sorry."

"What you said means a lot, and I'm going to do some soul searching. Who knows what I'll find?"

"Save some room for me and June," he says, and his fingers dance up my spine. "We like you."

"I like you two, too. Her more, obviously. She gives great manicures. My nails are so pink."

"Obviously. Wait until she does your makeup. You're going to feel really special. The ladies at the park complimented my eyeshadow for days after she made me her muse." He untangles our limbs and grabs our beers. "I think we need another toast."

"Oh?" I reach for my drink and hold it in the air. "What are we going to cheers to this time?"

"Second chances," Dallas says, and his gaze holds mine. "And the right things coming along at exactly the right time."

"Sounds like a Vertical Horizon lyric."

"Are you even old enough to know who that is?"

"Pretty sure that's considered classic music now, lone star. You're aging yourself."

"Lone star?" he asks

"Yeah. You know. Texas. Cowboys. Dallas. Yeehaw," I explain, and he grins at me.

"Wow. You're kind of a little shit."

We knock the bottles together. His eyes stay on me as we take a sip in tandem. They follow me when we move to the couch and go through the rest of the scrimmage photos. The moon gets higher in the sky and the night stretches longer and longer, and the whole time we're together, Dallas never looks away.

NINE

DALLAS

MAVERICK LEANS BACK on my couch and cracks open a beer. "How are things going with the nanny?"

I kick my feet up on the coffee table and stretch out my legs. "She's great. I don't know how I survived for so long without her. I'm sleeping better. I'm eating all of my meals, and I haven't felt this good on the field since my rookie year. June is so tired by the end of the day from being out and about, she falls asleep well before her bedtime."

"Where are they?" Reid asks. "I hope you didn't kick them out just so we could come over."

"They're at the movies. Maven told me to have an afternoon off before I fly out to California tomorrow for our first preseason game, so I am."

"Is she hot?"

I choke on a sip of beer and shoot Maverick a death glare. "Stop it."

"What? I'm just asking a question."

"You're trying to meddle in something that doesn't need to be meddled in."

He sits forward and rests his elbows on his thighs. A shit-eating grin stretches across his mouth, and he drops his chin into the palm of his hand. "I am not. I'm curious, Dal. That's all."

I know he won't give this up until I answer him, and I sigh. "She's fine."

Maverick blinks. He tilts his head to the side. "Fine? The weather is fine. Food is fine. *People* aren't fine. What does that mean?"

"You have a vivid imagination. Interpret it however you want."

I don't add the rest—it's too dangerous.

Fine is the furthest thing in the dictionary to describe Maven Wood.

Hot as sin would be more accurate.

A distraction.

Very fucking pretty, with muscular legs and big, blue eyes that sparkle when she's teasing me. A smile that notches itself in the center of my chest whenever she looks my way, and I've found myself staring at the spot on her neck, just above her throat, frequently and often. That obnoxious sliver of skin taunts me whenever she's wearing a ponytail or playing with her necklace.

There's nothing *fine* about her.

"Alright. Two can play that game, asshole. I'll find her on social media and judge for myself."

"How the hell are you going to do that?"

"Don't underestimate me, Lansfield. The FBI should hire me for my detective skills." Maverick swipes his phone off the arm of the couch and taps the screen. "You told us her name is Maven. She's Shawn's goddaughter, which means he definitely follows her, and if I scroll through his list of—bingo. There she is. Maven Wood."

"Are you thirty or thirteen?" I ask, alarmed.

"The devil works hard, but Maverick Miller searching for a

woman works harder." Reid laughs. "He's faster on the apps than me."

"Fuck, Dal. She's hot."

I know what her social media pages look like. I did a deep dive into them myself, clicking on every picture I could find so I could try and learn her whole story. There are ones of her on the soccer field in a white jersey. A few of her with friends on the beach, the ocean behind them and the sun making her skin glow. I found one of her and Shawn's wife, Lacey, at some charity event. She's holding a glass of wine and looking stunning in a black dress with a plunging neckline and the tiniest smirk on her lips.

I had to turn my phone off after that.

"Let me see." Reid jumps out of his chair and hurries behind the couch. He leans over Maverick's shoulder and whistles. "Oh, yeah. She's pretty. Click on that photo of her and the dogs. No, the other one."

"She plays sports too? God *damn*. Athletic women are my kryptonite," Maverick whines.

"You should message her, Mav, and introduce yourself. No one shoots you down," Reid says.

I know they're fucking with me. Joking around to try and make a point, but I'm still irritated for some reason. I take the phone from Maverick and bury it between the cushions next to stale Goldfish crackers. "Will you two quit it? Stop gawking at her."

"Uh oh." Maverick crosses his arms over his chest. "I think Dallas is jealous. He doesn't like that we're giving his girl attention."

"She's not my girl," I say, exasperated. "She's my friend and my employee. I like spending time with her. That's it."

Maven has been with us for three weeks, and we've settled into a routine that works so well, I find myself finally relaxing.

She's at the apartment by nine in the morning, and she doesn't leave until I get home from the stadium in the late afternoon. Sometimes she stays for dinner, handing over control at the stove after she burns the vegetables or sets a paper towel on fire. Her determination in the kitchen despite being an absolutely horrible cook is cute.

I give her shit and she throws it right back. The two of us work around each other to keep things moving as efficiently as possible for my daughter.

This past week, she's stayed at the apartment well past June's bedtime. We'll sit on the couch and talk until she starts to yawn and my eyes start to close. I feel bad for keeping her so late, but she never makes it seem like she's bored or looking for an excuse to leave.

I think she likes the company too.

"Can I ask her out?" Maverick asks, and something behind my ribs burns hot with his question.

"I will punch your teeth in if you try. You'd find a way to fuck this up for me, and June loves her. Maven adores June, too, and my therapist keeps telling me about the psychological benefits to JB consistently having a woman in her life. I don't know, y'all. There used to be this constant panic when I watched my daughter. My parents said it would fade as she got older, but it never went away. With Maven around, it's gone. It feels like I've been trapped underwater for so long, but now I can take a deep breath. I'm getting to the surface. It's been ages since things have been easy, but right now, they are."

"Sorry for giving you a hard time, Dal. We can see how much happier you are." Reid sits back in his chair and shoves his glasses up his nose. "You're lighter, too. Like a weight has lifted off your shoulder."

"It has. I know Maven's not June's mom, but she loves my kid already. She's giving her stability and the constant attention she deserves. Things are *good*. And it lets me see you guys more, too."

"Aw." Maverick leans over and kisses my cheek. "He loves us."

"Don't let it go to your head. Are y'all sticking around for the game tonight? I have some burgers I can grill and—"

The door to the apartment flies open. I crane my neck to look into the foyer, and I jump off the couch when I see Maven and June.

"Mae?" I call out. "What's going on? Are you okay?"

I hustle toward the door. I check June for injuries when I get to them, but I don't see so much as a scratch on her.

"Hi," Maven says, and her voice is strained. Her cheeks are pink and her eyes are red, and my heart hammers worriedly in my chest. "We're fine. I just... I messed up, and I feel like a horrible person."

"Talk to me. Are you hurt?"

"No, no. No one is hurt."

"Did you kill someone? Do we need to hide a body? I think I might have a shovel somewhere in the apartment." I take the backpack hanging from her shoulder and set it on the floor. "Wait a second. Is this another candy necklace situation?"

A soft laugh escapes her, and my shoulders relax. "No. We didn't terrorize any department stores today. June and I were in the movie, and she kept fidgeting. I asked if she needed to use the bathroom three times, and she said no. When we were leaving, I realized she had an accident. I forgot to bring a change of clothes with us, so I had to make the poor girl sit in her—" Maven takes a deep breath. "I'm sorry. I'm so sorry, Dallas. I feel horrible."

"Daddy!" June flings her arms around my leg, and I squat down to kiss her forehead. Her shorts are damp, but she seems unfazed. "We saw a movie."

"Did you? How was it?"

"There was a princess." June sighs and rests her head on my chest. "A pretty princess."

"We love princesses." My eyes flick to Maven, and she's gnawing on her bottom lip. There's a tug toward her. A yank, almost, to let her know she didn't do anything wrong, because I hate seeing her defeated and upset. "Mae, hey. It's okay. Accidents happen. When JB was younger, she had explosive diarrhea when we were at a birthday party."

"Explosive!" June repeats, and I laugh.

"Majorly explosive. Guess who forgot her diaper bag? Me. Getting home was a nightmare, and I had to throw away her car seat. Don't worry about it."

"Do you think she's traumatized?" Maven asks. "Do you think she hates me?"

"June? Do you hate Maven?" I ask my daughter point blank, and June frowns.

"I love Mae Mae," she says.

"See? Kid's already forgotten about it. She's got the memory of a goldfish. I'll give her a bath and put her in some clean clothes. She'll be as good as new."

"I can do it," Maven says quickly. "It's my fault. I told you to take the afternoon off, and I—"

"There's no such thing as taking the afternoon off when you're a parent. It's fine. Really. It'll take me ten minutes."

"I'm the one who messed up, and I'd like to be the one to make it right." Her eyes meet mine. "Please, Dallas."

Oh, fuck me.

I shouldn't like hearing her say that, but I do.

It messes me up. Catches me off guard and alters my brainwaves a little, because when June tugs on my shirt, I realize I'm staring at Maven like I've lost any and all intelligence.

Maybe I have.

"Okay," I say, and it feels like there's a frog in my throat. "Sure. Yeah. Thank you."

"I'm sorry again." She takes June's hand in hers. "You go and have fun. We'll stay out of your way."

"I don't want you to stay out of the way. Come to the living room when you're done. I'm making burgers, and my friends and I are going to watch the game. You should join us."

"Are you sure? I don't want to interrupt your night."

"You're not interrupting a thing. I'm glad you're here."

Maven smiles. "Okay. I'd like that a lot."

They walk down the hall and I watch them go, knowing my friends are going to give me absolute shit when they meet her.

TEN

MAVEN

"ALL CLEAN." I run a brush through June's wet hair and pull the brown waves back into the two pigtails she likes to wear. "You're as good as new, kid."

She twirls around in the sparkly pink skirt she put on after her bath. "Can I wear a crown?"

"Of course you can. You never need an excuse to wear a crown, and don't let anyone tell you otherwise." I grab a tiara off the floor and set it on her head. "There. Now you look just like the princess from the movie."

June hurries over to the dresser. She rummages through a drawer before running back over and handing me another tiara. "Yours."

"Thank you, June Bug." I smile and put it in my hair. "How do I look?"

"Pretty." She throws her arms around my neck and gives me a hug. "You're my best friend, Mae Mae."

The nice words lodge themselves in my heart, and I squeeze her tight. "You're *my* best friend, June. I'm sorry for not taking you to the potty today."

"That's okay." She pats my cheek and giggles. "I love you."

"I love you, too, kiddo." I pick her up and step over a pile of blocks. "Let's go find your dad. I heard he's making us burgers, and I'm starving."

We head down the hall, and the tension I've been holding onto starts to seep away. I know Dallas isn't going to bite my head off, and the longer I hold June in my arms and she talks about castles and dragons, and puppies, the more I know he was right.

She's already forgotten about what happened, and I need to let a little bit of that guilt go.

I slow my steps as we approach the living room and take my time so I can make sure we're not interrupting anything. I've heard about Dallas's friends, but I haven't met them. June calls them her uncles, and knowing she has an army of men who love her and care about her makes me happy.

It's exactly how my dad and Shawn are, best friends from childhood and a friendship that's lasted for decades. Sometimes it feels like I have two dads. Both of them are around whenever I need advice and are eager to jump in when I ask for help. I'm lucky to have so many people who support me, and so is June.

A laugh bounces off the walls and rings in my ears, and my lips tug up into a smile.

Dallas.

I'd recognize that sound anywhere.

It's good to hear him having fun. Between parenting and practice and the errands he's constantly running, he hardly gets a second to himself.

I've been taking up those precious seconds, too, hanging out at the apartment the last couple of nights and chatting with him about my college days and what it was like when he entered the league. He asked to see more of my photography and I asked to see the yearbook the team puts together at the end of every season.

Spending time with him is easy and *fun*.

He'll grin at me from across the couch. Hold his side when I make a joke. Wheeze with tears in his eyes after I show him a funny video until he finally settles down. He hugs me before I leave, his arms wrapping me tight and holding me there for one second, then two and three.

He's a good guy, and I'm not sure I've ever met a man like Dallas Lansfield before.

"Daddy," June says as we come around the corner into the living room, and I set her on the rug.

She takes off, giggling as she makes her way toward him. I lean against the wall and watch him scoop her in his arms and spin her around.

"There's my girl." His eyes flick over to me, and his smile grows. "Hey, Mae. Are you doing okay?"

"Yeah. I'm good."

"Good." He hooks his thumb over his shoulder and points to the two men perched on the couch. "These are my friends."

"I'm Reid," the first one says. He's smaller than Dallas, shorter and less broad, with red hair and thick glasses. Cute, too, with freckles across his nose and bright green eyes. His skin is fair and his smile is kind. "I'm the social media manager for the Titans."

"I've seen you around." I take the empty chair by the fireplace and cross my legs. "You're always staring at your phone."

"I don't know how you would notice that," Dallas teases. "You're always staring at your camera."

"Because it's my job," Reid and I say in unison.

"Great minds think alike," I laugh, and he lifts his beer in my direction.

"And that's Maverick Miller," Dallas says.

Overwhelming is too soft a word to describe him.

He's bigger than any hockey player I've ever seen, with tattoos down his left arm and a big red heart on the back of his hand. His dark hair is messy, his smile is boyish, and there's something charismatic about him that makes it difficult to look away. He's attractive, yeah, alarmingly so, but there's also an air of easiness in the way he moves. Like the earth would bend to him if he asked it to.

Maverick walks toward me with the smug confidence of a man who knows he's God's gift to the world and drops to his knees. He takes my hand and kisses my knuckles.

"Maven," he says with a deep and rumbly voice. "It's nice to meet you. I'm Maverick."

I sneak a glance at Dallas, and he's watching us. His jaw is tense, and his eyes are narrowed into tiny slits. He looks annoyed, but when I blink, the irritation is wiped clean from his face.

"You know, Maverick, you're exactly where every man should be—on their knees," I say.

"I'll stay here forever if you want. I'm a man who likes to deliver," he says with a wink.

"I think I'm going to pass. I can't handle another average encounter with a guy who thinks he knows what he's doing with his stick, but really, he can never find the net."

Maverick pops on his feet and grins from ear to ear. "You're good, Maven Wood. I like you already, but I can *always* find the net."

"We get it. Women love you. Zero complaints. Hooray for Maverick." Dallas sets June down, and she runs straight for Reid. "If you ever need anything while I'm not here, you can always call these two. Maverick lives on the other side of the building, and Reid can leave the stadium a lot easier than I can."

"It's nice to meet you guys," I say.

"The pleasure is all ours." Maverick stalks back to the couch and sits down, stealing June out of Reid's arms. "How do you like working for the Titans?"

"I love it. Being on the field is a totally different experience than up in the stands, and I think I took three thousand pictures at the scrimmage. I'm afraid I'm going to use up a whole memory card next week for the first home game."

"Just make sure all of your photos are of me," Dallas says.

"You're on the field less time than anyone." Maverick lets June play with the silver chain around his neck, and he fixes the tiara on her head. "No one wants to see your face."

Reid shoots me an apologetic look. "You're going to hear these arguments a lot. It'll be nice to have someone to suffer with."

"I'm going to start the burgers. Keep talking, and see if you get fed," Dallas says.

"Want some help?" I ask, and he smiles.

"From the girl who caught a paper towel on fire the other day in the toaster oven? I'd love some help. JB, you're going to hang out with Uncle Mav and Uncle Reid while Maven and Daddy cook some burgers, okay?"

June nods, too busy tracing the shapes on Maverick's arms to listen to him.

"Sorry, *Daddy*." Maverick smirks. "JB has a new leading man in her life."

"Insufferable," Dallas mumbles, and he gestures toward the kitchen. "Shall we?"

I jump out of the chair and follow him. He grabs a beer from the fridge, pops the top off with the hem of his shirt, and hands it to me.

That was hot.

"Thanks." I take a sip and set the bottle on the island. "Your friends are fun."

"They're something. Thanks for being a good sport with them. It's nice to see someone dish it back to Maverick for once and not drop to his feet." Dallas pauses and reaches for a plate. "He's smitten with you."

"He's... large."

"It's okay, Mae. You're not going to hurt my feelings by thinking he's hot."

"I do not think that."

"Liar." He slings a dish towel over his shoulder. "Everyone thinks he's hot."

"Everyone thinks you're hot, too," I blurt out for some stupid reason, and I cover my mouth after I've said it. "Can we pretend I didn't just call my boss hot?"

He puts his elbows on the island next to me and grins. "You think I'm hot?" he asks, and his voice is pitched low like a secret.

"I—no. I don't. Other people do." I fumble with my drink and take a sip. Dallas follows the bob of my throat as I swallow, and he won't stop looking at me. "I'm not one of them."

"Now you're just hurting my feelings." He sticks out his bottom lip and pouts. "Any other grievances you want to air? Are my peanut butter and jelly sandwiches shit?"

"Your sandwiches are incredible, and you know it. I hear you presenting them to June like they're a Michelin-starred meal," I laugh, and I shove his shoulder.

Dallas is too big for me to actually move—the man is a wall of muscle—but he makes a nice show of pretending like I did some damage.

"Be gentle with me, tiny fighter," he murmurs.

His fingers wrap around my wrist to stop me from trying to mess with him again. He holds me there, his eyes on mine, and I stop breathing.

We've touched each other before. Accidental grazes when he's reaching over me to get a mug from the top shelf. Quick brushes of skin when I slide past him to put June to bed or hand him a plate to load into the dishwasher. The press of his thigh into mine at the dinner table because he takes up so much space. Friendly hugs and his arm slung around my shoulder.

This is different, and it doesn't feel like we're joking anymore.

Anything I want to say catches in my chest. It turns to dust when his thumb runs along the vein inside my wrist. When his gaze bounces to my mouth and holds there, it's electric.

"Daddy!" June shouts, and I hear the pitter-patter of feet coming down the hall.

Dallas and I spring apart.

He drops me from his hold and turns away. I sit on the barstool behind me, and June barrels into the kitchen just as I catch my breath.

"Uncle Mav says I have to be a chaperone," June says.

"Uncle Mav doesn't even know how to spell chaperone," Dallas says, and he faces me again. His cheeks are pink, and he looks a little winded. I hold back a laugh because I feel exactly the same way, like I've been sprinting for miles and miles, no finish line in sight. "You good?"

"Me?" I ask. "Why wouldn't I be good?"

Because something definitely just happened between us, and we both don't know what to do.

His eyes fall to my mouth again, and I see heat behind the dark brown before he blinks it away. "Just want to make sure."

"I'm fine. Groovy, even. All is well."

"Good. That's good. I'm going to get the burgers going," he says, and he waves toward the balcony. "If you need me."

"I'll keep an eye on June and make sure she doesn't try to run through any glass doors or anything," I say, and his lips hook up into a smile.

There he is.

When Dallas heads outside to fire up the grill, I can't help but wonder what might have happened if June had walked in thirty seconds later.

ELEVEN

DALLAS

"I THINK you might be insane, Coach." I groan as I drag my body into the hotel. The air conditioning is a sweet relief from the warm California sun, and I shiver at the change of temperature on my burnt skin. "We got off a six-hour flight and we have our first preseason game on Sunday, yet you still insist on a full practice. My legs are going to fall off. I haven't run that much since I was a rookie."

"Preseason games don't matter," Shawn says, and he pats my shoulder. His fingers push into my aching muscles, and I think the fucker is doing it on purpose. "Why waste a practice day for something that won't reflect on our record at the end of the year? It's character building."

"It also builds sore hamstrings, a sore ass, and not being able to kick on Sunday," I grumble, and he lets out a sharp laugh. "I'm glad you find my misery funny, you dickwad."

"You'll be fine." He points to a couch tucked in the corner of the lobby. "Sit. I'll be there in a minute."

"Dammit. What did I do?" I collapse onto the furniture, and my sweaty limbs slip on the leather. I drop my practice gear on the floor and set my helmet on the cushions. "Whatever it is, I'm sorry."

A chorus of *oohs* come from my teammates as they pass me on their way to a long shower and stretch. Shawn put us through the ringer today, and I know everyone's plans to go out tonight just went out the window.

"Someone fucked up," Jett says, and he lets the other guys walk ahead of him. He ruffles my hair, and I swat him away. "You're in trouble."

"Yeah, yeah. Want to grab dinner tonight?" I ask.

"Sure. We can go before film review." His face softens and he takes the open spot next to me on the couch. "You doing okay being away from June?"

"It's not easy, but it's getting easier." I shrug, knowing he's probably missing his teenage brother. He took him in last year after their mother passed away, and he's struggled with going from the role of brother to dad. "How about you? How's Benny doing?"

"He's fine, but I feel like I'm constantly flying by the seat of my pants. Does that ever change?"

"Nope. It's been four years of that for me, and there aren't any signs of figuring out this whole parent thing anytime soon. You did a good thing, man. Young girls are a hell of a lot different than teenage boys, but I'm here if you ever need anything. You're not alone."

"Thanks, D. Appreciate you." He knocks his knuckles against mine and stands up. "Get some rest."

I give him a half-hearted wave and wait for Shawn to finish talking to our assistant coaches. He makes his way over, a clipboard tucked under his arm, and takes the large chair across from me.

"How are you doing?" he asks.

"Pretty broad statement there, Coach. Physically I'm feeling every bit like an athlete who's been playing professional football for eight years and just had a practice that was hard as hell; like I'm going to need a walker just to get from my shower to my bed to take a nap."

"What about mentally? It's your first time being away from June this season, and I wanted to check in."

"Oh." I give him a tired smile. "I'm doing surprisingly well. When I got back to the bus after practice, I had a dozen photos waiting for me."

"How are things with Maven?"

"Great. We hang out in the apartment before I leave for practice and again when I get home. She's cool, and June loves her."

I leave it at that, because Shawn sure as shit doesn't need to know I like spending time with her, even when my daughter isn't around.

It's like a void is being filled when I'm with her. Each day is a drop in a cup I didn't realize was empty.

It's good to have another friend.

"You're a good guy, Lansfield," he says. "I'm glad things are turning around for you."

"Me, too." I grin and reach for his hand. We exchange a handshake, and all feels right in the world. "Thanks for checking in on me. It means a lot."

Shawn stands up, and I pop onto my feet to join him. "Go rest before the film review tonight. I don't want to start the season with a blocked field goal attempt."

"Don't worry. I'll be there."

I wave and head for the elevators. The ride up to the thirty-sixth floor feels like it takes hours, and I've never been so grateful to make it into a hotel room before.

I'm exhausted from an early morning flight and the three-hour practice. Climbing in bed and sleeping until this evening sounds like fucking *heaven*, but I want to talk to June more than I want to relax.

I grab my phone and head to the window. I open the curtains and let the west coast sunshine flood the room. Just as I'm about to call Maven, a text from her pops up on my screen.

MAVEN

It's dinnertime over here.

I might have ruined the chicken we were going to have, so we had some pasta delivered.

Attachment: 1 image

A photo comes through, and I grin when I see it.

My kitchen looks like a war zone. June is in her booster seat, and there is tomato sauce all over her hands and face. Maven has her arm extended to take the photo, and she's just as messy. There are drops of red on her neck, and the front of her white shirt is stained. She's smiling from ear to ear, and half a spaghetti noodle is stuck to her cheek.

A laugh bursts out of me, and I've never called someone so fast in my life.

"Hey," she answers on the second ring.

"Jesus, Maven. Did y'all even eat dinner, or did it go everywhere?"

"We might have made a little bit of a mess. I'll make sure to clean it up before you get home, but I can't promise you won't be finding sauce in the crevices of the table for weeks."

"JB looks like a murder suspect. It's cute," I say.

"Interesting use of the word cute. I didn't know serial killers were your type."

"The heart wants what the heart wants. Have y'all had a

good day? Tell me what you did. Thanks for the pictures, by the way."

"I didn't send too many?" Maven asks. "I thought I might have gone overboard."

"Not at all. Keep them coming."

"Today was good. We went to the library and did story time. Then we stopped by the park, and June played in the splash pad. After our nap we took a walk around the neighborhood. Your daughter has an emotional support acorn now, by the way. I can't get her to part with it."

"Two weeks ago, she was obsessed with a rock. Now we've moved on to acorns. Kids are something else. Is she behaving?"

"She's an angel. Do you want to talk to her? I can FaceTime you."

"Do you mind? I'm so fucking tired, but I want to say goodnight before I take a nap."

The screen goes black, then Maven's face pops up. That noodle is still stuck on her cheek, and she doesn't look the least bit worn out after a full day of chasing around a toddler. Her eyes are bright. Her smile is wide, and she looks fucking *beautiful*.

"There we go. How's California?" she asks.

"Warm. Loud. Busy. I haven't missed it at all."

"Sounds exactly like D.C. only three thousand miles away."

"I'm glad to see the apartment is still in one piece. What happened to the chicken?"

"I might have burned it. It's no big deal. Just give me the Nanny of the Year award now. Speaking of..." The screen turns blurry, then I see June in her booster seat with red handprints all over her shirt. "Look who it is."

"Hi, baby girl," I say, and Maven flips the camera around so June can see me.

"Hi, Daddy. You play football?"

"I did. I was on the field for a little bit kicking. How was the library? And the park?"

"Mae Mae got me a doggie book. Daddy, can we get a doggie?"

"We'll have to see about that. I'm starting to think Mae Mae might be a bad influence."

"Hey." Maven's face comes back into focus, and she sticks out her tongue. "Watch your tone there, Lansfield, or I might leave this spaghetti sauce everywhere and forget to clean up."

"Just kidding." I grin and sit in one of the chairs in my room. "What's the plan for tomorrow?"

"I haven't gotten that far yet. Any suggestions?"

"June likes the farmer's market. The one in Dupont Circle is really good. The zoo is never a bad choice either. She could watch the panda bears for hours."

"Daddy," June says, and Maven shifts the camera back to her. "Come home soon?"

"I'll be home in three sleeps, JB. And when you wake up tomorrow, it'll only be two sleeps."

"Wow." She giggles and grabs a noodle off the table, flinging it at the wall. "I love you, Daddy."

A lump forms in my throat, and I swallow it down. I don't want her to see me get emotional, but *fuck*, I miss her so much. It's never easy being away, and I'm counting down the hours until we touch down in D.C.

Sunday night can't come soon enough.

"I love you too, princess," I say.

"How much?"

"You know the stars in the night sky? If you added all of them up—and there are billions and billions of them up there— I'd still love you more than that, June Bug."

"That's a lot of love," Maven whispers in her ear.

"A lot?" June asks.

"More than anything in this world. Be good for Mae Mae tonight, alright?"

"Alright, Daddy." She blows me a kiss, and I pretend to catch it out of the air. "Bye."

Maven pans the camera back to herself. "You look exhausted."

"Coach sent us to he—" I catch myself before the swear slips out. "He ran us into the ground today. The man is out of his mind."

"Shawn in coach mode is scary. Go take a nap. I'll send you a picture when she's in bed."

"Thanks, Mae." I smile and run my hand through my hair. "It's good to see you."

"You, too. It's weird being here without you." She pauses. "June misses you."

"I miss her, too." I stare at the screen. I should hang up, but something is keeping me there, looking at her and trying to keep the conversation going. "The guest room should be all set up for you."

"I saw. I can't wait to jump on that bed. It looks soft." Maven turns away from the camera and laughs. "I better go. June is trying to weasel her way out of the booster seat. If we could avoid any hospital visits, that would be great. JB, say good night to your dad."

"Night, Daddy! I love you," June says.

"I love you too, kiddo. Night, Maven."

"Night, *Daddy*," she jokes and I nearly drop the phone. "Sweet dreams."

Later, when I wake up from my nap and open the picture of Maven and June curled up in her bed, my heart skips a goddamn beat. I hate myself just a little bit for staring at the photo for longer than I should, because it doesn't feel like I'm being the good guy.

It feels like the exact opposite.

Like I'm about to break all the rules and play with fucking fire.

TWELVE
MAVEN

DALLAS TEXTED me last night and told me to meet him and June at the apartment this morning, but he didn't add anything else. I'm clueless about what's going on when I unlock the door to his place and walk inside.

"Hello? Anyone here?" I call out.

It's quiet for a Tuesday morning, and I imagine Dallas might be moving slower only two days after his first game of the year. He got back late Sunday night from California with a win under his belt, but he was up early yesterday. I left as soon as I was awake; with no practice, he didn't need my help with June.

We're back on schedule today, but I'm nervous as I kick off my sneakers in the foyer and line them up next to Dallas's high-top Nikes and June's strappy sandals.

Maybe he's going to fire me.

Maybe his laughter on the FaceTime call we shared while he was on the road was forced, and he's pissed I made a mess in his house.

Maybe he started dating someone and doesn't need me around anymore because he has another woman who can keep an eye on JB while he's gone.

There's a pressure in my chest as I think about someone replacing me. A twist in my gut as I imagine someone else getting to tuck June in at night and read her favorite bedtime stories, and I take a deep breath as I walk down the hall.

"Kitchen," Dallas's muffled voice calls back. "Come on in."

I make my way toward the sound of pots and pans clinking together. Johnny Cash croons from a speaker, and I stop in the entryway to the kitchen, caught off guard by the sight in front of me.

Dallas.

Shirtless.

He's bent over the stove. There's a pink apron tied around his neck and one of June's many tiaras is tangled in his messy hair. His black joggers sit low on his hips, and he's humming along to the song.

I stare at him, at the ease of his movements as he flicks his wrist and lifts the pan off the stove. I admire the muscles stretching from shoulder to shoulder and down his spine. The red tint to his back makes it seem like he just climbed out of the shower a few minutes ago, and I wonder if he's still warm from the hot water.

I realize I'm gawking at him, and I clear my throat.

"You're taking Casual Tuesday to a new level," I say, and he spins to face me.

The back of him was nice—deliciously so—but I'm not prepared for the front.

The apron stops well above his belly button. Abdominal muscles peek out from below the flowered pattern. A dusting of dark hair trails down his stomach to the waistband of his pants and disappears from view.

His body is made of sharp lines and sharp angles, hours of physical exertion spent crafting the sculpted slope of his limbs. He's a *man* in every sense of the word, and for half a second, I daydream about what it would feel like to be pressed against him.

"Hey," he says with his southern drawl, the syllable a little tired around the edges but still irreplaceably lovely. "There you are."

I blink, and I jerk my gaze away from the spot above his hip and back to his face. He must have caught me staring, because he smirks and tilts his head to the side, a twinkle behind the dark brown of his eyes.

"Hi," I say, and my throat goes dry.

"If you're going to eye-fuck me Maven, you could at least buy me dinner first."

"I am *not* eye-fucking you," I say, and I play with my necklace. "I've just never seen you without a shirt on, and it's revolting."

"Tell that to the tongue hanging out of your mouth," he jokes. "I'm making pancakes. What kind do you want? Regular? Chocolate chip? Blueberry?"

I walk toward him and nudge him out of the way with my hip. "I'll have whatever you all are having, which looks like chocolate chip. Perfect. Where's June?"

"Cleaning up her stuffed animals. We had a tea party yesterday, and the collection of bears and giraffes didn't get put away."

"That explains the tiara then."

Dallas shrugs. He leans against the counter and faces me. "It makes her happy."

Simple, easy, as true as the sky is blue.

If there was a Dad of the Year award, it would go to him.

No one else would even be in contention.

His love for June is pure and honest. It's full of mistakes and mess-ups and so many things not going right. But there is so much *good* in that love, too. Half-done nail polish on his left hand and tiny braids in his hair. The quiet moments where he holds her in the rocking chair, her head on his chest and his arms wrapped around her like he's protecting her from the world.

He'd move mountains to make her happy, a deep adoration that no matter how hard I try, I'll never understand. I can admire it, though. I can feel it in my bones when he tells her she's his favorite girl and hugs her extra tight before he leaves for the stadium.

It's the most selfless love I've ever known, and it makes me want to be a better person because of it.

"You're a good man and a good father," I say softly, and he watches me. "And if you want to fire me, I understand. You're doing what's best for your daughter, and I don't hold that against you at all."

"Fire you?" Dallas takes a step toward me. "What the hell are you talking about?"

"I don't know. Your text was vague, and I thought maybe you wanted to part ways."

"Maven." He sets down the spatula he's holding and puts his hands on my shoulders. "Why would I fire you? You're the good part of all of my days. June's days, too. I'm being vague because I have a surprise for JB, and I want you to come along, too."

"You do?"

"Yeah." His laugh is soft and shy, and he dips his chin. "If you thought I was going to fire you, I need to do a better job of showing you how much I like you being here."

"No, it's not that. I just..." I bite my bottom lip and reach out, tugging one of the strings of his apron. "Being here with you and June is so fun, and we're normally open with each other about things that are going on in her life and ours. I mean, I told you my period cramps were going to make me late last week, and you didn't even bat an eye."

"I grew up with a sister, remember? I bought a heating pad,

by the way. For you to use if you're ever here and in pain. It's in the guest room bathroom with some Advil."

"Oh. That is—thank you, Dallas. You didn't have to do that."

"Have to and want to are two different things, Maven, and I wanted to do it because I want you to be comfortable when you're here. Shawn was nice enough to give us today off from practice, too, so I figured the three of us could take advantage of the time off."

"That sounds fun. I'm sorry for assuming the worst. That was shitty of me."

"You're forgiven." He gives my arm a squeeze. "I'm not going to tell you where we're going, but I will say you need to take off your jewelry. I know how much you love that necklace, and leaving it on puts it at risk of getting ruined."

I touch the gold chain around my neck, aware that he's noticed I never go anywhere without it. "Want me to grab June?"

"Please. We'll eat, get her ready then head out."

"We make a good team, don't we?"

"No, Maven." His smile curls into something different. Secretive, almost, and I want to know what he's thinking. "We make the best fucking team."

"A SPLATTER PAINT ROOM?" I ask, and I look around the lobby of the building Dallas led us into twenty minutes ago. "How does it work?"

"It's easy. We throw paint wherever we want. On the canvas. At each other. You can use your hands or the brushes. It's supposed to be a fun stress reliever." Dallas kneels down and helps June step into the provided jumpsuit we're all wearing to cover our clothes. "JB. You aren't allowed to eat the paint okay? It'll make you sick."

"Okay, Daddy," June agrees.

"This might be the coolest thing I've ever done," I say.

"Way better than getting fired, right?" he teases, and I roll my eyes.

"Only marginally." I braid my hair into two pigtails and throw on the hat Dallas gave me to wear. "Do I get points if I get paint on your face?"

"No paint on my face. I have a game on Sunday. What if I can't see to kick because there's blue acrylic in my eye? We'd lose, and my career would be over."

"You've missed kicks before, buddy. And that's what these are for. To protect your pretty eyes." I grab three pairs of goggles hanging from a rack on the wall and toss two his way. "All bets are off when we go in there. The paint room is a lawless space, and I *will* kick your butt."

"If you throw paint at my face, Maven, you better be prepared for the consequences."

"Don't tempt me with a good time. You're going down, Lansfield. Right, June? We're going to get your dad."

"Yes!" she squeals, and I grin.

Ten minutes later and all geared up, we head into a large room. We're the only ones here, and from the way the owner keeps thanking Dallas for his generous donation to the business's nonprofit supporting local art programs, I have a feeling the privacy was prearranged.

"Daddy, look." June points to a splatter of red on the wall. "It's messy."

"Very messy," Dallas says, and he leads us over to a long table covered in dried paint. "And you know what the best part is? There are no rules."

"No rules?" she asks. "I can run?"

"You can run wherever you want, JB."

"Gonna get you, Daddy." June stands on her toes and grabs a

brush off the table. She dips it in the can of pink and swirls it around. Satisfied with how it looks, she pulls it out and flings it at him, giggling when it goes all over the jumpsuit covering his legs. "I did it!"

I pick up a brush and dip it in the green. I bring my wrist back and throw it at Dallas. The color lands on his chest, and I grin. "Got you, *Daddy*. You look like a watermelon."

"Christ," he mumbles. He blows out a breath and finds the largest brush on the table. "Y'all are in for it now."

"Run, June." I pick her up and sprint across the room. Her giggles echo in my ear, and soon I'm laughing, too. I feel a twinge of pain in my knee and my heart pounds in my ears, but I keep moving. "We can't let him get us."

"Closer," June squeals.

I duck behind a tall canvas sitting on a wooden easel just as Dallas launches the brush covered in yellow at us. He misses hitting us, but a drop gets on June's ankle.

"You snooze, you lose, Lansfield," I say, and we take off toward the other side of the room.

"Damn, Maven, I didn't realize you were this quick," he says, and it adds a pep to my step.

June and I reach the table with the paint cans first, and I hand her two brushes. I take three for myself and dip them all in the first colors I can find. We spin around, and Dallas is only feet away.

"Now, JB," I say, and we attack. Paint from all five brushes hit him at once, and I pump my fist in the air. "Nice job, kid."

"I got Daddy," June says, and I give her a high five.

"Colluding with the toddler gives you an unfair advantage," he says, and he wipes a glob of purple from his cheek. "Put her down, and let's settle this fairly as adults."

It's hot as hell seeing Dallas in his element. It might not be a football field, but his athletic mindset is coming out, and a dominant side of him I've never seen before peeks through.

It sends a thrill through me. It makes me want to push him and test him and see how far he'll go to win. If he's anything like me—and I think he is—he won't give up or go down without a fight.

This is going to be *fun*.

THIRTEEN

MAVEN

I GIVE him a slow grin and set June safely on the floor. "Rules?"

"We start at opposite ends. June says go. First one to the table and first to get paint on the other wins," Dallas says, and I nod.

"You're on."

We make our way to the edges of the room, and I stare at him. I crack my neck from side to side and stretch my arms, preparing myself like I'm about to do a grueling workout.

This isn't a soccer field and I'm not playing in one of the biggest games of my career, but I feel that fire in me. The determination that settles at the base of my spine, and it's a shame he doesn't know what's coming his way.

"Wait," he calls out from across the room. "What about your knee?"

"What about it?"

"I don't want you to hurt yourself."

"Oh, no. You don't get to start with the nice guy act now. My knee is fine. It's thirty feet away, and I'm not fragile. I'll be okay."

"Are you sure?" he asks, and it's genuine. Considerate and kind with sweetness lacing the question, and it's embarrassing how easily I almost melt.

"Yes," I say, but my voice wavers.

"Good. Then I won't feel so bad when I kick your ass."

"Kick ass," June repeats, and it echoes around us.

"Way to go, Dallas," I say, and he rubs his forehead.

Even from here, I can see a streak of green he smudges just below his hairline. It trails down his temple to his cheek, and he has no idea he's getting paint all over his face. It's fun to watch him be clueless for half a second, because he's usually so meticulous about everything else.

"No, sweetie. That's a bad word, and Daddy shouldn't have said it. I take it back," he says. "No cursing allowed."

"Are we doing this or not, Lansfield?" I ask.

He rolls his shoulders back and crouches down. It looks like he's about to snap a football. His eyes stay trained on me, and his wicked smile makes heat pool deep in my belly. "June, can you count down from three for us? Then say go."

"Okay, Daddy." June holds her arm above her head. "Three, two, one, go," she yells, and I take off.

Dallas's legs are lightyears longer than mine, and I know the only way I stand a chance of winning this silly game is if I'm quicker. I move as fast as I can. My arms pump the air and my feet turn over the concrete floor like my life depends on it. I reach the paint a half second before he does. I grab a brush just as he runs full steam into the table.

It's chaos.

The table flips over. Dallas goes tumbling with it, somersaulting in the air. Cans go flying. Brushes fall from the sky like rain. I'm knocked on my back, and there's a rainbow of color in my vision.

"Oof," I get out. Something heavy rests on my chest, and when I open my eyes, all I can see is green. "Am I blind?"

"Holy shit," Dallas wheezes. "That did not go as planned."

"I can see why we signed waivers beforehand."

"Are you okay?"

I pull the goggles off and realize the weight I'm feeling is him.

On top of me.

Paint drips from his cheek and his hair. His hips press into mine, and his hands are on either side of my head, holding himself up so he doesn't squash me.

"What the hell happened?" I ask.

"I might have run into the table," he admits sheepishly. "In my defense, I thought it was sturdier than that."

"In the table's defense, you're a one hundred and ninety pound football player," I counter, and his chest rumbles with laughter.

We're so close, that when he drops his forehead, it rests against mine. The paint on his skin fuses us together, and I wonder if we're going to be stuck like this forever.

"Sorry, I—" he starts to say.

"No, that's okay. I'm—"

We move at the same time. I lift my hips to try and roll away just as he pushes down, and I *feel him* between my legs. Thick, long. Half-hard and pressing against the inside of my thigh. My breath catches and my back arches, some subconscious part of me aching to be closer to him.

"Sorry," he says again, softer this time. It doesn't sound much like an apology, and I wouldn't accept it if it was.

"My fault," I whisper back, but neither of us move.

He's pinning me to the ground. His large body cages mine, and until he releases me, I'm stuck here.

But I'm in no hurry to leave.

Everything in me pulls tight and turns to liquid heat as I relax into him. I hear his staggered breathing. I feel his exhales on my face. I smell his cologne, and I wonder what he would taste like if I ran my tongue up the line of his throat.

It's nice.

Too nice.

Nice enough for me to want to stay a while. Loop my arms around his neck and lift my hips again, to see how deep he could get.

"Daddy," June says, and we both whip our heads to the side. "Smoochy kiss."

"Oh, no, June Bug," Dallas says hurriedly. He tries to get off me now, but my leg is hooked around his thigh and his hand is tangled in one of my braids. "We're not—"

"Mae Mae is hurt," she says with the stomp of her foot. "Kiss and make it better."

"She's not going to stop," he mumbles. "Maybe I should just..."

I nod, vaguely aware of my surroundings. I bite my bottom lip as our eyes meet. "It's okay. You, uh, can."

His attention moves to my mouth, and he lets out a soft sound that's reminiscent of a tortured moan. "Forehead?"

"Sure," I say, a little breathless. It feels like I'm floating, walking on the clouds toward something I can't quite see yet. "That's good."

He hums. The hand in my hair moves down and cups my cheek with alarming care. He tips his chin down, and his lips dance over my forehead.

It's faint. Hardly long enough to be considered a kiss in the first place, but there's still bursts of color when he pulls away. When his eyes dance across my face and his smile hooks up on the right side of his mouth, pleased with what he sees, my cheeks burn as hot as the sun.

"Not just good," he murmurs, and his voice is deeper than I've ever heard it. "Fucking perfect."

I have to get out of this position before I combust.

"Yay," June says. I look up and see her holding a half-full can of paint. "I win."

Before I can register what's happening, she dumps what's left of the blue on us and drenches our heads.

I cackle. I laugh so hard tears prick my eyes and my lungs gasp for air. "Oh my god. She's so smart."

"June Marigold Lansfield," Dallas says. He pushes off of me and rolls onto his back, grabbing his daughter by the waist and lifting her in the air with one arm. She squeals with glee, and I love that sound. "You are in big trouble."

"Sorry, Daddy. I said I win."

"You definitely win, JB," I say, and I stretch my arm out to my side. My fingers brush against Dallas's free hand, and when I go to pull away, his pinky hooks around mine, keeping me in place.

"Can't argue with that," he says. "Except there's not any paint on *you,* and that's not fair." He sits her on his stomach and gently presses his palm to her cheek, leaving behind a swatch of color. "There. Much better."

"Can we get ice cream?" she asks.

"Ice cream sounds delicious," I say.

"It's not even eleven." Dallas turns his head to glance at me, and he looks younger than he has in the month I've been working for him. His smile is wider. His eyes are brighter. There's a lightness to him, like a weight has been lifted off his shoulders. "You're not going to back me up on this, are you?"

"You manhandled me to the floor. I'm siding with June on this one, dude."

"Fine." He stands up and lifts June with him. When he's on two feet, he offers me a hand, and I accept it, standing too. "Ice cream it is."

"Thanks," I say.

"Are we good? After..." he gestures to my face.

"Yeah. Totally good."

"Okay. Good."

"Good," I agree.

He hitches another look at me before June drags him toward the door, talking about mint chocolate chip and cotton candy.

We *were* good, until he was on top of me.

Now all I'm thinking about is what his mouth would feel like on every other part of my body, and something tells me that's not good at all.

FOURTEEN
DALLAS

THERE'S nothing like a Sunday afternoon at UPS Field in September.

The energy radiating from the fans is through the roof today. Their roars work their way into the locker room. The walls shake and my ears ring. It's a sound I've missed during the off season.

I grin and pull on my helmet. My body thrums with excitement and anticipation. Electricity runs through me as I buckle my chin strap and take a deep breath, savoring the last few seconds of tranquility before we head into chaos.

It's game one of the regular season, and our first step on the journey to another Super Bowl ring. The dream of being back-to-back champions fueled us through training camp. It was the motivation to go undefeated in the three preseason games and earn us the title of Vegas's favorite to win it all.

I've been in the league for eight years, which is long enough to be able to recognize when a team has chemistry and when it doesn't. It's easy to tell when guys want to be there and are having fun, versus the ones who think they're better than everyone else and just want to collect a paycheck.

The fifty-two men around me fall into that first camp. They're special. Selfless and hard workers. It's an *us* not *me* mentality, and they're hungry.

Something big is going to happen this season.

I can fucking feel it.

"Alright, boys. Gather around," Shawn says, and the locker room quiets down as we crowd around him. "Welcome to day one. The road to February starts right now, and it doesn't stop until we have a trophy in our hands. There is going to be a lot of pressure on us this season—we have people telling us we're overrated. That we shouldn't have won last year, and there's no way in *hell* we're going to repeat our success."

That earns a grumble from the guys. There's a low growl of displeasure with the shit talking, and I mumble my disagreement with that opinion, too.

"Probably that blow hard who yells on his television show all the time," Sam Wagner, the stellar tight end we drafted two years ago, says under his breath. "He can fuck right off."

"There are also going to be people overinflating your confidence," Shawn continues. "They're going to stroke your ego and make you feel cocky and complacent. And, at some point in the season—maybe it's today, or maybe it's in week twelve—you're going to want to take your foot off the gas. You're going to want to get comfortable. And what do we think about getting comfortable, Lansfield?"

I lift my head and look around at my teammates. My brothers who have been with me through thick and thin. They were there the night I got the call about June. They stuck by me that first season as a single dad when I was barely sleeping, a shell of myself on the field and off.

They are the guys who have lifted me on their shoulders after a game-winning field goal and comforted me when I came up short, the kick going wide right and costing us the division title.

I'd go to hell and back for each one of them.

I use Sam's shoulder to climb onto a bench so everyone can see me. "Comfortable means we're not doing things right," I say, and my voice projects through the locker room. "Being the best is difficult. It's challenging and outside your comfort zone. The minute you think it's easy, we've already lost."

"Thanks, Captain," Shawn says, and I give him a salute. "This is going to be a long year. We all know the toll it's going to take on your physical and mental health. But when things get hard, I want you to remember this: playing the game isn't something you have to do. It's something you *get* to do. And what a fucking gift it is, boys, to line up next to the guys who sweat and grind with you day in and day out. Millions of people would kill to be in your position, but you are the lucky ones."

"Hell yeah," Jett calls out, and the team hoots in agreement. "I get to play with the best offense and defense in the league. The best coaching staff and special teams. I don't know about y'all, but three-time Super Bowl champ sounds a hell of a lot better than two-time Super Bowl champ."

"Hands in," I say, and everyone shuffles closer. "Our motto of the game is *lucky ones*. On three, gentlemen. One, two, three."

"Lucky ones," they all yell, and I grin from ear to ear.

"Let's get this win, boys."

There's a mess of grabbing gear and hitting the wall above the door on the way to the field. Of cheering and yelling, and I spot Reid in the middle of my teammates, videoing something he'll upload to social media soon. I hang back and enjoy the high of getting ready to do something I love.

"Lansfield. You good?"

I look up from my locker. Shawn is watching me, his hands on hips and his sleeves pushed up his arms.

"I'm great." I rifle through my bag and find my jeans. I pull out a piece of paper from the pocket and tuck it in the waistband of my athletic pants. "Let's get this win, Coach."

Seventy thousand fans greet me when I make it on the field for warmups, and I soak it all in.

I take my time giving out high fives to the kids waiting outside the tunnel. A member of the Titans ticket sales team thrusts a Sharpie in my hand and asks me to sign a hat. My head is on a swivel as I sort through the security guards, the physical trainers and medical staff setting up shop on the sidelines before I find who I'm looking for.

There she is.

Blonde hair pulled up in a ponytail and covered by a navy-blue hat. A white Titans polo and khaki pants that hug her legs damn well. A camera around her neck and an awed look on her face.

I jog toward Maven and stick my tongue out when she takes a picture of me.

"Photo of the game right there," she yells over the crowd.

"Hey," I say, and I pull her into a side hug. She's warm from the afternoon sun, and I tap her shoulder twice before letting go. "How's it going?"

"This is nothing like the preseason games. I'm not going to lie, I'm a little overwhelmed."

"Only a little? Pretty sure I almost shit myself my first game," I say, and she bursts out laughing. "Coach had to literally drag me from the bathroom."

"It's a bummer that wasn't included in the Cosmo article about your hair flipping. The women would be flocking to you," she jokes.

"I don't need any more women. I'm pretty busy with the two I have in my life."

"Oh?" Maven asks, and I have to lean in closer to hear her. "Are you?"

"Between you attacking me with paint and June always six seconds away from running into the coffee table in the living room, I'm closer to a heart attack than I was last year," I say.

"That might be true, but you're forgetting something."

"And what's that?"

She stands on her toes and cups her hand around my helmet. "You're also happier than you were a year ago."

"So much happier. Speaking of, I have something for you." I step back and pull out the paper I tucked in my pants.

"Is it your grabbable dick? Dammit, Lansfield, we're in public."

"Nope. Smaller. Much smaller," I say, and I hand her the note. "It's from June."

"Is it?" Her fingers brush against mine when she takes the paper, and I watch her carefully unfold the square. "Oh, it's beautiful."

I smile at the three stick figures. It's a loose interpretation of the three of us from the eyes of a preschooler. There's a sun in the upper right corner and a bunch of different colored scribbles that take over the rest of the page. JB asked me to write a message across the center: HAVE A GOOD FIRST GAME, MAE MAE.

With a little pink heart under it done by June herself.

"She worked very hard on it."

"The penmanship is impeccable and her spelling is top notch." Maven folds the note back up and slips it in her pocket. She tips her chin up and beams at me. "This is so sweet. Thank you."

"I was also tasked with inviting you over for pizza after the game. Please don't feel obligated to say yes. I know you've been spending a lot of time with us, and I don't want you to think I'm taking advantage of your time or anything like that."

"Of course I'll be there. There's free food—if anything, I don't want you to think *I'm* taking advantage of *you*." Her attention drifts across the field. She brings her camera up and presses the shutter button. After snapping a couple pictures, she admires the shots with a soft, proud smile. "Are you ready for today? The Renegades are good."

"Very good. We'll see how it goes. I'm sure it will take a little bit to get our nerves out."

"I'm rooting for you." She reaches out and squeezes my arm. Her fingers curl around my muscles, and her thumb drags across my jersey. It's nearly eighty degrees out, but I shiver at the contact. "I hope you have a great game."

"Thanks." I check the scoreboard and see there's only thirty minutes until kickoff. "I better get going. It's my first season as a thirty-year-old, and I need to make sure I'm limber."

"Limber." Maven laughs, and the sound is warmer than the sunshine hitting my face. "We can't have you pulling a hamstring. I'd never stop giving you shit."

"I can always count on you." I knock the brim of her hat and she swats at my hand. "Have fun today, Maven. I can't wait to see all the photos you take of the team over sausage and olive pizza when we're back at the apartment."

"Sausage and olive? That's my favorite."

"I know it is. Why do you think I order it every time?"

She holds up her camera so it's inches away from my face. This time I grin, and she snaps another photo. "You order my favorite pizza?"

"Duh. I can't have people who work for me not eating their favorite foods. That'll earn me a bad review on GlassDoor. Under accommodations you'll put: forces me to eat pepperoni pizza. Zero out of ten, would not recommend working here."

"Oh, people who work for you? Is that all I am?"

"All you are? No. You're also my friend. And I like to take care of my friends, which includes ordering their shitty pizza for them."

"Tell me how you really feel, lone star," she says and she nudges my side with her elbow. "I hope you're ready. I'm going to do a slideshow tonight. It's going to be six thousand photos from the game, and you can't go to sleep until you've seen every one of them. You'll be stuck there for hours and question why you ever hired me in the first place."

I grab a ball from one of the equipment managers and head for the centerfield line before Shawn can come out of the locker room from his pregame coach huddle and find me socializing for too long.

"Doubtful. There's nowhere else I'd rather be," I call out over my shoulder, and she smiles from ear to ear.

FIFTEEN

DALLAS

WE'RE TIED with thirty seconds left in the fourth quarter, and I fucking love when games go down to the wire like this.

Both teams' defensive lines have been good today. Aside from kickoffs, I've only been on the field twice for extra points. I made both of them with room to spare, but with how this drive is going, I have a feeling a field goal is coming soon.

I watch Jett maneuver past a cornerback and pick up two yards before he runs out of bounds to stop the clock. He's frustrated with the way he's getting shut down today, and he unclips his chin strap aggressively as he forms a huddle with the offense on third down.

"Lansfield," Shawn says, and he pulls his headset away from his ear. "Warm up. If we don't get the first down, we're kicking. I'm not taking any risks on fourth and inches."

"Got it, Coach."

I pop off the metal bench and pull on my helmet, making sure it's tight. I scoop up a ball and get the kicking tee positioned in front of the practice net on the sideline. A quick glance at the field tells me I'm going to be lining up around the forty-five-yard mark, and I grin.

I haven't missed a field goal in sixty attempts, and this one is right in my sweet spot.

Time to make it sixty-one in a row.

I swing my leg from front to back then side to side to loosen my hamstring. I twist my back next, groaning as my spine pops. When I turn to the left, I see Maven at the far end of the sideline.

Her attention is on the game. One hand is on her hip and the other holds her camera halfway up to her face. It's like she's in a trance, and I bite the inside of my cheek when she squats down to get a better angle for a shot of Jett and the rest of the boys.

Fuck, she's beautiful.

She's been on my mind since the paint room two weeks ago. I haven't stopped thinking about being on top of her and the soft curves of her body. And *goddamn* there are a lot of curves.

Her ass.

Her thighs and hips.

Her chest that pressed against mine.

Up until this point, I could pretend like she wasn't so fucking attractive.

I could ignore it when she walked around the apartment in tiny jean shorts, playing it off like the muscles in her legs were just part of my imagination.

Now I know she's a goddamn knockout. I know how perfectly she fits under me and what it feels like when she arches her back to get closer to me, like she's fucking desperate for it.

It's driving me out of my fucking mind.

"Hey." An elbow lands in my ribs, and I wince. I look to my right and see Odell Sinclair, one of our defensive linemen, staring at me. "What are you doing?"

I shake my head and stand in front of the kicking tee, trying to wipe my mind clean. I have a job to do, and I'm getting distracted by the hot blonde behind me. I pull my leg back and kick the ball straight into the practice net. "Nothing."

"You were staring at something."

"I'm watching the game," I say.

"The game that's on the opposite end of the field?" he asks.

"Okay, fine. I was checking the wind."

"The flags on the scoreboard aren't moving."

"You're a nosy motherfucker, aren't you?"

"Wait a second." He glances over my shoulder and grins. "You were looking at a girl. You never look at girls. Who is it?"

"I'm not looking at anyone." I fix my shoulder pads and shove him out of the way. "Mind your business and let me be."

"It's hard to mind my business when you're drooling, Cap."

"I am not drooling," I say emphatically.

"Sure looked like you were."

I ignore him and line up another kick. I put more punch behind this one, satisfied with how it feels against my foot. "Fuck off, Sinclair. I'm trying to do my job."

"Fine. Keep your secrets. I'll figure it out eventually. I always do," he says.

Shit.

She's the one person I can't get caught staring at, and especially not by the guy with the loudest mouth on the team.

I'm already on thin ice with her being June's nanny and a member of the Titans. It's a gray area I'm barely skating around, and one wrong move would ruin everything.

Interpersonal relationships with players and members of the team, in any capacity, aren't allowed. It's a stupid rule the league hasn't budged on, and they've drawn a clear line in the sand about who they'd side with if even a whisper of something off-limits made its way up to those with power.

They'd protect the players. The guys bringing in billions of dollars in profit every year. No one gives a shit about words like *consensual* or *love* when money is at stake.

We saw an example of that a couple years back when word got out that one of our assistant coaches was dating a player on another team.

Their relationship had been going on for years, and the news only came to light after a hotel video was leaked, showing them making out in a hallway. The assistant coach was fired, and her ten-year career went down the drain all because of some grainy footage from a shitty Hilton in Detroit even though Shawn fought hard to keep her onboard.

If Odell so much as joked about me looking at Maven, her ass would be gone faster than I can blink.

I could never do that to her. Not when I see the joy in her eyes when she's behind the camera and how much happiness it brings her.

I need to keep my distance.

It's better for everyone.

"You're up, Lansfield," Shawn says, and I give him a nod.

I've done this so many times, the second my cleats hit the field, I go into autopilot. It's like I black out, and all the sights and sounds around me blur away.

I stand behind the line of scrimmage and bend down to knock away a loose piece of grass. I lift my arm and stare at the goal post, my target straight ahead of me. The deep breath comes easily and calm washes over me as my teammates get in position.

Inhale confidence.

Exhale fear.

I repeat the mantra three times, grateful for the piece of advice from our team psychologist.

The whistle blows, and I roll my shoulders back. It's a quick snap, done so the defense can't call a timeout and try to ice me. I hate when teams do that shit. It only makes me want to beat them more.

Justin Rodgers, my holder, catches the ball easily like he always does.

I wind up and take three steps forward, my eyes focused only on the ball in front of me.

I punt it with everything I have as the time on the clock expires, leaning to the left as I watch it soar in the air.

I know the kick is good well before it goes straight through the goal posts with yards to spare, and I pump my fist. When the final whistle sounds and signals the end of the game, I'm swept into the arms of my teammates. Jett jumps on my back and nearly pulls us to the ground as he kisses my helmet.

"I'm so glad you're on my team," he yells over the cheers from the fans. "One and oh, baby!"

There's a round of congratulations and consolation hand-shakes with the Renegades players. I stop for a quick postgame interview with the local news station, and I let Reid record me doing a few stupid dance moves for some video recap he's putting together. I only get made fun of once, and I take that as a victory on top of the game win, too.

When the mayhem settles, I pull my helmet off. I flip back my hair and shake the sweat off the ends, and I see Maven watching me.

Our eyes meet, and a smile curls on her lips. She doesn't come any closer, but she does give me a thumbs up and a wink, an invitation to head her way if I wanted to.

"I'll be right back," I say to Reid, and he follows my gaze.

"Yeah, right." He laughs and pats my shoulder. "I'll see you in the locker room."

I jog toward her, accepting handshakes from other members of the team and the security guards tasked with keeping fans away from the field. She takes another picture of me as I approach her then moves the camera away from her face.

"Nice kick," she says. "Pretty sure that will be my photo of the game."

"It wasn't too much of a snoozefest for you? There was a whole quarter where no one scored any points."

"That's why sports are so fun; everything can change in an instant." Maven looks over my shoulder at the rest of my team. "Don't you need to head to the locker room?"

"I will in a minute. Could you grab June from the nursery? I'll meet y'all at the car after doing media stuff and we can head back to the apartment for pizza."

"Of course. How long do you think you'll be?"

"Hopefully not long, but no promises. Everyone gets excited after the first game of the season."

"As they should. Lord Dallas is here." Maven curtsies, and I give her a light shove.

"Go get my daughter, please, so we can get the hell out of here and go home. One of the best parts about having a kid is always having an excuse to dip out of things early, and I fully plan to do that every postgame press conference this season."

"We'll see you soon." She lifts her chin, and her grin is softer. "I'm proud of you, Dallas. Congratulations on your first win this season."

"Thanks, Mae," I say, and for some reason, the praise from her means more to me than from anyone else.

SIXTEEN

MAVEN

"HI, I'M HERE," I call out, flying into Dallas's apartment twenty minutes late. I kick off my shoes and make a beeline for the kitchen. The smell of bacon and coffee drifts down the hall, and my stomach rumbles. "I'm so sorry. Traffic was a nightmare this morning. There was an accident and construction and everything went to shit."

"Shit, huh?" Dallas looks at me over his shoulder from the sink and smiles. "Take a deep breath. I have awhile before I need to leave. Coach pushed practice back one hour. Your tardiness is allowed."

He drapes a dish towel over his shoulder and moves toward the oven. He pulls out a plate and sets it on the island. A pile of eggs, two slices of toast and bacon taunt me, and I almost moan.

"You shouldn't reward my bad behavior like this," I say, and I slide onto a barstool. I spear the scrambled eggs with a fork. "Soon I'm going to show up late on purpose just so you'll have a warm plate of food waiting for me."

"I wouldn't consider construction and unavoidable traffic bad behavior." Dallas pours me a cup of coffee, adding a splash of milk and half a spoonful of sugar. He stirs the drink then places it next to my plate. "Just unfortunate timing."

"Fair, but I still feel guilty."

"Sorry, I can't understand you through the toast you're inhaling," he teases, and I flip him off. "Take your time eating. June is in her playroom sorting through the eight dozen friendship bracelets she made last night. That's going to keep her occupied for hours."

"I want a friendship bracelet." I gesture to the one he's wearing on his wrist, a collection of different colored circular beads pressing against his tan skin. "Yours looks so cool."

"It does, doesn't it? I like having a piece of June with me when I head to the field."

"I would too." I tear off a piece of bacon and toss it in my mouth. "Thank you for the food, by the way. This is delicious. Way better than the PopTart I had on the drive over."

"Come on, Mae. You know how important a balanced breakfast is," Dallas says.

"I do, and that's why I appreciate your culinary skills. What time will you be home today?"

"Probably around five or six. After last week's win, I think Shawn might be less of an evil dick." He pulls a yellow Gatorade and a gallon of water from the fridge and sets them on the counter. "I'll try and get back as quick as I can so you're not sitting in traffic on the way back to your place. Why do you have to live so far away?"

"Because housing is more affordable on that side of town. We're not all multi-millionaires, remember?"

"Right." He adds a banana and a protein shake to his pile of food and looks up at me. "Maybe you should just move in here."

I burst out laughing. "Very funny."

"What? I'm serious."

My laughter dies in my chest. I stare at him, and my eyebrows knit together. "What are you talking about, Dallas?"

He walks around the island and takes the seat next to me. "I didn't think about the logistics when I asked for your help. Now I see how much time you waste going between my place and yours, and I feel bad. You sit in traffic for an hour and a half every day. That's absurd."

"Don't feel bad. That comes with living in the city, and I knew it would be a commute when I said yes." I turn and face him. My knees fit between his parted thighs, and I study his face. "Are you fucking with me about moving in?"

"I'm not. I swear. Come live with us, Maven."

He scoots his barstool closer, and my body warms at his proximity. I can see the freckles across his nose from a summer of training camp. The tendons stretching in his neck as he talks and the strands of his hair that have gotten lighter from hours spent at practice in the sun.

It's obvious he's attractive—everyone knows that—with a crooked smile that can make you weak in the knees. A boyish charm to the creases around his eyes and the dimples on his cheeks. In the quiet moments, though, like right now, he's not just handsome, some hot shot football player girls across America wish they could make theirs.

He's beautiful.

Stripped down. Honest. It's like he takes a mask off when he's here at home. There's a twinkle in his eye. A softness in his gaze. It's tender, vulnerable, and a side of him I'm lucky to see.

"I appreciate the offer, but I can't afford it. Your rent is probably five times what I pay."

"Who said anything about paying?" Dallas asks, and the right corner of his mouth turns down. "I wouldn't make you pay to live here."

"Absolutely not." I try to spin away, but he reaches out and stops me. His large hand curls around the seat so I can't move, and I huff. "That's not fair at all."

"Forget the rent for a second. Would you ever consider moving in?"

"Yes, but I would never want you to feel like you couldn't relax in your own home. If I'm here, that might make it difficult for you."

"You're going to have to give me more context than that, Maven. Are you going to play the drums at midnight or something?"

"No." I blow out a breath and wring my hands together. "I just... I can't help but notice there aren't a lot of women in your life."

"No," he says slowly with a raised eyebrow. "There aren't."

"I didn't know if that was because—" I swallow and look anywhere but his face. "If it was by choice."

"It is by choice. I don't date."

My gaze cuts back over to him. "You don't?"

"No."

"Why not?"

"I don't have any time, and I have a lot on my plate with June. I'm still figuring this parenting thing out, and I don't want her to ever feel like she's second to someone else."

"That... that's a good reason." I bob my head up and down, and I swear he smirks. "Do you do... other things?"

"Are you asking if I fuck people, Maven?" he says with a low voice.

"Yes," I squeak out, and this is not the direction I thought our conversation would go.

"I don't do that, either. Also by choice."

"Interesting."

"You sound disappointed."

I shrug, even though my traitorous mind begins to picture Dallas with someone. His hand under her skirt and his head between her breasts. A soft laugh as he makes her come, sweat on both their bodies and desire pulsing through them.

"I'm indifferent," I say.

"I'm very particular with the people I let get close to me. Women especially. But if you moved in, I wouldn't feel like I had to sleep with my door locked. I trust you." His voice turns gentle, the ebb of the tide as it pulls back to sea. "You're the first person I've felt comfortable with in a long time. Ever, maybe. I can be myself with you and... that's the best kind of friend I could ever want. Why wouldn't I want you around more?"

My breath catches in my throat. The air around us feels charged and electrified when his knee presses against mine. It's a magnetic force, because when I try to pull away, I can't.

"Oh," I whisper, and the gravity of his words hit me square in the chest. "You've become a friend of mine too. I hope you know that."

"I do, and I'm lucky. June loves you. She's happier when you're here, and so am I. It can be fucking lonely being a single parent. I've got Reid and Maverick, but they're young and single, and as much as they love JB, I know they don't want to sit here every night watching Bluey. Most of the other guys my age on the team are out partying during the week. Going to the strip club after a game and getting dozens of numbers."

"And that's not something you're interested in?" I ask, and a rush of heat climbs up my chest.

"I can't have that life anymore. I don't want it, either. I like coming home and hanging out with y'all. I like when you try to cook dinner before giving up and ordering takeout. I like having someone besides a four-year-old to have a conversation with

116

over a meal. And, do you want to know the best part?" he asks, and he leans in a little closer.

"What's that?" I ask.

"You haven't tried to take a picture of my dick yet."

"Stop." I choke on another laugh. "Someone's done that?"

"Yup. Mid-shower. Thank god the glass was fogged up, or I'd probably be on some Reddit thread that asked people to rate the size from one to ten."

"How would you rate the size?"

"I don't know. I haven't taken out a ruler recently to measure."

My eyes inadvertently dart to the front of his sweatpants. The gray joggers he likes to wear to the stadium stretch over his thighs and hug his muscles. Maybe I'm imagining things, but it almost seems like Dallas parts his legs a little wider, like he *knows* I'm looking.

And I am, a little bit.

I've seen him looking at me, and it's only fair I return the favor.

I just *know* he'd be a ten, and that makes me feel hot all over.

"Are you sure you want me to be your roommate?" I ask

"Yes," he says without any hesitation. "And you're not going to pay a cent either."

"But I—"

"Don't argue with me, Maven, because you're not going to win. I don't want your money, and that's final."

"What about your routines? Your schedule? I'd hate to be the extra person who throws a wrench in your plans."

"You're part of those routines. You spend all day here when I'm at practice. You ride with us to games and help put June to bed while I'm cleaning the dirt and grass off of me. We'd—I'd— love if you were here full time."

I consider his offer.

I don't want to make a snap decision, but he makes good points.

I'm here so much, my mail keeps piling up. I haven't dusted my dining room table in days, and I stopped trying to keep my plants alive.

And, most importantly, I *like* being here.

I like spending time with the two of them, and over the course of the last couple months, he's become a good friend. It's not just a boss and employee relationship, but something deeper. He's someone I feel comfortable around and safe to be myself—a girl who's not sure where she's going yet, but slowly finding her way.

"If I say yes, I think we need some rules," I say, and he nods for me to continue. "If anything starts to feel weird, I want us to take a step back. I want us to be honest with each other and openly communicate. I really like our friendship, Dallas, and I don't want to mess that up because I forget to do the dishes and you don't like it."

"Deal. What else?"

"Um." I rub my thumb across my neck, wishing I had my necklace to play with. I lost it after taking it off for the paint room, and I haven't found it yet. "This next part might be awkward, but it needs to be said."

He grins and rests his elbow on the island. "Go on."

"We're living together as friends, not as..." I clear my throat. "Not as a couple. We're both single, but we need to be aware of our surroundings. I like my job with you, and I like my job with the Titans. I don't want to compromise either just because—"

"We're in close quarters?" Dallas finishes for me, and I nod. "We're adults. We can find each other attractive without acting on it even if we see one another in a towel by accident. This is platonic. Another part of our business relationship, because now you're saving yourself time and energy."

"What about having people over? Do we need a code phrase for when we're bringing home a... a friend?"

"I'm assuming your definition of *friend* in this scenario is not the kind of *friends* we are." He pauses and rubs his jaw. "I don't want to tell you how to live your life, Maven, but I'm not comfortable having men I don't know in the apartment. Especially when I'm not here. If you want to do things with people, I'm going to politely ask for you to not do them under my roof."

My cheeks burn, and I wish I could hide my face. "I would never. I just didn't want to invade your space if you were... I don't know. Looking for a release at the hands of another person."

"The only guests I have over are Maverick and Reid," he says, and his ears turn pink. "I promise you won't come home and find me in any compromising positions. And you're obviously free to do what you like, just maybe not around me and June."

"June is my responsibility," I say. "That doesn't change if I move in, and I won't take advantage of your space by using it as a... a pleasure den."

"Our space," he says, correcting me, and I nod. "And please never say pleasure den again. Sounds like we belong in a horrible porno from the seventies."

"Right." I laugh. "Our space. Thank you. It's kind of you to offer your extra room to me."

"Don't mention it." He reaches out and ruffles my hair. "I better get going, roomie."

"That sounds so weird." I laugh and spin on the stool so he can jump off. "When should I move in?"

"Whenever you want."

"Is the end of this week too soon?"

"Nope." Dallas scoops up his pile of food and grins. "And I think we can agree to keep this between us, right? Shawn might murder me if he finds out you're living eight feet down the hall, and with the league's rules and everything—"

"Oh, god, yeah. It'll be our little secret," I say.

"I love secrets," he says.

The wink he tosses me as he leaves the kitchen makes me want to clench my legs together, and I wonder if I just made the biggest mistake of my life.

SEVENTEEN
DALLAS

I GOT BROS IN ONE AREA CODE

I need y'all to get over here ASAP.

PUCK DADDY

It's 8 a.m.

On a Saturday.

Have you lost your mind?

ME

Maverick. Did you change your name in my phone?

PUCK DADDY

Nah.

ME

How did you unlock it?

PUCK DADDY

Your password is June, which is the most obvious thing in the world. It's a wonder you haven't been hacked yet.

REID

What's going on, Dal?

ME

I don't have any shit for Maven here. I don't own face towels. I don't own candles. She's going to think I never have guests over.

REID

...but you never have guests over.

ME

Help. Please.

REID

Okay. What do you need me to bring?

PUCK DADDY

This might be the hangover talking, but it sounds like you're trying to impress her.

ME

I'm not. I just want her to be comfortable.

PUCK DADDY

LOL. He's such a liar.

Whoops. Sry. That was only supposed to go to Reidy Boy.

ME

Y'all talk about me behind my back?

REID

No.

PUCK DADDY

Yes.

ME

Ignoring that.

Can someone find me a candle and a face towel? And a loofah, too? Maybe a plant?

PUCK DADDY

The fuck is a loofah?

REID

I'll see what I can find.

ME

You're a good man.

FORTY-FIVE MINUTES LATER, Maverick collapses onto my couch and presses the heels of his palms into his eyes. "I'm hungover, jet lagged, and tired as shit."

"Sounds like a personal problem. It's not our fault you decided to go out last night after getting back from the west coast," Reid says. He sets a handful of reusable bags down on the coffee table and shoves his glasses up his nose. "Actions have consequences, and you deserve to suffer."

Maverick flings his arm over his face and sighs. "What are we doing?"

"Sprucing this place up." I rummage through the bags Reid brought and pull out half a dozen candles. I line them up and stare at the labels. "Reid, do you have a candle dealer?"

"You don't?" he asks dryly. "My next-door neighbor dabbles in candle making every now and then, and she was happy to give me some of her most popular scents. Gardenia is my preference, but you can pick what you want."

"Thanks. This is incredible."

"I'm confused why you're putting so much effort into this. Maven's been here a hundred times, Dal. She knows what your place looks like. She was practically your roommate already, just without the sleeping over part."

"I know, but some feminine touches would be good." I stack the pink face towels and matching washcloths next to the candles. "Like a plant."

"Who's going to take care of a plant when you're gone?" Maverick asks.

"Her, I guess. Don't women like plants?"

"Everyone likes plants," Reid agrees.

I stare at the one he brought over and put my hands on my hips. "What is it?"

"A snake plant. Studies show they've been known to remove toxins from the air over time. I have one at my place, and it's the only plant I've managed to keep alive," he adds.

"When did you become a botanist?" Maverick groans.

"I'm not." Reid walks over to the curtains covering the window in the living room and flings them open. His grin is smug when Maverick writhes in pain, and I laugh. "This dude on social media has a whole channel where all he does is talk about plants, and I decided to get some of my own. Snake plants are perfect for the guy who travels for work, and it's nice to do something besides stare at my phone all day."

"I never thought I'd be friends with two daddies. Human Daddy and Plant Daddy." Maverick moves his hands away from his face and gives us a slow grin. "Kind of makes *me* want to be a daddy. Dog daddy? Cat daddy? Thoughts, boys?"

"Stop calling yourself daddy. You're going to make my ears bleed." I throw a towel at him, and he laughs. "Can you get your ass up and help? Maven will be here soon, and I want this to be done."

"Only if you can remind me why you decided to ask your nanny to live with you."

"Because she spends hours every day driving here then driving home. She's paying a disgusting amount on rent for a place she's never in. We had a conversation, and we're well aware that we're moving in together as friends, not anything more. I trust her, and I know this is what's best for everyone."

"Dal." Maverick stands up, and his eyes look a little less glassy. He moves toward me with his long legs and long arms and clamps a hand on my shoulder. "Do you think it's possible you're trying to overcompensate here?"

"What am I overcompensating for?" I ask.

"Maybe you have feelings for Maven, and you're expressing those feelings through wanting to make your apartment look nice for her," Reid says.

"I don't have feelings for her. I just..." I sigh and take Maverick's spot on the couch. "I'll admit she's hot."

"Fucking finally," Maverick grumbles. "Took you long enough."

"I like spending time with her, but I'm also aware I *can't* do anything about it, and I don't *want* to do anything about it. My life is complicated as it is. Adding a relationship to it would be messy."

"Sounds like the definition of feelings to me." Maverick lifts his chin toward Reid. "Come on, Duncan. You're the relationship guy out of the three of us."

"I've dated two women in four years," he argues. "But, fine. I'll bite. Dal, it's normal to be attracted to someone you spend a lot of time with, especially because you've never had these kinds of interactions with women before. You're guarded. Careful about who you let close to you, and for good reason. This is the first time you're hanging out with someone who doesn't make you feel like you have to throw all your normal walls up, so you want to go above and beyond for her."

"That's alarmingly accurate," I say. "Everything just feels easy with Maven. This sounds so stupid, but it's like I'm safe with her. I *can* let my guard down and just... fucking *be*. We've known each other for awhile and have always been nice and friendly, but we've never been *friends*. I never thought she'd be someone who I could sit with on the couch and just shoot the shit with, but she is. She's down to earth, and I like that she doesn't give a shit that I play football. Like, if I lost my career tomorrow, she'd still hang around. I don't think I could say that for many people."

Reid hums, and I wish I could read his mind. "And you don't think that's the definition of having feelings for someone?"

"I think it's the definition of a friend," I counter firmly. "Because that's all we could ever allow it to be."

"Fine." Reid pulls out a pair of bookends from another bag. "But there aren't any rules about having fun, right? That's not off-limits?"

"What does that mean?"

"Fun," Maverick says. "It's something you do with your friends who you definitely don't have a crush on. And, in this case, maybe you flirt a little, too."

"Daddy!" June calls out, interrupting us as she runs into the living room.

"Hey, June Bug." I lift her up and bounce her on my knee. "What are you up to?"

She hands me a stack of friendship bracelets. The beaded jewelry matches the one she gave me last week as a good luck gift before my game, and my smile stretches wider. "For Mae Mae."

"Wow." I turn the bracelets over and see MEA MEA on the other side. "These are so cool."

"Will she like them?" June asks.

"Nope. She's going to *love* them," I say. "You can give them to her soon. Remember how I told you she's going to take the extra room next to yours?"

"Like a sleepover with Aunt January."

"Exactly like when Aunt January comes to visit." I hug her, happy she remembers when my sister stayed with us. "Uncle Mav and Uncle Reid are trying to help me pick out candles for her room. Which do you like?"

Reid hands the options over, and I bring them to June's nose. She makes a face at the first one, and all three of us burst out laughing. She shrugs at the second one, indifferent, and I agree. It smells like wet laundry. The third makes her grin, and she bobs her head up and down.

"Flowers," she says. "That one."

"Should we have gotten flowers?" I ask, and I toss the candle back to Reid.

"I mean, everyone likes flowers but—"

There's a knock on the door.

"She's here," Maverick says, and my hearts leaps up to my throat.

I jump off the couch and set June down. I check the mirror hanging on the wall and run my hand through my hair, hoping I don't look as disheveled as I feel.

I've never lived with a woman, and I'm out of my element.

Maven and I are going to be around each other constantly; in the morning before I leave for practice then again at night. On Sundays at the stadium and then after when we drive home together.

Home.

It feels oddly intimate. Like something I wouldn't want to do with any other person in the world.

Before I can register what the hell that means, there's another knock.

Reid and Maverick stare at me. June skips over to the foyer and stands on her tiptoes, trying to open the door. I shuffle forward and follow behind her, rolling my shoulders back and telling myself this is no big deal. That it's okay we're keeping our living arrangement a secret. That everything is going to work out perfectly.

Famous fucking last words.

I open the door and the wind gets knocked out of me.

Maven's standing there in a navy-blue dress with thin straps that show off the curve of her shoulders and the tan of her skin. Her hair is pulled back into a high ponytail that lets me see the length of her neck and collarbones that have no right to be as attractive as they are.

She tilts her head and smiles at me with warmth behind her eyes. I feel it in my chest when she looks at me. It's like a spark is catching and turning into a raging wildfire I can't control.

This would be easier if she wasn't so pretty.

"Hey." Maven leans on her suitcase handle, and I try not to focus on the way her dress rides up her thighs when she moves. "Fancy seeing you here."

I blink and clear my throat. "Hey."

"This is my friend, Isabella, who I mentioned would be helping me."

"Reid and Maverick are here. They can help, too."

"That'd be great. My furniture is in storage, but there are a couple of bags and boxes down in the car."

I nod, and my eyes move to her friend. "Hi," I say, and I hold out my hand. "I'm Dallas."

"I know." Isabella grins and shakes my hand. "I've heard a lot about you."

"Oh?" I lift an eyebrow, and that familiar easiness that comes with being around Maven locks in place. I glance back to my new roommate and smirk. "Something you want to tell me? I'm flattered I'm the center of so many of your conversations, Mae."

"Conversations like how you've had seventy-one nannies before me, and they all have a serious infatuation with your junk," she says innocently, and I choke on a laugh. "Don't let it go to your... head."

"You're a menace. Come on in, y'all."

I hold the door open so they can step inside. Two suitcases trail behind them, and I take the bag hanging from Maven's shoulder.

"Thanks," she says, and she tosses me another smile. Her attention shifts to June, and she bends down to kiss the top of her head. "Hi, June Bug. I'm so excited to be your roommate."

"Look, Mae Mae. I made a bracelet. It matches Daddy's!" June hands over the misspelled craft project, and Maven slips it on.

"It's so pretty." Maven turns her wrist from side to side and admires the pink and purple beads. "Thank you so much. I'm going to wear it all the time."

"Hope you don't mind being twins," I say, and I hold up my arm.

"What does yours say?" she asks, and I give her a sheepish smile.

"Doody. The other one says Duddy. We're working on our spelling."

"Maybe it was intentional." She slips past me toward the living room. I get a whiff of her shampoo as the hem of her dress grazes against my leg, and I do my best to not inhale. "Who's to say I didn't help her with them?"

"I see. Y'all have an alliance." I lean against the wall, and she looks at me over her shoulder. "And I'm just chopped liver."

"Prepare to be sick of us, lone star. You have no idea what you created by letting us live under the same roof. June Bug and I will rule the world one day, and we're starting with this apartment."

Maven flips her hair and disappears with a sly smile.

Maybe Reid and Maverick are right.

Maybe I should flirt a little.

It's harmless fun, and it's never going to go anywhere.

It might do me some good, and I can't imagine anyone better to indulge in than Maven fucking Wood.

EIGHTEEN
DALLAS

"CHEERS to our first night as roommates." Maven knocks her beer against mine. "I'd say today was a success."

"We're twelve hours in, and I can confidently say you're the best roommate I've ever had." I take a sip of my drink and wipe my mouth with the back of my hand. "But, to be fair, I've never had a roommate. The data might be skewed in your favor."

She lets out a soft laugh and pulls her legs to her chest. "What about Reid and Maverick? You never lived with them?"

"Nope. We've all had our own places for as long as we've known each other."

"How did you all meet? Is there some app for attractive men to match with each other and become best friends? It's probably called BroBond, and I bet their slogan is something wild, like, *connecting handsome homies*. Wait. No. Captivating Comrades, *where bros become family*."

I burst out laughing and rub my thumb down the neck of the beer bottle. "Did you just come up with that right now? That's fucking impressive. If the photography thing doesn't work out, you might have a career in marketing."

"For apps where hot guys become friends? Sounds horrible."

She beams and brings her beer to her mouth. "Now tell me how the greatest bromance of all time formed."

I lean back and drape my arm over the back of the couch. "I met Maverick years ago. We came into our leagues around the same time, and our agents organized this up-and-coming athlete interview with a local magazine. We got to talking, and the rest, as they say, is history."

"My favorite love story. What about Reid?"

"A former player for the Titans was making fun of Reid's glasses while he was trying to film our social media content. Dumb middle school shit, you know? I apologized on that guy's behalf, we got a beer after the game, and now he's my best friend."

"Cute. Does that mean they've always known June?"

"Yeah. They were here my first night with her, and they've been here every night I've needed them since. I feel bad for her; when she gets old enough to date, I think Maverick might actually deck anyone who tries to break her heart." I smile at the thought of my friend pinning someone against a wall. Years of brawling on the ice is going to spill over to protect his goddaughter from some douchebag who doesn't know how to treat a girl right. "And Reid would hack their computers and find a way to take control of all of their social media accounts."

"Sounds like she has quite the lineup to keep her safe."

"She does. Jokes on her, though. I'm never going to let her date."

"I remember my dad saying the same thing." Maven smiles at me over the rim of her bottle with wistful eyes. "I'm sorry to be the bearer of bad news, Dallas, but eventually your girl is going to grow up."

I freeze, my drink halfway to my mouth.

An ache settles in my chest as I think about fifteen, twenty years down the road. When June is old enough to have a life of her own with a person who loves her.

I guess I always thought it would just be the two of us, sticking together and figuring it out along the way because that's what we've always done, since the day she's been born.

That's not how it's going to be, though.

One day, I'll be replaced.

I'll be second, not first, and *fuck*, I'm already dreading when that happens.

I down the rest of my beer and stand up. "I'm going to need something stronger," I say through a strained laugh, and a rumble behind my ribs burns through me.

"Shit," she says, and her fingers wrap around my wrist in a gentle hold. "I'm sorry. This is supposed to be fun. I didn't mean to make it a depressing talk about the future."

"You didn't." I slip out of her grasp and head for the liquor cabinet situated against the living room wall. I rummage through the alcohol and some scotch. I grab a glass and pour it three quarters full. "These are things I should be thinking about, but I'm not. I guess I've been operating under the assumption that if I don't imagine them, they'd never come true." I shuffle back to the couch and sit down, taking a long sip. "Want some?"

"I've never had scotch before."

"Here." I scoot closer and she drops her feet to the floor. Our knees touch, and I offer her the drink. "It goes down easy."

Maven brings the glass to her nose and smells it. "What does it taste like?"

"It's woody. Which I know doesn't make a whole lot of sense, but just trust me."

She hums and dips her pointer finger in the drink. I watch, fascinated, as she brings the finger to her mouth. She wraps her lips around it and sucks down the tiny sample. Her eyes flutter closed and she lets out a soft sigh, a little puff of air, that goes straight to my dick.

"That's good," she says. "Really good."

"Told you," I say, and my voice is hoarse. My vision blurs when her tongue sneaks out and licks her lips dry. "It's my favorite drink."

"I can see why." She passes the glass back to me, a soft smile working its way onto her mouth. "Nice choice, lone star."

"Thanks." I tip the drink back and swallow down a long pull, deliriously wondering what a kiss from her would taste like. Sweet, probably. Like wicked, indulgent sin, too. "This one is strong, though. If you want more, just drink slowly."

"Looking out for me?" Maven teases, and color creeps up my cheeks. "Who's looking out for you? I'm not sure you showing up to the field hungover is the best life decision you've ever made."

"I've done far worse shit in my playing career than have a couple of glasses of alcohol two nights before a game."

"Is that so? How about I pour myself a drink and we can play a game of Truth or Truth?" she asks, and I'm warm all over.

I give her a casual shrug. "Okay. But only if you go first."

"Deal."

She grins and hurries to the cabinet. I watch her stand on her toes and try to reach a glass on the top shelf. Her shirt rides up. The cotton inches higher and higher up her spine, and I get a peek of skin that does more damage to my mental capacity than I care to admit.

When she turns her head and smiles at me over her shoulder with twinkling eyes, I think I go weak in the knees.

"Struggling there, sunshine?" I ask.

"Sunshine?"

"If you're going to call me lone star, I need a nickname for you."

"What made you settle on that one?"

"I don't know." I gesture to her hair then up and down her legs. "The blonde. The happiness. Just... all of you."

"I don't hate it." She dips her chin and bites her bottom lip. "Could you help me, tall and great football player?"

"Yes ma'am." I walk across the room and position myself behind her. My arm brushes against her cheek as I lean forward and easily grab an empty glass for her to use. "Didn't realize you were so short, half pint," I say in her ear, and her hair tickles my nose.

"It's a good thing I have you." She takes a step backward to give me room and ends up with her back pressed against my chest. "To reach everything I need."

"And what do I get?" I ask, and she spins around to face me.

"What do you want?"

You.

It hits me like a bolt of lightning, and it's the first time I've allowed myself to think of her as something more than a friend. As something that's not platonic, that's not my nanny or coworker, and I can't remember what it was like when I considered her something less.

It was silly to ever think I stood a chance against how goddamn perfect she is.

It's dangerous, this territory I've edged myself toward. Everything is hazy and fuzzy here, and every warning I've been listening to that says I need to stay away seems to disappear.

When she tips her head back and our gazes lock, that twinkle in her eye is gone. There's only heat now, and I know I should walk away. I know I should pull back and put some distance between us. I know I should find some space to clear my head.

But I don't want to, so I linger longer than I should.

I sink into thoughts of all the ways I'd have her.

How I'd fuck her, how I'd kiss her, how I'd admit how often

she's on my mind. What she'd look like naked in my bed and what she sounds like when she comes. How I could get her to say my name—a prayer, a fucking plea as she begged me for more.

I haven't been with a woman in years. My inspiration when I've jerked off has become nondescript; some combination of people I've seen. A vague outline of someone with generic features. Now, though, there's a crystal-clear picture in my head.

Her.

Every-fucking-where.

Her legs spread wide and a thigh hooked over my shoulder as I drive into her, again and again. The bounce of her tits and the pleased curve of her smile as she tells me *perfect. Right there. Don't stop.*

I blow out a breath.

I take a second to collect myself so I don't do something really fucking stupid and out of line, like ask her to bend over the couch.

Twelve hours in the same apartment with her, and I've lost all of my coherent thoughts.

I roll my shoulders back and give her a wry grin, knowing I have to keep it cool.

"For you to go first," I say, and I think a flash of disappointment crosses her face. "If I'm going to share all of my deep, dark secrets, I need to know just how deep to get."

Maven smirks. "As deep as you want."

NINETEEN
DALLAS

CHRIST.

There she is, totally unfiltered and totally herself.

Maven takes the top off the crystal decanter and pours herself a glass of scotch. I watch her hips sway from side to side as she walks back to the couch and sits down. When she gets settled on the cushions, she tilts her head to the side, an invitation to join her.

Who am I to say no?

I sit next to her, aware that we're closer than we were before.

"To sharing truths," she says, and she raises her glass in the air.

I reach for mine and knock it against hers, our second cheers of the night.

"First question: did your father have a heart attack when you started dating?" I ask. "Because I think I might when June does."

Maven smiles and runs her finger around the rim of her glass. "I didn't date anyone in high school, but I had a couple boyfriends when I was in college. Maggie, his girlfriend, gave him the whole speech about how if he doesn't let me live my life, I might start to resent him. I'm an only child, and he's always been sensitive and protective when it comes to me. But the older I get, the less scared he seems to be. He knows I can take care of myself, and I think that eases his mind."

"Are you dating anyone now?" I blurt out before I can stop myself. "Sorry. That was—"

"Part of the game, right?" She takes a sip of her drink and sighs again. "God, that's good. No, I'm not dating anyone. With my photography gig and being here with June, I don't have a lot of free time."

"Oh, shit. Are we cockblocking you?"

"You're not cockblocking me. If I wanted to, I could and would. But I like being busy and doing things that are bigger than me, you know?"

A sensation surges through me, and it feels a lot like relief.

Relief that she's not crawling into anyone's bed at night.

Relief that she could be anywhere in the world, and she picked here with me.

Relief that she sees taking care of my daughter as something important. Something valuable.

I grin like a smug bastard.

"I do know. That's why I like getting involved with the stuff the team puts together for the community throughout the year. Being an athlete is fun, but it's the people off the field that make this job worth it," I say.

"You're such a nice guy," Maven murmurs.

"I'm not always nice," I challenge, and she arches an eyebrow.

"Oh? Care to elaborate?"

I wouldn't be nice if I told her to get on her knees so I could fuck her mouth.

I wouldn't be nice if I asked who her pussy belonged to when I have my head buried between her legs, knowing fully well it's mine.

I wouldn't be nice if I told her to keep her eyes on me when I made her come.

This woman is under my skin now, and I don't think I'm ever going to be able to escape.

"On the field," I say, picking the safe answer.

"You're loyal."

"I try to be. If someone hurts what's mine—like my teammates—I'm going to make them hurt, too."

"That's a good quality to have. You're nice but fierce when it counts." She takes a sip of her drink. When she finishes swallowing, she drags her thumb over her bottom lip, and I've decided this is my new personal hell. "Can I ask you a question now?"

"Those are the rules of the game, aren't they?"

"Have you ever considered letting June go to an away game?"

I blink, caught off guard. It's not the direction I thought she was going to go, and I don't know how to answer.

"June's never seen me play in person," I say.

A crease of wrinkles form across Maven's forehead. Her mouth dips into a frown, and her eyes hold mine. "Never?"

"Nope. I thought she was too young the last couple of seasons. Now that she's older, I'd love it if she could come to a game, but the logistics would be a nightmare."

"How so?"

"If we were playing at home, I'd have to leave her with someone I trust, and the only people I do trust either live out of state, are already in the stadium on game day, or play for another professional sports team and have constant scheduling conflicts. An away game would be even worse. She'd have to travel, which she's never done before. When we got there, I'd have no one to watch her. It sounds like a recipe for disaster."

Maven stares at me, and her fingers tap her cheek. "What if I took her?"

"What?"

"What if I flew out and watched her for the weekend? I don't know what the rules are for traveling with the team, but we could fly on our own and meet you somewhere. I only photograph home games—I'm the newest one on the roster, so I don't get away game privileges yet. I'd already be watching June while you're gone, so it wouldn't be extra work."

"You—you'd do that?"

"Of course I would. It sounds like fun. She's going to have the coolest show and tell when she starts school."

"I never—" I stop to take a breath, and it feels like I'm dangerously close to crying. "Having June see me play wasn't something I ever considered to be a possibility."

Her face softens. "I put the preseason game on, and she loved it. She kept saying 'Daddy, Daddy' every time she saw you. She'd lose her mind if she got to see you in person with all your gear on."

"You think so?"

"I know so."

I nod, and a swell of emotion rises inside me. "Let me talk to the team and see what protocol is. After this weekend, we have back-to-back away games. Maybe y'all could come to the second one."

"You know I'm here for you, Dallas. If your daughter watching your game makes you happy, I want to make it happen."

"Thanks, Mae." I blow out a breath. "This game of yours is supposed to be fun, but I haven't been this emotional since I held June for the first time. Tell me something that will make me laugh. What's your worst hookup story?"

She grins. "You really want to know my worst hookup story?"

"Yes, because something tells me it's going to be good."

"You have to promise to not make fun of me."

"No guarantees, but I'll do my best."

"Fine." She sets her glass on the coffee table in front of us and turns to me. "There was this guy I was seeing during my freshman year of college. We had been on a couple of dates, and one night, I brought him back to my place. We were on my bed. I was wearing nice lingerie, and I thought we were going to have a good time. Without any foreplay or build up, he slipped inside me—and when I say slipped, I mean barely an inch—rolled his eyes to the back of his head, and told me he was finished."

I hide my laugh as a cough. "Just the tip, huh?"

"Tip is being generous. He had the audacity to ask if I finished, as if he couldn't tell I was as dry as the Sahara Desert."

"We're not the most observant creatures. You have to dumb things down for us."

"That's not even the worst part."

"What's the worst part?"

"When he pulled out, he pushed up onto his knees and..." Maven buries her face in her hands. "Peed all over my new mattress."

I drop my head back and laugh so loud, I wouldn't be shocked if I woke June up. "Stop it. Did he—was it a medical condition?"

"Nope. If it was, I would've been understanding, of course. After, he looked at the sheets and said, I quote, 'huh. Happened again. Gotta tell the boys. We keep a tally of how many beds we pee in.'"

I wheeze so hard I start to snort. Maven giggles beside me, and when I see her wipe tears from her eyes, I lose it all over again.

"Fucking hell," I say through a strangled breath. My abdominal muscles hurt from laughing so hard, and I try to calm down. "That is the most revolting thing I've ever heard in my entire life.

Did he—I cannot believe I'm asking this—help clean up the mess?"

"Nope. He told me 'this was fun,' and left. I never texted him again."

"I sure as shit hope not. Wow. There's a lot to unpack there."

She scoops up her glass and downs the rest of her drink like a champ. "Your turn. Tell me your worst hookup story."

"Ah." I run my hand through my hair and shrug. "I don't really have one."

"Everyone's been perfect? Lucky you."

"No. I mean, I don't date so—"

"What about one night stands before June was born? Quick fucks in the back of a club?"

I almost whimper at hearing her say *fuck*. "Nope. It's been a very long time."

Her mouth forms an O, and she scoots closer to me. "How long is long?"

"Long. I haven't slept with anyone since the night June came into existence. And before that, no one since college. Even back then it was only a few times."

Maven blinks. It looks like she's trying to do some tipsy math in her head, and it's the cutest fucking thing I've ever seen. "Seven years?"

"Eight, actually."

"And it's by choice? Because I'm sure there would be a line of women willing to give you a hand. Or a mouth. Or a—"

"Stop," I say, and she pulls back. "Sorry. I just... it's been a while, and hearing you say things like that makes it really fucking difficult to concentrate."

"I'm sorry," she whispers.

"Don't be, and thank you for the ego boost. Football has always been my sole focus, and now June is my number one priority. Maybe one day I'll find time to let go a little bit, but for now..."

"For now, you're practically a monk," she finishes for me.

"Sort of. I'm not a saint, Maven. I see things I like. Things I want but can't have. And sometimes it's really fucking difficult to keep my hands to myself."

"What kind of things do you want?" she asks, and it sounds like a dare. Like she already knows the answer, but she wants to hear me say it.

I've already dug myself deep into a hole by telling her all of this, so I might as well keep being honest.

"I thought about kissing you for the first time thirty minutes ago, and now I can't stop."

"Oh," she whispers. Her gaze drops to my mouth, and she licks her lips. "Would that be the worst thing in the world?"

"No. Fuck, no. It would be—" I blow out a breath. "We can't. I can't."

"I get it." Maven nods, and when she drags her thumb across her bottom lip again, I watch it like a starved man. "Do you want me to move out?"

"What? Of course I don't want you to move out unless you want to move out. I didn't suggest the roommate thing just so I could ogle you."

"You can ogle me. I've been ogling you. You have a very nice ass, Lansfield."

I laugh. "So do you. But I think you already know that."

"I do, but it doesn't hurt to hear it every now and then."

"Did we just agree that we can eye-fuck each other?" I ask.

"I think so. And they say romance is dead. Are there rules to this eye-fucking?"

"We can look, but we can't touch. We're friends, and I like having you as a friend. Anything more might get complicated with June and the team and the league and—"

"Someone would lose their job, and neither one of us wants that. So we're going to be on our best behavior and keep our hands to ourselves. I agree to your rules because it's the best for everyone. I don't want anyone to get hurt. Especially June. She's become my number one priority now, too."

My heart twists in my chest when I hear her say that. Maven is the first woman outside my family who's ever shown an ounce of interest in my daughter, and knowing how important June is to her makes me ache.

It reminds me that even though June's gone so long without any female attention, she has it now. It's from the most perfect person, and I can't imagine a better role model.

"Good," I say.

"Good." Maven stands up, and she looks down at me. "I'm going to head to bed before I get myself in trouble. Thirty minutes ago, I thought about kissing you for the first time, too, and now I can't stop either."

"Good night, Mae," I say as she heads toward the hallway to her room.

"Good night, Dallas." She pauses, and her grin turns wicked. "If you ever feel like breaking the rules and need a hand with something, you know where I'll be."

I groan and press the heels of my palms into my eyes. I stay on the couch longer than I care to admit, willing my dick to calm down and doing everything in my power to not imagine her spitting in her hand and jerking me off.

I fail miserably.

TWENTY

MAVEN

"HELLO?" I close the door to my dad's apartment and head for the living room. "Anyone home?"

"Mae?" My dad appears in the kitchen with a smile on his face. "What are you doing here, kid?"

"Hey, Dad." I throw my arms around him in a tight hug when I get close enough to reach him. "I thought I'd come by and say hi."

"You're not working?"

"Not today. Dallas got back from a road game last night, so he and June are spending the day together."

"And what a road game it was. Three and oh to start the season—I like those odds. Are you hungry?" he asks, already grabbing the ingredients for a grilled cheese. "Want to stay for lunch?"

"I'm starving," I say, and I take a seat at the island. "Do you want some help?"

"Nope. Talk to me. How is the nanny gig going?"

"It's going well. June is so easy. I don't have a lot to compare her against, but she's very smart. She's polite, and she always says please and thank you. She rarely acts out, and when she does, it's because of something that's easily fixable like hunger, tiredness or overstimulation. I was worried when I first agreed to help Dallas because this stage of life is such a big part of their development, but I think I'm doing a good job. I'm balancing the fun we have together with helping her learn things. Plus, she hasn't ended up in the hospital and I haven't been fired, so I think it's a win-win."

"That doesn't surprise me at all." He puts the bread and cheese in the pan and pulls a plate down from the cabinet. "You've always been a helper. The kid that wanted to make sure everyone knew how to do things. It makes sense that it's transferred to this role, too."

"I know I'm not her parent, and I'd never claim responsibility for who she is as a person, but she's teaching me things, too."

"Like what?"

"Like patience and empathy and different communication styles. It's not where I saw myself being at this point in my life, but I think it's exactly where I'm supposed to be."

"I'm proud of you." My dad smiles, and his eyes wrinkle in the corners. "I know I gave you shit for not finishing college, and I'm sorry for that."

"You gave me a lot of shit. I don't think you talked to me for three days."

"That's not true. It was a day, maybe. I couldn't bear not talking to you." His face softens, and he sighs. "All a parent wants is for their kid to be happy, and you seem so happy these days. Who am I to judge how you're finding that happiness?"

"Jesus, Dad." I blink away tears and wipe my eyes. "I came for food, not for damn waterworks."

"Twenty-two years with me, kid. You should know what you're getting into by now."

"I am happy. For the first time since my injury, I wake up and feel like I have a purpose. I know I'm not curing cancer or fighting for world peace, but right now, it's perfect, and it's enough."

"Aiden. Have you seen my—Maven!" Maggie walks into the kitchen and hugs me. I laugh into her arms and squeeze her tight. "This is the best surprise."

"Hi, Mags. I had the day off and figured I'd stop by. I haven't seen you all in a few weeks, and I missed you."

"Be careful. You're going to make your dad cry," she says, and she kisses the top of my head before pulling away. "We've missed you too. How are things? How's work? Why haven't I seen any of your photos from your first game?"

"I've been so busy. I send the photos to my supervisor, and I forget that other people want to see them, too. I promise I'll send some when I get home tonight."

"You better." She sits next to me and looks at my dad. "Grilled cheese?"

"Mhm." His smile melts into something secret. A private sort of devotion and adoration I feel expand behind my ribs the longer he looks at her. "Do you want me to make you one?"

"Of course I do. I'm on night shift today, and the only way I'm going to survive is with one of your famous sandwiches."

"You don't have to flirt with me, Mags." He leans over the island and kisses her forehead, and I scrunch up my nose. "I was going to make one for you anyway."

"Can we keep the PDA to a minimum when I'm around, please?" I ask. "My sanity thanks you."

They both know I'm just giving them a hard time.

I'm glad my family has expanded over the years, and I'm glad my dad is so happy.

My dad dragged his feet after my parents' divorce. He stayed single, busy as a part-time single dad and a full-time pediatric oncologist. I was worried he'd never find anyone else; he's a great guy, but he never put himself out there.

He didn't care about getting to know women and was oblivious to the people who practically threw themselves at him. Then Shawn signed him up for a photo shoot with a stranger, and that's where he met Maggie.

The two hit it off, had a night together I've *refused* to ask questions about, and now here we are. Six years later, and they're just as happy as they were when they first got together.

My dad likes to say his life changed that Valentine's Day, and I know the reason it took him so long to find love again was because he was waiting for Maggie.

Those two are soulmates. They might not wear rings and there might not have been a wedding, but they're in it for the long haul. Tied together through fate and destiny and a spread of half-naked photos, the more appropriate ones of which they framed and hung on the walls in the living room to commemorate their love for one another.

And Maggie.

She's funny and kind. Her heart is made of gold, and she lets me come to her whenever I need advice. She always keeps my secrets safe, and there's never any judgment when I ask her questions or tell her about the things I've done. She's never tried to fill the role of *Mom*, but I love her like she is one.

Then there's Shawn and Lacey, two best friends who fell for each other after an epic kiss on the big screen at a football game. With all this happiness around me, I realize, for the first time, that everyone I care about has a partner.

Everyone has that soul-crushing, head-over-heels kind of love that you read about in books. The infatuation where you could lose everything you have, but as long as you have each other, you know you'll be alright.

I wonder if I'll ever have that.

I wasn't sure if I wanted it, but when I see it in front of me, I desperately want to be a half of a whole with someone who looks at me like I'm their entire world.

"Hey. It's not my fault you showed up unannounced," my dad says, and he uses a spatula to transfer the sandwich out of the pan and onto the plate. "I'm allowed to flirt with my girl-friend in my apartment."

"Fine." I smile when he hands me the food. "Behave however you want."

"How do you like working for Dallas?" Maggie asks. "I did a deep internet dive the other night, and some of the stories about being around NFL players are kind of wild. Does he treat you right?"

"Dallas is literally the nicest guy in the world," I say. "He's never made me uncomfortable. I've liked getting to know him. The last couple of years have been isolating as I watched my friends finish out their college playing careers and move on to the next thing in their athletic journeys, and it's nice to be around someone who understands the joy and heartbreak sports bring."

He also asked me to move in, and, surprise, we're roommates now! The other night we were drinking on the couch and he was staring at me like I was his lifeline. Like I was keeping him afloat and I would've let him kiss me if he asked.

Maggie narrows her eyes. It feels like she can tell I'm hiding a dozen secrets, but she doesn't comment on them.

"That's good," she says, and she smiles brightly. "And how is his daughter? June, right?"

"The most adorable four-year-old in the world. I convinced Dallas to let us join him at an away game, so we're flying to Cleveland this weekend to watch him play. It'll be June's first time seeing her dad on the field in person. I ordered a special jersey for her, and Shawn got us some field access passes. Figured we'd surprise Dallas before kickoff."

Maggie reaches out and takes my hand in hers. "You're so thoughtful, Mae. That'll be an experience he'll remember forever."

"Yeah, well." I shrug, and my cheeks turn a faint shade of pink. "He's done everything by himself for so long, I thought it was time someone did something nice for him."

"You raised a wonderful woman, Aiden," Maggie says, and my dad grins.

"I know I did. How's that camera working for you, Mae? We can trade it out and get something nicer if it's not getting the job done."

"It's perfect, Dad. Really. I've taken some good photos with it, and ESPN even ran one of them last week in an article about the Titans."

"She's working her way up, folks." My dad hands Maggie a plate and rests his elbows on the island. "What about your apartment? Did the maintenance people ever come and fix that leaky faucet?"

I take a bite of my grilled cheese before I answer him. "Hm?"

"The leaky faucet in your kitchen. You said someone was going to repair it."

"Oh, yeah." I nod and take another bite. "All good there."

It's not technically a lie. I'm sure the maintenance people did come and fix it. I'm just not the one who signed off on the paperwork. Those problems belong to the new residents of 7F now, not me.

"We'll be at the next home game," Maggie says, and I'm grateful for the change in subject. "Shawn said he'd get us field access so we can see you in action. Lacey will be there, too."

"That will be awesome. I'd say we could all get dinner after, but with June and—"

"You have responsibilities, Mae, and that's okay. You know we're grateful for any pockets of time we can get with you, but we also love seeing you busy and doing something you love. It's good to see that excitement in your eyes again."

"It feels good," I agree, and my phone buzzes in my pocket.

I pull it out and see Dallas's name on the screen.

DALLAS

How's your day?

June is down for a nap, and I just realized how quiet the apartment is without you here.

There aren't any tornadoes whipping around me.

ME

Is that your way of telling me you miss me?

DALLAS

A bit, yeah.

Who knew I'd be a fan of chaos?

ME

I'm at my dad's and eating the world's best grilled cheese. I'll be back later.

DALLAS

Enjoy your afternoon. I just wanted to say hi.

ME

Hi, lone star.

DALLAS

Hi, sunshine.

I'll let you go. Catch you on the flip side, roomie.

"I'm not sure I've ever seen you smile like that before," Maggie says, quietly enough for only me to hear.

"I'm not smiling," I say.

"That's your second lie of the afternoon. Are you going to tell me what's going on?"

"Everything's fine. I'm…" I trail off, knowing I can't tell her, even if I want to. "Things are just good."

She hums in understanding and doesn't press any further, turning her focus back to her lunch. "Good. I like seeing you smile."

With everyone distracted, I read Dallas's text messages again, and my heart skips a beat when I realize I miss him, too.

TWENTY-ONE
MAVEN

"DO YOU HAVE HER SNACKS?"

"Yup. Extra Goldfish, too, because I know they're her favorite," I answer.

"And a change of clothes for when you land? In case the luggage gets lost?"

"Check. With a different pair of shoes in the unlikely event her favorite sneakers start to hurt her feet."

"What about a jacket? Her hat and gloves? Shit, do you think she needs boots?" he asks.

I look up and stare at Dallas leaning in the doorway. Worried shadows cross his face, and he gnaws on his bottom lip.

"Why in the world would she need gloves?" I ask. "We're going to Ohio in October. It's seventy degrees."

"What if a cold front passes through and all she has are shorts and T-shirts?" He exhales a ragged breath and pinches the bridge of his nose. "She'd freeze to death."

"What the hell is going on, Dallas?"

"I don't know." He walks into my room and takes a seat on the edge of my bed. He stretches back and grabs a fluffy pillow from near the headboard and holds it close to his chest like a security blanket. "I'm freaking out."

"Clearly." I shove a pair of socks into the zippered pocket of my suitcase and stand up, joining him on the mattress. "Talk to me, Lansfield."

"I'm really happy y'all are coming, but I'm also nervous. I'm thinking about worst case scenarios, and I want to throw up."

"Oh, that's why you're panicking? I thought it was because you had another nanny and daughter you're trying to hide from us."

"No." His laugh is soft and hesitant, but I take it as a victory. "This is her first time leaving the confines of D.C. What if your plane crashes? What if *my* plane crashes?"

"What if a meteor hits Earth? What if the dinosaurs get out of the theme park again?" I ask, and he levels me with an unimpressed look. "Sorry. I'm trying to lighten the mood, but I sound like an asshole. Look. I know you're anxious. Not only are you on the road for a game, but you'll have the added pressure of your daughter being in a world she's not familiar with. That's scary." I take his hand in mine and wrap our fingers together, holding him tight in what I hope he understands is a reassuring squeeze. "Do you trust me?"

"Yes," he says without hesitation, and his eyes meet mine. "I trust you more than I trust anyone else, Maven," he adds, and my stomach flip-flops when his voice dips to low and sincere.

It's one of the nicest things he's said to me. I know he doesn't give out that trust freely. You have to work for it, *earn* it, and being one of the select few to have it causes pride to zip up my spine.

I sit up a little straighter and give him a smile that turns distracted when his eyes drop to my lips and linger on my mouth before looking away.

I thought about kissing you for the first time, and now I can't stop.

154

His words come back to me like they have every night when I'm in bed—down the hall from the man I can't have—and hopelessly wondering what he's thinking.

I wonder if he thinks about me the way I think about him when we're next to each other on the couch. A television show will be on for background noise but we talk through it because we keep remembering stories to share: the funny things June said at dinner. Plans for the next day and a new recipe he wants to try.

Easy, seamless, the kind of talks where you have a two-hour conversation then lapse into silence that feels comfortable and right. An unhurried drift toward quiet contemplation and just enjoying the moment.

And, *god*, I want to kiss him, too.

Every day I spend with him, I realize I'm past considering him a friend.

I'm attracted to him, a connection forging between us with every brush of our elbows and every small smile we share over mashed potatoes and meatloaf.

I want him, and I hate that I can't have him.

I hate that I can't do anything besides admire the view. To flirt a little and appreciate the way his eyes roam down my body when I want him to do so much more.

"It's no different than any other day when you leave for practice. Or the other away games this season," I say when I find my voice again. "I'm still a phone call—and a hotel room door—away. Think of how fun it's going to be for June to be in a suite and watch her dad play football in person for the first time. It's going to be so special, Dallas."

He relaxes, and I know I'm saying the right things. The true things. He gets in his head about being a parent, and any time I get the chance to remind him how great he's doing at raising a tiny human, I jump at the opportunity.

He loves the praise and I love the way he lights up when I call him a good dad.

It makes me want to melt.

"You're right," he says.

"Of course I'm right." I nudge his shoulder with mine, and he squeezes my hand. "It's going to be fine. I know you were joking about plane crashes, but you do realize the statistical probability of that happening is—"

"Yup. You don't have to tell me, and maybe we shouldn't speak it into existence." His smile is shy, and he runs his free hand through his hair. A lock falls across his forehead, and I have the urge to brush it away. "I'm being a helicopter parent, and I'm sorry. I know you know how to do your job and take care of June—you do it damn well, Maven. Knowing this is another first we're crossing off the list has me wishing we could slow down time."

"Time is a bitch." I sling my arm around him and give him a sideways hug. "Imagine how different life would be if we had the ability to pause it and correct our mistakes or pick a different path after knowing the consequences of our actions. That's why we have to enjoy where we are right now; there's no going back."

"It's too early for this philosophical stuff," he mumbles, and I laugh. "You're wise beyond your years, Mae."

"I'm an old soul. Maybe I've already lived a thousand lives." I rest my chin on his shoulder and study the freckles across his cheeks. "How are you feeling?"

"I'm better now. Roommate. Nanny. Therapist and philosopher. I'm not paying you enough."

"I'd do it for free, you know." I rub my thumb across my neck, reaching for the necklace I still can't find. "I need to stop dragging my feet; our flight leaves in three hours, and I'm not finished packing."

"I'll let you get back to it. I'm going to say bye to June, then I'm heading out."

"Sounds good. I shared my location with you, by the way," I say, and Dallas frowns. "This morning, in our text thread."

"You did?" He pulls out his phone and I see my name pinned to the top of his messages. "Why'd you do that?"

"Because I wanted to. If I can't answer you right away, I want you to be able to see where we are."

His face softens into an expression of gratitude. The wrinkles around his eyes smooth over, and his frown melts away. "Thank you."

"Thank *you* for giving me your credit card this weekend. June and I are going to buy all the stuffed animals at the Cleveland Zoo gift shop. There are going to be so many giraffes around here, you won't know what to do with yourself."

"You know how much she loves the zoo. She's going to talk your ear off the whole trip." Dallas stands up and knocks me in the head with the pillow that's been resting on his knees. "Do you have y'all's tickets?"

"Yup. Two first class seats are safely tucked in my purse along with enough food to feed the entire plane." I nudge his shin with my foot. "Go say goodbye to your daughter. We're going to be fine. I promise."

"Okay." He drags himself to the door and looks back at me. Nothing about it is a quick glance; Dallas takes his time. He studies me from my head to my toes, and I've never felt so on display. "See you in Ohio, sunshine."

TWENTY-TWO

MAVEN

FLYING with a four year old was easier than I thought it would be.

It helps that June is perfect. She's the most go-with-the-flow kid I've ever met.

The flight attendants kept coming up to us and giving her goodies; an extra package of cookies. A pair of wings I pinned to the front of her shirt. A collectable airplane trading card to commemorate her first flight.

I took photo after photo and sent them all to Dallas, waiting impatiently as the shitty Wi-Fi did its best to deliver the snapshots at thirty-six thousand feet in the air.

I got a dozen messages back from him.

Tell her she can be a pilot, to the photo of her wearing the captain's hat during boarding.

Fuck protein today, I guess, to the photo of her eating the chocolate chip cookie that came with the inflight meal.

A morning nap? You have magic powers, to the photo of JB passed out, her head against the window and her mouth open.

My girls, to the photo of June and me when we touched down in Cleveland, followed by *I'm saving that one.*

I grinned for too long at that response.

After a quick ride to downtown Cleveland in our private car, I unload our bags in the driveway for our hotel.

"Daddy!" June screams at the top of her lungs.

I turn and see Dallas jogging toward us in his practice gear. A Titans shirt stretches tight across his chest, and black athletic shorts sit low on his hips. There's a backwards hat on his head, and my insides rearrange themselves when he scoops JB into his arms and spins her around.

"Hey, baby girl," he says. "How was your flight?"

"Daddy, we went in an airplane," she gushes. "We were high!"

"JB is a celebrity." I wave to our driver and wheel our stuff toward the lobby. "Even the people sitting around us talked about how well behaved she was."

"My superstar." Dallas blows a raspberry on her cheek, and she squeals. "Let me help you to your room, and we can put her stuff in mine. Ours are connected, and I figured June could sleep with me."

"Perfect." I brush my hair out of my eyes and fan myself. "Good thing we didn't bring her parka or snowshoes. It's warm."

"Yeah, until the freak snowstorm hits, and then you'll freeze to death because all you brought with you are those shorts." His gaze lingers on my legs before he takes my suitcase and drags it toward the revolving doors. "The guys want to see you and June before we head to practice."

"Me? Your cute kid I can understand, but why would they want to see me?"

"Because you're cool. Odell won't stop talking about that shot you got of him sacking the Tornadoes QB two weeks ago. He printed out a copy and wants you to sign it."

"You're joking." I trail behind him, a backpack slung over my shoulder and pulling June's tiny suitcase. "Pretty sure *Sports Illustrated* has way better shots of him."

"He likes yours the most," Dallas says, and that fills me with pride.

I've been working hard in my role, not because I want to make a name for myself, but because I want to be the best version of Photographer Maven I can be. I've spent hours researching angles and lighting and action photography. I've devoured every tutorial video on how to focus on the subject while still capturing their surroundings, and I can see an improvement in my craft.

I'm getting better. I'm learning how to move with the athletes, and I'm not afraid to get right in the thick of the action. My favorite spot is at the edge of the end zone where I can wait for a player to run at me full steam.

I'm starting to get that same sensation when I'm holding a camera as I did whenever I stepped out on the soccer field. There's excitement. The faintest hint of nerves. The thrill that I'm about to do something I truly love, and gratitude that this is my life.

I'm not the best sports photographer out there. Maybe one day I will be, but right now, I'm enjoying the ride, and god, it's been fun.

The lobby is chaos when we step inside. There are Titans players everywhere, and they take turns passing June around and giving her a kiss on the cheek. I know most of them, and I'm familiar with their numbers and positions.

Dallas still makes it a point to stand on a chair and introduce me to everyone I haven't officially met yet. There's a round of cheers when he lifts June in the air, and I smile as I watch them.

"Hey, punk," Shawn says, and he rests his arm on top of my head.

"What are you doing down here? I thought you'd be at the field already."

"Not yet. I was talking with my assistant coaches. How was your flight?"

"I'm sure it wasn't as nice as your charter plane, but not bad. June was awesome, and we didn't hit any traffic on the way over."

"Good. How are you doing, kid? I feel like I haven't seen you in ages."

"You see me on the sidelines all the time."

"That doesn't count, and you know it. I have five different people talking in my ear and can barely hear myself think on game days."

"I'm doing well. I'm having so much fun as a photographer, and I love spending time with June." My eyes cut back over to her and Dallas. She's telling him a story, and he nods along excitedly, like he can't wait to hear what else she has to say. "I'm really happy."

"Glad to hear it. I can't believe how your photography has taken off. You're getting reposted by some of the biggest sports websites, Mae. That's pretty damn cool. Lacey wanted me to ask you if you've started a social media account designated to your brand yet, whatever the hell that means."

"Not yet, but I know I need to get around to it."

"How are things with Dallas?" Shawn asks. "Is he giving you any problems?"

"None at all. He's so different from when I started helping him. He seems really happy, too."

"I haven't seen him smile this much since the season we drafted him. I know I wasn't totally onboard with the idea of you being his nanny, but you're doing a good thing by helping him with June. He's a nice guy, and he's had a rough time finding the support he needs during the football season. You stepped up when he needed it."

"No one deserves to feel like they're alone in the world," I say, and Shawn hums in agreement. "I'd do it again in a heartbeat."

"You're right." He checks his watch and grimaces. "Shit. I need to get to the bus. Darcy will get you the access passes for Sunday."

"Thanks, Shawn." I give him a hug, and I smile when he squeezes my shoulder.

"I'm glad we got to catch up, Maven. I know you don't have soccer in your life anymore, but it seems like you're slowly starting to figure out who you are. I'm proud of you," he says, and my smile stretches into a beam.

"I'm proud of me, too. Have a good practice."

"Ready to take her?" Dallas asks as I work my way back to him, and I nod.

"Yeah. Let me know when you're heading back to the hotel after practice. I'll make sure we're here."

"Thanks." He hands June to me, and she rests her head on my shoulder. "I'm glad y'all are here."

"So are we."

We stare at each other for a handful of seconds before one of his teammates comes over and asks if he'll run routes with him after he's done kicking. June's eyes close, and she starts to drift off to sleep, and I know it's time for us to go.

"I'll see you later," Dallas says, and I nod.

"Sounds good. You know where we'll be."

"Oh. Here." He pulls out a keycard from the waistband of his pants. "I already checked you in, so you can go on up. I opened the door between our rooms, but I'll close it tonight when we go to sleep. Do you have dinner plans?"

"No. I figured I'd order room service or something. You have a team dinner, right?"

"Not tonight, just tomorrow. Some of the guys are going out, but I'm not in the mood to do all of that. I was going to order pizza from this hole in the wall spot a couple blocks away and eat in the room. Want to join me after June heads to bed?"

"Like I'll pass up free pizza. That sounds great."

"Cool." He hooks his thumb over his shoulder and smiles. "I'm out of here. You two behave."

"Pretty sure we're going to take a very long nap. You're not allowed to draw any dicks on my face if you come back and we're still sleeping."

"What about a mustache?"

"Any face art will result in me kneeing you in the balls, so think about the consequences, Lansfield."

"Noted." He bends down and kisses JB on the cheek. "Thanks for making this possible, Mae."

"There's nowhere else I'd rather be."

When his gaze meets mine, I know he's thinking the same thing.

TWENTY-THREE
DALLAS

"HOW DOES the suite I arranged for Maven and June look?" I ask Darcy, our team assistant. I step to the side in the tunnel of Bearcats Stadium and lean my elbow against the wall. "I know today has been hectic. Can I help with anything?"

She caps her highlighter and smiles. "I went and checked it earlier this morning. There are noise canceling headphones in there for June, and the stadium chef got their food preferences. Everything's handled."

"Thank you for doing that. It's June's first game, and I want it all to be perfect," I explain.

"It's all part of the job, and I'm happy to help." Darcy waves and heads toward the visitors' locker room. "Have a good game, Dallas."

I make my way to the field. I want to get in some practice kicks before fans are allowed to enter the stadium. My leg is bothering me, and my quad muscles are a little tight after an awkward kick at practice on Thursday before we left for our trip.

I've stretched it, massaged and taped it, but there's still a lingering ache that's pissing me off. The more time I spend away from trainers' eyes, the better.

I'm sure as hell not going to tell Coach, either. If I give him any sign I'm in pain or struggling, he'll pull me without a second thought. With June in the stands and a tough game against a divisional rival, I refuse to spend the day on the bench.

"Hey, Dal," Justin Rodgers, our holder, says, and he squints up at me. "How are we feeling today?"

"Good." I knock my knuckles against his helmet in greeting and set the football on the kicking tee. "Beautiful afternoon for a football game, isn't it?"

There's not a cloud in the sky. I see nothing but a deep expanse of blue, and my lips twitch up into a smile. The world is still and quiet, and there's not even the slightest hint of a breeze in the air. At seventy degrees, the temperature is perfect, and I love days like this.

It takes me back to when I was a kid and playing with my dad in the park up the road from our house. Those afternoons in the early spring when we'd stay outside for hours until my mom yelled at us to get inside and we cooled off with sweet tea.

I wonder if June will ever play sports. If we'll move somewhere with an outdoor space that's not covered in concrete where we can run and play. The older she gets, the more I want to get out of the city. I want to find somewhere a little quieter, a little more open. A spot where she can be a kid with a long driveway to ride her bike and a fence for the dog she won't stop talking about.

Maybe there's a blonde there, too.

"Couldn't have asked for better weather," Justin agrees, and I'm pulled from the future I've started fantasizing for myself. "Way better than being here in December."

I swing my leg back and forth then toss him the ball. "You're from out west, aren't you?"

"Born and raised. I can't wait to get back out there when I retire. I'm going to buy a farm with mountains in the background and go off the grid. I'll become a cowboy." Justin grins and holds the ball in place. "Everyone loves a cowboy."

"Sounds like the dream." I wind up and kick the football. It ricochets off the goal posts, hitting the right then left, and comes up short. "God dammit."

"Chin up, Lansfield. You always miss the first one," someone calls out, and I turn around to find Maven and June walking toward me.

June is in a pink Titans jersey I've never seen before. My number—19—is smack dab in the center. Her jeans are rolled at her ankles to show off her favorite pair of pink Nikes, and her hair is pulled back in two pigtails that bounce behind her.

My eyes move from her to Maven, and my throat goes dry. My skin feels hot, and my heart races in my chest like I've been running for fucking miles.

She looks like a vision, and I take my time to admire her. I stare at her feet, at the high-top sneakers and the leather pants that hug her thighs and hips and leave nothing to the imagination.

Fuck.

I love her body.

And I love that she loves her body, too, and wants to show it off.

There are muscles and curves everywhere, a former athlete who embraces her shape rather than hides it. I'd die if she let me put my head between her legs. I'd go to heaven if she hooked a calf over my shoulder and let me touch all the parts of her she's proud of.

I move to her jersey—*my* jersey—that's tied above her waist. The light blue makes her skin look tan and soft, and I like how my number stretches across her tits and shows off even more of her figure.

Her blonde hair is in a high ponytail, pulled back so I can

see that spot on her neck I want to run my tongue up. The smile she's wearing nearly sends me into cardiac arrest, and I remember we have an audience.

"God damn," Justin murmurs, and I glance at him. He's watching Maven too, and irritation flashes through me. "She's fucking hot."

"No comment."

"Fuck you, Dal. You're staring at her like you're in the desert and she's a glass of water."

"I am not."

"Wanna bet? Hey, Maven," Justin calls out, and she waves. "Can I see the back of your jersey?"

"Oh, this old thing?" She turns around and walks toward us backward. Her hips sway from side to side, and it should be illegal for me to stare at her for this long. "What do you think?"

I think my time of death is going to be just before 11 a.m. in the middle of a fucking football field.

There's my last name stretched boldly across her shoulders like it's hers, too.

There's her round ass, covered by tight leather.

There's the back of her neck, a few strands of hair sticking to her skin.

Christ. I need someone to revive me.

"It's nice. What do you think, Dallas?" Justin asks, and he elbows my side.

"Hm? Oh. Yeah. Nice," I repeat, and I wonder if I have those cartoon hearts in my eyes.

I've never had a woman I like wear my jersey before. Lacey doesn't count—she was using it to get someone else's attention.

My teammates with partners talk about how it's such an ego boost. How they get possessive when their girl shows up and someone else tries to look at her, and I never understood why.

I get it now.

It makes me think she's *mine*, and I dare anyone else to try and get her attention.

Staying away from her is getting harder and harder to do. I congratulate myself whenever I make it through another day without doing something idiotic like pushing her against a wall and kissing her until morning.

Seeing her in my jersey, though, makes it difficult to remember my rules. It makes it difficult to remember why getting involved with her is a bad idea. It makes me want to say *fuck it* and deal with the consequences.

Maven spins back around and grins. "Thanks, guys."

"What are you doing here?" I ask, and I pick up June. "I thought y'all would be in the suite."

"We'll get up there eventually. I wanted to surprise you and let you have a minute with June before the game starts, so Shawn got us field access for warmups."

Fucking hell.

A couple of years ago, Shawn made us all take a test to learn what our love language is. He said it would be good team building and a way for us to show appreciation for each other.

I learned mine are acts of service and quality time, and the guys all made fun of me. They joked that there are plenty of places out there where I can get whatever kind of service I want.

But this is exactly the kind of gesture that sends my heart racing.

Someone showing up and doing something with me and for me. Giving up their time to do something that might seem small to them, but it's a mountain to me.

I didn't think holding my daughter in my arms on a football field two hours before kickoff would be the nicest thing anyone's made happen for me, but it is.

And it's because of her.

I cover June's ears and exhale. "Fuck, Maven. This is—"

"What you deserve, and what's going to keep happening as long as I'm around." She pulls something out of her pocket and smiles as she waves a sheet of paper in the air. "I'm getting all the guys to sign her ticket, too. I figured you could frame it and hang it in her room."

I squeeze June to my chest and shake my head. The more she talks, the harder it gets to breathe. "She's lucky to have you in her life. I'm lucky, too. I'm going to get you the biggest Nanny of the Year trophy for Christmas."

"Let's get a photo," she says, and she slides up next to me. I drape my arm around her and she rests her head in the crook of my shoulder as she pulls out her phone. "I'll photoshop the trophy in."

"Say cheese, JB."

"Cheese!" she shrieks, and Maven takes the picture of the three of us when we're mid-laugh.

"That's going to be a keeper," I say.

"Without a doubt." She tucks her phone away and looks up at me. "You know you always miss your first kick in warmups, right?"

"What?" I follow her line of sight and stare at the ball leaning against the goal post. "No, I don't."

"Yes, you do. You always come up short, and you favor the right side."

"Are you watching me, Maven?"

"You warm up five feet away from where I'm doing my job," she argues. "Don't flatter yourself. It's not like I'm watching *you*."

"You're watching *me* though, aren't you, Maven?" Justin asks innocently.

"I definitely am," she says, and I hear the teasing tone in her voice. "You're my favorite guy on the team, Justin."

"Shucks. You're my favorite photographer," Justin says.

The fucker has the balls to blush at her compliment, and I glare at him.

"Daddy kick the ball?" June asks, interrupting their flirting, and I'm grateful for her.

"I sure am, baby girl. Do you want to watch?"

"I want to kick," she says, and I set her back on the grass. She takes off toward the ball, giggling the whole way.

"Take a break for a few, Maven. I'll watch her," Justin says, and he winks at me as he chases after June.

"Nice jersey," I say to Maven when we're alone.

"I stole it from your closet," she admits. "I ordered the little one for June, but mine got delayed. I had to improvise."

"Always quick on your feet." I toss a ball to her and she catches it, taking a few steps back. "I can't believe you're here."

"I'm sure the suite is going to be nice, but it's way more fun being down in the action. Plus, June can work out some of her energy before we try to sit for four quarters."

"How was y'all's morning?"

"Great. We had breakfast, then we did a walk around the hotel before heading over. JB won't stop talking about how she gets to see Daddy play today to anyone who will listen, including our server at the pancake house. I tipped fifty percent because June wouldn't let her get back to work."

"That's June for you. She wants to be friends with everyone. Darcy made sure there are noise canceling headphones in the suite in case the game gets overstimulating. There's also going to be plenty of ranch dressing so you can dip your sliders. I swear, you're the only one who likes that shit."

Maven freezes. Her arm is pulled back, about to throw the ball to me, and she blinks. "You asked for extra ranch?"

"Yeah. We filled out a sheet with food preferences, and I made sure to include it. It's no big deal, and it's not like I didn't already pay for the suite. The least they can do is add some additional condiments."

"How did you know I love ranch?"

"You use it on everything, woman. Sandwiches. French fries. Pizza—god, the Italians would burn you at the stake."

"Sounds like *you* might be watching *me*," she says softly, and I take a step toward her.

"I definitely am. Is that okay?" I ask.

Maven's cheeks are flushed, and she nods. "It's more than okay."

"Good." My teammates start to file on the field, and I glance over my shoulder. "I should get back to it."

"We're going to hang out on the sidelines for a bit," she says. "We won't be in your way, will we?"

"You're never in my way, Maven."

"Let me go grab JB before someone mistakes her for a moving target. It would be really shitty to start the afternoon off with her getting knocked in the head with a ball."

"Eh, builds character. Y'all have fun today."

"You too, Dallas. Have a good game."

Maven brushes past me. She heads for the end zone and gives me another view of her ass. I reach out and wrap my fingers around her wrist, stopping her before she can get any further away.

"You should know, Mae, since you're wearing my jersey, it's yours for the rest of the season," I say lowly, and she lifts an eyebrow, intrigued.

"Is that so?" she asks, and I rub my thumb across her pulse point. Her breath catches, and she looks down at where we're joined. "I didn't realize there were jersey wearing rules."

"I'm making my own rules. If you put on another guy's jersey, I'm going to have to take it off of you."

"That sounds like it could be fun." Her eyes twinkle, and she smirks. "I've always liked a challenge. Now that I know how to rile you up, I might have to see just how far I can push."

"You might like a challenge, but I always win."

"We'll see." She wiggles free from my grip, and her fingers graze down my chest as she pulls away. I bite my tongue so hard, I think it might bleed. "Best of luck with that, Lansfield."

Maven tosses me one more wicked grin, and I have to cover my groin with my helmet. When she takes June from Justin's arms and heads to the protected part of the field, she makes sure to wink in my direction.

I don't know what game we just decided to play, but if it's anything like our *look but don't touch* agreement, I think we're going to have a hell of a lot of fun.

I don't give a shit if I win or lose, because either way, I get to go home to her.

And she's a fucking prize.

TWENTY-FOUR
DALLAS

"WE MEET AGAIN."

"It's almost like we're roommates or something," I say.

"How are you doing after the loss on Sunday?" Maven asks. She sits next to me on the couch and hands me a drink. "You looked pissed after the game and I haven't really seen you since."

She's not wrong.

We got back late on Sunday night after our flights were delayed and we all went straight to bed when we got home. On Monday, I overslept, and she was already out with June. She sent me a message that said they were heading to the library and she'd see me that night.

On Tuesday, she went to dinner at her dad's place. She didn't get back to the apartment until past ten, and by then, I was already in bed.

June had a doctor's appointment this morning, and I only saw Maven long enough to hand off JB before I headed to the stadium for the longest practice of my life.

I've missed her.

"I'm doing better, but I'm still pissed." I accept the beer from her and take a sip. "I think I went in with really high expectations for how things would go, and I got distracted. I haven't missed a kick that close in years."

"The streak for most consecutive field goals made has come to an end. You'll find a new record to break."

"Longest field goal in history would be nice."

Maven pauses. "I saw you deactivated your social media account," she says slowly.

"I did. I like that you keep tabs on me, Mae. You're such a little stalker."

"Yup. Stalking you twenty-four seven." She stretches out her legs, and her feet end up in my lap. I drape my arm over her shins and sigh. "I was worried about you. Do I need to hunt down some internet keyboard warriors and let their moms know they're being jackasses?"

"No." A laugh slips out of me, and I'm grateful for her joke. It feels like I've been wallowing in self-pity the last few days after the loss, and it's nice to think something is funny. "I just needed some peace and quiet. Things get loud a lot of the time, especially after a loss, and blocking everyone out helps. Maybe it's cowardly, but I don't care."

"It's not cowardly at all. It's called protecting your mental health, and it's important."

"Wish the league felt the same way," I sigh.

"The league sucks. I remember when Shawn had a panic attack on the sidelines during one of your games. You guys were understanding of what happened, but he was still fined for leaving the stadium early. Fucking bullshit."

I smile at the fire in her voice. The protection of the people she cares about comes through each word with fierce determination. She's not just saying it to cheer me up, either. The commissioner himself could be sitting in the room with us and she'd say the exact same thing to him.

I fucking love it.

"Total bullshit," I agree. "I've never understood why they care so much about protecting this masculine stigma. We might be rough on the field, but we also cry. We get sad. We pretend like the things fans yell at us don't bother us, but when someone tells me they wish I'd jump off the top of a building and die after missing a field goal in a football game—as if there aren't bigger fucking issues in the world—it gets to me."

"No one should have to deal with that." Maven reaches over and takes my hand in hers. "I support you, Dallas. And I hope you know the apartment is safe. You can be yourself here. You can be yourself around *me*. You can cry. Scream and yell. Whatever it is that you have to bottle up and keep hidden while you're on the field or in front of cameras, you're allowed to let it out here. I want to see it."

"Are you sure about that? You understand what it's like being an athlete. There are highs. But there are also a lot of lows. It's complicated. Messy. Ugly, too, and no matter what face I put on when we get defeated, I still end up in those dark places when people try and highlight my flaws. And if they ever said anything about June—" I trail off and shake my head once. "I don't know what I'd do."

"Don't keep them in. Give them to me. I like messy. I like complicated. I like flaws—*all* of them." She smiles at me so sweetly, so genuinely, I feel it behind my ribs. It's an ache that's never been there before. Like I'd do anything to make sure she smiles like that again. "Especially yours. Don't go to the dark places alone."

I stare at her, and for the first time, I feel seen as a player and a father.

Heard.

Understood.

It's scary to show parts of yourself to someone else, but I like her having them. I'd give her everything, if I could, and I feel like she'd do the same for me.

"Thank you," I say, and my voice is barely above a whisper. I squeeze her hand, and she rubs her thumb over my knuckles. "What is it with us and conversations turning deep as shit?"

"No clue." She laughs and untangles our hands to take a sip of her beer. "Guess it means we're comfortable around each other."

"Yeah." I nod and drag my eyes away from her face. "I guess we are."

"Speaking of comfortable, I hope you don't think June is bad luck. Her first game and you lose? It's got to be an anomaly."

"Nah. This one is on me." I play with the bracelet around my wrist and smile. "Besides, I only believe in superstitions when it comes to winning."

"What do you mean?"

"Whenever I wear my blue socks instead of my white ones, we win. When I eat a cookie the night before a game, we win. And, most recently this season, whenever you and I hang out together on a Friday night and drink a night cap, we win on Sunday."

"You know what? We didn't drink on Friday in Cleveland. We only ate pizza. It was good pizza, but clearly not game-winning pizza. Dammit, Dallas. Why didn't you tell me sooner? I would've run out to the convenience store and grabbed some Natty Ice."

I grimace and clutch my beer bottle to my chest. "I'd rather take the loss than drink that shit. I haven't had a Natty Ice since college. I've moved on to more refined choices."

"You really need to add tequila to your liquor cabinet."

"Is that your drink of choice?"

"Yeah. If you want something actually refined that's not watered down foam, I make a mean tequila sunrise."

"She's a bartender too, ladies and gentleman," I say, and Maven launches a pillow at my head. "Is there anything this woman can't do?"

"Many things. I can't fold a fitted sheet."

"No one can."

"I can't change a tire," she says.

"Easy. I'll teach you."

"I can't make breakfast without burning toast."

"Toast is overrated. Bagels are much better."

"I could never get a tattoo, no matter how much I want one."

"What?" I set my beer down and turn toward her. "You don't have any tattoos?"

"Nope. I'm terrified of needles."

"Isn't your dad a doctor?"

"He is, but that doesn't mean I have an infatuation with needles. Do you have a tattoo?" Her eyes bounce to my arms. "I haven't seen any, and I've been around you when you're shirtless a dozen times."

"Revolting, right?"

"The fucking worst."

"You haven't been around me when I'm pantsless, though," I say with a grin. "It's hidden."

"You have a pair of lips tattooed on your ass, don't you?"

"That sounds like something Maverick would do, not me."

"Okay, so not an ass tattoo." Her gaze moves to my legs. "Your thigh?"

"Mhm. It's a collection of random shit that's important to me."

"Oh." Maven sits up, and her feet drop to the floor. "I'm probably not allowed to see it, am I?"

"Probably not." I take a deep breath, because what I'm about to do is dumb. The stupidest fucking thing on the planet, and I say it quickly so I don't lose my courage. "But I'll show you."

"You will? I promise I won't touch you. I'll act horrified. Disgusted, even."

"That's what every guy wants to hear before they drop their pants," I joke, and she rolls her eyes.

"Your rules, not mine, buddy."

"Fair. No laughing, though."

I stand from the couch and hook my thumb in the waistband of my sweatpants. I shimmy them down my hips and let the cotton fall to my feet.

"I don't see anything," Maven whispers.

"I'm not there yet." I pull up the left side of my briefs and expose my thigh. "Tada."

She scoots across the cushions to get a better look, and I didn't realize how intimate this would be. She's on her knees so she can study the ink on my skin, and her nose is almost pressed into my leg.

I can smell her shampoo—flowers, I think, with the hint of vanilla. I can make out the darker blonde strands in her hair; auburn, almost, and much richer than the light yellow on the top of her head. I can see her long fan of eyelashes slowly blinking as she tilts her head to the side.

"What are they?" she asks. "There are so many things."

I tap the numbers on top. "June's birthday in Roman numerals." My finger moves to the pink and yellow bouquet that covers the lines of my quad muscles. "Lilies, because they represent new beginnings, and, well, finding out you have a daughter after she's been born is a big fucking new beginning." I touch the small collection of random doodles around the flowers. "An old record, for June Bug. A peach, for my home state. A taco—that one was a drunken mistake thanks to Maverick and Reid, and I'm never listening to them again."

"What about this one?" She drags her thumb over my skin, and I let out a shaky breath. "Shit. I'm sorry. I didn't mean to—"

"It's okay. You can."

Her nails trace the storm cloud with a rainbow peeking out from behind it, and I have to stare at the ceiling instead of focusing on the way the tips of her fingers are soft and delicate.

Maybe it's because I haven't been touched like this in fucking years and I've been starved for this kind of attention and care.

Maybe it's because it's her.

Maybe it's a combination of both, because I think I'd like her to touch me forever.

"It's beautiful," she says.

"Rainbows after rain. Cheesy, 'better days are ahead' kind of thing."

She tips her chin up and I bring mine down, our gazes on a collision course. She looks at me with wide eyes and pink cheeks, and I try. I try so goddamn hard to not think of her as anything but my friend, but my imagination runs wild, and I can't stop it.

I imagine her kissing the places no one's seen in years. Inking her name right below June's birthday, so I have something to represent the two best girls in my life. Just a few months with Maven, and she's already won that award.

I imagine her pulling off my briefs and sucking my dick. Her tongue running up the length from base to tip and seeing how deep she can take me down her throat. It wouldn't be awkward. She'd probably make a joke. I'd laugh, then she'd roll her eyes, giving me a few last seconds of sanity before she obliterated me into a million little pieces.

"I love it," she finally says. She wiggles backward, two cushions away, a safe distance that lets me look at her again without thinking I'm going to die. "And I like that they're secret, too. Only someone who really gets to know you would ever discover them, and when they do, it's like the world goes from black and white to color. That's special."

Maven keeps her attention on my leg, and I see a look in her eyes that wasn't there when my sweatpants were still on.

Hunger, if I had to guess, in a way that no one else has ever looked at me before. It's not determination to win a prize but more like desire. It's like she needs me, and that makes me feel bold as hell.

I rest my hand on my thigh. If I moved three inches to the right, I could wrap my fingers around my cock. She knows it, too, because the side of her mouth hitches up. It's a smirk, a taunt, a fucking *dare* to see if I'll do it.

I've never been so close to jerking off in front of someone in my life.

"I showed you mine," I say, rough and low. "Are you going to show me yours?"

"What do you want to see?"

I huff out a laugh. "That's a loaded question."

Maven tilts her head to the side. "Why do you think I asked it?"

She's putting the ball in my court, and no matter how much I want to lay her out on this couch and fuck her smart mouth, I have to keep my wits about me. We're dangerously close to slipping off the edge of something that would change everything between us.

"Where would you get a tattoo?"

"I haven't thought about it." She chews on her bottom lip, and I so badly want to sink my teeth into her and find out what she tastes like. "My ribs, maybe."

Eyes locked on mine, Maven pulls her shirt over her head and tosses it away. She points to the spot on her bare skin, and a sound that can only be described as a pathetic whine leaves my mouth. My vision blurs. My lungs close up, but I don't fucking dare look away. I know without a doubt I'd drop to my knees and worship at her feet if she asked

180

"That's a good spot," I whisper, and they're the most difficult words I've ever said in my life.

"What do you think?" she asks, and it's an invitation to admire her.

I drop my gaze to her throat, and she holds her hair off her neck. My eyes travel down to the green bra she's wearing, to the round tits that fill the lace and almost spill over, and I decide right then and there I want to buy her one in every color.

"Perfect," I say, but it comes out like a rasp. "Fucking perfect."

She plays with the strap of her bra and drags it down her shoulder. "I'm glad you think so."

"I think I need to see from a different angle, though. Just to be sure. Lie back. Please."

There's a minute of readjusting.

She scoots around and lays on her back. Her hair scatters across the pillows. Her feet rest on the cushions and her thighs part, like she's waiting for me.

"Now what?"

"Can I touch you?" I ask.

"Yes," she says without hesitating. "You can do whatever you want to me."

There isn't enough time to do everything I want to do to her.

I sit on my knees and move toward her until I'm between her legs. I hook one hand around her ankle and give her a tug to drag her closer to me.

I lean forward until my chest is above hers. She's breathing hard, and I am, too.

"I'm not going to kiss you," I tell her, but it's more for myself. My self-restraint is hanging on by a thread.

"Okay."

"I'm just going to touch. Only for a second. I'm a friend helping out a friend with an important life decision, should they choose to do it."

"Exactly. A second doesn't count, especially when it's from a friend," she agrees. "And you might be the best friend I've ever had."

I laugh at that. She smiles, and her grin is the confidence I need to spur me forward. I rest my hand on her skin. My fingers fan out across her ribs, and my thumb brushes along the underside of her bra. I can feel her heart racing, and the chaotic beat matches mine.

"Right here," I say. "Right here would be sexy."

"What should I get?"

"A heart." I draw the outline on her skin. "Or some flowers. Hydrangeas, maybe, because they represent emotion. Gratitude. The desire to understand. That's you, Mae."

I take my time to draw an imaginary flower. With each petal, I get closer and closer to slipping my fingers under the lace of her bra. Her breathing turns ragged and her left leg falls off the couch to make more space for me between her thighs. I scoot forward, closer to her, and my hips almost press into her pajama shorts.

"What color?" she asks, threading her fingers through my hair, and I know she's trying to keep me here, just like I'm trying to keep her here too.

"Blue." Before I can stop myself, I kiss the spot I just touched and suck on her skin. She moans softly, and I've never heard a better sound in my life. "Pink." I move to her nipple and blow on the flimsy piece of fabric keeping me from taking her in my mouth. "God, Maven. You'd make anything look perfect."

I'm hard. My dick throbs, heavy and aching, and it takes every ounce of the control I've spent years perfecting to not touch myself while she watches.

"So much for not kissing," she teases.

"You make it very fucking difficult to follow the rules."

"I'm sorry."

"No, you're not."

"No, I'm not." She gestures to the front of my briefs, and everything inside me burns hot and wild. "Are you going to do something about that?"

"Yeah. Die a slow death while I think about you with tattoos on your body. While I think about you in general, honestly."

"I've always wanted to be someone's muse." Her palm moves from my hair to my cheek, and she rubs her thumb along the line of my jaw. "Am I allowed to tell you that I'm glad we found ourselves in this position? Am I allowed to tell you I've been thinking about you less as a friend and more as someone..." Maven trails off, and the sentence hangs in the air.

I know the words she's not saying, because I'm thinking them, too.

Someone I care about.

Someone I want to take to my bed and hold tight through the night.

Someone I want to spoil and shower with gifts and attention.

Someone I think I might be falling for.

"Yes," I say. I turn my cheek and press my mouth to the center of her palm. I savor the breathy exhale she lets out when I do it again. "I'm thinking it, too."

We stare at each other, and I'm not sure how much time passes. It might only be a matter of seconds but it feels like hours. The world stands still when I'm with her, and it's like we're the only two people in the universe.

"I should..." I slowly climb off her and sit on the other end of the couch. I'm still hard, and it's impossible to take my eyes off of her. "You're so beautiful, Mae. And I don't just mean like this." I gesture up and down her body. "I mean all the time."

She sits up and fixes her bra, sliding the strap back up her shoulder. "So are you. I feel lucky that I get to see these sides of you, Dallas. You're perfect."

"I'm far from perfect." I pull up my sweatpants and adjust myself. "But I'm glad you're the one I can show those imperfect parts to."

"Should we make drinking and shedding our clothes a weekly thing?" Maven asks. "Or are we pretending this never happened?"

"We probably shouldn't make it a weekly thing, but I'm sure as hell not going to forget about it anytime soon."

"Good." Her eyes move from my chest to my stomach then further down. "I'm not, either."

"I don't want to be the one to walk away, because I don't want you to think I'm walking away from you. But the longer I look at you, the less I trust myself to behave. So I'm going to get up and go to bed. I think you should too."

She hums and stands from the couch, towering over me. I lift my chin to look at her, and she smiles, a dangerous, sensual thing. "Whatever you say, *Daddy*. Good night."

I bite my fist when she walks away, and whatever strand of self-restraint I have left just got even shorter.

TWENTY-FIVE
MAVEN

"THIS GAME IS SO GOOD," Cassidy, one of the other photographers for the Titans, yells out over the sound of the hometown crowd. "There's nothing better than extra football."

"First overtime game of the season." I take a break from capturing photos to stretch my neck and glance over at her. "We have the best job, don't we?"

"Every time I think about quitting, I'm reminded that I'm getting paid to watch football. Ten seasons in, and I can't imagine doing anything else."

"Do people ever criticize you? Do they tell you to get a real job?" I ask.

"All the time. But then I post pictures from the Super Bowl with the guys, and everyone's jealous. It's like men are allowed to exist in sports spaces without being questioned about their career. When a woman does it, they can't wait to get rid of us," she says.

"I've noticed that, too. I'm glad the guys on the team are so supportive of the women on the Titans staff, but the men on the internet can be brutal. Someone said the photo I shared of Sam Wagner two weeks ago looked like something their toddler could take. Which is funny because SportsCenter used it as their lead off image on the primetime show. FishandBeer4269 can fuck off."

Cassidy laughs. "Welcome to the hellish side of working in an industry men think is their thing. Throw in actually knowing the rules of the game, too, and they positively *hate* us."

We walk from the far side of the field to the end zone where the Titans will be trying to score so we can be in the best position for any game-winning drives. A field goal will allow the Grizzlies to have a shot with the ball, but a touchdown ends the game.

I know Jett's going to do everything in his power to make sure their opponents don't get an opportunity to squeak out a victory.

"You're nannying for Dallas, right?" Cassidy asks, and she adjusts her camera strap as we pass the logo at centerfield. "How's that going?"

"It's great. His daughter, June, is four. Have you met her? She hangs out in the nursery during games, and the cutest girl I've ever met."

"No, but I've heard about her. He's private about his personal life, and it's been that way the whole time I've been here. It's so different from what I'm used to seeing. Guys like him—the ones who know they're hot—always tend to be boastful about their conquests. They parade women in and out of the stadium like a flavor of the week. Not Dallas, though. He's a mystery I can't figure out."

I bite my tongue and hold back from telling her I have him figured out.

Sort of.

I've learned what gets him riled up. I know that he's never greedy about anything in life—he's the most selfless man I've ever encountered. But when he looks at me, it's like he's allowing himself to be selfish for the first time.

I can still feel the phantom touch of his mouth on my body. The soft, warm kiss he pressed to my ribs and the way he sucked on my skin. He left behind a little pink mark I stared at for too long the morning after, wondering what a matching one would look like between my thighs or on the column of my neck.

He was so *hard*. His length strained against his briefs and left nothing to the imagination. It was as if touching me got him excited, and I almost hooked my leg around his waist and pulled my shorts off so he could sink into me.

It would have been good.

Deliciously good, because everything he does is magical, a gentle soul who would take his time. Who would listen and learn and be thorough, making sure to take care of me before taking care of himself.

I'm so attracted to him, and it's not just a physical pull when he takes off his sweatpants. It's not just when his inked skin is on display or when the tension between us grows to a near breaking point.

It's there in the quieter moments too. The mundane moments. The smaller, less assuming moments like when he hugs me when he gets home from the stadium then nudges me away from the stove, a teasing grin sliding into place. The secret moments when he looks at me when he jogs on the field and lifts his chin in greeting, a new addition to his warmup routine that wasn't there in the preseason.

He's slotted his way into my life and I've slotted my way into his. It's funny to hear people call him a mystery when he's become the most sure thing I've ever known.

"He's something," I say, and the words catch in my throat.

I busy myself and adjust my camera lens. I scan the field and watch the Titans offense huddle together. They win the coin toss and elect to receive.

"What are you hiding?" Cassidy asks.

"I'm not hiding anything."

"Bullshit." She elbows my side and smiles. "You're hooking up with him, aren't you?"

"Sh," I hiss, and I look around to make sure no one is listening. I breathe a sigh of relief when I realize we're alone. "I'm not hooking up with him."

"If it makes you feel better, I've been dating Jett for four years. The rules are such bullshit, and I hate that we have to keep it on the down low."

"I'm sorry, *what*?" I gape at her. "I've never even seen you two talk to each other and you're telling me you're sleeping together?"

"Frequently." Cassidy grins. "Football players are so fun, minus the bureaucratic stuff that comes with being involved with them. How does a team photographer have any impact on what the quarterback is doing on the field? It's not my fault if he throws an interception."

"That's so true, but Dallas has always been a rule follower. I don't think he'd go against his moral code just to sleep with me. He can find that release somewhere else."

"I'm sure he can, but never say never. That boy can't stop looking at you."

"What are you talking about?" I ask, and lower my camera.

Cassidy gestures to the group of players standing on the sidelines. I sort through the defensive linemen and medical staff until I find Dallas. He's glancing our way. His eyes bore into me like he's tracking my every movement, and my heart skips a beat when he lifts his arm and waves.

My lungs constrict and it's difficult to take a deep breath when his lips twitch into a silly little grin. I wave back, distinctly aware that while he should be paying attention to the field, he's paying attention to me instead.

Something else that's new this season.

"It's not the first time, either," she adds.

I've worked a few games with her, and I know I can trust Cassidy. She shows up to work, does her job and minds her own business. Whatever secrets I want to protect won't end up being whispered to anyone else if I tell her, and it might be good to get them off my chest.

"There's something happening with Dallas, but I'm not sure what to call it," I explain. "We know it can't happen, yet we're both getting really bad at trying to stop it."

"Maybe you shouldn't try to stop it. The heart wants what the heart wants, right? Besides, if you're the reason he has more pep in his step this season, then keep doing whatever you're doing. It's working. Live your life, Maven. If that means doing it with the hot football player that's looking at you like you're his source of oxygen, I'm only going to cheer you on."

I laugh and my shoulders relax. I'm glad I have someone I can talk to about this. "Thanks for your support, Cass. I'm not sure the members of management would agree, but I'm grateful for your stamp of approval."

"What are coworkers you see once a week for?" she laughs. "Looks like we're finally getting this overtime period underway."

"Do you ever worry about Jett out there?" I ask. I squat and bring my camera to my face. "He takes some nasty hits."

"I do, but I remind myself he's been hit a thousand times before. His protective equipment always works, and the trainers we have are the best in the business."

"True." I groan when Jett gets sacked and loses three yards on the play. "Dammit. Come on, guys."

We watch the second down result in a pickup of only a yard, and the Titans offense is facing third and twelve well past the fifty-yard line. Out of the corner of my eye, I spy Dallas warming up into his practice net. He doesn't look the least bit phased, and I admire his ability to stay calm under pressure.

He's exactly the same way as a parent, too.

"Dallas can kick far, but this would be too long even for him," Cassidy says. "And a field goal doesn't win it. The Grizzlies would still get possession."

"He'd probably like to try after last week. He was really beating himself up, and he blamed himself for the loss. Such bullshit," I mumble under my breath, and she hums in agreement.

"Because it's easy to cheer for people when they're success-ful. Everyone has to—*hell yeah!* Go, Jett, go," Cassidy yells, and we jump to our feet.

We watch as Jett evades a defender. He fakes left then goes right, finding an open route up the center of the play. His linemen and guards keep the Grizzlies defense away from him, and there's nothing but wide-open field ahead.

"He's doing it," I cheer, and I sprint to the section of the end zone he's heading for. My finger never moves from the shutter button, capturing picture after picture of his game winning score.

His teammates flood him as soon as the refs signal the touch-down. They form a line, sitting on the ground for their celebration as Sam Wagner, the tight end, sprints up. He pretends to lock them into a roller coaster car. They lean forward then backward, their arms waving chaotically as the rest of the Titans surround them.

"I love that celebration the most," Cassidy laughs, and I nod.

"Same. Their best work this season, to be honest."

"Look at them. They're like little kids in the candy store."

"I'm going to head to the tunnel so I can get some shots of them after their post-game interviews," I say, and she waves.

"Sounds good. I'm going to hang out here and snap a few solo photos of Jett."

"Of course you are," I tease, and she sticks out her tongue. "I'll see you in a bit."

I jog to the tunnel, dodging reporters and security personnel. I want to snag a good spot before the media tries to flood the area, and I know it's going to be jam packed in here in a matter of minutes. I find a spot tucked away from the main path where I can lean against a wall and catch my breath, waiting for the team to make their way inside.

The coaches come in first like always, and Shawn gives me a high five before he heads to the locker room. The players who dressed out but didn't play follow him.

The defense comes after, helmets in their hands and relief on their faces—it's obvious they're glad they didn't have to take the field again. There's a break in the action, then the rest of the guys file in. I look up from my camera as Dallas walks into the tunnel.

It's like time stops when I see him.

His gaze meets mine, and he ignores his teammates. My heart pounds in my chest as he makes his way over to me.

"Great game," I blurt out, even though he hardly played. Three extra points and no field goals makes for a boring day on the sidelines for him. Still, he's happy, the euphoria of victory written in his scrunched nose and lazy, easy stride. "Your leg looked great out there."

"Are you watching me, Maven?" he asks.

He props his elbow against the wall above my head. His other arm hangs by his side and his helmet almost presses into my leg, but he still seems too far away.

I know he's lighter and leaner than some of the guys on the team, but he's not small. He takes up too much space, an intimidating, overwhelming presence that makes it difficult to think straight.

I can smell the sweat and grass clinging to his jersey. I can see the smudges of his eye black on his cheeks. I can feel him inch closer to me, and the toes of his cleats knock against my sneakers.

To anyone walking past us, we're just two people talking. Shooting the shit as I congratulate him on another victory. There's nothing wrong with what we're doing, but blood still pounds in my ears. I can't look away from him, and his attention never wavers from me, either.

"Always," I answer, and he gives me a wicked, dual-dimple smile that makes my heart skip a beat.

Dallas fumbles with something under the collar of his jersey. There's a flash of gold and I watch as he pulls out a necklace—*my* necklace. The one I thought I lost two months ago and gave up trying to find.

He's wearing it without a care in the world, and something about his smug confidence tells me he's had it in his possession for a very long time.

"Seems like I have a good luck charm with me," he says, rough and low. He holds up the M and keeps his eyes on me as he kisses the letter then runs his tongue over the chain. It feels like he's running his tongue over *me* and the places of my body I desperately want him to touch. "I think I'm going to wear it every game."

Holy shit.

I reach out and graze my fingers over the jewelry. I give it a soft yank and he careens forward, nearly stumbling into me with a breathy laugh I feel deep in my stomach. His eyes gleam with delight as he stares at where my fingers press into the hollow of his throat.

"It looks better on you than it does on me," I tease.

"Impossible. You look good in everything."

"Yeah, but you—" I snap my mouth shut.

You look like the man of my dreams.

"Are you going to finish that sentence?" he asks, and I bite my bottom lip. His eyes drop to my mouth and hold, a flash of heat sparking across the brown of his irises.

"I shouldn't." I let go of the necklace and stare at the way it hangs from his neck. It's shorter on him, almost a choker, and I didn't know I had an attraction toward men in gold chains until now. "How long have you had this?"

"Since the day after the paint room. You left it on the kitchen counter. I meant to give it back to you—I put it on as a joke, but then I forgot about it and..."

"And you've been wearing it since."

"All day, every day." He lowers his chin, and his mouth is mere inches from my ear. His breath is warm on my skin, and I shiver. "I like having something that reminds me of you. Can I keep it?"

I'm tempted to throw my arms around his neck and kiss him right here, in front of the entire team. It's like he's staked a claim on me. Marked me as his and marked himself as mine, too.

"Yes," I say. "Because you look hot as hell wearing it."

"She finally admits I'm hot," he murmurs, a teasing lilt to his words. "Only took three fucking months. I should've shown it to you sooner."

I laugh and he grins, a beautiful flash of teeth and crinkles around his eyes. "Don't let it go to your head, Lansfield."

"It already has, sunshine. Admit it, you're obsessed with me."

Someone hollers behind me, and it breaks the spell Dallas has me under.

It doesn't look like we're *just talking* anymore. We're standing far too close. We're touching, and I know how our positions could be interpreted. I take a step to my left, and I can breathe a little easier when I'm out of his orbit even though I miss his proximity.

"Something like that." I clear my throat and fix the strap of my camera around my neck. Dallas stares at my throat before he glances away. "I'm, uh, going to get some final shots of the team then grab June from the nursery. Want to text me when you're ready to meet at the car?"

"Sounds good. They don't need me in media tonight, so it shouldn't take too long." He smiles and rubs his jaw. "I can't wait to get home."

"Me too," I whisper.

My heart twists in my chest, an obnoxious whir as he tucks the jewelry safely away and taps my shoulder, a secret only we know.

TWENTY-SIX
MAVEN

I'VE BEEN fidgety all day.

It's like I'm brimming with the anticipation of something I can't quite shake.

My social media exploded after my photo of Jett's game winning touchdown went viral. It's been impossible to keep up with the notifications and influx of comments, and I'm so glad I set up a designated account for my photography before the game.

The traffic has been spurred on by Dallas, too.

I've scrolled through two dozen news outlets, and under each photo of mine that gets posted, there's a comment from his official account asking them to give me credit.

This picture was taken by @mavenwoodphotography

Photo by @mavenwoodphotography, member of the Titans

Hey, @espn—can you tag the photographer, please?

By Monday night, I had twenty thousand followers. A week later, and I'm closing in on fifty thousand. It's a whirlwind, an absurd response all because I was in the right place at the right time while doing my job.

I can't sit still, and I'm restless. I lounge on the couch and try to flip through a romance novel even though my attention is pulled elsewhere. The apartment is too quiet. My mind is too muddled with thinking about Dallas and June and the necklace he's still wearing. Now that his secret has been discovered, he lets it hang freely against his shirt.

I don't know how I missed seeing it before.

The chain is like a beacon, and my stomach somersaults every time the jewelry catches in the light and flashes across the room.

The two of them are out shopping because June is outgrowing everything in her closet. It's sending Dallas into a tailspin. He paced around the kitchen last night, talking about curfews and driver's licenses. I'm pretty sure I heard him mumble something about a 401k under his breath, and I lost it, laughing hysterically until he pulled the sink nozzle out and sprayed me from across the counter.

Then he couldn't stop looking at my wet T-shirt and the way it clung to my skin.

He left the room after, his cheeks pink and his eyes full of liquid heat.

I sigh and set a bookmark in place. I stand up and do a lap around the living room. I like it so much better when Dallas and June are here, and even though I like to be alone and crave that independence, it feels like something is missing when they're gone.

A burst of adrenaline and courage hits me as I round the coffee table. After days of pushing outside my comfort zone, my body buzzes with curiosity. If this excitement is coming from doing something I'm only decently good at, what would it be like if I tried something I was *very* good at?

I hurry to my room and rifle through my dresser, pulling out athletic clothes. I trade my jeans for a pair of soccer shorts and my sweatshirt for a sports bra and tank top. I grab the cleats that have been sitting untouched in a box in my closet, and a ball I haven't kicked in months.

Before I can change my mind or think too long about what I'm doing, I slide my keys off the kitchen counter and head for my car.

The park is only a few blocks from Dallas's apartment, and I've driven past the soccer fields a hundred times. There is always a wistful tug in my chest when I see the goal and the center circle. Flashes of memories come to me as I remember what the grass feels like under my feet and the joy of victory. It's like I can still hear the crowd, an echo in my ear that's becoming fainter and fainter the further removed I get from the sport I love.

The parking lot is empty. Late afternoon is turning into early evening and the time when families are getting ready to sit down for dinner together. The sun hangs low in the sky and the field almost looks like it's glowing. The grass is golden, the nets are a burnt orange, and it's a beautiful sight.

I take a deep breath and climb out of the car, bringing the ball with me. I walk to the sidelines and swap my sneakers with cleats. I lace them slowly, the habit of double knotting and making a perfect bow coming back to me like it hasn't been months since I last slipped my feet in the white Nikes. I put my hands on my hips and stare out in front of me.

The sense of dread creeps up my spine and spiderwebs across my back. It's always there when I look at the place I used to call home. The place that brought me solace and joy. It wraps around me in a vice-like grip, a nearly suffocating fear and the clear image of what happened last time I put on my cleats at the forefront of my mind.

I sigh and hang my head. My shoulders sag, and I know no amount of adrenaline will get me to step a foot further.

"Maybe next time," I whisper into the autumn air, and I turn back to my car. I walk ten feet before my phone rings, and I stop to answer it. "Hello?"

"Hey," Dallas says, and even through the phone I can hear his smile. The curve of his mouth and the soft timbre his voice takes when he talks to me is all too familiar. "June and I just got home, and I'm going to make dinner. "Where are you?"

"Nowhere."

"Nowhere?"

"I'm out."

"Out," he repeats slowly. "That's vague. Are you okay?"

"Yeah." I nod even though he can't see me. "I'm fine."

"You don't sound fine. Is this one of those hostage situations?"

"No." I laugh and plop down on the grass, reveling in the breeze. "It's silly."

"Try me."

"I'm at the soccer fields."

He's quiet on the other end, but I think I hear a soft hum. "Which ones?"

"The ones behind the playground up the road."

"Stay right there."

"What? Dallas you—"

The line goes dead. I sigh and pull my legs to my chest, watching the clouds roll by.

Ten minutes later, Dallas's SUV parks next to mine. I lift my chin and smile when I see June sprinting toward me. She's wearing a Mia Hamm jersey and tiny cleats, and the thought of her liking something I like makes tears prick my eyes. I stand and scoop her up, spinning her around and burying my face in her hair.

"Hi, Mae Mae," she says, and her arms hug my neck.

"What are you doing here, June Bug?"

"Daddy said we come visit you."

I look over my shoulder and see Dallas jogging toward us. He has a soccer ball tucked under one arm and a pair of dirty cleats on his feet.

"Hey, Mae," he says.

"Hi." My heart moves to my throat when he beams at me. "You didn't have to come down here."

"I know we didn't, but we—I—wanted to." He leans forward and pinches June's cheek. "Why don't you go kick the ball for a few minutes, JB? I'm going to talk to Mae Mae, then we'll play, okay?"

"Okay, Daddy." June kisses my forehead and I set her down, rolling the soccer ball a few feet away. She kicks it, clapping her hands together as she takes off for the goal.

"I didn't know she liked soccer." I tilt my chin to look up at Dallas, and he's already looking at me. "Those cleats are the cutest fucking thing I've ever seen."

"I told her you play, and she wanted to watch a million videos. We've kicked on the balcony before, but I think she might be obsessed with it now." He turns his chin and watches his daughter, a soft, reverent smile on his lips. "I tried to find a Maven Wood jersey, but I came up empty handed. I hope Mia is a good runner up."

My bottom lip quivers, and I take a deep breath. "She can borrow one of mine next time, but Mia is always a good runner up."

Dallas sits on the grass. His long legs stretch out in front of him, and I join him. "What's going on?"

"I don't know. The apartment felt so empty with you both gone, and I had this idea that I'd come up to the field and kick around for shits and giggles. Except, I got here, and I just couldn't."

"What are you afraid of?"

"Failing," I blurt out. I've thought it, but it's the first time I've voiced it since my injury.

"Just because you're scared to do something doesn't mean you're going to fail."

"I know. It's just hard to be here and not associate it with who I was before. But when I'm not here, it feels like a piece of me is missing. It's like my heart is playing tug of war, and I'm doubting myself."

"I wish I could show you how June and I see you. Then you'd never doubt yourself."

"How do you see me?" I ask, and I've never wanted to hear the answer to a question more in my life.

"You're the most incredible person in the world." Dallas lies on his back and crosses his hands over his chest. "You're fearless and you work hard. You never give up, even when everything is going against you. You've got a kind heart, and you care about others. Every day with you, Maven, is a good day. The *best* day, and if I had to pick a woman I hope June grows up to be like, it'd be you." He turns his cheek and looks up at me. His mouth splits into a grin, and I feel it in every empty part of myself. "It's okay to be afraid, but I never want you to think you're not capable. Do you remember how you told me you like messy? You like complicated?"

"Yes," I say, and I lay down beside him.

"You're safe with me, too. You're allowed to mess up. If you fall, you dust yourself off and try again tomorrow. Maybe next time you'll get a little further. Maybe it'll take you a month before you even kick a ball again, but guess what? I'll be out here with you every day until it feels *right*."

Hearing his words feels a lot like flying. Like my feet come out from under me and lift me off the ground. I reach over and touch his cheek, wanting to make sure he's real. That he's here with me, his heart of gold and kindness and understanding in every fiber of his being.

"Where did you get the soccer ball?" I ask, and his eyes trace over my face.

"You've never looked in that closet in the hallway?" he teases, and I shake my head.

"No. I always assumed it was stuff you wanted to keep private. It wasn't mine to snoop through."

His gaze softens into a grateful look that almost cleaves my heart in two. "I bought it the day after you told me about your injury. We weren't as close as we are now, but I could see that fire in you. I wanted to have one in the apartment, just in case you wanted to try to play again."

There's a split down the center of my chest. I've had attention from men before. The handful of people I've dated have sent me bursting bouquets. The guy I was with for six months at the end of my sophomore year bought me a bracelet.

This, though, is the first time someone's done something for me because they *wanted* to, not because they felt like they had to. A gesture not for him, but for me, an invitation that will never expire.

"You might be the nicest person I've ever met," I whisper. My thumb strokes his cheek, and he sighs. "What did I do to deserve you in my life, Dallas?"

"I ask myself that every day. You're my best friend, Maven. You know that, right?"

I nod, a bob of my head, because words are too hard to use right now. I hold his gaze, though, so he knows he's my best friend, too.

"I take care of the people I care about, and you're on that list, right below June. Some days you take the top spot, not because I love my daughter any less, but because what I feel for you is different than what I feel for her." He shakes his head. "I'm always going to be in your corner."

I swallow. He's so beautiful in the dusk light. Soft and earnest and a man who's done a lot of great things, but the best is yet to come. And as the sun dips lower in the sky, there's a moment where he also looks like he's *mine*.

"I think I want to try," I say. "Right now. Will you try with me?"

"I'd do anything with you, Maven," he says.

He stands up and dusts the grass off the back of his shorts. My necklace rests against the collar of his shirt, and he offers me a hand. I take it and our fingers thread together as he lifts me from the ground in an easy, gentle pull.

I stare at the ball between us, and I touch my toes to the hexagons. I exhale and give it a kick with the inside of my foot. Electricity surges through me as the ball rolls ten feet ahead.

It's far from the goals I've scored. The penalty shots I've knocked down to send my team to the Final Four. It's not even as monumental as the kicks kids do. The old Maven would laugh at how silly it is that I'm staring at the ball like it's made of gold. But it's *something*, and something is better than nothing.

"I did it," I say, and turn to Dallas. "Can you—"

"Whatever you want. Whatever you need. Let's go, sunshine."

Dallas jogs after the ball, running backwards so he can keep his eyes on me. Every few feet he looks behind him to check on June, too. He taps the ball back, and I touch my cleats to it a few times, getting reacquainted with the magical way the leather feels.

I pass to him, a harder kick that has my blood pounding in my ears. He laughs and chases after it, stopping it with the back of his heel.

"Look at you," I say, impressed.

"Look at *you*," he says. "A fucking rockstar."

"I wanna play," June says when she runs up to us, and she kicks her ball to me. "Can you pass to me, Mae Mae?"

"Of course I'll pass to you, JB."

We spend the next twenty minutes in a triangle, passing to one another and running after the ball when someone kicks it too far. My stomach hurts from laughing so much. When June grabs Dallas's leg and steals the ball out from under him, running all the way down the field and scoring a goal, I lift her in the air like she just won the World Cup.

We stay out there until the sun sets and the stars start to come out. When we call it a night, our legs tired and our breathing heavy, I realize my happy place finally feels happy again and I've never felt more powerful.

TWENTY-SEVEN

MAVEN

"GOING SOMEWHERE?"

I look up from the rideshare app and see Dallas sitting on the couch with a picture book in his hand. June is in his lap, and they're wearing matching tiaras that sparkle in the early evening sun.

"Hey," I say, and smile at the pair. "I'm meeting Isabella for drinks. Is that okay?"

"You don't have to ask my permission to do things, Mae. The apartment is yours, too, and you're free to come and go as much as you want."

"I know, but I should've checked with you first. In case something came up with your schedule."

Dallas chuckles. "When has anything come up with my schedule in the three months you've been here?"

I bite my lip to hold back a smile. "Not once. Maybe you should live a little."

"Maybe. But I like being here best." He sets the book down and cradles June to his chest. "Where are y'all going?"

"This wine bar over by Georgetown. Isabella knows a server there and was able to get us a table. I won't be late, though. I know you have an early flight to Seattle tomorrow, and I don't want to disturb you when I get back."

"You won't." He pauses, and his eyes track down my body in a slow perusal of my outfit. He starts at my crop top and moves to the leather skirt that hits the top of my thigh. He lands on my knee-high boots, and he lets out a soft puff of air. "Wow."

"Is it too much?" I pull on the hem of the skirt and try to make it longer. "I've only been in overalls and khakis between here and the stadium. This is the first time I've worn something nice in a—"

"Nothing about you could ever be too much. You look beautiful."

His compliment warms my skin. It lands in the center of my chest and stays there, making a home for itself next to all the other nice things Dallas tells me. All the words of affirmation he has been whispering in my ear when I need them most.

You can do it.

I'm so proud of you.

"Beautiful," June agrees, and her eyes flutter closed. She puts her thumb in her mouth and drifts off to sleep, using Dallas as her pillow. He doesn't seem to mind.

"See? Kids never lie," he says. "Can I see the back of your outfit? Please?"

I do an exaggeratedly slow circle and take my time. I'm teasing him a little bit, but it's only fair to make him suffer when he's sitting there in gray sweatpants that have no right to look as good as they do.

"Like this?"

"That's perfect, Maven."

I blush at the praise and nearly trip over my feet. When I complete the spin, Dallas is sitting on the edge of the couch. His cheeks are pink, and the color reaches down his neck. He sets June on the cushions and stands, stalking toward me.

"Do you like what you see?" I ask, playing with fire.

"No."

"Oh."

I turn my cheek, embarrassed, only for him to curl his fingers around my chin. He tilts my head back until our gazes meet.

Dallas bends down, and his mouth brushes against my ear. "I love what I see," he says, dark and low.

"Maybe I wore this outfit for you," I find myself saying, and this isn't part of our game. This is real, honest truth I want him to hear. "Maybe I wanted you to miss me while I'm gone."

"You could wear a sack, Maven, and I'd still miss you." His hand drops to my hip, and his fingers press into the small sliver of exposed skin at the hem of my shirt. "Will you let me know when you get there?"

"I will."

We stand there and stare at each other. My phone vibrates, telling me my driver is close, but I'm reluctant to walk away. It feels like something important is happening between us. Like a declaration is on the tip of his tongue, and I desperately want to know what it is.

I could kiss him if I wanted to, and *fuck*, I want to.

I haven't let myself imagine a life where Dallas and I could be together, not totally, but with the way he's watching me, with the way his fingers press into my skin and refuse to let me go, I think he wants to kiss me too.

"Anything else?" I ask.

"Yeah." He bends down and kisses my cheek. It's a soft graze of his lips, the exact replica of what he did at the paint room, but it's cataclysmic enough to spread through me like a wildfire. "We'll be counting down the minutes until you're home."

I didn't know how much I needed his touch again. Now that I have it, I'm addicted. My breath catches, and my hand wraps around his wrist. I drag my thumb down the line of his vein and let myself have one more second of this little world we've carved out for ourselves.

My phone buzzes again, and a text tells me my driver is downstairs. "I should go. I can't lose my five-star rating."

"We certainly wouldn't want that." Dallas squeezes my hip once then takes a step back. "Have fun, Mae. Call if you need anything."

"Are you going to stare at my ass again?"

His mouth twitches, and one dimple pops on his cheek. "It would be criminal not to."

"I'm all for law abiding citizens." I wiggle out of his hold and turn around, looking at him over my shoulder. His eyes are fixed on my hips, and there's no shame in his appreciation of my body. "For the record, I'm going to miss you, too."

"Thatta girl," he says with a wicked grin, getting the last word, and I don't stop blushing until I'm out on the street in the fresh air.

THE WINE BAR is loud for a Thursday night. Isabella and I are tucked away in a corner, yet I can't hear myself think over the pulsing music.

"Am I getting old, or does this feel more like a club and less like a place to do merlot flights?" I ask.

"This is my fault. We should've gone somewhere away from campus. There are too many attractive college kids here with fake IDs, and it's making me think I need to start an under-eye skin care routine," she says, and we both laugh.

"We were kids too, once upon a time. Two years ago, we would've fit right in."

"And now you're taking photos for the best football team in

the NFL and I'm coaching high school soccer. We're career women chasing our dreams and climbing into bed before 11 p.m."

"How times have changed. A toast to being badasses. And doing things even when they're scary."

We clink our glasses together and take a sip in tandem. I lean back in my chair and look around. The atmosphere is something I used to enjoy, but now it makes me miss the peacefulness of Dallas's apartment.

"How's it going with the hot dad?" Isabella asks over the rim of her glass. "Please tell me you two have fucked."

"There's been absolutely zero fucking."

"What?" She frowns and tilts her head to the side. "He's single. You're single. He's a millionaire who lives eight steps away from you, and you're not taking advantage of it? What am I missing here?"

"Technically I'm not allowed to take advantage of it. The NFL is strict about players fraternizing with members of their organization, and I'm pretty sure sliding into bed with the star kicker and fucking him goes against almost all of the rules the league has in place."

"Fuck the league," she exclaims, and she hits the table. Our plates rattle, and I laugh at her enthusiasm. "It's not fair you can't climb him like a tree."

"It's devastating, really. The man is like a Greek god," I sigh. I've thought about what it would be like to drop to my knees in front of him more times than I can count. "But I know he's being good because he cares about me and my job, and I'm respecting his boundaries."

"You at least flirt with him, right? I saw the way he stared at you when I helped you move in—he couldn't take his eyes off your ass. It can't be all work and *no* play."

"There's flirting." I hide my smile behind a sip of wine. "It's a game. We know nothing can come of it, but we like to push each other."

"And who's winning?"

Him.

By a landslide.

I can still feel the kiss he pressed to my ribs and the warmth of his breath over the lace of my bra. I hate that I'll never know what his mouth feels like on the rest of my body.

"We're pretty evenly matched," I tell her, and swirl my wine around. "I just wish he wasn't so nice."

Isabella puts her elbow on the table and rests her chin in her hand. "Is being nice a bad thing?"

"It's a terrible thing, because now I like him. A lot. If he were some asshole, I could think about fucking him once then leaving. But that's not the case with Dallas. He's literally the epitome of the perfect man. He's kind. He remembers things and goes out of his way to make me smile. The more I'm around him, the more I can see myself falling for him, and I don't know how to stop."

"Shitty rules aside, if you were allowed to go after him, would you?"

"Yes," I say without hesitation. "Or, I would try. He doesn't date, and maybe I'm naïve in believing I can be the one to change that, but I think I could. We've had these moments together. They're not big or grand or anything other people would swoon over, but they're special. He wears my necklace under his jersey, Isa. And the other day, I went to the soccer field for the first time since my injury, and he asked what I needed. How he could help. Then he kicked a ball around with me for an hour."

"Whoa," she breathes out, mesmerized. "You always said you wouldn't step foot back on a field."

"I know, but I had this urge to try again. When I got there, I couldn't do it. I was seconds away from giving up when Dallas showed up and..." I shrug. "With him by my side, I felt like I could."

"Why am I getting emotional over this?" She wipes her eyes and laughs. "I really hate that you two can't be together."

"I do, too. I also kind of hate that I love my job. If this career wasn't taking off or I had a toxic work environment, I'd quit. But I don't want to. This role has become a part of me, and I won't give that up for a guy."

"It's too bad he couldn't give up his job."

I snort. "Yeah, right. Who the hell would walk away from a career that pays six million dollars a year?"

Isabella chokes on her drink. "He makes *that* much money to kick a football? I was totally kidding about him being a millionaire. I had no idea he was that rich."

"Absurd, isn't it? I nearly had a heart attack when I looked up his net worth online. Did you know he wasn't even drafted? He took a call from the Titans after the final round, signed a shitty rookie contract, then worked his way up to the starting spot. Now he's the best kicker in NFL history."

"Is his daughter's mom in the picture? Is he single because he has some secret fetish that wards off women? Why else is he alone?"

"No," I laugh. "I don't know the whole story about June's mom, but she's not around, and she's never been mentioned. He's done everything by himself up to this point."

"Admirable. We were around a lot of football players when we were college athletes, and Dallas seems like one of the good ones."

"Good doesn't even come close. I was late to his apartment once because of cramps, and this fucker bought me a heating pad and stocked the medicine cabinet with ibuprofen so I wouldn't be in pain. He's attentive, and no guy has ever had such a hold over me."

"Sweetie, that's not a guy. That's a goddamn *man*. You know that translates to the bedroom too."

A rush of heat inundates me. I imagine us tangled in sheets with sweat-soaked skin and panting breaths. My calf around his hip and his hand between my legs. Slow, lazy circles that tip me over the edge with his name on my lips when I come. A muffled laugh into my neck as he asks for another and whispered praise when I give him what he wants.

It would be undeniably sexy, the chemistry between us reaching scalding levels. But something tells me it would be tender, too. A light-hearted joke when I trace the lines of his muscles. A bashful smile as he hold himself over me, apologizing if he's a little out of practice.

It would be *us*.

"You're thinking about it, aren't you?" Isabella asks, and I hide my face in my hands.

"Yes," I groan. "I can't help it."

"At least you have something to imagine when you get off tonight. I have to rely on shitty dating apps and boys who wouldn't be able to find my g-spot even with a spotlight on it. Enjoy your daddy, Mae. The rest of us are suffering."

I burst out laughing. "I'm sure you could ask his best friend for a hand if you're desperate. Everyone knows Maverick Miller has the reputation of being the city's biggest playboy."

"I'm not hot enough for Maverick Miller. I'd probably take my shirt off and he'd say, 'that's it?'"

"Oh, he would not. He's such a nice guy, Isa. The other day I walked in on him and Dallas getting their nails painted by June. I saw photos from his game later that night, and he kept the polish on."

"What about the nerdy one? He's cute," she says.

"Reid? Very cute, and very obsessed with the person who runs the Thunderhawks social media accounts. He has a vendetta against her. For the guy who volunteered with me at the animal shelter last month and cried as he held a litter of puppies, I'm surprised he's so hellbent on taking her down."

"So many men in your life, so little time. What's it like to be God's favorite?"

"I am hardly his favorite," I laugh.

"Okay, maybe not, but I'm glad to see you so happy again, Mae."

"Me too. I'm learning that sometimes it's okay to go through hell. It makes the other side so much better."

"Like rainbows after rain," she says, and I nod.

"Yeah," I agree. "One more drink, then I'm going to head out. Dallas has an early flight tomorrow, and he's a light sleeper. He'll hear me get back to the apartment, and I don't want to disturb him too much."

"You're so considerate to lover boy." Isabella grins and reaches for my hand across the table, but all I can think about is that tattoo on Dallas's leg and how I'd give anything to see the rest of his body.

TWENTY-EIGHT

MAVEN

I TURN on my side and stare at the wall, frustrated.

I can't sleep.

The glasses of wine and good conversation are still flowing through me, and I can't get my mind to shut off. My thoughts keep drifting back to Dallas like they do every night. Flashes of imagination and fantasy as I wonder what it would be like to stumble into bed with him. How *good* it would be and how much I crave him.

I sigh, restless, and grab my phone off the bedside table. It's just past one in the morning, and I don't think I'm going to settle anytime soon. I push up on my elbows and glance out the window, wondering if some fresh air would do me some good.

Tossing the sheets off my legs, I stand and pull on a pair of socks. The apartment is quiet when I open my bedroom door and walk down the hall, but something tells me I'm not the only one awake.

I make a pit stop at June's room. I peek inside and find her on her back. Her pink sheets are pulled up to her chin, and her favorite stuffed animal, Mr. Bear, is tucked safely against her chest. I watch her breathe deeply, lost to a child's dream, and an enormous wave of love hits me.

Before starting as her nanny, I was never sure I wanted children. When I'm around JB, though, it makes me want to be a parent. It makes me want to have someone to look after and care for, helping to mold them into a human who might change the world.

Three months with June, and I can't imagine my life without her in it. Dallas and I haven't talked about what the future looks like or how often he'll need or *want* me after this season, but I'm already dreading the day I have to walk away from their family.

"Sleep well, June Bug," I whisper, and head to the kitchen.

The light above the stove is on, and I smell coffee. My eyes catch on a Post-it note stuck to the cabinet, and I smile when I see an empty mug beneath it.

On the balcony if you want to join.

My secret spot is yours too.

-D

I pour myself a cup and make my way toward the balcony doors. A gust of wind greets me when I step outside, and the faintest October chill hangs in the air. I take a deep breath when my feet hit the concrete, and it's like my brain turns off for the first time all day.

My eyes find Dallas on instinct, and I'm drawn to him.

He's impossible to miss, shirtless and leaning over the railing of the balcony with a steaming mug in his hand, but I know I'd find him even in a crowd of people.

"Been waiting for you," he says. He looks at me over his shoulder, and his mouth curves into a double-dimpled smile. There's a crease on his cheek from his pillow, and his hair is sticking up in six different directions. "Come here."

I'm a weak woman, and there's nothing this man could ask that I wouldn't do.

Our arms touch when I stand next to him. Our shoulders brush, and the heat from his body wraps me in a warm embrace.

"Hi," I say.

"Hey, sunshine. How was your night?"

I rest my elbows on the metal ledge, mirroring him, and stare out at the city below. "It was good. I'm glad I got to see Isabella."

"How do y'all know each other?"

"We played at Georgetown together. She's the first person I met on campus my freshman year, and we just kind of clicked."

"It's good to have friends like that. They're harder to find the older you get, so keep the good ones around."

"You have lots of friends. Are they all good?"

"I know lots of people," he counters. "There's a big difference. I would only consider a few to be friends."

"I'm honored to make the cut."

"Who says you're on the list?" Dallas teases, and I roll my eyes.

"I must've imagined you calling me your best friend, then."

"You know you take the top spot, Maven."

We settle into silence and bask in the stillness around us. The rest of the world is asleep but we're wide awake and brimming with the comfortability of being around a person you adore.

There's always so much laughter when I'm with Dallas. So many jokes and stories, an endless supply of humor and good things, but I like when it all gives way to gentle quiet. When we can just *be*, without all the worries and responsibilities that come with being us.

"How's your knee feeling?" he asks after several minutes. "Any pain after the other day?"

"Nope. I'm fit as a fiddle. Maybe we could go back to the field next week when you're home from Seattle."

"I'd like that."

"I didn't wake you up, did I?"

"No." He brings his cup to his mouth and grins. His friendship bracelet slides down his wrist, and I didn't realize he still wears it like I wear mine. "I have a lot on my mind, and coffee at midnight seems to be the only antidote to overthinking."

"This is my first time indulging in your method, but so far, I like it. Is there anything you want to talk about? You know I'm happy to listen."

"What isn't there to talk about? We lost again last week. I'm boarding a plane and flying across the country in six hours." His eyes cut over to me, and he pops a shoulder, something left unsaid. *You.* "There's a lot going on upstairs, but being out here helps."

I hum and tilt my chin up to admire the twinkling stars. "I can see why this is your secret spot. It's beautiful, and I feel like there's a sense of clarity out here. I could stay forever and never get sick of it."

"Yeah," Dallas says. I turn my head to look at him, and he's already staring at me. A torn expression takes over his face and the late night moonlight bathes his bare torso in shades of silver and gray. His goofy grin is gone, and it's replaced with a soft smile I feel behind my ribs. My fingers itch to trace the column of his throat. The lines of his body and the sculpted slopes of a physique perfectly crafted from hours of exercise and exertion. "It's the most beautiful thing I've ever seen."

Me.

He's talking about *me.*

His eyes twinkle, and he keeps his gaze locked in place, a sure thing in a world full of maybes. That pressure behind my ribs expands, a weight on my chest the longer I look at him, and it's hard to take a deep breath.

"My view isn't so bad either," I reply.

It's quiet enough for him to shrug it off and pretend like he didn't hear me. I expect him to ignore it, to let it slip by, another admission from a silly girl with a silly crush on the man she can't have.

Instead, he steps closer.

I can hear his breathing—slow and steady until it changes to rough and ragged when the cotton of my shirt presses into his tan, bare skin. A nearly silent gasp falls from his mouth when neither one of us pulls away, and I wonder what else I could do to hear that sound again.

"Maven," he murmurs, sweet like honey.

I wish he'd find a way to whisper my name like that every second of every day.

It's reverent. Secret. *Loving.*

He doesn't talk to anyone else like that, and I know I'm the lucky one.

I tip my head back. He reaches out and cups my cheek with his free hand. His thumb is warm as it runs down my jaw and hooks around my chin, a spot I think might be his favorite. I sigh and close my eyes, trying to find more of his touch, if only for a second.

"Fuck," he says around an exhale before it gets snatched up by the breeze.

"I wish you would," I say, turning my cheek and biting the pad of his thumb.

His laugh is made of pure delight, a beautiful, wicked thing I feel deep in my belly.

"Seeing you like this makes me lose my mind. It makes me want you in all the ways I can't have you."

"Would it really be so bad if you lost your mind?" I ask. "If you lost it with me?"

"You're the only person I'd want to lose it with." Dallas takes a step to his left and puts distance between us. His sigh is heavy and anguished, as if space is the last thing on his mind. "But I have to think of someone other than myself."

"You *always* put others before yourself, Dallas. What would you do if you could be selfish for once? This is your secret spot —tell me a secret."

"Sometimes I can't remember what my life was like before you were in it," he whispers. "Everything about you has been unintentional and the biggest surprise. I'd go through eight hundred nannies if it meant finding you again."

"Eight hundred?" I whisper back. "That's too many. Imagine all the pictures of your dick the internet would have."

"It would be worth it. You've filled all the quiet and lonely parts of my life, Maven."

"Is that a bad thing?"

"No." He pauses and dips his head. Pink spreads across his cheeks, and I reach for his hand. Our fingers thread together and I squeeze once, a gentle assurance that I'm here. That I'll *always* be here. "It's the best thing."

It might be night, but the edges of his smile are as bright as the sun.

Something stirs inside me. It's new, this feeling. A sensation I can't describe but can only associate with other things I've come to adore—every good day I've had with him. My necklace hanging from his neck. Burnt toast and drives home from the stadium. Stolen glances under streetlights and small talk.

It hits me with the force of a wrecking ball, and it's like the universe narrows down to a single entity: him.

"I might not be able to have you how I want," I say softly, and his grip on my hand tightens. "But I'm so lucky to have you."

"Of all the sports teams in the city, you stumbled into mine." Dallas chuckles, a wisp of a laugh that sounds starkly beautiful under the inky night sky. "I'm not one to believe in divine intervention, but someone up there saw that I was struggling, and they sent me the best gift I could ever ask for. You."

"We have got to stop having these emotional conversations. Why can't we talk about the weather like normal people instead of spilling our guts like lunatics?"

"Where's the fun in that?" His arm drapes over my shoulder, and he gives me a sideways hug. "Watching you turn into a blubbery fucking mess is one of my favorite things."

"Asshole," I grumble under my breath, and I swat at his chest. "Speaking of fucking messes, you're going to be a nightmare on your flight. Shawn is going to kill you when he sees the dark circles under your eyes."

"Ah, well. It's worth it. Life is short—you have to tell people how you feel about them."

I swallow. "You've filled the sad parts of my life, Dallas. You've taught me how to be happy again."

"You would've gotten there on your own, Mae."

"Maybe. But I've gotten there a lot quicker because of you."

"That's what friends are for. They help pick you up when you're down and remind you why you started in the first place."

"Friends," I repeat. "Right."

We stand there, side by side, and as the night stretches longer, I've never hated a word more.

TWENTY-NINE
MAVEN

MY PHONE RINGS just as I'm slipping into bed on Friday night. Dallas's name comes across my screen as a FaceTime call, and I answer right away.

"Hey."

"Hey, Mae," he says.

"How was practice?"

He flicks on the lamp in his hotel room, and his face comes into view. There's dirt on his forehead, and even with the dark circles under his eyes, he's smiling.

"It sucked majorly. Shawn made us do laps until our legs gave out. Less than forty-eight hours until kickoff, and we're out there clocking four miles."

"That man really doesn't care how tired you are, does he?"

"He doesn't give a fuck." Dallas collapses into the chair by the window. He rests his head against the glass and takes a deep breath. "Everything's better now, though. I'm talking to you. How are my girls?"

"I'm good, but June is fast asleep."

"Dammit. I thought I'd be back in time to say goodnight to her." He sighs and scrubs a hand over his face. Disappointment is evident in the droop of his mouth, and I feel horrible for telling him that news. "Guess not."

"I'm sorry, Dallas. She knows you're going to call first thing in the morning."

"It's not your fault. The time zone change always throws me off, and I thought I had an extra hour to spare."

"I bet if you asked Shawn, he'd let you have your phone at practice so you could see her before she goes to bed."

"I'm sure he would, but I don't want him making exceptions just for me. Lots of guys have kids, and they miss saying good-night to them too. I'm not special."

"No, you're not, but I'm sure your teammates would like that opportunity."

"We'll see. How was your night? What are you doing?"

"It was good. I just got in bed, and I'm going to do some reading."

"Which book? The one with all the red tabs you left by the couch?"

I stare at him, and my mouth pops open. "How do you know about the tabs?"

"Confession. I've been reading your books," Dallas says with a sheepish smile.

"Which books?"

"All of them. The one you forgot on the kitchen counter the other day. The ones you have next to your bed. I can't put them down."

"Stop." I laugh and sit up. I bring my legs to my chest and rest my chin on my knees. "You're fucking with me. There's no way you read my romance novels."

"Why? Because I'm an illiterate football player?"

"Because they're love stories with all these grand gestures and sweeping declarations. There isn't any blood or guts or anything you would find interesting."

"Blood and guts are overrated," he says.

"Why didn't you tell me? I have a whole bookshelf you can look at if you want."

"Sneaking them from you is way more fun."

"This makes so much more sense. My bookmark was in the wrong spot the other night, and I thought I was imagining things when I picked it up yesterday."

"Sorry. Next time I'll make sure it's on the right page. What do the tabs mean?"

"It's a way of keeping track of things I like in the book. They're color-coded. Blue represents something sad. Orange is for the things that make me happy. Pink is for the quotes I love."

"And red?" he asks, and I swallow. "The one I shoved in my suitcase has a lot of red tabs in it."

"Um. Those are things I find hot. Scenes I'd like to try or think I'd enjoy," I say shakily.

"Oh." He leans forward in his chair and stares at me through the phone. "The toy scene? When they were out at a restaurant?"

"Yeah." I nod, and I think the room might burst into flames. "It's my favorite part."

"I liked it too."

"I didn't know you were into toys."

"Why wouldn't I be into toys?"

"I don't know. Doesn't it take away some of the power from the guy?"

"Full disclosure: I've never been with a woman while she used one," Dallas says, and his cheeks are red. "But I imagine it would be sexy. I'd get to watch her get off on her terms. I could see the things she likes and learn from her. I mean, yeah, she's the one in control, but think about when she asks to be fucked with it. Who gives a shit about power?"

A conversation about sex toys and romance novels is *not* what I was expecting when I answered his call, but I can't deny that I like it. Hearing him talk so unabashedly and openly about something he'd be into is turning me on.

"What are you thinking about right now?" I ask.

It's a daring question, but I'm done caring about lines and boundaries. We both know what direction this is headed, and if he wants to put a stop to it, I'm giving him the opportunity to bow out. To find an excuse to hang up and pretend this never happened.

Except his pupils are blown wide. The phone is four inches away from his face, and he's hanging onto my every word. He's invested in this, and my lips curl into a slow, bold smile.

"Something I'm not supposed to be thinking about." His voice is low and strained. It cracks on the last two words, like he's trying with all his might to step away but just *can't*. "I'm thinking about you, Maven. I'm always fucking thinking about you. How I wish you were here. How much I miss you."

"What would you do if I were there? Would you finally touch me, Dallas?"

"I can't touch you," he says, and the look on his face is ragged. Desperate and irritated and mad at the world. "But fuck if that doesn't mean I don't want to."

I roll onto my stomach and prop my phone up against the pillows. With the dip in my thin tank top and the change in position, I know I'm showing off some cleavage when I face the camera. "This is okay, right? You're not touching me. You're just looking."

"You found a loophole," he murmurs, full of praise, and I blush at the attention. "You like me looking at you, don't you?"

"Yes," I admit, and I play with the thin strap of my top. "It makes me feel wanted."

"I want you more than I've ever wanted anyone else, Mae. In another world, you'd already be mine."

The confessions fuel the fire in me. The slow heat that

builds up my spine mirrors the heat in his eyes. He's watching me with bated breath, like I'm giving him oxygen.

He might have called us friends, but after tonight, we won't ever be friends again. We're going down a road there is no turning back from.

"I'd like that," I whisper. "I'd like that a lot."

"Would you do something for me?" Dallas asks, and I nod. I'd do anything for this man. "Go to my bedroom."

"Why?"

"You'll see."

I pad down the hall as quietly as I can. I slide into Dallas's room and lock the door behind me, unsure of what he's about to ask me to do. "Please don't tell me there's a body in here."

"I took all the bodies with me. Go to my closet. There's a box on the top shelf. See if you can reach it."

I head across the rug to the walk-in closet. I have to stand on my toes to grab it, but I finally sweep it into my arms. "Why am I looking at a box addressed to you?"

"Bring it to the bed."

"You're so bossy." I jump onto the mattress and cross my legs. "What is it?"

"Something I think belongs to you."

I frown and pull off the top of the box. My mouth drops open when I see what's inside. "Oh my *god*. You have my vibrator."

His grin is delicious, and I wonder what it would feel like pressed to the inside of my thigh. "I do."

"I've been looking for this all week! I got a refund after I claimed it was never delivered."

"It was delivered all right. You must have left my name in the address box after you ordered something for the apartment. Imagine my surprise when I opened it up and saw *that*. I thought it was a joke at first, but then I realized it was probably yours."

I'm close to panting. My fingers grip the box so tightly, my knuckles turn white. Any embarrassment I might be feeling disappears, and it's replaced with a white-hot need. A need to slip my hand in my shorts. A need to release this tension I've been carrying for *months*.

"I had to get a new one. I could only live with a hot football player for so long before I gave in and ordered the top-of-the-line model."

"You deserve the top-of-the-line model. Maybe you should use it."

"Of course I'm going to use it."

"Maybe you should use it right now," Dallas says. "And I could watch."

I suck in a sharp breath. "What about your rules?"

"I'm not allowed to touch you, but you can touch yourself. That's not against the rules."

Heat flares through me. "Now who's the one finding loopholes?"

"Do it in my bed. If I can't fucking taste you for myself, I want to smell your come on my sheets when I get home."

Jesus Christ.

That's the hottest thing a man has ever said to me.

I'm almost rendered useless as I try to open the packaging with my teeth. "Goddammit. They don't make these things easy to get into."

"Having some trouble there?" Dallas pulls off his shirt, and I'm momentarily distracted by his stomach and the muscles across his chest. He stands up and walks to the hotel room bed, getting comfortable. "Take all the time you need, honey. You're worth the wait."

Honey.

That's new.

I like it.

"Don't you want to shower?"

"I'll shower after. Want to watch you come first."

God, what I would give to hear that whispered in my ear.

I lean the phone against the pillows and scoot back so my whole body is in the frame. "How's that? Can you see me?"

"Perfect," he says. "You're perfect, Maven."

"Clothes? On or off?"

Dallas makes a strangled sound. "I want to say off, but if I do, I might charter a plane back to D.C."

"On, then. But I'm going to take off my shirt."

He bobs his head, and I pull my top over my head. I throw it to the side and watch his reaction to seeing me topless for the first time.

"Jesus," he whispers. "Can you—" he squeezes his eyes closed before they fly open again, like he's afraid to miss something. "Can you get closer? I don't mean to be so demanding, but your tits—"

"Yeah?" I get on my knees and crawl toward the camera. I run my hands over my breasts and push them together. Dallas groans, and I bite back a smile. "You like them? I never pegged you for a boob guy."

"With you, I don't give a shit what it is. Your fucking elbow turns me on."

"There's probably a market for that."

His chuckle is soft and light, and *god,* I wish he were here with me right now. "Probably."

I pinch my nipples between my fingers and drop my head back. "Fuck. I haven't really touched myself in a while."

"You haven't?"

"I've been busy. Have you touched yourself recently?"

"Last night," he admits. "Or, this morning, I guess. After our talk on the balcony. Those fucking shorts of yours drive me insane, Maven."

"You know I'm not going to apologize."

"Of course you aren't. God damn, sunshine. Your tits are incredible. I bet they'd bounce when I fucked you, wouldn't they? They'd look nice and pretty when I covered them with my come."

It's my turn to groan. I imagine being on my knees in front of him, my mouth open and his come all over my body. His fingers running down my throat and across my chest. "I'd let you do that, Dallas. I'd let you do anything to me."

"Anything? You'd let me fuck every hole of yours? Make them mine? Ruin you so much that you couldn't walk in a straight line at a game while millions of people were watching? I might be a little out of practice, but I still know how to fuck you like you deserve."

I nod feebly. I thought I was going to be the one controlling this, but I guess not. I reach for the toy and click it on, getting used to the vibrations.

"All of me," I say. "It's all yours."

I bring the toy down my stomach. Dallas's right hand disappears, and I hope he's touching himself.

"Go slow," he demands, and his voice is thick with lust. "It's been a while, and I want to enjoy this. Enjoy you. Too fast and it'll be over in a second."

"I'll go slow." I drag the vibrator up my thigh and over the front of my shorts. "As slow as you want."

I touch my clit for the first time, and I jolt forward. The intensity is mind-shattering. Even on the lowest speed, I see stars. There behind the fragmented colors and the precipice of bliss are images of Dallas.

Him, on his knees, begging *please*. His mouth on my neck and his heart in my hands. Shimmering, twinkling dark brown eyes and a smile that makes me weak.

"Look at you. You're fucking drenched for me," he says like a prayer.

"You sure this is for you, hot shot?" I smirk, and begin to move my hand in a slow circle.

His breathing hitches when my back arches off the mattress, and I bring my chin down to look in the camera. The intensity behind his gaze is so ferocious, I can feel it three thousand miles away.

"I dare it to be for someone else, Maven," he says. "We both know you bought that toy so you could touch yourself while you thought about me."

THIRTY

DALLAS

I'M GOING cross-eyed from looking at my phone screen, but I'm afraid to blink. I don't want to miss a second of watching Maven fucking Wood touch herself.

Fucking hell.

She's the hottest woman I've ever seen.

I'm obsessed with her body when she has clothes on, and seeing her like this—half naked and letting out soft sighs—firmly cements the thought in my useless brain.

Her tits are incredible, and every time she arches her back off the bed and finds a spot on her body she really likes, it makes me want to bite the soft skin of her chest. It makes me want to take one of her nipples in my mouth and suck until she's squirming under me and begging for more.

Her pajama shorts—that goddamn scrap of fabric that haunts my dreams—keep getting wetter and wetter. The cotton is practically translucent, and I can see her sharp hip bones and the outline of her pussy through the material.

She's teasing herself, taking her time as she runs the vibrator up her body then back down. Every flick of her wrist that brings her hand back between her legs makes the spot a little damper.

Responsive.

I want that wetness on my mouth. On my tongue and covering my hands. I can't wait to get home on Sunday and smell the scents she left behind. They'll be a reminder that I might not be next to her, coaxing the orgasm out of her myself, but at least I had some sort of role in her pleasure.

"Tell me the truth, Maven. Who do you think about when you use your toy?"

"You," she whines, and smug possessiveness pulses through me. "Of course I think about you. I wish you were touching me right now."

"So do I, pretty girl," I rasp, one hand around my dick. I've never been this hard in my life and I give myself a few quick strokes, dangerously close to blowing a load. "I'd make you feel good."

"Can I see you?" she asks, and she runs her tongue over her bottom lip like she's fucking starving for a sight of my dick. "Can I see how hard you are, Dallas? Please?"

That sweet little please is my undoing.

I scramble to flip the camera around and drag my hand over the head of my cock. Pre-cum soaks my thumb, and I use the moisture to give myself another rough jerk before resting my palm on my thigh.

I turn the phone to the side so she can see my whole length. I've never had phone sex or sent a dick pic before, and I hope the angle is okay.

Should I show her my balls, too? Do I touch myself while she's looking, or do I sit here like a statue and let her see how fucking hard I am without doing anything else?

"Jesus," Maven whispers, and that must be a good sign. I must've done something right. "You're so big. You don't even fit in the frame."

"Stop flattering me, Mae," I say through a laugh. "I'm already going to think about you when I come. You don't have to inflate my ego."

"You're the biggest I've ever seen. I'm not sure how you'd fit."

I'm not sure how you'd fit.

That means she's thinking about us being together. The mechanics of being in bed and what position would work best.

I have to squeeze my eyes shut because the more I look at Maven, the more I imagine her tight pussy swallowing me down. Riding three of my fingers before I sank my cock into her and the heavenly stretch when I bottomed out.

Fuck, I want to fill her up.

"We'd make it fit," I growl, and I don't recognize my own voice. It's rough and hoarse, and I'm barely holding on. I've never been this turned on in my life, and knowing she's feeling the same way has my brain even more scrambled. "You'd take every inch like a champ, Maven. Because you're so fucking good."

She moans, and she increases the speed on her vibrator. My eyes fly open and I watch her again, tortured that I can't use that fucking toy on her myself as her mouth forms an O.

Her chest is scarlet and her knees open wider. There's enough space between her parted thighs—those *fucking thighs*—for my whole body, and I'd love to have her calves hooked over my shoulders while I buried my face in her pussy.

I know she likes praise. I've seen the way she reacts when I tell her how well she's doing. She lights up, eager to hear more, and it doesn't surprise me that she likes it in bed, too.

I'm suddenly hit with the realization of how inexperienced I am. I'm the first to admit my sexual encounters can fit on ten fingers, and while I've never had any complaints, I really hope I'm doing this right.

"I don't think I can go slow anymore," she pants, and her left hand grabs her tit. She squeezes her nipple between her fingers then twists, and I make a mental note of what she's doing. Of what she likes. "I need to come, Dallas. Are you close? I want to get there together."

"Don't worry about me. Pull your shorts to the side and make yourself come, Maven. You've done so well going slow for me, and I want to see what your cunt looks like when you get off thinking about the man you can't have."

I don't know where the *fuck* these words are coming from or if she even likes them, but I'm committed now. I watch, mesmerized, as she listens to me.

I almost lose consciousness when she circles her clit with the toy.

The wind gets knocked out of me when I hear the slick sounds of how wet she is.

I think I go to heaven when she uses her fingers to spread herself open.

"Dallas," she says around a breathy exhale, and that's the nail in my coffin.

As if I ever stood a fucking chance.

I close my eyes and jerk my cock four more times before I fall over the ledge of a mountain and spill all over my hand. My chest heaves and my lungs constrict as I try to suck down some air.

I will my body to calm down, but my limbs are heavy. My vision blurs, and I've forgotten my name. There's a mess on my stomach and hips, and I feel stickiness on my palm. When I crack an eye open, I find Maven watching me with flushed cheeks.

"Hi," I say, unsure of what happens next.

"Hi," she says back, and her mouth pulls up into a soft smile.

"Did I—was I—"

"Oh." Her eyes sparkle, and she bites her bottom lip. "Best I ever had."

"You're just saying that. The bar is men peeing on your mattress, Mae."

"No." She puts her chin in her hand, and her smile stretches wider. She looks perfectly sated and perfectly beautiful. "I'm serious, Dallas."

Jealousy runs through me.

I know I'm not allowed to be pissed that she's had a life before me—I have a daughter with someone else for fuck's sake. But knowing other guys have seen her like this makes me want to mark her and claim her as mine. It makes me want to throw my entire rulebook out the window and step away from the moral high ground.

I take a deep breath. "Are we good? I didn't just massively fuck up our—"

"If you say friendship, Lansfield, I will find a way to murder you from here," she says. "We're perfectly fine. That was incredible. *You* were incredible. What fun is it to be attracted to someone and not do anything about it?"

I reach for my discarded shirt and wipe my hand clean. "I thought I was supposed to be the older and wiser one."

"You're certainly older."

I laugh and drop my head against the pillows.

This all feels so normal, so *easy*, and I don't have an ounce of dread that I might have done the wrong thing. We've been teetering toward this for a while now, and if I should be feeling any shame, I'm not.

I was selfish for once, greedy and goddamn determined, and it paid off.

I want to do it again.

"I miss you," I confess.

"I miss you, too," she says, and she tucks a piece of hair behind her ear. "What are you going to do the rest of the night?"

"After that? I'm spent. You ruined me. I wish I could go to bed, but I have a stupid team dinner."

"When are you—"

A knock cuts her off. I stare at my hotel door and frown.

"Are you in there, Lansfield?" Shawn asks loud enough for me to hear, and I drop the phone.

"Fuck. *Fuck*," I hiss. "I need to go."

"Is that Shawn?" she asks, and I nod.

"Yes, and I prefer if he didn't know I just watched you orgasm all over that toy of yours." I jump up and pull my shorts to my hips. I shove my dirty shirt under a pillow, and my heart races in my chest. "Jesus Christ. Talk about cockblocking."

Maven laughs, and she stretches out on my bed. She's still naked from the waist up, and even though I know she's taunting me, it's hard to draw my eyes away. "You might want to put a shirt on, buddy. Shawn gave me that necklace."

"*Fuck*," I mumble again. I dig through my suitcase and yank a hoodie over my head. "I'll text you later."

I hustle to the door and fling it open, leaning casually against the wall.

"Lansfield."

"Hey, Coach."

Shawn narrows his eyes. He looks me up and down and crosses his arms over his chest. "Who were you talking to?"

"What?" I ask, feigning innocence. "No one. I was going through some of the routes we're running on Sunday. It helps when I say them out loud."

He hums. "First time I've heard of this new ritual of yours."

"Maybe you should pay more attention. What's up?"

"How's your leg? I noticed you were hobbling on some of those laps this afternoon, and I wanted to make sure your foot and knee were okay."

"I'm fine. Just a little sore from a long flight, but it's all good."

"You're being really fucking weird," Shawn says, and he looks over my shoulder. "Is there someone in your room? You know that shit doesn't fly with me at away games."

"There's no one here. Seriously. And thank you for checking on me, but I'm fine. Ready for a good night of sleep."

"Okay." He relaxes, and I'm glad I said the right things to get rid of him. "Team dinner is in an hour. Don't be late. Almost two months into the regular season and the rookies still don't have a concept of time. Help me out with that, will you?"

"You got it. Need anything else?"

"No. I—" his phone rings, and he pulls it out of his pocket. "Hang on. It's Maven."

I almost fall off the wall. "What does she want?"

Shawn holds up a finger. "Hey, Mae. What's up? I'm just here with Lansfield. Huh? He does look a little flushed." He pulls the phone away from his ear and looks me up and down. "Are you running a fucking fever?"

"No," I say firmly. "Don't listen to her."

"Thanks for letting me know. Love you too, kid." He hangs up and glares at me. "Why is my goddaughter telling me you might be ill?"

"Because she's a little shit," I grumble. "I'm not sick. I'm not injured. I'm tired. I miss my daughter. I don't want to lose another game, and some peace and quiet before I'm surrounded by fifty-two rambunctious assholes when I only got a few hours of sleep last night would be really nice."

"Alright," Shawn concedes, and he takes a step back. "I'll see you downstairs in a bit."

I shut the door and put the deadbolt in place. My shoulders sag as I hear his footsteps retreating from my room.

That was a close fucking call.

I walk back to my bed and pick up my phone, firing off a message to Maven.

ME

You're a damn menace, woman.

MAVEN

You love it.

ME

I do.

There's no way to come back from *watching someone I live with get off on FaceTime,* is there?

I think we just dug ourselves into a hole, and I don't know how to climb out of it.

I'm not sure I even want to.

THIRTY-ONE

DALLAS

SPENDING FRIDAY NIGHT on the couch with Maven is always the highlight of my week, and tonight is no different.

I just don't know how I'm supposed to look her in the eye after watching her come with that goddamn toy.

My *hottest things I've done in life* list is short, almost nonexistent, if I'm being honest, but that video call takes the fucking cake. It's the most spontaneous I've ever been. I've replayed it over and over again in my head. I've tried to commit it to memory, because I don't want to forget a single second.

I can still hear her moans and the way she said my name mid-orgasm. I can still see her wrist moving in a slow, lazy circle as she ran that vibrator up every inch of her body.

I didn't know I could be jealous of a sex toy for fuck's sake, but I was. Knowing it got to touch her while I had to watch idly from the sidelines was torture.

I'm going out of my fucking mind. The only way to put myself out of this misery is to jerk off, and every thought I have when my hand is wrapped around my dick is so depraved, I'm embarrassed to take the seat next to her.

We've been around each other plenty this week. We've had

dinner with June every night and worked in tandem to get her tucked into bed. There was co-narrating JB's favorite story as she drifted off to sleep, and washing and drying pots and pans like a team.

But now we have to sit side-by-side and chat about our day like I haven't admired her cunt and she hasn't seen my dick.

It's totally fucking fine.

"Why are you standing there?" Maven asks, and she looks up at me from the couch. The smile she's been wearing all night dips into a frown. Little creases form across her forehead, and I have the urge to smooth them out with my thumb. "Is everything okay?"

"Peachy," I answer as I hand her a beer. "How was your day?"

"June and I went to the neighborhood Harvest Festival and ate kettle corn until our stomachs hurt. She won't stop talking about Halloween and what costumes she wants to wear."

"What does she want to do? Last year we were princesses— Mav and Reid dressed up and came with us, too. The year before we did Peppa Pig."

"Stop. All three of you wore princess dresses?"

"Is there any other way to do it?" I pull out my phone and toss it to her. "Password is 5863. There's a whole album for Halloween."

"Oh my *god*. You're wearing a wig. That is a serious commitment."

"You can't walk around in a sparkly dress and not wear a wig, Maven."

"Sorry. I don't know the Halloween protocol around here. Pretty sure I was at the bars last year to celebrate the holiday."

"Do you want to join us?" I ask, and I don't know why I didn't consider that she might already have plans with someone other than me and my four-year-old kid. "We can pick out another group costume. We can all go as Barbies or something."

"Oh." Maven dips her chin, and that smile is back. "As long as I'm not intruding."

"You're not. I promise."

"Okay. Then, yes, I'd love to join you." She motions to the couch. "Are you going to stand all night?"

"No." I take a seat at the far end of the sofa, and there's enough distance between us to be respectable to a fucking priest. "Just taking my time."

"What's the topic of conversation tonight?"

You, naked in my bed, and how we can make that happen without someone losing their job.

I shrug. "It's your turn to pick. Two weeks ago, I rambled for thirty minutes about fantasy football draft positions, and you fell asleep. I'm not making that mistake again."

"It wasn't you. While your speech about why the kicker's field goal distance to awarded points ratio was passionate, it was my own fault. I was exhausted."

"I appreciate you looking out for my ego, Mae. Pick something good, please. Practice was brutal again today, and if you start talking about the difference between shades of chalk, I'm going to be out in two minutes."

"Okay. Something good." She stretches out her legs and rests them in my lap, just like she always does. There's hesitancy in her voice, and I brace myself. "Am I allowed to ask about June's mom?"

Her question catches me off guard.

It's a conversation I always find a way to dance around. No one knows the real story—not even Maverick and Reid—and I've been content to keep it that way.

But I've already shown Maven all these other parts of me, and this feels like the last thing that's missing. The final puzzle piece, and I want her to have it.

"Yes," I say, and I set down my drink. I wrap my hand around her ankle and rub my thumb up her calf. Touching her, even in this platonic, nonsexual way, settles me, and I sigh when she scoots closer. "You know I'll tell you anything."

"She's not in the picture, is she?"

"I haven't talked to her since the night we were together. Lawyers have handled everything between us. I was celebrating an away game with some of my teammates. We went to this dive bar away from the Vegas strip, and I met a woman who didn't seem to know who I was."

It all comes flooding back to me.

My teammates have one night stands all the time.

They have multiple women in and out of their hotel rooms. A list of numbers for every city we touch down in. I've never been a fan of all that attention, though. It's not because I'm waiting for The One or some other bullshit like that. I don't like people thinking I'm high and mighty just because I'm on television once a week.

It was different the night June was conceived.

I was amped up from a great win, and nothing could rain on my parade. I gave into that attentiveness. I welcomed the free drinks and the free food. It was all consuming, but it was particularly nice from the mysterious brunette who kept flirting with me.

Instead of walking away and slipping into bed alone like I normally did, I stuck around.

"What happened?" Maven asks gently, and I take a deep breath.

"I asked her back to my room. I was still on a celebratory high and didn't think twice when she told me she was on birth control and not looking for anything serious. I wasn't either. I mean, fuck. I knew I'd be inking a big contract during the summer. I was in the prime of life. I had no responsibilities. No one to answer to. It was me and football, and that was it."

"Until it wasn't?" she asks, and I nod.

"Nine months later, I received a call that told me I was going to be a father. June's birth mother handed over parental rights and custody in exchange for not asking for any money. And the craziest part? The only reason she slept with me was because she needed to cross off *bag a professional athlete* from her bachelorette scavenger hunt list."

"Oh, Dallas."

I thought someone was fucking with me when I got the call.

I requested multiple paternity tests and receipts from doctor's visits. I had an investigator do a deep dive into her past to see if she had done this before, because up to this point, I had been *so fucking careful.*

The one time I let go, only for a night, my entire world changed. I've been locked up ever since, too afraid to step a toe out of line.

"There was resentment at first," I admit. "Toward her. Toward June. It's not like I wanted to live this luxurious life on yachts with models or anything like that. You know that's not my scene."

"Are you sure? I thought I saw some photos of you in Saint-Tropez," Maven jokes, lightening the mood, and I pinch her shin.

"Not me, I'm afraid. Before I got the call about June, everything was easy. Everything was simple. My whole future was planned out for me: I was going to play in the league for a decade and a half, then I'd settle down. I'd always wanted to be the fun uncle, never a dad."

"But now you're a dad."

"Yeah. All of a sudden, I was building a crib. I was singing lullabies. My priorities changed, and it was scary at first. Fuck, it's still scary. Most days I'm not sure I'm equipped to be a father. But now that I'm here on the other side, I hate myself for being so mad about June in the beginning. She's the greatest gift I've ever been given. I love her so fucking much, and I hope she knows that. When I look at her, I know she's going to be the only person in my life who's ever going to love me wholly and completely. She's the only one who will ever love me for me, not for my career or how many games I play."

I tip my head back and stare at the ceiling. The lights blur, a watery mix of yellows and whites, and I squeeze my eyes shut.

"Sorry," I mumble. "This whole deep as fuck thing is getting really fucking old."

"Don't you dare apologize to me," Maven says with ferocity. The sofa dips, and the next thing I know, she's wrapping her arms around me in a hug. "I'm so proud of you, Dallas. You've grown as a person. As a father. June knows how much you love her. You tell her as much by showing up every single day, and she's going to love you back long after you retire and people forget who you are. New records will be set. Your accomplishments will start to fade away. But she's still going to come home every night, excited to see you, because you're her *dad*, and you're doing a damn good job."

"Christ." I slip my arms around her waist and bury my face in her hair. "Now you've started the waterworks, Maven. God dammit."

Her laugh rumbles against my chest, and I hold her even tighter. "We're going to have to buy a new couch at the end of the season. Something a little happier than this one, because it's seen some shit."

"If furniture could talk." I sigh and pull away, resting my chin on top of her head. My hand runs down her spine then back up, and I'm so glad she's here.

"You're wrong, you know." Maven untangles herself and looks up at me. "June's not the only one who likes you for more than your career. I do too. And whatever woman you end up with one day will as well. You're the kindest, most gentle man I've ever met, and if you lost football tomorrow, I'd still think the same thing."

What if I want to end up with you? I think, and I wish I could hold her again.

"Thanks, Mae. That means the world to me."

She sits back on her side of the couch and smiles. "Thank you for sharing with me."

"Thank you for listening. This isn't the direction I thought our night would go. I had a surprise for you."

"A surprise?" she asks excitedly. "What is it?"

"Since you won't stop complaining about the drink selection in this house, I figured I needed to step up my game." I stand and head for the liquor cabinet. I open the doors and pull out a bottle of tequila. "It's from Mexico."

"Oh my god. I love that brand." She reaches for the bottle, and I hand it to her. "This is the fancy shit. I'd never buy this for myself."

"Which is why I bought it for you."

"Spoiling me, Lansfield?"

"Taking care of someone I care about," I say, correcting her.

"Want me to grab some glasses?"

"No." I turn the cap and look down at her. "We don't need them."

"Are we going to throw it back old school?"

"Sort of. Sit on the edge of the cushions."

Maven wiggles to the end of the couch and rests her feet on the floor. "Now what?" she asks, and it's softer than before.

"Tip your head back," I tell her roughly, and her eyes widen in understanding as she tilts her chin up.

I hook my fingers around her chin and stroke her jaw. I bring the bottle to her mouth and she opens her lips, her tongue out and ready.

Her smile is coy, but she doesn't speak. She waits patiently, and I pour a small taste of liquor on her tongue.

"Swallow," I say, and she does so immediately without batting an eye. A groan works its way up my throat, and my sweatpants grow impossibly tight. "Christ, you're good, aren't you?"

"I try to be."

"You're so good, Maven." I press my thumb on her bottom lip, and she moans. "Open again."

She keeps her gaze on me and slowly opens her mouth, waiting for what comes next. I'm making this up as I go, and when I move my hand to her throat, I can feel her heart racing under my touch.

"Doing okay?" I ask, wanting to check on her.

"Never better," she says.

I pour another round of tequila in her mouth—more this time—and watch in amazement as she stares at me. There's not so much as a grimace on her face and her eyes twinkle. She squeezes her thighs together, and I think she's enjoying this.

"Fuck. I wonder what you'd look like with a mouthful of my cum," I murmur. "Beautiful, I bet. Taking everything I give you. Swallow nice and slow. Let me watch you."

Her neck bobs, and the tequila glides down her throat. Once her mouth is empty, her tongue sneaks out. She licks away a lingering drop of alcohol that hangs on the corner of her lips, and I'm hot all over.

"Not wasting a drop, are you?" I ask.

"Never." Her eyes bounce to the front of my sweatpants. "I wouldn't waste a drop of *that* either."

"I know you wouldn't. You're greedy, aren't you?"

"For you? I'm fucking ravenous, Dallas."

I grin and close my hand around her throat, applying the slightest bit of pressure. This woman is from my dreams, and it doesn't surprise me when she arches her back to get closer. "You want more, pretty girl?"

"You know I want all of it."

We're not talking about tequila anymore.

I want all of it too.

"Lie on the sofa. Prop up your head," I tell her, and she scrambles to get into the position.

The strap of her sleep top falls down her arm and catches at her elbow. Her chest rises and falls like she's been running for miles, and I can see her hard nipples through her shirt. Maven stretches out, lazy like a cat, and rests her head on the pillows. A smile works its way to her mouth, and I want to kiss it off of her.

If I can't have her in my bed, this will have to do.

I climb onto the couch and straddle her, my legs on either side of her hips. My erection presses into her, and instead of pulling away, she nudges her thighs open so she can feel more of me.

"Are you just going to sit there and stare at me all night, or are you going to do something?" she asks with the smug defiance I love about her.

"Two sips of tequila, and she's feisty. I never pegged you for a lightweight, Wood."

"It would be a lot nicer if you *did* peg me, Lansfield."

A laugh bursts out of me, and it makes her giggle, too.

"God, I like you," I say softly. "I like you so much."

"I like you, too. I like you more than I've ever liked anyone else."

The heat from moments ago cools and turns softer.

I tuck a piece of hair behind her ear, and she turns her cheek to kiss my palm. Overwhelming desire sweeps over me, and I can't remember why I've stayed away from this woman. It's like I'm permanently stuck in her orbit, and I hope I never have to leave.

This is the part where I kiss her, right?

I want to.

I think I might die if I don't.

She's looking up at me with those big blue eyes and pink lips, and I want her to stare at me every night like that.

We could figure it out. No one would have to know. I hardly see her at the stadium, and when I do, she's too busy taking pictures to notice me. I always notice her, though.

"Maven," I whisper, and she licks her lips, like she knows what's coming. "I—"

A wail travels down the hall and cuts me off. My head snaps toward June's room, and panic rushes through me.

"Shit," I curse, and I try to pull myself off of Maven. The tequila spills, and my foot gets caught under a cushion. "I need—"

"You need to calm down first," Maven says, and she gestures to where I'm still hard. "I'll get her."

"But she—"

"I've got it, Dallas. Really." She pops off the couch and takes the bottle from my hands. "You trust me, right?"

"Yes," I say, and I crane my neck, hoping I can see what's going on. "More than anyone in this world."

"Good." She bends down and kisses my forehead. "You're not alone, remember? Let me do this for you."

"Okay." I nod, and that same swell of emotion that hit me earlier sweeps me up again. "Thank you."

She jogs away, and after a minute, her voice drifts toward me. She's singing a soft song, and I imagine her holding June in her arms. Rocking her back and forth just like I do as she quiets the nightmares.

It hits me, then, as I think about someone else taking Maven's spot one day down the road.

She's irreplaceable.

Not just as a nanny or someone behind the camera at foot-ball games, but as the woman I want by my side until the end of time.

I'm totally and completely head over heels for her, and I need to figure out a way to fucking have her once and for all.

THIRTY-TWO

DALLAS

"WHAT THE FUCK IS GOING ON?"

I look up from the menu I'm holding and stare at Maverick. "Hm?"

"It's a Saturday night. You're supposed to be at dinner with your team at the hotel, *Captain*. But here we are, at a restaurant I've never heard of, watching you pick which steak you're going to eat." He snatches the menu out of my hand and slams it on the table. "You're going to get the filet, like you always do, and if you don't tell us what's going on in the next six seconds, I'm going to lose it."

"You're not dramatic at all," I draw out. I glance over at Reid, hoping he'll think Maverick is out of line, but he only blinks back at me. "Okay. I need advice, but what I'm going to say cannot leave this table. If word gets out, I swear to god I'll end both of you."

Maverick reaches for me and hooks his pinky around mine. He gestures for Reid to do the same, and soon the three of us are holding hands over a candlelit table and a five hundred dollar bottle of wine.

"Swear on my life," he says, and Reid nods in agreement.

"What's going on, Dal?"

I'm breaking a dozen team rules by being here.

I should be with the rest of the Titans watching *Miracle on Ice* in the hotel's banquet hall before tomorrow's home game, but I snuck out after our film review session. I claimed I had a headache and needed some fresh air.

It's only half a lie—I did need some fresh air. I also need some room to figure out what the fuck I'm going to do with my coworker-turned nanny-turned roommate-turned best friend-turned current inspiration for all my filthy fantasies.

I was never supposed to fall for her.

She's the one woman I can't have.

The rational part of my brain—the part that understands the severity of consequences and doing things I'm not supposed to —is telling me to let it go. To give it—*her*—up.

But my stupid fucking heart can't get onboard.

I laid in bed last night, tossing and turning while considering the possibility it's the attention that has me in a goddamn tizzy. But then I remembered how warm I feel when she laughs. How much better life is when she's around, and I know it's not just any woman.

It's her.

"Maven," I say, and I run my fingers down the stem of my wine glass.

"What about her?" Reid asks carefully, and it makes me wonder if he and Maverick have talked about my feelings toward her when I'm not around.

"I—we—she—" I snap my mouth closed. "Y'all are going to make fun of me."

"We are not," Maverick says. "Did you guys make fun of me when I waited naked on the couch of that girl I met at the bar, only for her parents to walk in and surprise her for her birthday?"

"No, but—"

"And did we make fun of Reid when his screen time was eight hours a day one week, all of which was spent hate-watching Thunderhawks posts with that catchy little song they play when they win?"

"No, and I—"

"We give each other shit, Dallas, but we'd never make fun of something that's clearly important to you."

"Okay." I nod and down the rest of my drink. I'm stopping after this one otherwise I'm going to pay for it tomorrow, but I need a little liquid courage. "Maven and I have had a lot of moments over the last few months. She's become one of my favorite people in the world, but lately, things are different."

"Different how?" Reid asks, and he rests his elbows on the table. "Good different?"

"Yes," I say right away. "We, uh, had this FaceTime call last week. I told her I was reading one of her romance novels. She found the vibrator she bought that I was keeping in my closet for her. We might have watched each other get off and—"

"Oh my god," Maverick hisses, and he scoots his chair closer. "You had phone sex and we're just now hearing about it? What is wrong with you?"

"Yes, we had phone sex and it was..." I laugh and dip my chin. My cheeks flood with heat. "It was the hottest thing I've ever done, y'all. Watching her touch herself was unreal. Then last night, I was literally on top of her on my couch and pouring tequila in her mouth. If June hadn't had a nightmare and inter-rupted us, I would've kissed her."

"Wait. You two haven't kissed?"

"No. I'm not allowed to kiss her."

"Why not?" Maverick asks.

"Because she could lose her job if anyone found out. Shawn had to fire an assistant coach a couple years back because of an inappropriate relationship. He'd fucking *murder* me if he found out Maven and I were a thing."

"So don't let them find out," Reid says, like it's the easiest fucking thing in the world.

"Besides the whole team ethics thing, if we did get together and broke up, what would that mean for June? I'm not just dating for myself. I have to think of her, too."

"You're making a lot of excuses for why you shouldn't be with her," Maverick says. "Forget the league—you have ten more years in you, tops. Forget June—she'll be old enough to understand emotions soon. Forget about ethics and rules and all of that shit. At the end of the day, Dallas, what's going to make you happy?"

"I can't—"

"You can. You think about others too damn much. What the fuck do *you* want?"

Her.

"I want her," I admit, and I lift my head to look at them. "Y'all know I prefer to keep people at a distance, but Maven found her way into my life, and I don't want to ask her to leave. I know we could get in trouble, but I want to do it anyway. The consequences aren't anything compared to how much I—" I blow out a breath, and my laugh borders on hysterical. "I'm fucking falling for her, and I haven't even had her yet."

"Hell yeah you are, man." Maverick slings an arm around me. "Your cheeks look like they must hurt from smiling so much. You've always been a happy guy, but this is different."

"You look at her like she's the sun," Reid adds, and he hugs me too.

"No. She's the stars. Always there. Shining and bright, even when everything in my world goes dark. I'd stay up all night just to see her."

I feel like I've been fumbling through life the last four years.

Stumbling along and searching for any source of light but coming up short. Then she ran into me, and now all I see are colors.

"God. Look at our boy growing up." Maverick wipes his eyes and scrubs his hand over his face.

"*Jesus,* Mav. Are those tears?"

"Shut up. We're not making fun of each other, remember?" He grabs a napkin and blows his nose. "I'm just so fucking happy for you, Dal. I'm happy June has a role model besides the dipshits we can be. I'm happy Maven is so *good*. She's funny, man. Not in that way where she's trying to impress you, but actually fucking funny. And she likes you back. This is what you deserve."

"You think so? I'm afraid I'm going to tell her and she's going to laugh in my face."

"In no world do you tell her how you feel and she says she doesn't feel the same way," Maverick says.

"What do I do? Do I tell her now or wait until after the game?"

"If the worst-case scenario happened to you in the game tomorrow, would you die wishing she knew how you felt?" Reid asks.

"Yes," I say, and I'm already on my feet, decision made. "I'm going to see her. Right now."

Maverick jumps up. "Hell yeah you are. Go get your girl, Dal."

I pull on my jacket and throw some cash on the table. "I love y'all. Thanks for being in my corner."

"Always." Reid puts his hand over his heart and sighs. "Look at our boy growing up. Let us know how it goes."

"We want to know every single detail," Maverick says with a sly grin.

"No, we really don't," Reid practically begs.

"Fuck off," I laugh, and I make my way outside, ready to be home with her.

GETTING a rideshare on a Saturday night is nearly impossible.

Two drivers cancel on me, and by the time I pull up to my building, it's been over an hour since I left the restaurant.

June's definitely asleep, but I know Maven will be awake. I don't know if I should give her a heads up that I'm coming up or just surprise her.

I think if I text her, I might lose all the momentum I have.

The ride up to my floor is unbearably long, and when I'm finally standing outside my door, I take a deep breath.

I slip inside as quietly as I can and kick off my sneakers. The sound of the television in the living room echoes down the hall, and I follow the noise. I stand in the entryway and see Maven on the couch.

Her phone is in her hand and her bottom lip is caught between her teeth. It looks like she's thinking hard about something, but before I have time to wonder what it is, my phone buzzes twice in my pocket. I pull it out and find messages from her on my screen.

MAVEN

Hi. I hope the hotel is fun. The apartment is always so lonely when you aren't around.

Can you hurry home, please?

I love that she calls my place home, and I type out a quick reply.

ME

Hey, sunshine.

> Kind of sounds like you miss me.

I watch her reaction, and I feel victorious when she smiles and answers right away.

MAVEN

> Only a little bit. Don't flatter yourself.

"Just a little bit?" I ask.

Her phone goes flying. She lets out a noise that's somewhere between a screech and a squeal, and I double over laughing when a shoe comes flying at my head.

"What the *fuck*? Dallas?" Maven clutches her chest and stares at me like an ax might be coming for my head next. "Are you insane? Who the hell sneaks up on a woman alone in an apartment you absolute asshat? You're lucky I put my dinner knife away, or that pretty face of yours would be all marked up."

"You think I'm pretty?"

"Fuck you. You almost gave me a heart attack, and it's a miracle you didn't wake up JB."

I clutch my side and wheeze. "I'm sorry. I didn't think that through. I was trying to be romantic, and it came off as incredibly serial-killery."

"Uh, yeah. I feel like you might rival Ted Bundy with that entrance." She pulls the blankets off her legs and stalks toward me with her hands on her hips and the cutest angry face I've ever seen. "What are you doing here?"

When she gets close enough to reach, I grab her arm and tug her toward me. Her chest presses against mine, and I cup her cheek with my palm.

"I missed you too."

Maven blinks, and I swear her eyes sparkle. "That's why you came here? To tell me you missed me?"

"Among other things."

"Like?"

"Like that I can't get you out of my head," I say, and my words crack around the edges. "I think about you, every second of every day. I've tried really fucking hard not to, but I can't stop, and I'm done pretending like I can. I'm weak, Maven, and you've ruined me. I never stood a chance when it came to you."

Her breath catches and she parts her lips. I stare at her, and a flash of color catches my attention. I take a step back, and that's when I realize what she's wearing.

A jersey.

My jersey.

With nothing but bare legs underneath it.

"What are you—" I run my fingers across the neckline and down the front, tracing the numbers that sit over her chest. She arches her back and her breaths come out in soft, strangled pants. "Why are you wearing my jersey, Maven?"

"Because," she whispers, and her fingers hook in the belt loop of my jeans. "You said it was mine for the rest of the season. It makes me think I could be yours, too."

Seeing her like this, I don't want to be smart.

I want to be reckless.

I want to be out of my mind.

I'll worry about the trouble we'll be in tomorrow.

Right now, all I want is her.

This woman is mine. Fuck the consequences.

"Tell me to stop." I settle my hand over her heart. "Tell me to leave you alone."

"No." Our chests press together, and there's fire in her eyes now. "I'm done playing games."

"Fuck it. Fuck staying away. Fuck shouldn't. I don't just want you, Maven. I fucking need you like I need air. Can I have you? Please let me have you."

"Yes," she says, and that single word rearranges my entire

world. "You can have me. All of me, Dallas, because you've always had me."

I crash my mouth into hers.

It's violent and chaotic. Rough and possessive, and I need her to know that if this is my last minute on Earth, I'd be happy to die right here, her lips on mine.

She's soft. *So fucking soft.* A soft mouth. Soft curves. Soft hands that find their way into my hair and tug on the pieces by my ears.

I work my palm up to the curve of her elbow, her neck then her throat, looking for any spot I can touch. I want to feel her to know that she's real and that I really get to have her in every way I've hoped.

Maven mirrors me. Her fingers press into my muscles and the curve of my jaw, and she lets out a laugh that I swallow down greedily. Her laugh turns to awe when I run my hand up her bare leg. It melts to desire when I lift her in my arms and walk us blindly through the living room until her back presses against a wall.

She answers enthusiastically, with teeth and tongue and legs wrapping around my waist. Her heels settle into the small of my back, urging me closer, and I know when I'm buried ten inches inside her, it still won't be close enough.

It's like we know exactly where the other is going to go next. She tilts her head to the left and I go to the right. I bite her bottom lip and she opens her mouth wider, letting me soothe the sting with my tongue.

I think I'm on fire, and I've never been so eager to burn.

The kisses turn less frantic and more indulgent. We slow down, knowing we have all the time in the world. I savor the curve of her mouth and the moan she lets out when I squeeze her tit. She hums when I grip her ass with my free hand, and my fingers sink into more soft skin that's going to haunt my dreams for years to come.

"Fuck, Maven," I say, coming up for air.

"Why did we wait months to do this?" she asks, and she rolls her hips. A strangled sound leaves my mouth, and she laughs softly, pleased with herself. "This is so much more fun than looking."

I dip my chin and kiss her neck. "You're driving me fucking wild in this jersey."

"Does that mean you're going to leave it on when you fuck me?" She runs a hand down my chest and cups me through my jeans. "So I know who I belong to?"

"Jesus." I drop my forehead against hers and squeeze my eyes shut. Her thumb drags up the zipper, and I swear I see fucking stars. "I'm not going to fuck you tonight. I want to tell you that now."

"You're not?" Her voice turns hesitant, and I pull back so I can look at her. "Did you—am I—"

"Don't you dare finish that sentence. You know you're perfect, Maven. I'm not fucking you tonight because when I do, I want to take my time. When you touch me, I'm not going to last very long. It's not you—well, it is you. You're a fucking goddess and—"

Maven cuts me off with another kiss, and I don't remember what I was saying. "I don't care how long it lasts. Take me to your room, Dallas," she murmurs against my mouth.

So I do.

THIRTY-THREE

DALLAS

I ALL BUT kick my bedroom door in.

It hits the wall and I wince, waiting to see if I just woke June up with the loud noise.

"You're definitely not getting your security deposit back," Maven whispers into my neck. She presses a kiss just below my ear, and my grip under her thighs tightens. "You know I love JB, but if we have to stop this before we even start, I'm going to be pissed, Lansfield."

I breathe a sigh of relief when I hear nothing but silence down the hall. "We're clear."

"Thank god."

I shuffle into my room and close the door behind us. I make sure to lock it just in case. The walk to the bed feels like it's miles long, and when I drop Maven on the mattress, I finally get a chance to really look at her.

Her blonde hair is a mess and her cheeks are pink. There's a red mark on the column of her throat, and I grin smugly, thinking about her at the game tomorrow. She'll be standing on the sideline with a souvenir I left behind, and not a single fucking person will know.

"You're a vision, Maven," I say, and I pull my shirt over my head. Hunger flashes in her eyes as her gaze roams down my torso.

She scoots back on the comforter toward the headboard and holds herself up on her elbows. Her feet drag across the sheets, knees bent and thighs wide. "Come here," she says, softer than before.

I crawl across the mattress to her. When I'm close enough to reach, I bend down and cup both of her cheeks. I kiss her again, with my tongue and with my teeth because I'm desperate for more of her.

When I pull away, my attention bounces to the jersey bunched around her chest. I'm torn between wanting her to wear it forever and ripping it off. I move down her body to the sinful black thong I didn't notice before, but now I want to tear it to shreds.

"I've imagined what this would look like," I say, and my throat is dry.

"Have you been thinking about me, Dallas?" she asks with a sly smirk.

"More than I care to admit. Never in my wildest dreams did I think it would be this good. And I haven't even touched you yet."

I position myself between her legs and run my palms up her thighs. They're just as glorious as I thought they would be; creamy white. Silky smooth. Muscular and curvy. Being suffocated while my head is between them is the only way I want to go.

My hand moves up to her thong. I brush my knuckles along the front seam and find it already wet. I give her pussy a light tap before I curl my fingers in the waistband of the lace and snap the elastic against her skin. Maven hisses and drops her head back, and I stare at the spot on her neck that's been distracting me for days.

"Maybe you should hurry up and actually touch me," she says around another soft moan when I massage her thighs with both hands. She grips the sheets next to her hips, and her legs open wider. "Or I might do it myself."

I lean forward. My body covers hers, and I drag my teeth up her throat. "Fucking needy, aren't you?" I whisper in her ear. "Are you wearing anything under my jersey, pretty girl? Take it off and let me see."

She scrambles to pull the jersey over her head, and I sit back on my heels to watch. I'm at a loss for words when I see a matching lace bra, black as night. She's a daydream, and I have to take a deep breath.

"Do you like it?" she asks, playing with one of the straps and with my sanity.

"Yeah," I say, but it's more like a croak, and I adjust myself over my jeans. I'm so fucking hard, and I need some relief. I rub my palm across my length, imagining her chest covered in my cum. "Can you just wear that from now on?"

"If that's what the boss wants. What else do you want?"

All of it.

Everything.

You, in a million fucking ways.

Maven is easily the hottest woman I've been with. She's confident and sexy in a way that tells me she knows exactly what she likes and exactly how she wants things done. She's the one with the power here, and I'm going to do my best to keep up.

"You know it's been a long time since I've been with some-one. I want this to be about you, Mae. Not me. Lay down," I say, and her mouth curves into a beautiful smile.

She gets comfortable on her back, and her hair is scattered across the sheets. One leg is propped up and the other is out straight. I have the urge to take a photo of her. To make it my lock screen so I can see her whenever I want.

I unbutton and unzip my jeans, yanking them down and getting rid of them. I run my palms up her stomach toward her chest. She lets out a shaky breath, and I take her tits in my hands.

"Look at you," I murmur. I pinch both nipples, and she moans. "I want you to tell me what feels best, okay? What you like and what you want more of. Can you do that for me?"

"Yes," she gasps. "I like that. Right there."

"Good. So good." I reach down her body with my right arm and cup her pussy possessively. "And already so wet. Does wearing my jersey turn you on, Maven? Do you like to pretend I'll come home and find you in it, then bend you over the couch and fuck you like you were mine?"

"I've done a lot of things pretending you'd come home and find me."

"Like what?" I ask, and my thumb finds her clit. She cries out, and I move the hand on her chest to cover her mouth. "Shh, honey. If you want me to take care of you, you have to be quiet."

"I'm trying, but it feels so good," she says, and her voice is muffled. "No one has ever taken their time before. They usually just jump right into it."

I freeze, and our eyes meet. "Never?"

She shakes her head, and I lower my hand. "Never."

"No one has made you come just by touching your tits?" I ask, and I pinch her nipple again.

"No," she whispers, and she bites down on her bottom lip.

"And they've never fucked your pretty cunt with their fingers until they had your come all down their hand?"

"No." She squirms and reaches for me, tracing the outline of my dick through my briefs. I jolt forward and almost fall on top of her, the sensation already too much. "Is that what you're going to do, Dallas? Are you going to please me in a way that no one else ever has?"

Jesus fucking Christ.

This woman is unbelievable, so unfiltered and so unabashedly herself, even when she's half naked. I don't stand a chance of walking out of this room alive.

"You've been with boys, Maven, who don't know how to take care of you. But I do." I hook my fingers in her underwear. I pull the lace down her thighs and toss them away. "I've read your books. I've watched you get off. I know exactly what you like."

"Prove it," she says, like she thinks I won't, and the dare makes me grin.

"Fucking brat." I lie on my stomach and use my thumbs to spread her open. She's already so wet, and I can feel myself leaking in my briefs. "I need to find a way to shut you up." I drag one finger through her, and she moans so loudly her whole body raises off the bed. "That'll do it, won't it? I'm going to tease you like you've been teasing me for fucking months."

I lift her legs so her knees are bent and I circle her clit in the slow circle I know she likes. It's torturous to take my time and not just sink into her, but I see the way she's getting wetter. With my left thumb still moving in slow motion, I slide my right pointer finger inside her to my knuckle and match her moan.

"*Fuck.* You're so goddamn tight."

"Told you," she whines. "You're not going to fit."

"I'm going to fit. I'm just going to have to get you ready so you can take every inch." I curl my finger, like I'm beckoning her toward me, and she gasps. "There?"

"*Yes.* Don't stop, Dallas."

"Going to add a second finger, okay?"

"You better."

I smile and kiss the inside of her thigh, adding my middle finger with a firm push. My laughter dies when I feel her stretch around me. "Goddamn, pretty girl. If this is how good you feel on my fingers, what is it going to feel like when my cock is inside you?"

"Heaven." Maven's hand tips my chin to look up at her. Her whole body is flushed and her eyes are glazed over, but she's never been more beautiful. "It's going to feel like heaven."

"Can I taste you? Please?"

"God, yeah." She flops back down and threads her fingers through my hair. "Show me how badly you want me."

Heat burns through me, and I thrust into the mattress with her command. There's no way I get through this without finishing in my briefs, a fate I've already sealed for myself, but I don't give a shit. Not when her legs spread wider. Not when she knocks my hand out of the way and replaces it with her own as she holds herself open for me.

I scoot forward and lick up her entrance. A choked noise that sounds like a delighted sob escapes her. Determined, I hook my arm around her thigh and drag her closer, my nose pressed against her. I bury my tongue inside her pussy and fucking feast.

I've done this once or twice, but it's never been like *this*.

Never with moans and her pushing my tongue deeper inside her like she'd die without it.

Never with my hips lifting and fucking the mattress, pretending like I'm fucking her each time my cock grinds against the sheets.

Never with sweat on my forehead and my fingers bruising her skin.

"*Yes*," she hisses. "That's good, Dallas. So good. You like eating pussy, don't you? You're not such a nice guy after all."

Arousal blazes through me. "Only your pussy, Maven," I say. I circle her clit with my tongue and press three fingers inside her. My free hand rubs her stomach in soothing circles when she cries out. "And you want to talk about not being nice? Look at *you*. The sunshine girl likes to be bad, doesn't she?"

"Close," she says through a strained breath when I curl all three of my fingers. She reaches out and wraps her hand around my length. The cotton of my briefs rubs against me, and I groan at her touch. "So close. Are you going to come with me?"

"Yeah, honey. I'm going to come with you," I say low in her ear, and she tightens around me. "There you go. You're doing so well, Maven. Let me see how gorgeous you are when you come."

Maven lets out a moan I steal for myself. Her body shakes and her breathing turns ragged and uneven. I feel her chest heave as I slow my fingers and work her through the high until she goes limp and pliant under me.

"That—I—" she tries to say, and she finishes with a sigh. "Yes."

I pull my fingers out of her and massage her thighs, calming her down. "Good?"

"The best." She gives me a tired, satisfied smile. "Did you—?"

"Almost. But not yet." I move back down her body. "Let me clean you up first."

"Are we going to—*oh,*" Maven whispers when I lick her again. "Dallas. I can't."

"You sure about that?" I ask from between her legs. "Come on, Mae. We both know you're not a quitter."

I move slower. I'm more thorough. I find the rhythm she likes best with my tongue. I mimic exactly what I did with my fingers, and I see her body giving in again.

"Circle my clit," she says. "I like that—*yes. Fuck, Dallas.* Right there."

I love that she's not afraid to tell me what she wants. I love that she's greedy about it.

"On my tongue this time," I say, and I shove one hand down my briefs. I grip myself, jerking up and down as her breathing gets harder. "Let me imagine what it's going to feel like on my cock."

Maven moans, and a second orgasm races through her. She rides my tongue like it's her own personal toy. She reaches out and tugs on my necklace, and that's what does me in.

I gasp and squeeze my eyes shut. I thrust into my palm and use her thigh to steady myself. Warm liquid covers my hand, and I groan, months of tension finally leaving my body.

Neither one of us says anything for a handful of minutes, and when I lift my chin, she's smiling at me.

"Dallas," she says, and I move for her.

I wipe my hand on my jersey, not caring about the mess. I kiss her roughly and sigh when she wraps her arms around me and pulls me close.

"You okay?" I ask against her mouth, and she nods.

"Nothing about you could ever be considered just okay, and that includes the aftermath of what you did to me. I'm on top of the world."

I blush and kiss her neck. "Such an ego inflater."

"Can I stay in here with you tonight?" Maven asks.

The responsible thing to do would be to head back to the hotel. After lying about a headache, I know someone's going to be checking on me at the crack of dawn, but I don't want to leave her. Not when she looks up at me with hopeful eyes.

"You can stay in here every night," I say. "I do need to get up early and try to sneak back into the hotel before our team breakfast, but I won't leave without saying goodbye."

"Okay." She runs her hand down my back and settles her palm between my shoulders. "You're my favorite person in the world. Did you know that?"

"I had a feeling. Only because you're mine, too."

"Shower then bed?"

"Good idea. I should try to get some sleep. With you next to me, though, I doubt that'll happen."

"I'll behave. You have a big game tomorrow, and I don't want to be the reason you lose."

I laugh. "If we win, though, we're going to have to do that before every game. I might have found my new favorite meal."

Maven grins and drags me to the bathroom. Something in me pulls tight at the intimacy of the moment, and I start to wonder if this could be a forever kind of thing.

THIRTY-FOUR

MAVEN

THE FIRST HINTS of sunrise are only just beginning to sneak through the curtains when I open my eyes. I see the muted grays and dull whites, and I bury my face into the warm mass beside me, not ready to start the day.

"Morning," Dallas says, and his voice is rusty with exhaustion.

"Already?" I groan, and I huff out a sigh against his chest.

"That's how the calendar works." He drops a kiss to my forehead and wraps his arms around my waist. "How'd you sleep?"

"Did we even sleep? It feels like I just closed my eyes," I grumble, and untangle myself from the mess of limbs and wrinkled sheets. "What time is it?"

"Too early, but I need to start getting ready. The team breakfast is at eight, and I can't have anyone finding out I didn't sleep at the hotel. You can go back to sleep, though. June should sleep for a while."

"What happens if you don't sleep in the hotel? Does the principal put you in detention?"

His laugh is deep and rumbly, and he squeezes me tight. "No, but Shawn could bench me. I haven't missed a game since I entered the league, and I'd like to keep that streak going."

"Such a rule follower. Is there any streak or record you don't have?" I ask, and push up on my elbow.

My heart lodges itself in my throat when I look down at him, and I have to swallow down the sensation that settles in my chest when his gaze meets mine. Dallas was sexy last night with his rough words and heated eyes. A man of desire and need finally taking what he wants.

He's terribly beautiful in the light of day, with soft edges and gentle touches. Wild, messy hair and a crease on his cheek from his pillow. His neck is covered in the pink marks I left behind after our shower last night, and I want to connect them all to see what I could draw.

His eyes are glassy, a little fogged over, as if he's stuck in a trance or a haze, but he stares at me. He stares at me like I'm something precious. Like I'm the most important thing in the world.

"Why are you looking at me like that?" he asks. He reaches up and tucks a piece of hair behind my ear, and his fingers dance across my jaw, in no hurry to pull away. It's easy, tender affection. The kind that makes butterflies flutter in your stomach and your cheeks hurt from smiling so much. "Are you okay?"

"Yeah." I nod, and I've never been so sure of something in my life. "I'm perfect."

His smile matches mine, a slow and indulgent thing full of teeth and crinkled eyes. It warms me, and when he leans over and kisses me, I sigh. It's gentler than I expect it to be, but I guess that's what happens when you quell that frantic, urgent need for someone after wanting them for so long—you feel like you finally have all the time in the world.

"I really wish I didn't have to leave." He rests his forehead against mine, and now that he's closer, I can see the flecks of gold around his irises. Light swatches of color that make the room infinitely brighter. "I could stay in bed with you all day."

"We have tonight," I say, and I drag my thumb across his swollen bottom lip. I might have bitten it too hard when we tumbled back into bed. "And tomorrow. And the day after that. But I know this isn't really your thing, so if it was just last night, well, it was fun."

"Fun?" he repeats slowly, and his eyebrows pull together. "What do you mean *my thing*?"

"This." I gesture between us and the mess we've made. Half the pillows are missing, and the comforter disappeared hours ago. "Dating. Hooking up. I don't want you to feel obligated to act a certain way just because you had your head between my legs."

His mouth twitches. "I see. Give me a second."

"Where are you going?" I ask, and the mattress sinks as he hops off the bed. He doesn't bother with clothes, and I don't know if I should frown at how mysterious he's being or admire his ass as he walks away. "Oh, god, is this the equivalent of dining and dashing? You ate me out and now you're leaving before things get awkward?"

"Your unfilteredness is one of my favorite things about you," he says, and he disappears into the walk-in closet.

"What else is on that list?"

Dallas comes back into the bedroom a minute later, and there's a stack of papers clutched tightly to his chest. "Take a look and find out."

"What are those?"

"You'll see," he says, and he drops the pile in my lap.

I pull the twine holding them all together and postcards

scatter everywhere. I pick up the first one and run my fingers over the corners, studying it like it might hold some sort of clue as to what's going on.

It's from California, a vintage style design with tall palm trees and a bear on the front. I turn it over and see Dallas's handwriting on the back.

> M-
>
> I always get June a postcard from every away game.
> It makes being away from home a little easier, and I thought I'd start the tradition with you, too.
> It's silly, but I have this idea that one day when she's older, we'll pull them out of a shoebox and I can tell her about the cities I got to see and the people I got to meet.
> We're really lucky to have you in our lives, and I hope you stick around for a long time.
> -D

"California. This is from your first road game," I whisper.

Dallas nods and rejoins me on the bed. He scoops me into his arms with ease and maneuvers our positions until he's leaning against the headboard and I'm leaning against him. Settled, he kisses my cheek and drops his chin to my shoulder.

"Read the next one," he says.

My hands shake as I turn it over. It's another letter to me, longer than the first, and his handwriting is smaller so he can get in all the words he wants to say.

> M-

I'm not sure I'll ever give these to you. If I do, there's something I want you to know.

You've only been with us for a month, and already, I can see the impact you're having on June.

She's always been happy and outgoing, but she's different when you're around. She's braver and more willing to try new things. I know that's because she feels safe with you.

You two sing loudly. You play in the fountain at the park. You skin your knees and you come home with sunburn on your shoulders. Maybe I should be mad at you for living a little dangerously, but then I see the smile on June's face—on your face too—and I know I could never be mad at you. Not for a single second.

JB has needed someone like you in her life. Someone vivacious and bold. Carefree, but also able to discipline and be firm when needed. I heard you scold her the other day when she ran into a kid on the playground and didn't apologize. You told her why what she did was wrong, but you soothed her after.

That's good parenting.

Good nannying, I guess I should say.

I know you say you don't have a clue what you're doing (I'll admit you're fucking terrible in the kitchen, but god, it's cute to watch you try), but you're wrong, Maven.

You're doing so well, and I'm so grateful for you.

-D

I'm greedy for the next one, and my laugh bursts out of me when I read it.

> M-
> I have a bone to pick with you.
> Those goddamn jean shorts you wear around the house? They're the bane of my fucking existence.
> They're entirely too tight, and they make your ass look good.
> Too fucking good.
> Can't you walk around in a sack or something? My productivity has gone out the window.
> (Don't, though. I dream about your thighs, and I'd be sad if I didn't get to see them again.)
> -D
> p.s. (addendum after our FaceTime call, scribbled frantically in the airport): you're going to be the death of me, woman. I think it's time to invest in the sex toy market and buy you a thousand vibrators.

I reach for the final one, and it's the shortest of the bunch.

> M-
> I miss you.
> _Fuck_, I miss you.
> -D

"Why?" I ask, and the question hangs heavy between us.

"I've always said I don't date because I'm focused on football. I don't want any distractions or things that will interfere with my job. But lately, I realize that's not true—you're the biggest distraction of all and I'm having the best season of my career. I think I've been using excuses because I just hadn't found the right thing yet. Because when I look at you, Maven, I'm alive for the first time in years. I feel like I was made for you, and I feel like you were made for me too. I'm all in on this. On you."

A crack goes straight down my chest. It's like when lightning strikes a tree, a quick burst of light then a burning flame. I turn to face him, and his face is brighter. Assured and confident. In a world of what ifs and endless possibilities, he and I are a definite yes.

It's not an *I love you*—it's too soon for that—but in a way, it's better. *Deeper.* A level of admiration I've never had before that goes far beyond those three words.

"I *was* made for you," I say. I bring my fingers to his neck and touch the necklace pressed against his throat. I move to his chest and settle my hand over his heart. "And I'd like to stay here for a long time."

"As long as you'd like, sunshine."

Our gazes lock and hold, a beat of tranquil silence before we both attack.

I'm not sure who kisses who first, just that we're both there, meeting halfway. A laugh falls out of us at the same time. It gets scooped up and carried away when I tackle him and we both fall backward, a mess of grins and wandering hands.

"How long until you need to leave?" I ask into the crook of his neck, and he lets out a stuttered exhale.

"I should've left ten minutes ago, but I'm past caring," Dallas says, and I hum in firm agreement.

"Can I touch you? Can I taste you?"

He stills, and his throat bobs with a slow swallow. I didn't get a chance to last night—he wouldn't let me. It was a pride thing, not an unwillingness thing, he told me bashfully, but now his nod is unyielding. Aggressive and definite, and I pull away to look at him.

"Yeah, Mae," he says from low in his throat. "You can touch me."

"What do you like?" I ask, and I climb off of him.

He props himself up on the single pillow that's left, one arm behind his head and the other sitting low on his stomach. "I—" he dips his chin and shudders out a breath. "Anything. Anything you do will feel good."

"I want you to feel better than good, Dallas."

I sit on my knees and lean forward, taking the head of his cock in my mouth. His groan is strangled, and he reaches out, fingers curling in my hair. I think he's afraid I might disappear.

I wrap my fingers around his length and stroke him up and down. He's the biggest I've ever had, thick and heavy in my hand. It takes me a second to get used to his size, but when I do, his sigh is etched with pleasure. He lifts his hips a fraction of an inch off the bed, meeting my hand and asking for more.

Dallas is always so controlled—so put together and so full of self-restraint on the field and off. Seeing him like this—greedy, selfish and desperate—might be my favorite side of him.

"Maven," he croaks, and even in the heat of the moment it's laced with reverence.

I take him back into my mouth, fully this time, and I work his cock as deep as I can. My eyes prick with tears and I breathe out of my nose, but I smile victoriously when I reach the base of his shaft.

"Christ. *Fuck*. I don't—how are you—god, okay. I'm—"

His words die and his grip on my hair tightens when I add my hand, and gently drag my teeth halfway up his length. A string of expletives follow when I squeeze then twist my wrist.

"That. Keep doing that. Please," he begs.

I squeeze my thighs together, turned on by his enthusiastic

reactions. I sneak a glance and find him watching me, his mouth popped open and awe burning in his eyes.

Dallas pulls his arm out from behind his head and reaches for me, nudging my knees apart and slipping his hand between my legs. "You like this, don't you, pretty girl?" he asks, and slides a finger inside me. I moan against his cock, and his chuckle is anything but teasing. "Where do you want me to come, Maven? Down your throat? On your tits? Tell me, because you're driving me out of my fucking mind, and I can't last much longer."

I pop him out of my mouth and continue to stroke him. I run my fingers through the pre-cum leaking from his slit and bring them to my mouth, savoring the saltiness. "My tits," I say, and before I can explain myself, Dallas is flipping us around.

I land on my back and he kneels over me, his hand giving himself quick jerks.

His entire body is flushed, a deep scarlet that looks like he should be lounging under a sunset. His movements are rough, sloppy, and when I rest my hand on his thigh, over his tattoo, and reach for his balls, he loses it.

Warmth covers me from my stomach to my neck, and Dallas falls forward, bracing himself on the headboard. His breathing comes out in choked breaths, and I rub his leg, helping him calm down.

"Fuck," he says. A bead of sweat rolls down his stomach, and I sit up and lick it off. "You're perfect. Can I keep you?"

"That's the orgasm talking. I hope my mouth is better than your hand."

"Significantly." He drops his head back and stares at the ceiling. "I really fucking hope we win today."

"You're thinking about football right now?" I ask, and his lips curve into a grin. "I guess I need to step my game up."

"I'm thinking about football, because if we win, we're doing that every fucking Sunday morning. And it would be a shame to waste such talent."

Later, when Dallas kicks a sixty-seven yard field goal that goes down as a new NFL record, he points to me over a sea of people and makes a heart with his hands, another secret only we share.

THIRTY-FIVE

MAVEN

THE APARTMENT IS SUSPICIOUSLY quiet when I get home on Wednesday night.

June doesn't run to the door to greet me like she normally does. All the lights are off. I stand in the foyer, listening for any signs of life, and find none.

"Dallas?" I call out. I kick off my boots by the door and worry rushes through me. "JB?"

"Kitchen," he answers, and the pressure in my chest releases half a degree.

I walk down the hallway carefully, unsure of what I'm going to find. I nearly jump out of my skin when he comes around the corner and startles me.

"Dammit," I say. "What the hell is with you and trying to scare me?"

"Sorry." Dallas grins and drops a kiss to my forehead. "June is at Maverick's for the night, and I'm making us dinner."

"Did I miss a memo?" I follow him into the kitchen and slide onto one of the barstools. It smells delicious in here and I inhale, trying to figure out what he's making. "Was I supposed to be here earlier? Do you have somewhere to be?"

"Nope. He volunteered to keep her at his place tonight so we could be alone. I've been busy since Sunday with all the media shit, and I know you've been watching her all day, every day, without any of my help. This is my way to thank you."

"Breaking the NFL record for longest field goal will do that to you. This is sweet, Dallas, but you don't have to thank me for doing my job. For doing something I want to do," I say, and he walks around the island to give me a drink.

Dallas wraps his arms around me and rests his chin on the top of my head. I sigh into his chest and my body relaxes under his touch.

"I know I don't have to thank you," he says. "But I want to."

I bury my face in his shirt and smile. The cotton smells like garlic and onions and it's all so familiar. So easy, like we've been doing this for months. "You know I love June, but I'm excited to be alone with you."

He pulls away and cups my cheeks. A drop of tomato sauce hangs in the corner of his mouth, and I reach up and wipe it away with my thumb. "Me, too."

"What are you making?"

"Spaghetti. Your favorite." His grin is crooked and his dimples pop, sharp stars on sharp cheeks. "And some garlic bread, too."

"Now you're just spoiling me. Is there anything I can do to help?" I ask.

"Nope." Dallas nods toward the drink in front of me. "Tequila sunrise. I hope it tastes okay."

I take a sip and it's citrusy on my tongue. I lick my lips and hum. "Delicious. He's an NFL record holder, folks, but he's also a bartender."

Dallas laughs and moves back to the stove. He lifts the boiling pot of water and dumps it in the colander in the sink. I like watching the ease of his movements. The strain of his biceps as he does mundane things like grabbing plates from the cabinet and grating parmesan cheese. There's something settling in his confidence, and I smile when he slides the food my way.

"What?" he asks, and he sits beside me. He twirls the pasta around on his fork with his right hand and rests his left hand on my thigh. "Why are you looking at me like that?"

"Because you're nice to look at." I moan around a piece of garlic bread. "I think your cooking might be my favorite thing about you."

"Didn't think I'd ever be jealous of bread, but I haven't gotten you to make that sound."

"The night is young, Lansfield."

We eat while we talk about their Monday night game next week. We argue over Halloween costumes for twenty minutes before Dallas reluctantly gives in to my idea. He scoots my stool closer to him and I hook my foot around his. When we drop our empty plates in the sink, my stomach is full and my heart is happy.

"You wash and I'll put them in the dishwasher?" he asks, and his hip nudges mine.

"You got it, boss."

"Can you make sure you actually rinse all the food off? Not a half-assed job that leaves sauce everywhere?"

"Wow. Three minutes ago you were talking about how wonderful I am, and now *this*? It's bullshit." I laugh when he pokes my side, and I grab the faucet to defend myself. "Wash them yourself."

I turn on the sink and spray him, drenching his hair and upper body. A drop of water rolls down his cheek and he blinks at me, breaking into a slow grin.

"You fucked up, Maven," he says with sparkling eyes.

"I didn't mean to," I say, and I try to dart away.

Dallas is faster, with longer arms and quicker reflexes. He grabs me and tosses me over his shoulder. I squeal as he leads us down the hall.

"Like I'm going to believe that," he laughs, and his wet shirt soaks the front of my jeans. "You should've thought about the consequences."

"Why?" I whisper in his ear. "I like being bad."

He almost trips over his feet, and his hand moves from my ankle to my thigh. "You're a menace."

"What about the plates?" I tease, and he opens the door to his bedroom. "Washing dishes is one of your favorite pastimes."

"I think fucking you into the mattress might edge it out, so I'd like to give that a shot."

Dallas drops me on his bed. I bounce twice and look up at him, watching in amazement as he peels off his shirt. He tosses it aside and crawls onto the sheets, his gaze never leaving mine.

"Hi," I say, and I trace the muscles on his shoulders.

"Hey." He reaches for the hem of my shirt and looks at me. "Can I?"

"You've had your tongue inside of me, Dallas. Yes, you can take off my shirt."

"Just wanted to be sure," he mumbles, and he tugs the clothing over my head. "Because I'm still not sure what I did in life to deserve this with you."

I tuck those words away for later. There's a time to fawn over them, to feel a giddy swoop in my belly when I think about his gentle soul, but it's not right now. Not when his thick length strains against the denim of his jeans and he's looking at me like a predator looks at their prey: like he wants to consume me.

I pop open the button of his pants and he pulls them off, leaving him in black briefs. I smile at the edges of his tattoo peeking out and he guides me onto the pillows with a soft push.

He undresses me, tugging my jeans down my thighs and

tossing them aside. When I'm lying under him in nothing but my bra and underwear, he hums.

"You really are the hottest thing I've ever seen," Dallas says. He leans forward and takes my breast in his mouth, over the fabric of my bra, and I moan. "You drive me out of my fucking mind."

"Yeah, well—" I gasp when he bites my nipple. The sharp sting of his teeth is just enough to feel good. "Look who's talking."

"Stop distracting me." He moves to the other side of my chest and sucks that breast, too. The cotton of my bra clings to my skin, sinfully wet from his mouth. "Going to get you off first."

"No objections from me."

I reach out and run my palm up his thigh, needing to touch him. I drag my thumb down the front of his briefs where he's already hard. Before I can go any further, his fingers curl around my wrist and he brings my arms over my head.

"Don't. If you do that, I'm not going to be able to fuck you, Maven, and I think I might die if I don't get to sink into your tight pussy. Hold onto the headboard, honey. Let me make you come."

"If that's what the boss wants," I say, and my eyes roll to the back of my head when he licks my neck.

He moves down my body, kissing across my chest then my stomach. He shoves my legs apart and positions himself between my thighs. There's nothing considerate or sweet about him right now, and I love that he loses his mind around me.

Dallas hooks his thumbs in the waistband of my underwear and shimmies them down, humming his approval when I lay in front of him naked from the waist down. His touch dances up my thigh, pressing into the muscles and moving his hand further and further until he's inches away from where I need him the most. He's teasing me, making me wait, and I hate him a little bit for it.

I lift my hips and he chuckles, his eyes cutting away from my legs to my face.

"Impatient." His thumb circles my clit, and I feel like I've been electrified. My entire body tingles with sensations when he drags his thumb through my slick arousal and parts me. "So fucking wet. So fucking pretty."

The compliments make me blush, and I squirm on the sheets. "Dallas."

"Tell me what you want."

"You, inside me."

He presses a single finger in me, giving me what I want, and I feel a slow ripple of ecstasy everywhere. "So fucking tight too."

My knees fall open and I welcome him in. His second finger is better than the first and his third is the best yet. Just when I'm about to ask him for more, he sucks on my clit, and I think I go to heaven.

"Fuck," I call out, and I feel myself already teetering close to the edge. "Dallas."

"I love when you scream my name like that. Like I'm the best fucking thing you've ever had," he says, and his words vibrates against me.

He is, I think. *The best I'll ever have.*

He curls his fingers and my hand shoots forward. I press his face into me as I grind into him, seeking release. His chuckle is deep, and when he bites the soft flesh of my thigh, I couldn't care less about how desperate I look.

"You gonna come for me, pretty girl?"

His words are like magic. Pressure builds at the base of my spine and my vision goes hazy. There's nothing but bliss on the horizon.

"There you go. Ride my face, honey, and take what you need."

The *honey* does me in, because it's so *him*.

I squeeze my eyes shut as white-hot pleasure rips through me. It's overwhelming and mind-numbing, and instead of letting me fall down from the high alone, Dallas works me through it, whispering about how good I am until I'm a mindless heap on his bed.

I take a deep breath as I come back to earth. "You're something else," I murmur, and I turn my head to look at him.

Dallas strokes himself over his briefs. His chest is red and his eyes are dark and hooded. He wipes his mouth with the back of his hand, and I see the wetness I left behind.

"Look who's talking. If I had known you tasted this sweet, I would've knocked down your door months ago," he says. "That first day you were here, when you were wearing that pretty little dress and spun around the balcony—I would've taken you then."

A flash of heat burns through me as I imagine us out there, in a place anyone could see.

"No, you wouldn't have," I say, and I push up on my elbow. I unclasp my bra and watch his pupils go wide. "You're too good to have done that."

Dallas's smile is wicked, and he pulls off his briefs. Before I can blink, he lifts me and spins us. He ends up on his back and I end up on his lap, straddling him. His hard cock presses into my ass, and I wiggle my hips, eager for more of him.

"I'm done being good, Maven. I've been dreaming about you on top of me for days, so here's what we're going to do. You're going to sit up and spread your legs nice and wide. Then I'm going to fuck you, and you're going to watch while you take every inch of my cock."

THIRTY-SIX

DALLAS

I'M a different man when Maven is around.

It's like I have this urgent need to fucking possess her. To stake my claim so no one else can ever have her. And when she's inches away from my dick with a body that would make even the most religious man sin, I'm fucking *feral*.

Maven stares down at me with wide, blue eyes, and she looks every bit like a queen sitting on a throne. I'd build one for her, if she asked. Her back arches and she rolls her hips again, teasing me. Taunting me. *Using* me. The circular motion has her grinding into my abdomen muscles, and it's the sexiest thing I've ever seen.

I hold onto her thighs and blow out a breath. My last bit of intelligence is hanging on by a thread, and I need to say the smart things before I turn into a pile of fucking rocks.

"Condoms," I blurt out, and a smile curves on her lips. "There are condoms in the bedside table. Grab a dozen of them. There's no way one is going to be enough."

"A dozen? That sure is ambitious."

"Have you seen your tits? Or your goddamn thighs?"

Maven laughs, a soft swoop of air that nestles its way next

to my heart. I really would do anything to hear that sound again. She leans forward and brings her mouth close to my ear, and I'm practically panting as I wait to hear what she has to say.

"I want to feel you, Dallas," she whispers, and my throat goes dry. There are spots in my vision, and a strangled noise leaves my chest. "I'm on birth control, and I take it every day. I'm sure you're hesitant because of your past, but I want you to know, if you ever want to give someone that trust again, I'd like for it to be me."

There's such care and consideration in her words, and a fire blazes through me when I realize she's letting me be the one to decide how this goes. I've been in this position before and I know there are consequences from heat of the moment decisions. One of them is four years old and sleeps down the hall from me.

But when I think about what could happen this time around, there isn't any fear. Not even a little bit. I think about worst-case scenarios, and none of them seem like a worst-case at all.

Another kid who's as incredible as my daughter?

A family with Maven?

That sounds like the fucking dream.

"I trust you," I say. I reach up and cup her cheek, wanting her to hear the sincerity in my voice. "I trust you so much, Maven. But are you sure you want to be reckless with me?"

"All I want to do is be reckless with you, Dallas."

"I don't think I've ever been smart around you. Not for a single second." My thumb presses just below her hip bone, and I massage the soft skin there. "I'm clear on all tests."

"Me, too. I haven't been with anyone since I started working for you. Long before that too."

"Okay." I lick my lips, knowing she really was mine that very first day. "Just us."

My last bit of self-control snaps when she runs her hands up my stomach and settles them over my heart.

I lift her so she's hovering over me. I rub my cock against her clit and coat my length in her arousal. When her steady breathing turns to ragged pants that tell me she's ready for more, I guide her onto me.

We hiss in unison when the tip of my cock pushes inside her entrance. Maven grips my shoulders and her nails dig into my skin, leaving half-moon marks behind. I wish she'd leave them on my neck, too, so I could show them off at practice tomorrow. So I could boast a little bit and gloat that I'm the one who got the girl.

It's excruciating to go so slow, to take my time and move inch by inch, but I have to. I *have* to, because otherwise this will be over too soon, and I'd savor it forever, if I could.

"There you go," I slur, and I feel drunk. I'm barely two inches inside of her, and I'm already mindless. "That's good, Maven."

"Dallas," she begs, and my name has no right sounding so filthy coming from her mouth.

"I know. I know, baby. *Fuck.*"

"I don't think—it's too much—I—"

I cut her off with a kiss and lift my hips, nearly bottoming out in her. "You can. We're going to make it fit. You know why, pretty girl?"

"Why?" she whispers, and her eyes meet mine. She looks just as wrecked as I feel, and I swear my dick twitches inside of her at the sight. "Why, Dallas?"

"Because you're mine, Maven. Now sit down, honey, and take what's yours."

She lifts onto her knees. Her pussy glides up my dick like she's about to climb off of me, but then she spreads her legs a little wider. She sinks down, all the way down, and she fucking takes me just like I asked.

I'm not sure I'm even breathing. I think my heart stops and then jolts back to life when she bends from her hips and drags her tongue up my chest.

"So tight," I manage to get out. "So wet. And all for me."

"Look." Maven curls her fingers around my chin and strokes my jaw. I melt under her touch. "Look at us together."

I follow her gaze, and I don't know where to stare first.

I watch her pussy work me up and down and my tongue almost falls out of my mouth when I see her drenched fucking thighs. My eyes dart to her chest, to her tits bouncing as she rides me. I find the sheen of sweat on her neck, and I want to lick it away.

I rest one hand on the small of her back, just above the curve of her ass. Holding her steady, I sit up and capture her nipple in my mouth, desperate to taste her.

"Am I doing okay?" I ask, and my teeth scrape over the pointed peak.

"You're doing so well, Dallas," she whispers. "You're so good. No one fucks me like you do."

That unlocks some animalistic side of me I didn't know I had.

I hate everyone who came before me and I'm going to make sure there's no one after me. I want to be the best. The only.

"Can we switch positions? I want to fuck you from behind."

There's a gleam in Maven's eye as she slows down. As her movements turn lazy, unhurried and indulgent. She runs her hands up her body. Her palms cup her tits, and I'm close to asking if I could watch her do that for an hour or two.

"I'd like that," she says.

I pull out of her and groan at the loss of contact. She stretches out across the sheets, positioning herself on her hands and knees and lifting her ass in the air like a fucking offering. Like I could take that too, if I wanted.

"Here?" I ask, and my fingers dance down her spine. I brush across her ass cheeks, and she moans. "Has anyone ever taken you here, Maven?"

"No. But you can."

Fuck.

A hundred new images pop up in my brain, and I grip my dick. The jerky strokes I give myself do nothing to ease the ache, and I'm so hard I think I could get off just by staring at the curve of her backside.

"Next time," I rasp. I massage the valley between her shoulder blades then ease her down until her chest is flush against the mattress. "Next time, I get to see what all your holes feel like."

It's easier to slide inside her this time. The angle lets me get deeper, and her body has already warmed up to me. Her ass bounces when I thrust into her, unrelenting, and her soft groans only encourage me to move faster and harder.

It's heaven. Fucking heaven.

When I drive into her and hit the spot she likes best, she says my name like a prayer. Like she'd scream it, if I asked her to.

"Perfect," she muses. "Such a good boy for me."

Christ. That's the hottest thing anyone has ever said to me.

"I want you to come." I reach between her legs and tap her swollen pussy, chuckling when she squirms against my fingers and grinds against my cock. "How do I get you there?"

"Harder. A little harder," she whispers, and it sounds like she's barely hanging on to her sanity too. "You're not going to break me, Dallas. Fuck me like you mean it. Please."

"Fucking filthy and desperate for my cock." I slam into her with full force and she cries out. "Like this?" I thrust again, and when she clenches around me, I circle her clit in the pattern she likes. "There you go. Let me feel you, Maven."

She moans my name and comes apart piece by piece. With

every jerk of my hips, she falls a little more until she tumbles over the edge completely. I feel the moment she stops fighting it, when she welcomes it, and I know I'm close too.

"Come in me, Dallas," she says, and her eyes meet mine over her shoulder. Satisfied. Beautiful. *Mine.* "Make me yours."

With her last bit of energy, she meets me thrust for thrust, and seconds later, I detonate.

My limbs give out and I spill inside her. I'm hot all over, and it feels like I'm burning alive. I grip the base of my cock, panting as she takes every drop from me. I collapse onto her and an exhale shakes my body.

"You ruined me, woman," I say.

Maven wiggles out from under me and rolls onto her back. She stares up at me, and that burning sensation moves to my chest. "Should I apologize?"

"Don't you dare."

"Was it worth the long hiatus?"

"And then some." I lie next to her and drape my arm over her stomach. "Thank you."

She wrinkles her nose and touches my necklace, playing with the gold chain. "For what?"

"Being gentle with me."

"I'm not sure there was anything gentle about what we just did. I think I heard a screw pop loose on your bed frame."

I laugh and tug her across the sheets until she's pressed against me. I bury my face in her hair and sigh happily. "I don't just mean the sex."

"I know." She rubs her hand up my arm and she kisses my cheek. "Thank you for trying with me. Thank you for trusting me."

"There's no one else I'd rather try with."

We're quiet for a minute, catching our breaths and letting our heart rate slow down. I think I drift off to sleep, but then

Maven runs her hand through my hair, and my eyes flutter open.

"I miss June," she says softly. "Do you think we should tell her about us?"

"I'm not sure. It's not like she's meeting you for the first time; you're a constant in her life. But I think it's probably for the best to keep this between us for now. I don't want to put any more risks on the table, including a kid who doesn't know what a secret is." I pause and stroke my thumb down her throat. "I hate that we have to hide this. If your job wasn't on the line, we'd be out in the open. I'd show you off to the world and let everyone know you're mine. You know that, right?"

"I know." Maven smiles. "But sneaking around is going to be fun, and I'm glad I get you all to myself."

"You never struck me as the selfish type, Mae."

"I never was. Then you came along."

Later that night, long after rounds two and three and while the rest of the world sleeps, I feel the change.

I have nothing to base it off of. No experience to measure it against. But when I hold Maven in my arms as she drifts off to sleep, it feels a lot like those books she reads.

Like the start of falling in love.

THIRTY-SEVEN
MAVEN

"I DON'T WANT to be a snowman."

"At least you're not a fucking reindeer. I have *hooves*."

"It makes sense that I'm a carrot. Out of all of us, I definitely have the biggest—"

"Boys." I snap my fingers, and three heads turn and glance at me. "Are you all *really* still complaining about the costumes your daughter and goddaughter picked out?"

"No, but—"

I put my hands on my hips and give them a disappointed look. "June has been so excited for tonight, so you know what we're going to do? We're going to wear the outfits. We're going to smile and take pictures with all the kids who want one, and when June asks if you had fun you're going to answer with a resounding *yes*. Do I make myself clear?"

Reid, Maverick and Dallas hang their heads. "Yes, Maven," they say in unison, and I smile.

"Great. We're leaving in ten minutes, so put on your happy faces." My attention bounces to Dallas, and I bite back a laugh. "Your tail is messed up, Dal. It's off center."

"Because this onesie was made for people who are under five

feet. It's so tight, you can practically see my dick," he says, and he adjusts the gray fabric. "If I get arrested for indecent exposure, y'all are paying my bail."

"Bold of you to assume your dick is big enough for people to see," I say. I toss my hair over my shoulder and leave the living room and Maverick and Reid's cackling laughter behind. "Might want to bring a magnifying glass with you. It'll help."

I push the door to June's room open, and I lean against the wall. She's fixing her pigtails, and she lights up when she sees me.

"Mae Mae!" She darts over with her purple cape trailing behind her, and she motions for me to pick her up. "Look at the new crown Daddy got me."

"Hi, Princess June." I lift her and spin her around. "Your new crown is so pretty. I love the jewels. Are you ready for some candy?"

"I want a Kit Kat," June declares. "And a Snickers."

"What about some Reese's?" I ask. "Those are my favorite."

"No." She wrinkles her nose. "I don't want peanut butter."

"You love peanut butter, silly." I grab her candy bucket off her small desk and flip off the light. "You stole my PB&J sandwich the other day."

"No, I didn't," she giggles, and I tickle her sides.

"Are you fibbing, JB? Tell me the truth, or everyone will turn to ice!"

"I stole it, I stole it!" She covers her face, but she peeks at me through her tiny fingers. "It was yummy."

"I'm glad at least one of us got to enjoy it. Are you ready to see Daddy's costume?"

"He's a reindeer! Like Rudolph."

"Exactly like Rudolph, June Bug, and he's the happiest reindeer in all the land. In fact, he told me he'd like to be a reindeer forever. What do you think? Should we say a couple spells and let him keep his tail?"

"No! Not forever."

"Okay, okay. We'll let him stay Daddy."

I bounce her on my hip as we walk down the hall, and I can't believe how big she's getting. She's almost a half inch taller from when I met her, and I can tell she inherited her dad's height and long legs.

"Mae Mae." June tugs on my sleeve, and she points into the living room. "Look."

I stop in the entryway and almost keel over with laughter. All three guys are on the floor, in positions as if they really were the characters they're dressed as. Dallas is on his hands and knees. Reid is sitting on his ass, and Maverick lies on his back looking so realistic, I have to do a double take.

"Boys. Your princess is here," I say, and they all wave.

I bite my bottom lip when Dallas looks at me, and I know even with all his complaining, he'd dress up again in another ridiculous costume for JB's benefit in a heartbeat.

"I want to ride the reindeer," June says, and I set her on the ground.

She skips over to Dallas and he puts her on his back.

"Bet she's not the only one who wants to ride the reindeer," Maverick says under his breath, and Dallas shoots him a look.

"Watch yourself, Miller," he grumbles, and crawls toward the kitchen. "JB, Daddy can't do this for very long. His knees hurt."

"Wonder why that is," Reid jokes, and his phone buzzes. He jumps up, patting his onesie, trying to find it. "Dammit. Why don't these things have pockets?"

"Because they're made for children who don't have cell phones. You don't have to work tonight, do you? I saw all the content you posted on the social media pages earlier today. What else is there to do?" I ask.

"He's not working—he wants to stay up to date on the Thunderhawks account," Maverick explains and throws himself on the couch. "It's like a war between those him and their poor social media manager."

"It's not a war, it's my job," Reid explains, and he sounds exasperated to be having this conversation again. "My boss chewed me out the other day for not having nearly as much engagement as some of the other teams, so I'm trying to emulate what they do."

"You have to admit whoever runs that account is impressive," I say, and Reid glares at me. "I'm obviously on Team Reid here, but growing an expansion team's following to almost three million people when they haven't had a winning record yet is pretty significant."

"I'm not saying she doesn't do her job well." He stands up and shoves his glasses up his nose. "I just would like for *our* account to not get roasted by her."

"Maybe you need to step your game up, Dunc," Maverick says, and puts his hands behind his head. I've never seen someone make a carrot costume attractive before, but Maverick Miller is a different breed. "Our record sucks and the people still like our content."

"Maybe *you* need to step your game up," Reid throws back, and I laugh at the argument between the two. "Those hat tricks don't mean shit if you can't make the playoffs."

"Uncle Reid!" June screeches, and Dallas comes crawling back into the living room. He winces, but he keeps moving across the carpet until he reaches the couches. "Can we go get candy now?"

"We're going to get so much candy, June Bug," Reid says, and he relieves Dallas from his duties. "C'mon. Let's go get your shoes. I think Uncle Mav wants to help."

"Uncle Mav does want to help," he says, and jumps to his

feet. He looks between me and Dallas. "Behave, you two. We can only distract her for a few minutes before she gets bored."

The three of them shuffle through the apartment, and I join Dallas on the floor.

"You look like you're in pain," I say, and I brush a lock of hair away from his forehead. "Aren't you a professional athlete? Carrying a forty-pound kid shouldn't be too strenuous for you."

"It shouldn't, but when she's grabbing my shoulders and digging her feet into my sides, it's a little more difficult." He reaches out and cups the back of my head. His fingers thread through my hair, and I sigh. "Missed you while I was gone."

"For the six seconds you were away?" I joke, and he nods. "Please. We can't turn into one of *those* couples after only two weeks."

"You're right." Dallas kisses my forehead and wrinkles his nose. "I did not miss you while I was gone, and I can't wait to leave again."

"Okay, I take it back. I hate that." I crawl into his lap and rest my head on his chest. "I missed you too."

"We probably have five minutes before those three come charging back in here." He loops his arms around my waist and rests his chin on my shoulder. "How was your day? Where did you disappear this afternoon when I got home?"

"Good." I smile and glance up at him. There's stubble on his cheeks. The other day when I joked that he should do No Shave November because he'd look hot with a beard, he tossed out his razors. "I went to the soccer fields."

"Oh?" Dallas gives me a hopeful smile. "How'd that go?"

"Really well. I didn't tell you because I wanted to make sure I could do it on my own, you know? You being there for the first time..." I dip my chin and bury my face in his fuzzy onesie. "I wouldn't have been able to do it without you. But I wanted to know I could do it again."

"Of course you'd be able to do it again. And you don't have to play a full-length game every time you get out there. Hell, some days you can just sit and stare at the goal. Progress isn't linear, Mae, and what's most important is that you did it."

"Have you ever thought about coaching?" I ask, and I pull a piece of lint off his shoulder. "After you retire? I think you'd be really good at it, because your motivational speeches make me think I can run through a brick wall."

He laughs. "Calm down, Kool-Aid man. You're not the first person to tell me that, but when I retire, I think I'd like to finally make time for myself. And June. And—" he cuts himself off, but we both know what he was going to say. *You.* "I've given enough of myself to the sport. When it's time to go, it's time to go for good."

"And when is that?" I ask curiously. "You know I want you to play for as long as it makes you happy, right? If we have to hide our relationship for a while, then so be it."

"I don't know when retirement will be. Two years from now? Maybe three? I almost threw in the towel at the start of this season. And then you assaulted me in the tunnel and barged into my private meeting, and here we are."

"Asshole." I poke his side, and he laughs. "I think the words you're looking for are that I changed your life."

"Yes," Dallas says, and he wraps his fingers around my arm. He presses a kiss to the inside of my wrist, and I sigh. "You really did."

"Warning," Maverick booms down the hall, and I slide off of Dallas's lap. I smooth my palms over the skirt of my dress, and he follows my hands with heat behind his eyes.

"Do they know about us?" I ask.

"Maverick and Reid? Yeah. They weren't really surprised, given I told Maverick I'd punch his teeth in if he tried to ask you out."

I burst out laughing and stand, offering him my hand. "You're ridiculous."

Dallas lets me lift him off the ground and tilts my chin back. Our gazes meet, and he kisses me, a slow press of his lips that has me really regretting the decision to go out and trick-or-treat when we could stay here instead.

"I wear your necklace, and you wear mine," he says, and his thumb rubs up my neck. His hand settles around my throat, and heat rushes through me. He adds the slightest bit of pressure, and I have to squeeze my thighs together. "I dare anyone else to try and take you away from me."

"Hey," Maverick says, and we jump apart. "Knock it off, love birds. There are children present."

"Yeah," Dallas snorts. "You."

"I'm sorry. It's really hard to take you seriously when you're wearing that ridiculous costume," I say, and Maverick smirks.

"Reid and I have a bet on how many numbers I can score tonight. His guess is less than five, but I really think I can pull off at least twelve."

"Your fucking ego is something else." Dallas kisses my cheek and elbows past Maverick. "Let's go, y'all, before all the big candy bars get taken."

"You're staring," Maverick says to me, and I blush.

"I am not."

"Yes, you are." He grins. "Take care of our boy's heart, Maven. He's been waiting for someone like you for years. He's always been happy, but now he's..." Maverick shrugs and adjusts the green stem on his head. "Now he's on top of the world."

When Dallas gets back on his knees and June tugs on his antlers, his gaze cuts over to me. His face lights up, and his smile is the brightest and widest of the night. It hits me square in the chest, a scary thing that takes my breath away, and I know I'm on top of the world, too.

THIRTY-EIGHT

MAVEN

THE NOVEMBER WIND whips through UPS Field, and I shiver on the sidelines.

I never thought I'd miss late summer and its thick humidity, but with the freezing rain pelting my face, I'd give anything to be warm. I stopped feeling my toes two quarters ago, and my hands are like icicles.

"This fucking sucks," Cassidy says from beside me, and I nod in agreement.

"Miami sounds nice, doesn't it? This four seasons weather is bullshit," I answer, and my teeth chatter.

I can't believe the fans have stuck around, but with the Titans down three with one minute to go, I think they're hoping to catch a miraculous comeback. The defense huddles together on the field, and Dallas stands off to the side, stretching his leg. It's fourth down, right on the twenty-yard line, and he'll be kicking a field goal after the timeout.

I distract myself from the uncomfortable playing conditions and hold up my camera. I click the shutter button, snapping a photo of the guys with their arms draped over each other and making last-minute play calls.

I shift the lens to the right and take half a dozen pictures of Dallas rotating his hips. A smile dances over my mouth as I watch him in his own little world, and there's not an ounce of strain on his face.

If anyone got a hold of my laptop, our relationship would be a dead giveaway. There are hundreds of photos of him—in his uniform, warming up with a goofy grin on his face as he interacts with the fans of the game. After a win in the tunnel to the locker room, his head tipped back and his helmet lifted in the air. Mid-jog onto the field, looking at me and catching me in a stare just as I catch him staring at me too.

It's hard to believe Dallas and I have only been together a month because it feels like it's been years. I care about him so much, and if this is how I feel after only such a short amount of time together, it's terrifying to wonder what it'll be like in six months or a year.

The refs blow the whistle to resume the game, and the sharp sound shakes me from my daydreams of June, Dallas and I in a house outside the city, with a big yard and maybe a dog too.

The players break from their huddles and line up on the line of scrimmage. Their breaths come up in wisps of white, and a hush falls over the crowd. Dallas swings his right leg forward then back five times. He lifts his arm and checks the wind before closing one eye and lining up with his target.

His pre-kick routine has been the exact same in every game over the last eight years. Looking my way and tapping his hidden necklace is a new addition this season, though, and it's my favorite.

The ball gets snapped, and Justin Rodgers barely catches it. Dallas pulls back and kicks just as the defense leaps off the ground. A player from the opposing team lifts his arms and bats the ball out of the air. The tips of his fingers knock it onto the field, and there's a mad scramble of white and black jerseys.

Everyone slips and slides across the damp field. Mud sticks to legs and arms, and grass goes flying in every direction. I should be taking photos, but I'm too busy holding my breath and watching the play unfold, the live ball still without an owner.

Amidst the confusion, Dallas is the one to scoop it up. There's panic in his movements as he looks left then right. I see the moment he spots a teammate downfield, and he pulls his arm back to heave a Hail Mary toward the end zone.

I can't wait to give him shit for his spiral when we get home.

As soon as the ball leaves his hands, a Wildcats player charges toward him from the side. Dallas doesn't see him—maybe because of the rain, or maybe because he's not paying attention—and before anyone can warn him, he's being leveled on the ground in one of the worst hits I've ever seen.

A gasp goes through the stadium. It's so quiet, you can hear a pin drop. Dallas lays on his back, his arms and legs out to the sides like a starfish, but he's not moving. I can't even see if he's breathing.

"Medic," someone screams, and I think it might be a Wildcats player. "We need a medic."

The atmosphere shifts, and we go from zero to one hundred in less than a second. Chaos unfolds around me, and a fight breaks out on the field when Justin lunges for the player that hit his teammate. Shawn sprints from the sidelines and his assistant coaches trail behind him. Still, Dallas doesn't move, and my world starts to come crashing down.

"Maven," Cassidy says, quick and sharp, and she shakes my shoulders. "Where is June?"

"What?" I ask, and I watch the injury cart roll out from the tunnel. "She's in the nursery."

"You have to go and get her."

"No," I say firmly, and I shake my head. I can't imagine leaving Dallas, even if I'm just here on the sidelines.

"You have to get her," she says again, gentler this time. "They're probably going to take him to the hospital for a concussion or a—" she trails off and doesn't finish the sentence. "She needs to be with you."

Hospital.

Concussion.

June.

Dallas's words from last week come screeching back to me, and tears sting my eyes.

"You're my favorite person in the world," he tells me, just like he does every night. He tucks a lock of hair behind my ear, and he hooks his fingers around my chin. "But I need you to promise me something. Can you do that, pretty girl?"

"It's hard to agree to a promise if you don't tell me what it is first." I trace the outline of his abdominal muscles, and his skin is warm under my touch. "Or is it a secret?"

"No. It's just not what I'd prefer to be talking about when you're naked."

I smile and push up on my knees. I throw a leg over his thighs and straddle his hips. "What would you prefer to be talking about?"

"How badly I want to bend you over the bed." Dallas leans forward and kisses my chest. "How I want to fuck you into the mattress and keep you here forever."

My breath catches in my throat, and I cup his cheeks with my hands. When his eyes meet mine, I swear the brown twinkles.

"You can talk to me about that as much as you want. I'm not going anywhere, Dallas."

His soft smile turns into a full-fledged grin. "I'm glad you're not going anywhere, because I might give you my last name one day. Might put a shiny ring on your finger, too, and tattoo your name on my leg with all my other favorite things."

"You'd never," I say, and I let out a squeak of surprise when he lifts me off his legs and spins us so my head rests against the pillows.

"I would. Which is why I need you to promise me something. If I get hurt in a game, I need you to take care of June."

"What?" I sit up and meet his gaze. "What are you talking about?"

"You saw what happened last week in San Diego. Their safety, J.J. Hanson, went into cardiac arrest on the field after a brutal hit. That could just as easily happen to any of us. If it does—if it happens to me —I need you to promise me you'll look after June. I love Maverick and Reid, but I trust you the most, Maven. I know you'll take care of our girl."

I wait for him to laugh. To say he's just joking around, but he doesn't, and I start to cry. He's as serious as can be, and that terrifies me. I can't imagine a world without Dallas in it, and I never want to.

"Okay," I whisper. I wrap my arms around his neck and pull him close. His body rests on top of mine and I can feel his heartbeat, a reminder that he's very much alive. That he's okay, and that he's always going to come home to us. "I promise."

"Thank you," he says, then kisses me.

His cheeks are wet, and there's more behind the press of his lips and the way his hand shakes as he holds the back of my head. He doesn't say anything else and neither do I. We stay like that, in the quiet, still night, just the two of us, until the sun starts to creep over the horizon.

The memory fades to reality, and I wonder if it was all a dream. I'll blink and Dallas will be on his feet, laughing with his teammates and winking in my direction. I wait. I wait and I wait and I *wait*, but he's still there on the ground, and my heart cracks in two.

I know you'll take care of our girl.

I pull my camera off my neck and hand it to Cassidy. Out of the corner of my eye, I see the players from both teams dropping to their knees and lowering their heads. There's an AED in someone's hands, and I turn my back on the field.

If I look, I won't leave.

And I *have* to leave.

I sprint to the tunnel and hit the button for the elevator a thousand times before it arrives. When I get to the doorway of the nursery, I find June playing with dolls with Benny, Jett's younger brother. She's oblivious to what's going on, and I'd do anything to keep it that way.

"Maven?" Ms. Ann, the head of the nursery, asks. "What are you doing here?"

"Dallas," I say, and it's difficult to talk. "I need June."

Her eyes widen in understanding and she nods. "June, it's time to go," she calls out.

June looks up and sees me. Her face breaks into an ear-splitting grin, and she dashes my way.

"Mae Mae," she says, and I lift her up. She wraps her arms around my neck and kisses my cheek. "Hi."

"Hi, kiddo. Are you having fun?"

"Benny and I drew lots of pictures. I drew a cat and a doggie. Now we play with dolls and have a tea party!"

"That sounds like the best day." I fix her jersey and the sight of Dallas's numbers across her chest makes me choke up. "We're going to leave a little early, okay?"

"Okay. Do we go home?"

"We're going to go home, but we're going somewhere else first."

"Oh. Okay. Can I have my backpack, please?"

I force out a smile and grab her pink bag. "Tell Ms. Ann thank you."

June waves and blows a kiss. "Thank you."

"Was it bad?" Ms. Ann asks quietly.

I nod and bite my bottom lip. "He got tackled on a blocked field goal. He wasn't moving when I left."

She squeezes my hand. "He's going to be alright."

I nod again and wipe my eyes. "Thank you for watching her."

"Mae Mae sad?" June asks, and she touches my cheek. "Why are you crying?"

"I'm okay, princess."

I don't want to freak June out, so instead of sprinting like I want to, I walk calmly toward the elevators and wonder what the protocol for this situation is.

They normally take players into the blue medical tent for concussion evaluations with neuro-trauma consultants, but with how severe the hit looked and Dallas's lack of movement, my bet is he's going straight to the hospital. Dallas told me the name of the one the Titans use, and I try to remember what it is.

I have to make a split decision. Do I take June to the hospital? Do we go to the apartment? Do we wait here and just hope for some news? Before I have a chance to decide, my phone lights up. A number I don't have saved in my contacts is calling me, and I answer right away.

"Hello?"

"Maven? It's Maverick. Where are you?"

I almost sob when I hear his voice. "I'm with June. We're almost to the players' garage."

"Don't move. I'll meet you there."

The minutes feel like hours, and when Maverick rounds the corner, I start to cry again.

"Hey," he says, and his face is pale. He pulls me into a hug, his arms wrapping around both June and I. "I'll take JB to my apartment. You should be there when he wakes up."

"Is he—" I don't know how to ask this next part. "Do you think he will?"

"I saw his hand moving on the stretcher. That's a good sign.

My guess is he got the wind knocked out of him. Definitely concussed. Maybe a broken rib, too. The guy is a twig."

"Compared to you," I grumble. "I think he's a wall of muscle."

"You should see me without a shirt on, then." Maverick winks, and for the first time in ten minutes, I relax. "You'd think I was Superman."

"Superman!" June echoes.

"Superman!" Maverick says again, and he takes her from me. He lifts her over his head and pretends to fly her around. "You're coming home with me, kid."

"No Daddy?" she asks, and she looks around, trying to find Dallas.

"Daddy has to do some work things because he's very important," he explains. "But when you wake up, he'll be there. How does that sound?"

"Okay, Uncle Mav." She squeezes his cheeks, and she giggles. "Home."

Maverick cuts his attention back to me. "Text me with updates?"

"I will. Thank you for taking her."

"Dallas's girls are my girls, too," he says. "I take care of what's mine."

"You're a good guy, Maverick Miller. One day, you're going to make someone very happy, and ten million hearts will all break because you're officially off the market," I say, and I turn toward the garage. "I'll let you know when I hear more."

He and June wave goodbye, and when I slide into Dallas's Mercedes, I know I'm no longer being strong just for myself.

THIRTY-NINE

DALLAS

MY ENTIRE BODY ACHES.

I crack open an eye and bright light floods my vision.

I hear a beeping noise, but it's way too fucking quiet for a football game.

There's a throbbing pain in my head, and it hurts to take a deep breath.

"The fuck?" I mumble, and I look around.

White walls.

Medical equipment.

A shitty television hanging in the corner playing a shitty soap opera and a whiteboard on the wall.

Tile floor and the smell of cleaning solution.

Hospital.

I'm in a goddamn hospital.

Panic creeps up my throat. I hold my arms out in front of me and wiggle my fingers. I lift my legs and wiggle my toes.

All accounted for, and I sigh in relief.

I lift my jersey and check my torso for any bleeding. All I find is a red spot the size of a fist. I climb off the bed, and it feels like I've been hit by a truck. I'm halfway to the door before it opens and five different people walk in.

Doctors with white coats. Nurses in scrubs. Shawn brings up the rear, still in his Titans gear, and my heart sinks to the ground.

"Sit," he barks out, and he points to the bed.

I know listening to him is how I'll get out of here faster, so I plop down and fold my arms across my chest.

"I'm Doctor Anderson," one of the men says. He's young, like he might be close to my age, and I see a hint of a tattoo peeking out from the collar of his scrub top. "Do you know why you're here?"

"Well, doc. I have all my limbs. I'm breathing on my own, and I don't see any stitches on my body. I'm going to guess I have a goddamn concussion, but I feel fine. I *am* fine. Can we cut this bullshit out?"

"I'm going to do a SAC test and ask you some questions to determine the severity of your injury," Dr. Anderson says. "Would that be alright with you, Dallas?"

"I don't have much of a choice, do I?"

"Not unless you want to spend the next couple of days here under our watch."

"Fuck, no. Ask away."

"Can you tell me what day it is?"

"It was Sunday. I'm assuming it's still Sunday."

"Okay. And what about the actual date?"

I sigh and rub my forehead. The throbbing is still there, and I think someone might be pounding on my skull.

"November," I say after a minute. "November something."

The doctor hums, and the woman to his right jots something down on her clipboard. "Who's our current president?"

"Uh. I don't know."

"Can you list the months of the year backward?" Dr. Anderson asks.

"December. November. October." I close my eyes. It's too bright in here. "August. No. Wait. September, then August. July. June. May. April. Uh. March. February. January."

"Good. Who were you playing today?"

I open my eyes and stare at the floor. "I don't know."

"Do you remember the score?"

"No. But if I'm here I really hope we fucking won."

"Dallas, you have a concussion. It's mild, based on the short-term memory loss you've experienced and your sensitivity to light and sounds."

"I'm not sensitive to light," I argue.

"You can barely keep your eyes open. You also lost consciousness on the field," Dr. Anderson says, and the blows keep on coming.

"Christ." It hurts to take a deep breath. "And my ribs?"

"One is very bruised. On your right side."

I turn and look at Shawn. There are stress lines on his cheeks and he seems years older than when I last saw him. "What the hell happened?"

"What was the last thing you remember?" he asks, and he shoves his hands in his pockets.

I try to sort through the memories, but it's like I'm seeing flashes of things, not the whole picture.

"It was raining," I say slowly. "A bad snap. I think I picked up the ball. Then everything gets fuzzy."

Shawn sits on the edge of my bed, and everyone files out of the room except for Dr. Anderson. I don't know why they're acting like this is top secret. I'm sure the internet is already speculating about what's wrong with me, and a thousand people have probably come up with the wrong diagnosis.

"Your field goal was blocked."

"God dammit."

"Then you recovered the ball. It was kind of a mess out there with the mud. One of the Wildcats defenders came at you from the side after you threw a pass and then he tackled you."

"When I didn't have the ball?" My blood boils, and I stand up. "Who was it?"

"Sit your ass down," Shawn says firmly, and I scowl at him. "We're still reviewing the tapes—and I'm sure the league is too. It was close, Dal. It's hard to tell if he didn't know the ball was out of your hands and already committed to the tackle, or if it was intentional."

"Okay, so it was just a hit. No big deal."

"Hard enough to lose consciousness. You were breathing, though. We didn't need an AED or anything like that. You started to come to when we got you in the ambulance, and now here we are."

"Oh, god." I feel sick, and I put my head in my hands. "June. Where's June? Where the fuck is my daughter?"

"June is fine," Shawn assures me. "Maverick has her. He took her to his apartment."

I don't know how long I've been here. Hours? Days? Imagining her waiting for me all alone and confused makes me want to rip the door off the hinges and escape without looking back.

"What about Maven? I need to see Maven."

"What?" he frowns. "Why do you need to see her?"

"Because I just—" I look around. "Where's my phone? *Shit.* Can you call her? Can you get her here?"

"Calm down."

"Don't tell me to calm down," I say fiercely, and I shrug his hand off my shoulder. "Where is she?"

"She's in the waiting room. She came from the stadium."

"Can you—please, let me see her." I look at the doctor. "Is that okay?"

"Of course," Dr. Anderson says, and I sigh in relief.

"Is there something you need to tell me, Lansfield, because now would be the time," Shawn says, and it sounds like a warning. "I'm giving you the chance to come clean with me."

I shake my head. I don't have enough coherent thoughts to know my own name let alone what I need to tell him. "I just want Maven."

He sighs but stands up. "Do not leave this room."

When he disappears, I look up at the doctor. "How long am I out for?"

"You'll enter the NFL's concussion protocol. There are five phases, and movement between the phases is determined by the team's medical staff. Players are typically out for nine days, but most come back the next week."

"Am I going to have any permanent damage? Why did I lose consciousness? I've been playing football for decades, and I've taken way worse hits than that," I say.

"The medical answer involves stress on the brain tissue and the electric discharge of nerve cells," he explains.

"And the dumb person answer?"

"The body is delicate. I think it was a freak accident spurred on by a cheap shot and an awkward angle."

"You saw it?" I ask.

"I might have been in the breakroom when it happened and the game might have been on." His lips twitch. "As for permanent damage, I don't see any cause for concern. You'll have a headache for a few days. Light might bother you. Your short-term memory should come back soon, but it could be a few weeks."

"Well, that's lovely, isn't it?" I grind my teeth together, but there's nothing I can do about it now. "Is my neck okay?"

"It is, and you have full range of motion in your extremities."

"Please don't tell me I have to stay here overnight."

"You don't. I'm just waiting for your team personnel to get here and then I can discharge you."

"Thanks. Sorry I'm being an ass. I appreciate your help."

"You're allowed to be frustrated." The doctor smiles, and he tucks a pen in his coat pocket. "We played football against each other."

"No shit. Really? When?"

"Back in high school. I was a senior when you were a freshman, and you smoked us on your way to the national championship."

"Small world." I reach out and shake his hand. "Dallas."

"Jordan."

"Nice to meet you. Is that why you went into the medical field?"

"Yeah. I saw too many of my teammates get hurt and were misdiagnosed, so I decided to do something about it. Never thought I'd get a call on my lunch break informing me that Dallas Lansfield was coming in on a stretcher."

"Aw, shit, man. I know y'all work hard around here, and I'm sorry for cutting into the limited free time you have."

"Don't worry about it. Do you have someone who can stay with you? Who can take care of you?" he asks. "You shouldn't be alone for the first twenty-four hours."

"Yeah." I blow out a breath. "I have—she's, well, I—"

"Maven?" he finishes for me, and I nod. "Mind if I hang around until she's here so I can give her some information?"

"Please. But she's going to be pissed at me. Don't judge her by how upset she is."

"Nah." Dr. Anderson grins. "That just means she cares about you."

"My coach doesn't know the details about our relationship. He *can't* know."

311

"Doctor-patient confidentiality," he says. "My lips are sealed."

The door flies open. Maven comes storming inside, and it's so much like that day she stormed into Shawn's office I swear it feels like we're back there.

Then I see her wet hair and her smudged make up. Her eyes are red-rimmed, like she's been crying for hours, and her cheeks are pale, and I need to touch her immediately.

"Come here, sunshine," I say softly, and she bursts into tears.

She sprints to me and wraps her arms gently around my neck. I hold her, stroking her hair and rubbing her back. Her skin is cold, and I bring her even closer, trying to warm her up.

"I was so worried about you," she whispers, and her tears hang on my neck. "You were on the ground and not moving, and I—" she hiccups and buries her face in my jersey.

"I know. I'm so sorry. I'm alright, though. I'm here. It's okay."

"I got June from the nursery. I didn't think I should bring her. Maverick has her at his apartment." She pulls back and holds my cheeks with both of her hands. Her eyes sweep over my face, and she's never been more beautiful. "Is it really you?"

I rest my forehead against hers. "Yeah, baby. It's really me."

"I remembered that talk we had, and I thought about you leaving me and I—"

"That's never going to happen. *Never.* You hear me, Maven? I'm going to come home to you and June every night."

"Sorry," Jordan says. "I don't mean to interrupt, but your coach—"

Maven pulls away from me and sits in the chair beside the bed. She wipes her eyes and sniffs just as Shawn enters the room.

I hate this distance between us and I want to pull her back to me. I want to put her in my lap and scream *yeah. She's mine. Fuck your rules.* But I can't. I can't and I fucking *hate* it.

Shawn looks at us. I know there's a question there. I can see it in his eyes and I feel it hanging in the air. He doesn't ask it, though, and turns his attention to the doctor instead.

"Do you spend a lot of time with him?" Jordan asks Maven, and she nods.

"I'm his daughter's nanny."

I hate the way she says it like that, like it's her defining quality, and I want to blurt out that she's so much more.

She's a role model. A leader. A teacher.

She's compassionate and kind. Funny and sarcastic. Loud, all the time, but the kind of loud that makes me hate the quiet.

She's beautiful. A complete show-stopper when she wears makeup and flowy little dresses that show off her legs. But she's also gorgeous when I drag her into the shower. When I wash her hair and smudge her lipstick off with my thumb.

She's the reason for all of my good days.

"Dallas will need to rest for a day or two, and you'll need to keep an eye on him," Jordan says. "After that, he can get back to short walks and watching television. Only Tylenol during the first twenty-four hours, then you can move on to Advil, if needed. He should be close to normal by day three, but monitor symptoms. If things get worse, you need to get to the emergency room."

"Is there anything we should avoid?" Maven asks, and she rests her elbows on her knees. "Things that might make the concussion worse?"

"Bright lights. Loud sounds. He's wincing right now and doesn't even realize it." Jordan chuckles. "Don't push the recovery. It doesn't take long, but you have to let the brain heal."

"Got it." She stands up and smiles. "Thank you, Doctor."

Jordan glances at Shawn. "Want to meet me at the desk and I'll get the paperwork for you all to sign?"

"Sounds good." Shawn clasps my shoulder. "Glad you're alright."

"Would you miss me, Coach?" I tease, and he pinches me.

"Not in the fucking slightest." He gives Maven a quick hug. "You doing okay?"

"Better now," she says. "Thank you."

He hums. "No practice until Wednesday. We'll start the concussion protocol then."

"*Wednesday?* But that means I won't be ready for Sunday's game."

"You're not playing."

"My streak—"

"You'll start a new one. Non-negotiable, Lansfield," Shawn says, and he walks out.

"I'm sorry," Maven whispers, and she squeezes my hand.

"It's not your fault." I bring her hand to my mouth and kiss her knuckles. "Will you give me a second? I'll meet you in the hall."

"Sure." She smiles and slips out of the room.

"Here's my card if you need anything," Jordan says when we're alone. "Like I said, you'll be fine in a few days."

"Thank you. And thank you for not saying anything to Shawn."

"Don't mention it. You're lucky to have someone like her. You're clearly very important to her."

"She is to me, too. Do you have someone?"

"Nah." He gives me a sad smile. "I did, once upon a time. But I left the small town in Colorado for the big city, and she stayed put."

"Shit. Sorry, man."

"It happens."

I pull my jersey over my head. "Do you have a Sharpie I can borrow?" Jordan hands me one, and I sign my name over my number. When I'm finished, I hand it to him. "Appreciate you looking out for me. Y'all are superheroes."

"Wow. Thanks, Dallas. If you go down the hall and make a right, you can exit without having to go through the lobby. Just in case you want to avoid the chaos."

"Got it." I wave and find Maven waiting for me outside the door. "Ready, pretty girl?"

"Yeah." She smiles and stands on her toes. Her lips brush against the corner of my mouth, and she puts her hand in mine. "Let's go home."

FORTY

MAVEN

"JUNE IS ASLEEP," I say.

"Thanks for being on bedtime story duty," Dallas says.

"It's the highlight of my day." I look down at him and put my hands on my hips. "How are you feeling?"

"The exact same way I've felt the last two weeks. Great." Dallas reaches up and pulls me into his lap. We go tumbling back into the pillows on the bed, and I laugh. "I've played a game since then, and I have no lingering pain. You need to stop worrying about me."

"I just want to make sure because I care about you."

"You helped a lot, Mae. You're the only reason I smiled those first three days after the concussion. Without you, I would've died of boredom."

"That would have been a tragedy."

"Maybe next time I get hurt you could walk around the apartment in a nurse's outfit."

"If I did that, you'd never let yourself get better." I rest my head on his chest and sigh. "I'm sorry your sister and niece couldn't make it up here."

"Me too. The weather is bad all up and down the east coast,

and their flights have already been canceled twice. It's too much of a headache for them to keep going to and from the airport, so I told them not to worry about it. If we make it to the Super Bowl, I'll fly them out."

"Guess that means you're going to be stuck with my family for Thanksgiving tomorrow. I'm sorry for all the chaos that's going to ensue."

"Are you sure it's okay that June and I come to your dad's place? I don't want y'all to go out of your way for us."

"It's not going out of our way at all." I run my fingers across his jaw and drag my nails through his beard. He shivers, and I smile. "Lacey and Shawn will be there. My mom is bringing her partner. My dad and Maggie, too, of course, and there's plenty of space. June and I will leave for the stadium when you do so we only have to take one car."

Dallas hums and lifts the hem of my shirt. He rubs along the underside of my bra with his thumb. "It's going to be very difficult to be around your family and not touch you like I want."

"You're going to have to try, buddy. There are going to be knives out, and it would be great if we could get through the meal without Shawn trying to stab you."

He laughs and tucks his chin into the crook of my neck. "Do you think your dad will care that you're dating me? I'm not sure how I'd feel about June dating someone eight years older than her."

"He'd be a hypocrite for caring; he and Maggie are over a decade apart. But my dad likes you. He thinks you're a nice guy. The only things he'll want to know are if you make me happy, and if you treat me right."

"Do I make you happy, Maven Wood?" he asks low in my ear.

"You do. Very happy. That's all that matters. Fuck the age difference."

"You make me happy too." Dallas's touch moves to the other

side of my chest. His fingers brush over the fabric of my bra. "I've missed you. Feel like I haven't had you in days."

"We had phone sex when you were out of town last weekend." My eyes flutter closed when he pulls my shirt over my head. He takes the cups of my bra and folds them down, pushing my breasts up. "You took a pair of my underwear with you, remember?"

"Fucking ruined them, too. But it's not as good as the real thing." He hums and dips his chin, taking me in his mouth. His tongue swirls over my nipple, and I let out a soft exhale. "I know how much you like being touched. Being teased."

"Dallas," I whine, and I squirm in his lap. He's growing hard under me, and I reach between us to stroke his length.

"Is there something you want, Maven? Use your words, pretty girl." He bites down and I cry out. "Do you want to come just from this?"

"Yes. No." I drop my head back and let out a frustrated groan. "I want you in me."

"Where? Here?" he asks, and he moves his hand to my mouth. He presses two fingers on my tongue, and I close my lips around them. "Or here?" He pulls my sleep shorts to the side with his other hand and presses a single finger in me.

I nod, unable to speak, but wanting to encourage him to do *more*.

Dallas chuckles and pulls his fingers from my mouth.

"Let's take these off so I can look at you," he murmurs, and I lift my hips. He slides my shorts down my legs and throws them to the side. My bra comes next, and I'm naked in front of him. "There you are."

"Do you like what you see?" I ask.

"I love what I see." Dallas yanks his shirt off then reaches across the mattress and drags me to the end of the bed. He opens my legs and kneels on the floor. "Lie back."

"You don't have to. You know I can come by—"

"I'm doing this because I want to. Eating your pussy is a fucking dream." He spreads me with his fingers, and I always forget how intimate this is. There's no place to hide, and he can see every part of me. "Put your feet on my shoulders, baby. Let me enjoy."

"Well. If the boss insists."

I flop onto my back and close my eyes. I don't even have a chance to get comfortable before three fingers work into me, and I squirm on the sheets.

"Just as tight as I remember, and just as pretty," he says appreciatively, and heat floods my body with the compliment. "Pink. Wet. Fucking Christ, woman."

I reach out, desperate to touch him, and I thread my fingers through his hair. He starts the same way he always does: slow, with a gradual push and a curl. A light touch of his thumb, and a hum of approval when I lift my hips and work him deeper inside of me.

"Greedy," he says, and he nips at the inside of my thigh.

"You would be too if you knew how nice your fingers are."

"Which do you like better? My fingers, or when I do this?"

Dallas adds his tongue. He mimics how I used my toy all those weeks ago, and I think I've died and gone to heaven.

"*That*. Definitely that. For someone who doesn't have a lot of experience, you're alarmingly good at this."

"Maybe I watched videos. Maybe I read every single book you have on your bookshelf. Maybe I researched."

"You're such a liar."

"Am I?" he asks, and he takes my hand out of his hair. He guides my fingers to my chest, then down my stomach and to my pussy. "Or am I not too proud enough to admit that I might need some help to make sure you scream my name when you come?"

Hell.

This man is crafted from every woman's fantasy. He gets off from my pleasure, and it's the hottest thing I've ever experienced.

I open my eyes and look down at him. His face is flushed and his breathing is ragged. His pupils are blown wide, and his erection is so hard, I'm afraid he might be in pain.

"You don't need help, Dallas. You're perfect," I say, and he blushes even deeper with the praise. "I told you that you're so good. That you take care of me like no one else ever has. And that's true. Look how wet I am. It's all for you."

His throat bobs and his grip on my thigh turns almost painful. "Hold your pussy open for me," he says roughly.

I smile at his determination and use my thumbs to spread myself open. He picks back up with his rhythm. Three fingers inside me. A tongue torturing me. A palm on my breast, twisting my nipples.

Dallas is patient. He doesn't rush. He doesn't make me feel like I'm taking too long. When he pulls away from my chest, I know he's touching himself, and that nearly does me in.

"Close," I say, and I writhe on the sheets. "Dallas, I'm so close."

"I know you are, baby. I just felt you clench around my fingers. You're almost there, and you're doing so well."

I lose it. I moan, long and low, as I come undone on his tongue.

"That's it," he says, and he laps at my entrance like he's been starving for weeks. "Give me one more, Maven."

I feel exhausted. Utterly spent, like my bones are going to split in two. "I can't," I whine.

He gives my clit a light slap, and my back arches off the bed. "Come on, pretty girl. For me? Please?"

It takes everything in me to not scream. The sensation is too much. I bring my hand to my mouth and bite down on my knuckles as I unravel again. The pleasure is white-hot and all-consuming as it races through me for a second time.

"That was—" I stop to take a breath. "You could teach a pussy eating class."

He grins and licks his lips, proud of himself. "Yeah?"

"Yeah." I push up on my elbows and look down at him. He's got one hand in his briefs, and it's my turn to lick my lips. "Can I see?"

Dallas nods and stands. He hooks his thumbs in the waistband of the cotton and shimmies them down his thighs. There's a deep swoop in my belly when I look at him. Arousal, yes—he's God's gift to the world with his thick cock and a body crafted of soft muscles.

But there's something else, too. Something deeper. More poignant. Like the longer I stare at him, the more disbelieving I am that this man is *mine*.

"Come here," he says, and I stand on shaky legs. He kisses me and runs his tongue along the seam of my lips. My mouth opens for him, and I moan when I taste myself. "Give me your hand."

I let him take my palm and wrap my fingers around his shaft. We stroke him together, his hand guiding mine, and he groans. After a few tugs, I drop to my knees.

"Can I?" I ask, and he shakes his head.

"No." He grabs a fistful of my hair and tugs. My neck jerks back, and I gasp in surprise. "Spit on it, then get on the bed with your ass in the air. I'm going to fuck you into the mattress so hard, you won't be able to walk at the game tomorrow. You're going to have to tell anyone who asks that you took every inch of my cock like the good slut you are."

Oh.

Possessive Dallas is my favorite Dallas.

I bring my mouth over the head of his cock. I spit and drag

the saliva down his length until it covers from base to tip. I look up at him and break out into a slow grin. Two can play that game.

"Yes, Daddy."

I've never seen a man move so fast.

Dallas lifts me in his arms like I'm as light as a feather and hauls me back onto the bed. He bends me over until my face presses into the sheets, and I'm more turned on now than when his head was between my legs.

"This is going to be quick." He nudges my thighs apart with his knee. "Because you drive me out of my goddamn mind in the best fucking way."

He slams into me, and I almost fall over. I grip the headboard to keep myself upright, and my teeth clamp down on the corner of a pillow. He's rougher than he normally is, but I've never felt safer in my entire life.

"Harder," I say, and he grants my wish. He's so deep, and my eyes sting with tears. "More."

"Touch yourself," he grunts, and his hand rests between my shoulders to keep me down. "Want to feel you come on my cock."

I'd do anything this man asks.

My fingers slide up my thigh, and I find relief. He's not going to last long, and there's no way I am either.

Not when he digs his nails into my skin and marks me.

Not when I hear the sound of our hips meeting and the low groan working its way up his throat.

Not when he curls over me, his mouth near my ear, and whispers how he's so proud of me.

Not when a bead of sweat rolls down my neck and he licks it away.

And when he smacks the swell of my ass just as he thrusts into me, I freefall.

He follows me, my name a garbled string of letters and sounds as his movements still. As his breathing slows down. As he pulls out of me and collapses onto his stomach, reaching for me the moment he hits the mattress.

"Hi," I whisper. I brush the hair away from his forehead and press a kiss to his eyebrow. "Are you alive?"

"No." He opens one eye, and he looks dead to the world. "You killed me."

I laugh and snuggle into his side. "How does your head feel?"

"I think I might be reconcussed." Dallas grins. "If I can survive *that*, I'm definitely back to one hundred percent."

"Good." I close my eyes and rub my hand down his arm. "When we can move again, we should shower then try to get some sleep. Tomorrow is going to be a long day."

"It's going to take me five to seven years to recover. But you're right. With lunch and then a 4 p.m. kick off, we're going to be dragging our feet this time tomorrow."

"I'm glad I get to spend Thanksgiving with you and June. Even if we are exhausted."

"Me, too. Family is important to me, and I'm excited I get to spend time with yours. I know they can't know we're together, but one day they can, and I'm going to make sure there's no doubt in their minds I'm the right person for you. Because you're the right person for me."

Dallas feels like a fairy tale. And when I drift off to sleep, his arms around my body and our hearts beating in unison, I know one day, I could love him wholly, and it would be the easiest thing I've ever done.

I'm already on my way there.

FORTY-ONE
DALLAS

"IS SOMETHING WRONG, Maven? You're walking a little funny."

If looks could kill, I'd be dead. She glares at me as we ride the elevator up to her dad's apartment, and I fight back a grin. I love when she gets feisty.

"This is your fault," she hisses under her breath.

"I told you what was going to happen. You're the one who didn't believe me." The doors open, and I take June's hand. "Listen to me next time," I add over my shoulder.

Heat flares behind the sharp blue of her eyes. The apples of her cheeks turn bright red, and when she nearly trips over her feet, I laugh. I walk down the hall slowly, swinging June's arm back and forth. We're going to need a minute for Maven to pull it together.

"It's number twelve," she calls out. "There's probably some sort of decoration out front."

She's not wrong. I stop us in front of a door that's covered in three dozen paper turkey hands. I tilt my head to the side and try to read some of the names.

"What is all of this?" I ask.

Her shoulder brushes against mine, and she traces over the scribbled coloring job of one in the top right corner. It looks like it could be one of June's drawings that I have hanging on the fridge at home. "Decorations from his work."

"He deals with cancer, right?"

"Pediatric cancer," Maven says softly, and my heart sinks to the ground. "Spirits can always be down this time of year, especially for kids, so he finds ways to make people happy. Turkey hands. Paper snowflakes. There's probably a box of all the past mementos in the storage closet. He knows it's not the most profound thing in the world, but sometimes a distraction is nice." She looks down at June, and her eyes shimmer with tears. "I've only been around JB for four months, and I feel like she has a part of my soul. Like she's mine. I can't imagine what that pain would be like if something happened to her."

She is yours, I think.

This thought has been coming to me more and more frequently these days when I see the two of them together. When I watch the patience Maven has and her ability to turn situations into teachable moments, I know with absolute certainty she would be the world's best mom.

June got sick when I was on the road last week. She had a fever and kept vomiting. I was five seconds away from buying the first plane ticket home, but Maven told me she had it handled.

And she did.

Not once did she complain about losing any sleep or the amount of laundry she had to fold. It was no big deal, a small bump in the road over a long stretch of smooth highway.

"I see where you get it from," I say.

"Get what?" Maven asks.

"Your kindness and selflessness. It's why you altered your life just to help with mine."

"Oh." She smiles and lifts one shoulder in a shrug. "I don't know if I'd consider that selflessness. Helping someone I care about is the bare minimum."

"If that's what you think is the bare minimum, I can't wait to see what you consider going above and beyond."

"Stick around and you'll find out."

I'll stick around forever if you let me.

"Daddy." June tugs on my arm. "Can we go inside? I wanna see the parade."

Maven pulls out her keychain and turns the lock. "Sorry, JB. I'm slacking. We're here," she calls out, opening the door with her hip and stepping inside. She unzips her jacket and hangs it on a rack. "Hello?"

"You're here!" Lacey bounds across the living room and almost tackles Maven in a fierce hug. "I haven't seen you in *weeks.*"

"That's my fault," I say with a sheepish grin. "I've been keeping her very busy."

"With work," Maven clarifies, and I wink at her. "I'm so happy to see you, Lace."

"You, too. You look good." Lacey hugs me next then ruffles June's hair. "Are you behaving yourself, Dallas?"

I grin. "Not at all."

"That doesn't surprise me." She takes the pot of mashed potatoes I'm holding and gestures us forward. "We're all in the kitchen. Do you want something to drink? Probably no alcohol before the game, right, Lansfield?"

"Depends. Do you want to watch your husband yell at me for being an idiot?" I ask.

"Don't tempt me with a good time." Lacey's grin is sly. "I almost wore another one of your jerseys today just to piss him off a little."

I laugh, remembering the time she asked for one of my

jerseys to wear to a game before she started dating Shawn. I guess it was the nudge he needed to realize how he felt about her.

I never got the jersey back. I wonder where it is.

"You know I would've lent you another one," I say. "Anything to rile the old man up."

Out of the corner of my eye, I see Maven's smile slip a little around the edges. She touches her neck, undoubtedly looking for her necklace, and I touch mine on instinct.

"Everything riles him up these days. I don't think he got a lick of sleep when you had a concussion," Lacey says. "Don't tell anyone, but you're secretly his favorite."

"What about the parade, Daddy?" June interrupts.

"We have it on in the kitchen. Come on, I'll take you," Lacey says, and the pair walk ahead of us.

"Hey." I reach out and hook my pinky around Maven's. "Are you okay?"

"I'm fine." She glances at me. "Why wouldn't I be?"

"I don't know. You seemed a little pissed when Lacey mentioned the jersey thing. You know she and I never—"

"I know." Maven sighs and shakes her head. "It's stupid. I'm fine. Really."

"Come on, pretty girl," I say softly, and I run my thumb over the back of her hand. "Tell me what's on your mind."

"I wasn't pissed, I was jealous. Jealous that she got to wear your jersey," she explains. "Which is such a dumb thing to be jealous about because I love Lacey, and you have a literal child with another woman, but I think about these people who have had you before me, and I wish it were me. I wish I had found you sooner."

I give her a slow grin and tug her behind a corner, out of sight. "The first away game you and June came to, you walked onto the field in my jersey. Justin was warming up with me,

remember?" I ask, and she nods. "He called you hot or something, and I was so pissed that he was looking at you. So, yeah, I
know what you mean about jealousy."

"Oh." She looks up at me and smiles. "I guess I shouldn't
wear his jersey to the game this afternoon then."

"You can do whatever you want, sunshine," I say, and pull
her toward me. It's reckless to be acting like this where anyone
can see us, but I don't care. "Because you're mine. At the end of
the day, you don't go home with any of the boys who might try
and get your attention. You go home with me."

Maven hums and rests her hand low on my stomach. I blow
out a breath and close my eyes. It's wild how one touch from her
gets me all worked up. "I like when you get like this," she
murmurs. "Like you'd burn the world down for me if I asked."

"You wouldn't need me to. I'd just hand you the match and
let you do it yourself. But I would. I would, Maven. There's
nothing you could ask for that I wouldn't do."

She touches my cheek and drags her thumb down the line of
my jaw. "I'm going to remember that."

"I'll keep reminding you," I say, and in a fit of absolute idiocy,
I spin her and press her against the wall. I cup the back of her
head before it can hit the hard surface, and I kiss her.

I kiss her like my life depends on it and she kisses me back
with all of her might. Her hand tangles in my hair and my hand
works its way under the skirt that's been distracting me since she
zipped it up this morning, and if this is how we get caught, I'd
die a happy fucking man.

"Where'd all your responsibility go?" she asks, and her
mouth moves to my neck. She sucks on my skin, and I hiss.

"Out the fucking window. If you see it, can you bring it back
to me?"

"No. I like you like this."

My hand freezes halfway up her leg. "Are you wearing

fucking *thigh highs,* Maven? When the hell did you put these on?"

"When you weren't looking." She bumps her nose against mine and grins. "Do you like them?"

"I'm not sure if I want to get on my knees and worship you or be angry that I have to wait until we get home to have you," I growl.

"Your knees would be preferable."

"Stop." I snap the top of her stockings against her leg and the moan she gives me is soft. "I'm walking away from you now."

"Okay."

"Like. Right now."

"Is that why you're still holding my ass?" she asks.

I blow out a breath and take three steps back. "I hate that skirt."

"You do?"

"But I'm going to buy you one in every color. Those stockings too. Max out my credit card, Maven."

She laughs. "Come on, lone star. Let's go stand a respectable distance apart and pretend like we're not sleeping together. It's going to be a blast."

I follow her to the kitchen and I'm greeted by a half dozen faces. I recognize most of them, but a few are new to me.

"Hey, y'all," I say, and I wave to everyone. "Happy Thanksgiving."

"Happy Thanksgiving, Dallas." Maggie walks around the kitchen island and kisses my cheek. "We gave June some chocolate milk. Is that okay?"

"That's perfect, thanks." I look over and see her sitting on a chair, swinging her legs back and forth. Shawn points out something on the T.V. and she nods before bursting into a fit of giggles. "Let me know if you need me to watch her, Coach."

He looks at me over his shoulder. "I like her more than I like you, Lansfield."

"Most people do." I stick out my arm toward Aiden, Maven's dad. "Nice to see you again, sir. Thanks for letting us join you."

"Sir?" he asks, and he shakes my hand. "Do I really look that old?"

"Shoot. No. I didn't mean it like—"

"Relax. I'm just giving you a hard time. Aiden is fine." He grins and clasps my shoulder. "What do you want to drink?"

"Water would be great. Can I help with anything?"

"You can sit down and get off your feet." Aiden points to the chair at the end of the island. "You have a big game today."

"Dad has you on his fantasy football team," Maven explains, and I laugh. "The more points you get him, the more he'll like you."

"I'm going for at least six field goals today then," I say.

Everyone jumps into action to get the turkey carved and the stuffing in a serving dish. Maven and I set the dining room table and Lacey pulls two pies out of the oven. The potatoes we brought are added to the buffet line, and just as the clock strikes eleven-thirty, we dig in.

"These potatoes are amazing," Maggie says. "Maven, you made these?"

I snort into a bite of green bean casserole. "She wishes she did. Your daughter is not great in the kitchen, Aiden."

"No, she's not. Never has been. She started a fire once. I walked out of the room for eight seconds and came back to flames." He laughs and takes a sip of his wine. "She has other strengths."

"Like stealing candy necklaces?" I ask innocently, and a foot kicks my shin. "Hey. Don't injure the NFL player."

"Don't be a d-i-c-k," Maven says sweetly.

"I forgot about the candy necklace. Being a girl dad is tough, man." He pauses and looks at his daughter. "But it's also the best thing in the world."

I lift my glass. "I'll drink to that."

"Speaking of best things in the world, we started a tradition a couple of years ago," Shawn says. "We go around the table and say one thing we're grateful for. It doesn't have to be long-winded. Just a reminder about how good life can be, you know." His eyes bounce to me. "You don't have to join if you don't want to."

"No way. I'd love to join. Just don't make me go first."

Gratitude gets tossed around. Words like health. Family. Love. Patience. Some come with a small story. A reason for why. Others don't. And when it's my turn, I know exactly what I'm going to say.

"First, thank you for having me and June here. Family is important to me, and to be surrounded by one so full of love and appreciation for each other is a gift. If I had to pick one thing I'm thankful for this year, it would be Maven," I say, and her mouth pops open. "I'm not just saying that because of present company or trying to get in anyone's good graces, but because it's the truth. I didn't know what the start of this season would look like as far as my playing career went, and the only reason I still get to wear a jersey this afternoon is because of her. Fantasy points or record-breaking field goals wouldn't be possible without her."

Under the table, she rests her hand on my thigh. She squeezes my leg and bites her bottom lip. "I'm thankful for the right things coming along at exactly the right time," she says softly.

"I'm thankful for ice cream!" June yells, and the heavy moment breaks when everyone laughs.

"What kind of ice cream, June?" Maven asks.

"Vanilla!"

"Good choice, kid," Lacey agrees.

I grin and set my napkin on my empty plate. When I glance across the table, I see Shawn watching me.

There's a look in his eyes I've only seen a handful of times, and none of them were good. It's like there are little daggers behind his gaze, and it sends a shiver down my spine.

It feels like we might have just gotten caught.

FORTY-TWO
MAVEN

"I CAN'T BELIEVE we're starting off December with a loss," I say to Cassidy as we put our camera equipment away. "How do we go from winning on Thanksgiving by thirty-five to losing by twenty today?"

"Jett's going to be pissed," she says under her breath. "He's been in a slump lately. I don't know what's going on. Ever since he's taken in his brother, his stress management has gone to shit. It's not going to get much better after this game. We've lost more this season than in the last two years combined. The media is going to crucify him."

"Has he talked to anyone? The team psychologist? Shawn?" I ask.

She gives me a look. "Come on. You know it's ingrained in their minds that asking for help is weak, which is fucking bull-shit. He looks so sad in all the photos I took of him, and I don't know what to do."

"Maybe I can see if Dallas can talk to him. Just to let him know he's there if he needs someone to listen. It's not parenting advice, but lending an ear as someone who has been there before."

"That would be great, Maven." Cassidy squeezes my arm and smiles. "I appreciate it. What are your plans for Christmas?"

"Nothing too exciting," I say. "I'll stop by my dad's place and spend some time with him. June's wish list is miles long, and I think Dallas is getting her everything she's asking for, so our morning will be pretty packed. What about you?"

"We're hoping Shawn gives the guys a few days off for the holidays. If he does, we're going to fly to Florida to see my family."

"That would be so fun. I hope you get to go. A couple days off would help everyone recalibrate before we head into the final stretch before the playoffs. I can't believe we're almost at the end of the regular season."

"Time flies, doesn't it?" She looks past my shoulder and waves. "I'm going to go. Your man is coming, and I'm going to go find mine."

I laugh and give her a quick hug. "Alright. Hey. Tell him to keep his chin up. These things come in waves. Look how much better Dallas is feeling this season."

"I think that has less to do with the waves and more to do with the blonde who keeps him in check." Cassidy winks and grabs all of her bags. "See ya next week, Mae."

I turn around and find Dallas in his street clothes with June asleep in his arms. She looks so small with her head on his shoulder and a tiny fistful of his shirt in her hand, and I smile when I see them. I can't help it.

All of my worries melt away as he walks toward me, and I feel calm when he crowds my space. When his sneakers knock against mine and he taps my hip twice before stepping a half foot away.

He has that steadying sort of presence. It's why he's such an incredible athlete and such an incredible father; when he pulls you into his orbit, you're automatically at peace.

"Hey," I say, and his mouth tugs up in a lazy grin.

"Hey, sunshine."

"Sorry about the loss."

"It happens. There have been plenty before it. There will be plenty after it. Are you ready to go? We're making tacos for dinner," he says. "And then homemade s'mores. They were a request from Sleeping Beauty here."

"Sounds like the perfect night to me. Want me to carry her?"

"Nah. I got her. You know I miss her when I'm out on the field." He twirls his keys around his fingers then pats his pockets. "Shit. I left my phone in my locker."

"Do you need it?"

"Yeah. My agent is sending me over a potential endorsement deal with a major sports drink, and I told him I'd call him in the morning before practice to discuss details."

"I can go grab it. I don't mind."

"Are you sure? All of the guys should be cleared out by now, so you won't see anything you don't want to see."

"And if I want to see something?" I grin when he narrows his eyes in my direction. "Just kidding. Where is it?"

"On the top shelf. Stand on the chair if you can't reach, half pint. Let me take your bag." I hand him my camera equipment, and he winces. "You carry this around all day?"

"Calling me weak, Lansfield?"

"No, I'm calling this stuff heavy. There's got to be a lighter camera out there."

"There probably is, but my dad got me this one. I like using it."

"We'll get you a little wagon to pull all your stuff around in," he says, and he adjusts the strap on his shoulder. "There has to be a market for that."

"A wagon. I wouldn't get made fun of at all." I laugh and

head toward the locker room. "I'll meet you in the garage in a few."

It's eerily empty on the walk toward the locker room. When the Titans lose, everyone tends to clear out pretty quick. They like to be pissed about the defeat in private. It doesn't surprise me that only forty-five minutes after the end of regulation, there's not a soul to be found.

I wave to Paul, the security guard who's been working for the team for three decades. He sits up on his wooden stool and puts down his mystery book when he spots me.

"Maven. Do you need something?" he asks.

"Dallas left his phone in his locker. Do you mind if I run in and grab it?" I flash my badge and he laughs.

"Put that silly thing away. I know who you are." He keys in a code on the punch pad on the wall then nods toward the door. "Go on in. It'll be quiet. I'm the last one left."

"When do you get to leave?"

"After the final security sweep. Should be any minute now."

"Then I'll move extra quick." I wave and slip inside.

The door shuts behind me, and I look around.

I've never been in the locker room before. It's only open to coaches and select members of the press in an effort to protect the player's privacy.

I get it. With smartphones and social media, pictures and quotes can be shared in seconds. Conversations and situations can be taken out of context. Before you know it, someone has a P.R. nightmare on their hands that shouldn't have started in the first place.

I know I said I'd be quick, but I take my time as I walk around the perimeter of the room. The carpet is plush and freshly vacuumed. The walls are a nice brown. The Titans logo is proudly displayed in the center, and everything smells clean, not like the sweaty balls and grimy uniform stench I thought would hang in the air.

The player's lockers are a different story. I see the personalities in the way they organize their jerseys. In the pictures and personal items they have taped up. Some display their large families. Others are of significant others. Sam Wagner has eighteen photos of his dog in a bandana, and I need to ask if I can meet him.

I spot Dallas's cubby, and I smile.

His cleats are lined up in a neat row and his jerseys are in color-coded order. There's a dirty clothes hamper that's almost overflowing, and his helmets are stacked into a pyramid.

I grab the chair sitting in front of his locker and jump on it. My hand sifts around the top portion, searching for his phone. The tips of my fingers graze it, and as I start to drag it toward me, my knuckles brush against something that feels like paper on the side paneling.

I frown and lean forward to try and see what it is, then my breath catches in my chest.

It's a photo.

Of me, June and Dallas at the splatter paint room.

We took it before we left to get ice cream. Our cheeks are squished together and there is acrylic everywhere. I'm laughing. June is sticking out her tongue. Dallas is grinning, and his face is mid-turn, like he's trying to look at me.

I stare at it.

And then I stare at it some more.

It feels like an eternity passes before I dare breathe again.

We look like a family.

A happy family, and it makes me emotional.

It's dangerous to have that picture up there. Anyone could see it. They could find it and make their own assumptions about its significance.

I want to know what *he* thinks when he looks at it.

Walking back through the locker room feels like an out of body experience. I smile at Paul and make my way toward the player's garage. I find Dallas leaning against the hood of his car and looking up at the ceiling.

His hair is still wet from his shower. His joggers are low on his hips, and his feet are crossed at the ankles. He looks peaceful, lazy, almost, and when he lowers his chin and meets my gaze, his smile is dazzling.

"I put your camera stuff in the car," he says. "June is passed out in her car seat. That kid can sleep anywhere."

"Great." I swallow and nod. "Thanks."

His grin slips into something of concern, and he walks toward me. "What's wrong? You look like you've seen a ghost."

"I got your phone." I set the device in his hand and step away. "You have a picture of me in your locker."

"Oh." Dallas rubs the back of his neck, and the chain of my necklace sneaks out from under the collar of his plain white shirt. "Yeah. I do."

"Why?"

"Why?" He laughs, like it's the most obvious thing in the world. "Because you and June are my favorite people, and I like looking at y'all before I take the field. Because it's my reminder that even when things go to shit out there—like tonight—I get to come home to you. To her. And everything else doesn't really matter."

"How—" I swallow again, and the question is heavy in my throat. "How long have you had it up?"

"I hung it the day after the art room. After I touched you. After I kissed you. After I realized that no matter how hard I tried to fight it, I was never going to be able to stay away from you."

"And if someone saw it?"

Dallas shrugs, unbothered. "I'd tell them the truth. That I'm falling for you."

"What about the rules?"

"Fuck the rules."

I choke on a laugh and close the distance between us. I wrap my arms around his neck and kiss him. His tongue runs along my lips and I part my mouth, opening for him. He groans when I sink my teeth into his bottom lip, and it's like he's been waiting for this moment all day.

Falling for me.

God, I'm not just falling for him.

I'm jumping. *Leaping.* Willingly and hopefully. He's carved out a part of my heart, and if he were to walk away tomorrow, he'd have it forever. I'd never get it back.

I love you.

I feel it in the center of my chest when he looks at me.

I feel it when we're on the couch and he uses my hair to practice his braiding skills, wanting to get the hairstyles June asks for right.

I feel it when we're in crowded spaces and he finds a way to touch me. To let me know he's there.

I feel it on the field during a game. Seventy thousand people, and he always finds me.

I've never said those three words before, but with Dallas, I'd scream them. I'd yell them from the mountaintops so everyone could hear.

"I'm falling for you, too," I whisper, and his lips pull into a smile.

It's a beautiful thing, and I feel it when he does that too. When he kisses me like he'll never get another chance.

"One day, my locker will be covered in photos of you and me. And June."

"Like Sam and his dog."

"Exactly like Sam and his dog," Dallas chuckles. "We should go. I don't want June to wake up and think we left her."

"It's probably best to avoid any traumatic experiences."

His palms fall from my face, and he threads his hand through mine. He's warm and soft. The most sure thing in the world.

"Let's go home, honey," he says, and his thumb strokes across my knuckles.

I imagine photos of us over the fireplace. A couple frames on my bookshelf. A wedding dress, maybe, and a couple of kids, too.

Home.

That might be the best word of all.

FORTY-THREE

DALLAS

I HEAR feet pounding down the hallway and whispered voices. I fumble for my phone and check the time.

Just past five thirty, and right on schedule.

I smile as I scrub a hand over my face and try to wake myself up before the start of the busiest day of the year. I'm fucking exhausted and running on three hours of sleep, but I'm so damn excited for today. Nothing beats watching your kid's face light up when they open the presents they've been waiting for.

The footsteps stop just outside my door, and I hear more whispering. A soft giggle slips under the crack of the frame. I pull the covers over my head and pretend to hide just as the door flies open.

"Oh no," Maven says. "Where the heck did Daddy go?"

I shouldn't love that she calls me that, but *fuck* does it do something to me when she does.

"He's hiding!" June squeals.

"Should we check the closet?"

I listen to them and grin like an idiot under the white duvet.

Maven stayed in my room until two, her head on my chest and my hand between her legs. We fucked under the stars—

twice—then stayed wrapped around each other for hours after, talking about anything and everything and nothing in between.

I would've kept her here longer, but with June eager to open Christmas gifts and an internal alarm clock that barely lets her sleep past six on a good day, I knew she'd be up earlier than usual. I didn't want to lock the door to keep her out, but I also didn't want her to barge in and find us in a compromising position.

Thinking about that conversation makes me want to die.

"Daddy?" June calls out. "Where are you?"

"Wait a minute, JB. I think I know where he might be."

I know it's coming, but I still groan when something solid lands on my stomach. I pull back the sheets and wrestle with the wiggling four year old in my arms. "Christ, you're getting big, kid. I guess the broccoli is working."

"Daddy!" she screeches, and she kisses my cheeks. "Merry Christmas."

"Merry Christmas, baby girl." I snuggle her against my chest and look up at Maven. "Hey, Mae."

"Hey, lone star."

I pat the spot next to me, wanting her close, and she climbs onto the mattress. She's wearing a ridiculous onesie with reindeer and candy canes all over it, but it's the cutest fucking thing I've ever seen. Her hair is a mess and her eyes are bloodshot. There's a mark on her neck, just above her collarbone, where I sucked on her skin last night until she was panting my name.

Beautiful.

So goddamn beautiful.

"Can we do presents?" June asks, and she plays with my necklace.

"You know the rules," I say. "Food, then presents, then the soup kitchen. You have to eat your eggs before you can play with your new toys."

"Soup kitchen?" Maven asks. She leans on the stack of pillows behind her and brings her legs to her chest. "I thought the Titans were finished with all their community engagement events for the year."

I forgot that she hasn't spent the holidays with us before and doesn't know our traditions. Time flies with her, and it feels like she's been around forever.

"This is something I do on my own," I explain. "It's the soup kitchen downtown near the homeless shelter. I go every year. They serve a free meal three times a week, but on Christmas Day they do a huge feast. It's open to anyone, no questions asked, and I donate all the food for it. June came with me last year and loved it, so I'm bringing her with me again."

Maven blinks. Her mouth pops open, and she scoots a few inches closer to me. "You do all of that?"

"Yeah." I run my fingers through June's hair and try to work out some of the knots from her bedhead. "I haven't told you much about my family, have I?"

"No. Is there any bad history there? I thought you and your sister got along well."

"We do, and there's lots of love. My parents worked hard and made ends meet when I was growing up. We never missed a meal, and we always had warm clothes when the weather turned cold. When it came time for the holidays, though, they weren't able to spend the money on the newest toys or stock the living room full of gifts. I got made fun of at school because I didn't have the video game consoles or new sneakers everyone else had. I told myself that if I made it to the NFL, I'd not only provide for my family, if I had one, but for other families, too. I think it's easy to get swept up in the luxury of having all this money, but what good is it if you don't spend it to help other people, too?"

She rests her chin on my shoulder and blinks up at me.

Her fingers touch the line of my jaw, and I sigh. "You are the most extraordinary man I've ever met. I wish I could go with you."

"Next year." I squeeze her thigh, a promise of what's to come. "You'll come with us next year."

"Smoochy kiss!" June says, interrupting us, and Maven's cheeks turn pink.

"Sorry, JB. Your dad and I—"

"Maybe we should," I say quietly, and she frowns.

"I thought we were keeping this a secret. Kissing in front of her defeats the purpose of that," Maven says.

"It does. And I'm not saying we should make out in front of her or anything like that, but it would be nice to hold your hand when we're watching a movie. To have both of you in my arms where you belong."

"Oh." Maven bites her bottom lip and nods. "I'd like that."

"June." I spin her in my lap so she's facing both of us. "You know how Mae Mae spends a lot of time with you?"

"She's my best friend."

"Would it be okay if she spent lots of time with me too?"

"Is she your best friend, Daddy?"

"Yes." My eyes meet Maven's. "She's my best friend in the entire world. I like her very much, and she's very special to me."

"More than Uncle Mav and Uncle Reid?"

"In a different way."

June taps her cheek, deep in thought. "Okay, Daddy. We can share."

"And maybe I can kiss her?" I ask.

"Smoochy kisses only," June says, and she claps her hand. "Kiss, Mae Mae."

"Feels like there's a lot of pressure with an audience here," Maven jokes, and my hand rests on the back of her head.

"Better not mess up, sunshine." I smile and press my lips to

344

hers. I taste her toothpaste, and I hum when she melts into me. "Ten out of ten."

"I think you deserve a gold star," she murmurs.

I keep it short, just long enough so it doesn't make June uncomfortable or encourage her to ask questions. When I pull away, Maven's eyes twinkle.

"Merry Christmas, Dallas," she whispers, and she tugs on my necklace.

"Merry Christmas, Mae. Best I've ever had."

"A NEW BIKE?" June tears off the wrapping paper of her last gift. A bow goes flying, and the living room floor is an absolute disaster. "It's pink!"

"Your favorite color. Look at this." I lean over her and squeeze the horn. She giggles and tries for herself. "People will hear you coming for miles."

"Will you teach me to ride it, Daddy?"

"As soon as it gets a little warmer, we'll go down to the trail by the Potomac and practice. You'll be a pro in no time," I tell her.

June turns around and hugs me. Her little hands grip my shirt, and I smile as she does her best to squeeze me tight. "Thank you."

"You're welcome, sweetheart." I glance at Maven and lift my chin. "I have something for you, too, Mae."

She frowns and crosses her arms over her chest. "I thought we said we weren't doing presents."

"We did, but I lied."

"Is this going to be a personality trait of yours, Lansfield?"

I grin. "Never."

"That's good, because I also lied to you." She reaches under the couch and pulls out a rectangular box. "Right under your nose for weeks, and you had no idea."

"You little menace. Let me go grab yours."

I jog to my room and grab the box sitting on the top shelf of my closet. When I come back into the living room, Maven and June are cuddling on the couch, and *god*, I love to watch them.

They get along so well. They have ever since that first meeting, and I love that Maven never babies her. They have full conversations, and Maven asks for June's opinions on so many things. My daughter has always been her number one priority, and I know that even if I never made a move, even if I never gave in and kissed her, she would've stuck around for as long as possible, just to spend time with JB.

I sit next to them, and I reach over and wrap my fingers around Maven's ankle. I rub my thumb up and down her calf, and she sighs.

"You first," she says, and she hands over the package. There's tape everywhere, and the wrapping paper doesn't cover the corners. "June helped."

"No wonder it's so well done." I rip off the paper and turn the box over, reading the description. "A digital picture frame? What does it do?"

"I know we text each other and send pictures all the time, especially when you're on the road, but this will keep them all in one place. You can plug it in when you're at your hotel, and it will cycle through all the images. I can also send a photo straight to the device with a caption, and it'll pop up on the screen. It's not much, but I know you don't like to be away. I thought this might make things a little easier and keep all the memories in one place."

My fingers curl around the edges of the box and my vision blurs. I sniff and tip my head back to stare into the ceiling lights. My exhale is jagged and it feels like I swallowed a shard of glass.

"Daddy, are you sad?" June asks, and she climbs into my lap. "Why are you crying?"

"I'm not sad, baby girl." I set the box down and rock her against my chest. "I'm just happy. Really happy. These are happy tears." My gaze locks with Maven's, and she's smiling from ear to ear. "Thank you. Thank you for everything. We're so lucky to have you in our lives."

I love you.

I love you so fucking much.

It burns through me like a raging wildfire and fucking *consumes* me.

I've never felt this way about anyone before. If someone asked me to describe it, I wouldn't know how. It's a lot like coming up for air after being stuck underwater. My lungs feel full. My vision is clear, and I can finally fucking see.

When I look at her, when I make her smile and laugh, it feels like I have a purpose greater than football. Like my life has meaning.

This woman did what no one else has ever done: she snuck her way in. She fixed me and healed parts of me I never knew were even broken, but she also ruined me along the way.

I'll never be able to have anyone else.

"I'm the lucky one," she says.

I swallow and wipe my eyes with the back of my hand. I'm going to be a fucking *mess* when I use this on our next road game. The boys are going to make fun of me for hours, and I can't wait.

"JB, could you give Mae her present, please?" I ask.

June scoots across the couch and takes up residence in Maven's lap now. She hands over the box, and Maven kisses her forehead. The two work together to pull off the paper, and Maven's hand freezes when she reads the name on the box.

She takes a deep breath and slowly opens the top. Her shoulders shake when she sees what's inside, and she whips her head up to stare at me.

"Dallas."

"Maven."

"Are these—" she pulls the tissue paper back and gasps.

"What is it?" June asks, peering around her arm curiously. "A doggie?"

"Cleats," Maven whispers. "New soccer cleats."

"I started going to therapy after my injury. My therapist thought I needed something to renew that love of the game. A fresh start to wipe the slate clean," I explain. "He suggested I get new cleats because they weren't tied to the past experiences. I know you aren't sure where you want your future to go with soccer, but when you decide, you'll have your own fresh start, too."

She blinks, and I know she's trying to stop the tears from falling, but they come anyway. Loudly and aggressively, until there's snot hanging from her nose and her cheeks are bright red.

Fuck, I love her.

"Thank you," she hiccups. "They're beautiful. They're perfect. What did I do to find a man like you?"

"The first step was accosting me at the field," I murmur, and I pull her and June into my arms, hugging them tight. "The second was loving my daughter. The third was just being you, Maven. Because that's enough."

If someone were to ask me when I knew she loved me back, I'd pinpoint this moment, right here, with tears on her eyelashes. The way she looks up at me as if I hung the moon, and for her, I'd die trying.

FORTY-FOUR

DALLAS

THIRTY SECONDS.

We're thirty seconds away from saving our season and making the playoffs.

If our defense can hold the Bobcats to two more stops, we'll live to see another day.

If they don't, we're out, and that's it. No more football until September.

It's been years since we've missed the playoffs, and I don't want to start down that losing road again. It was a long grind to get back on the side of victory, and getting defeated today would be demoralizing.

"Come on, boys," Jett yells, and he jumps up and down on the sidelines next to me. "What play do you think they drew up?"

"Quarterback sneak. I've watched enough film of these fuckers to know they have the highest success percentage with it too. They only need three yards, and they'd be idiots to run anything else."

The whistle blows, and a gust of January wind rips through the stadium. Jett and I step closer, and I shiver under my Cape

Coat. His fingers dig into my bicep, just below my shoulder pads, and if I wasn't so fucking cold and so fucking nervous, it would probably hurt.

Everyone at UPS Field is on their feet. I spot Maven at the other end of the sideline, her camera at the ready and a beanie over her blonde hair. She's too zoned in on the game to notice me, and I reluctantly drag my gaze back to my teammates to watch our fate play out.

The ball gets snapped, and the Bobcats quarterback grabs it. He's a small guy and quick on his feet. An absolute hellion to defend, but he hesitates—something he never does—and one of our linemen barrels into him before he can take more than three steps.

The ball pops out of his arms and lands on the field, fair game for anyone to grab.

Both teams of coaches start screaming and pointing, then Odell Sinclair, the biggest guy on the field at two hundred and eighty pounds, scoops up the pigskin and starts charging toward the opposite end of the field.

"Holy shit," Jett screams, and he runs down the sideline. "Go, Odell, you unbelievable mother fucker."

The dude has the slowest 40-yard dash time in the league, and I've never seen him run more than ten yards at practice. But here he is, passing the fifty, then the forty, then the thirty. There's block after block in the back field. Our defense prevents the Bobcats players from chasing him down, and he has nothing standing in the way of our end zone.

"He's doing it. Mother of fucking god, he's doing it," I yell, and when he crosses the goal line, I throw my jacket off and storm the field with my teammates.

It's pandemonium.

You'd think we just won the Super Bowl by the way we

descend around Odell. We jump up and down and act like the biggest fucking idiots on the planet, but I don't give a shit.

We're going to the playoffs.

"Where did you learn to run like that?" I ask Odell, and I wrap him in a tight hug.

"By trying to keep up with your skinny ass," he yells, and I think he breaks one of my ribs when he squeezes me.

A dozen reporters work their way into our circle. There are video cameras and microphones everywhere. Shawn and Odell both get drenched with the Gatorade cooler. Stadium security tries to keep the rapidly growing crowd away from the players, but they're doing a shitty job.

I hug my teammates then scan the field, looking for Maven. She's snapping photo after photo of the celebration, but when she spots me, she grins from behind the camera and breaks out into a run.

Goddamn she looks incredible, and a bolt of possessiveness rips through me as some of the other guys try to get her attention. I swear to god my dick twitches when she ignores them and keeps her eyes trained firmly on me.

When she's close enough to reach, she leaps into my arms. I spin her around, and to anyone else, it would probably look like we're two friends celebrating. Reveling in the high of the moment of a great fucking game. But I can feel the way she leans into me. How she wiggles in my hold and sighs against my neck.

"Great game," she whispers in my ear.

"I'm not going to have a voice tomorrow." I laugh and bury my face in her hair for the briefest of seconds before I set her back on the grass. "I like that you're here for these moments."

"Me too." She pops her hip to the side and I stare at the curve of her thigh. "My eyes are up here, Lansfield."

"Sorry. You're really fucking distracting, and I have this weird attraction to you. When I see you, I want to do unspeakable things to you."

"Yeah?" She tilts her head back and looks up at me. "Maybe you should do them."

"What? Here? In the end zone?"

"I didn't know you were into exhibitionism."

"I think I'd be into anything with you." An idea forms in my head, and I feel my cheeks turn red at the thought. I swallow and lift my chin toward the tunnel. "You want to go celebrate?"

Maven steps toward me, and our toes touch. "If by celebrate you mean go home and do whatever it is that has you blushing like that, then hell, yeah, I want to celebrate."

"Do you have Maverick's phone number saved in your phone?"

"Why? Is he planning on joining us?"

"Absou-fucking-lutely not. His dick is probably twelve inches long. I wouldn't stand a chance."

Her laugh is light, and it warms me up. "Here," she says, and she pulls her phone out of the back pocket of her khakis.

I find Maverick's name and send him a message.

ME

It's Dallas.

Can you grab June from the nursery and take her to your place?

Want to celebrate with M.

MAVERICK

Hey, Daddy. I got you.

Let it be known I'm missing out on going to the bar with a five-foot-ten goddess, but you know I'm weak when it comes to my goddaughter.

ME

For the love of God, do not ever include my daughter in the same sentence as your sexcapades ever again.

MAVERICK

lol. Like you're not going to fuck in the back of your car or something.

ME

Or something.

I'll swing by later.

MAVERICK

??? What does that mean?

Dallas?

Goddamit I hate you.

Kidding. Love u very much. Go wild, kids.

"Thanks," I say, returning her phone to her, and I give Maven's arm a tug. "Let's go. We have to move quick."

"Where are we going?"

"You'll see."

I can't bring her with me into the locker room through the front entrance, so I veer left to a small hallway off the tunnel. It's a hidden corridor no one ever uses, and I'm glad to find it empty. I punch in the code for the door to the right, and hold it open with my foot.

"Get in," I say, and give her a gentle push forward.

"Dallas," Maven hisses. "I'm not allowed to be in here."

I take her hand and lead her through the back part of the locker room. I crane my neck to make sure no one is following us, and I shrug. "Don't give a shit."

"Are there cameras in here?"

"No." I tug her into the shower room. I take the stall closest to the exit and pull the curtain closed behind us. "What do you say, sunshine? Do you feel like being a little crazy with me?"

"This is why you were blushing. I told you I wanted you to lose your mind with me, Dallas. Of course I feel like being a little crazy with you." She grins, and it's a wonderful fucking sight.

"Here, give me your camera. I'm going to hide it in my duffle bag so it doesn't get ruined." I look out the curtain and see that the coast is clear. "Wait here."

I hustle through the locker room and carefully shove the camera in my bag. I hide it behind the rest of my stuff so you can't tell what it is, and I make it back to the showers just as the first wave of my teammates start to file in.

When I get to the stall, Maven is standing there naked. Her clothes are in a ball on the small bench and her hands are on her chest, running down her body.

"Thought I'd get a head start," she says roughly, and I groan at the sight of her.

"Fucking beautiful," I grind out. I pull my jersey over my head and toss it on the ground. Fuck if it gets wet. "Touch yourself while you wait for me to catch up."

She licks her lips and spreads her legs. Her palm moves down her stomach in the slowest motion I've ever seen.

"Like this?" she asks innocently, and I think I rip my compression shorts in half when she slides a finger inside herself and moans.

"Just like that," I say, and I lift her up. I reach behind her and turn on the water before backing her against the wall. "You're wet already, aren't you?"

"Your football uniform really does something for me." She brings her finger to my mouth and traces my lips. "Do you want a taste?"

"Please."

"Open up," she says, and she presses her finger on my tongue.

I suck on it and groan when I taste her. "So fucking sweet, Maven. I want more."

"Where's the rest of the team? How long do we have?"

"Who knows? After a game like this, we all kind of do our own thing. Shawn knows he won't be able to hold our attention for more than five seconds, so we reconvene at practice tomorrow." I bend down and kiss her, and she wraps her arms around my neck. "Lean back a little, honey, so I can slide my fingers inside you and get you ready for my cock."

Maven's legs loosen around my waist, putting space between us, and I hum my approval. I'd normally take my time with her. I'd lay her out and tease her, licking every inch of her body until she made a fucking mess, but right now I'm feeling greedy. A little bit frantic and wild, and I push two fingers inside her just as cheers echo through the door to the shower room.

"Oh, god," she whispers, and she rolls her hips, adjusting to the stretch. "That's—yeah. *Yes,* Dallas. Right there."

I curl my fingers at her enthusiasm and she arches her back. Her legs open wider for me, and I smile against her mouth.

"That's so good, Maven," I murmur. "You always take my fingers so well."

I'm usually a man made of control, but seeing how the guys looked at her as she walked toward me on the field made me need her.

I had to have her.

Immediately.

"Dallas," she whispers, and I love that my name sounds like she's close to begging me for what she wants. "Your teammates are going to come in. Someone could hear us."

I've never hooked up with someone in the locker room before, but it's the hottest fucking thing I've ever done.

The water dripping down our bodies as her chest presses against mine.

The possibility of getting caught.

It's torturous in the best fucking way.

She must think it, too, because she clenches around my fingers. I imagine her clenching around my cock, and I get even harder.

"Let them," I say through a rasp. I dip my head and bite her neck. A smug grin works its way to my mouth when she hisses. "And make sure you say my name nice and loud when you come, Maven. I want the whole team to know whose fingers make you feel good."

"So much for keeping this a secret." Her laugh dies in her chest when I add a third finger. "Fuck, Dallas. I want the world to know you're mine."

Goddamn.

The door to the shower room opens, and I don't bother trying to figure out who's on the other side of the curtain. I can't concentrate. Not when she reaches down and wraps her hand around my dick. Not when she strokes me under the stream of the water. Not when she leans forward and presses her heels into the small of my back, asking for more.

"Okay," I whisper, and I kiss her collarbone. I ease my fingers out of her and step us away from the wall. "Okay, baby."

Her blonde hair is stuck to her face. Her skin is pink, and her eyes gleam with delight. I line up with her entrance, and she nods, encouraging me along. I bring her down my length slowly, and I brace one hand on the wall, next to her head.

She's so fucking tight. I've fucked her dozens of times and I'm still not used to how *good* it feels when her pussy takes me all the way to the hilt.

Maven moans, and it's loud enough to draw attention to us.

"Oh, shit," someone says from a couple stalls down.

"Hot damn. I guess we're really celebrating," someone else adds.

"I bet it's Bellamy. He's got a new girl, and they can't keep their hands to themselves."

"Should we leave? Let them have their fun?"

"No way. Maybe this is part of the fun."

"You hear that, pretty girl?" I whisper in her ear. "I think they know I'm yours. But maybe we should be sure."

I fuck her—hard. I thrust into her without abandon. She meets my every move eagerly, and her tits bounce as she takes me inch by inch. It's like we're racing to see who can get the other there first, and she's going to win. I give my best effort, though, when I press my thumb against her clit and circle in a slow rhythm that has her grinding into me.

"I'm close," she says, and her nails drag down my back. "Keep doing that. Please."

"I got you. You can let go, Maven."

Her body shudders against mine. Her breaths come out in quick little pants followed by a long, low moan that's so sexy, so fucking *needy*, I follow her over the edge.

I can't see straight. My legs shake and spasm. I wrap my arm around her and bite her throat as I spill inside her.

"Dallas," she whispers only for me, and my hand slips off the wall she says my name. "God, I love when you fill me up."

Fucking Christ.

This woman.

"I think you're every one of my fantasies put together," I say, and I rest my forehead against hers. I try to take a deep breath, but it feels like there's dust in my lungs. "You really were made for me."

I love you so fucking much.

It's there on the tip of my tongue, like it's been every day since Christmas. I know I can't say it now. Not when my dick is softening and she's falling asleep in my arms with heavy limbs, but *god*, I want to.

"What?" she asks, and her eyes flutter closed. "Why are you looking at me like that?"

"Just happy." I kiss her forehead. "That's all."

"Thoroughly fucked, is more like it."

"That, yes. You worked my dick like a fucking champ." I peel a piece of wet hair away from her cheek and tuck it behind her ear. She blushes, and I smile. "It's a little more than that, though, too."

"Dallas?"

"Yeah?"

"I'm happy too."

"Thoroughly fucked, you mean?" I ask.

"A little more than that, though, too."

I grin into the curve of her shoulder. I should be exhausted. Spent after a good game and a good fuck with the girl of my dreams. But I'm not.

I'm on top of the fucking world.

FORTY-FIVE
MAVEN

"THERE'S a rumor going around the locker room I think you might be interested in," Dallas says, and I look at him in the bathroom mirror.

I lift an eyebrow. "Oh? What is it?"

"Word is someone was having a threesome in the showers after our last win."

He leans against the wall lazily. I can tell he's exhausted from a long practice before the Titans head out west for the first playoff game, but he still gives me a slow, sleepy grin that makes my heart skip a beat.

"Really?"

"Yup. I might have added a little fuel to the fire by saying I saw two women leaving with a mysterious player, because Shawn gave us a look at Thanksgiving, and it makes me think he knows about us. Or suspects something at the very least," he says.

"Wait, what?" I ask, and I spin to face him.

"Yeah. When we all shared what we were thankful for. He was watching us—me, really. And... I don't know. It felt like he knew something he shouldn't."

"Has he said anything to you?"

"Not a word." Dallas shrugs. "Maybe it's my imagination."

"Okay, so we'll tone down the way we look at each other when people are around, then. Who do your teammates think it was in the showers?"

"Bellamy is still the frontrunner, and there's talk of Sam Wagner, too. Bets are being made, and I saw Odell put five hundred bucks in an earnings pool. I almost feel bad for the guys, but then I remember Sam kicked my ass in sprints earlier today, and I figure he'll be just fine."

I laugh and put in my earrings. "They'd never suspect Dallas Lansfield, the rule follower."

"No, they wouldn't." His eyes roam down my body and liquid heat flares behind his gaze. He pushes off the wall and walks toward me with commanding steps that have me squeezing my legs together. "God damn, woman. That outfit is hot."

"Do you like it?"

I spin around and show off the sweater dress I bought two weeks ago. The black fabric hugs my curves and hits mid-thigh, well above my knees. I paired it with boots and tights, and when Dallas blows out a breath and reaches for me, I feel sexy as hell.

He runs his hands down my back and palms my ass. His fingers squeeze my cheeks and press into the soft flesh. A groan slips free from his chest, and his appreciation for my body makes me feel even sexier.

"Please don't tell me you're going to be around men tonight," he says roughly. "Please tell me you're going to a convent."

"Why?" I stand on my toes and hold the back of his neck. "Jealous, lone star?"

"When you look like this? Very." He lifts me onto the counter in one easy swoop of his arms and sets me down on the marble. "I'd kill anyone if they tried to touch you."

"You couldn't even kill the spider in June's room last week." I drag my nails down his chest and his hips buck forward. "There's no way you'd kill a man."

"If he touched what was mine, I wouldn't hesitate."

Mine.

My stomach twists in pleasure at the thought of him defending me. Of him using his athletic prowess to ward off anyone who went a step too far. Six months ago, I wouldn't have said it was a turn on of mine—I'm independent. I always have been, and I can take care of myself.

But why should I have to when there's a man made by the gods who could do it for me?

"I promise you won't have to visit jail tonight. I'm having dinner with Maggie and Lacey at this new Italian restaurant in Dupont Circle. With the holidays and the end of the regular season plus the start of the playoffs, I haven't seen them in a while. I need some girl time," I say.

"Getting our nails done together isn't enough girl time for you?" He holds up the manicure June did for him a few days ago. The pink polish is chipped, and there is a fresh coat of purple on his pinky and thumb. "We could go shopping."

"Your effort is commendable." I kiss his nose, and he smiles. "It's weird to call them my friends because they're so much older than me and attached to the parental figures in my life, but they are. Maggie started dating my dad when I was sixteen, so she was there during those awkward teenage girl years where I felt like a fish out of water."

"God. I'm never going to be ready for those days." Dallas closes his eyes and takes a shallow breath.

We will be, I think.

I almost say it, because when I think about the future, I see Dallas, June and myself together. Picking out outfits for JB's first date and hearing the horror story of her first kiss. Tackling braces and acne and her first period. I want to be there for every milestone, no matter how big or small.

"She needs to learn cursive first," I say, and he laughs. "One step at a time."

"You're right. How are you getting there and back? Do you want me to drive you?"

"Rideshare. It's too much of a hassle to come and grab me when you have June. That involves car seats and patience and an hour out of your night. But thank you very much for offering."

"You'll call me if you need anything?"

Dallas is a helper. The kind of man who likes to be depended on and needed. I lean into that sometimes, by asking him to open a jar. To reach something that's too high for me. He always gets a little smug. A little more self-assured and rolls his shoulders back. It's never cockiness but more like he's *proud* that he's wanted.

God, I want him so much.

In every way imaginable.

"I will," I promise, and I wrap my legs around his waist. "You know I always need you."

"Not like that." He dips his chin and kisses my neck. He smooths his hands up my thighs, and I part my legs wider. "But I guess like that. God, Maven. Let me keep you forever."

And ever and ever.

Let's grow old together.

"That's an awfully long time. I hope you don't get sick of me."

"Never."

Dallas brings his mouth to mine, and the kiss is full of fire. It's scorching hot, but I sort through the need we have for each other and find the dash of sweetness and the splash of love he always adds to his affection. It's hidden. Secret. A sprinkle of tenderness amidst the deep glide of pleasure sweeping up my body.

I can feel it in the way he holds the back of my head to deepen the kiss.

The reverent way his fingers brush across my chest.

The smile he's giving me—I can't see it, but I know it's there. In the curve of his lips. In the scrunch of his nose and the wrinkles near his eyes. Pure, undiluted bliss.

It's in his reluctance to pull away. In the way he whispers my name, regretful to let go, as if we'll be separated for days instead of hours.

Perhaps my most favorite of all is the care and consideration he uses when he takes my heart in his hands. Gently, like he plans to guard it for the rest of his days.

MAGGIE AND LACEY are already at the restaurant by the time I get there.

One orgasm and a traffic nightmare later, I stumble inside slightly winded, slightly frazzled, but happily satisfied.

"Hi," I say when I slide into the booth across from them after we exchange a round of hugs. "I'm so sorry."

"Don't worry about it," Lacey says, and she reaches out to grab my hand. Her wedding bands are cool on my skin, and I smile down at the glittering diamonds. "Everything okay?"

I bite my lip and try to hide my smile. "Everything's great. These last few months have been the busiest of my life, and I feel like we're finally starting to slow down. Except for tonight, clearly, because I'm way behind schedule."

"I think we need to make a toast." Maggie pours us each a glass of wine, and we hold up our drinks. "To the woman who has never watched a kid before, but is successfully navigating the role and *nailing* it."

"And," Lacey adds, "to the woman who's made a name for

herself as an up-and-coming sports photographer for a top NFL team."

"Okay. How much did Dad and Shawn pay you to say these things?" I laugh and we knock our glasses together. "It's totally unnecessary. They're my jobs. I'm not out here operating on people's brains or diagnosing sickness like you all are."

"Knock that shit off. We don't measure our successes against each other. What's new? How's June? Is Dallas doing okay?" Lacey asks. "That boy is something else, isn't he?"

"Dallas is..." I blush and take a long sip of wine. "Great, yeah. A very thoughtful guy."

"Thoughtful enough to leave a hickey on your neck?" Maggie grins and lifts her chin toward my throat. "Did he even try to hide it under the turtleneck?"

"Oh my god," I hiss. "It's not—we're not—"

"If you even *try* to lie to us, we're disowning you, Maven. We've known for weeks." Lacey puts her elbows on the table and grins. "Spill."

"*Weeks?* You're joking."

"The friendship bracelets? The way you two looked at each other at Thanksgiving? How he picked you up after the playoff clinching win and didn't give a shit about anyone else? It's not hard to put two and two together," Maggie says, and I don't hear any judgment in her voice.

"Does my dad know? *Shit.* Does *Shawn*?" I ask, panicked.

"No and no. Come on. Those two are oblivious as hell," she says, and I relax marginally. "Your secret is safe with us."

I take a deep breath and finish off my glass of alcohol, needing some courage.

I can trust Maggie and Lacey—I've always trusted them.

I've told them intimate details about my life no one else knows. They've answered my questions and I've never felt any shame in sharing my curiosities.

"What I say at this table cannot leave this table." I look at both of them, and they nod in agreement. "Dallas and I are seeing each other. We've been seeing each other for a couple of months."

"Oh my god, Mae." Maggie stands up and hurries to my side of the booth. She drapes her arm over my shoulder and hugs me. "That's so exciting. Give us the details."

"We, uh, are also kind of living together," I say, and I laugh when Lacey's mouth pops open. "It's a long story that involves how much I was paying for rent and how little time I was spending at my apartment, and it just kind of happened. We started spending time together, one thing led to another, and here we are."

"Is it serious?" Lacey asks. "I've never seen him with a woman before."

"We're not just sleeping together, if that's what you're asking. I mean, we're definitely doing *that,* but I'm falling in love with him." My heart moves up to my throat as I say it out loud, and my fingers curl around the edges of the table. "Is that insane?"

"I knew I wanted to spend the rest of my life with your dad after only one night together," Maggie says gently. "Sparing you the details, that night was about more than just sex. In less than twenty-four hours, he made me feel safe. He showed me how I deserved to be loved. You don't need years to know you found the right person."

"But we're at such different points in our lives. I dropped out of college. He's a professional athlete with a daughter. I'm still figuring out what I want to do going forward, and he's settled in. It works now, but what about in five years? In ten or fifteen? I don't want him to feel like he's settling with me."

"Settling? Maven, that man has smiled more this season than he has the last four years combined," Lacey tells me. "And I think a lot of the time, people get caught up in the *ever after* part of being happy. What's wrong with just being happy right here, right now? None of us can control the future. If things are good, if things with Dallas are what you've dreamed about, then who cares what five years down the road will look like?"

She's right.

I don't have a lot of experience to go off of—the few guys I dated in college are boys compared to Dallas—but I know what we have is special. It's full of hope and healing and encouragement and support. Communication and listening. It's tender and soft but loud and vibrant.

It's the most wonderful thing in the world.

"Yeah." I nod and smile. "Things are good. When I'm with him and June, I really feel like I'm part of their family. Not as Mom, but as something... I don't know. Just as special."

"It's hard to figure out how to define that role," Maggie says. "That's how it was for me with you and your dad. You have a mother who is wonderful and thoughtful and very present, and I'd never dream of taking that title from her. But June doesn't have a mother. Not one that's involved. Maybe in a couple of years you'll slide into that role naturally. Maybe you're starting to already."

"This sentimental stuff is heartwarming, but tell us the *really* good details—how is he in bed?" Lacey asks with a wicked grin, and I blush. "That hickey on your neck speaks volumes."

"Fantastic. Mind-blowing. He doesn't have a lot of experience, but he's so eager to learn. He reads my romance novels and *researches*. I don't know how he goes from sweet one minute to literally ripping my shirt off in the next, but it's the best I've ever had. Not just because of our physical attraction, but because there's an emotional connection, too. It's like we can read each other's minds and anticipate what we need. I've never felt such a deep affection toward someone before."

"Protect that," Maggie says and she squeezes my shoulder.

"Fight for it. Take it from someone who spent years in a marriage where I never once had those feelings toward my partner; that kind of love is special."

"When I'm with him, I feel like I can fly. Is that how it is for you all?"

"Yes," they answer in unison, and I laugh.

"That's what happens when you're with a man who supports you," Lacey continues. "It's how it should be, but women get so used to making excuses for why we aren't happy in a relationship. We blame ourselves and think those sorts of feelings are unobtainable, when, really, they're the most natural thing in the world when you're with the right person."

Dallas *is* the right person. He's the right person for me right now, and he's going to be the right person for me in thirty years.

Long after football and photography and any other passions we share, he's going to be there, welcoming me home with open arms, because he is mine, and I'm hopelessly and completely his.

FORTY-SIX
MAVEN

I KICK off my boots and tiptoe down the hall when I get home just past ten. I turn the corner into the living room and wince when a floorboard creaks, only to find Dallas on the couch.

"I'm awake," he says. He lifts his head from the pillows and opens his arms. "Hey, pretty girl."

"Hi." I smile at him. "What are you doing? It's late."

"Reading a book from your stack and taking notes."

I laugh and walk over to him, lying next to him so our chests press together. "How was your night? I missed you."

"I missed you, too." He kisses the top of my head and wraps his arms around me. "Our night was good. We had burgers for dinner. June wanted ice cream even though it's January, so we looked like two fools running down the street to the grocery store."

"What flavor did you get?"

"Asking the important questions. Chocolate chip. Your favorite. There's extra in the freezer." He gestures to the liquor cabinet with a lazy wave of his hand. "Do you want a drink? We haven't made much of a dent in that bottle of tequila."

"No." I sigh and rub my hand across his pectoral muscles. "I had a few glasses of wine at dinner, and I'm just at that point where everything feels nice and lovely."

"I bet you are. Your face is pink." Dallas touches the curve of my cheek with his thumb, and the skin-on-skin contact warms me instantly. "How are Maggie and Lacey?"

"Good." I pause and bury my face in his bare chest. "They might know about us, but Shawn definitely doesn't."

"You told them?"

"Only after they noticed the hickey on my neck. Thanks for that, by the way."

Dallas chuckles and pulls me closer. "How do you feel about them knowing?"

"Good. I mean, it was bound to happen eventually, right? And they gave me some good advice, so I don't regret telling them one bit."

"Advice?" I feel him frown against my forehead. "Do we need to talk about anything?"

"No, no. Nothing like that. I just pointed out how we're kind of at different stages in life, and I didn't know if that's something to be concerned about." I close my eyes and sigh. "I don't want you to wake up one day and think you can do better than me. I know I don't have a degree. I know I'm not some famous model or athlete or clay bowl maker."

"Can you name a famous clay bowl maker?" he asks.

"No, but that's not the point. You're older. Your life has already been decided for you—you're a dad. First and foremost, and no matter what else you do after football, you'll always be *that* before anything else. And I love that about you, Dallas, because you're the best dad in the world. But I don't want you to think I'm this wild, unstable girl who doesn't know what she's doing, when you so clearly do."

"Maven." He nudges my shoulder and eases me on my back. He sits up and looks down at me. "I knew exactly who you were when I kissed you the first time, and the last words I'd ever use to define you are unstable and wild. Are you more spontaneous than me? Without a fucking doubt. Do you have less filter than some people? At times, but you also know when to rein it in and take a breath."

"I'm scared," I whisper. "I like you so much, Dallas. And June is my world, too. I never want to lose you both."

"Do you know what I think about when I wake up?" he asks, and he tucks a piece of hair behind my ear. "I think about how happy you make me. How wonderful you are with my daughter and how you love her like she's yours. I think about your kindness and patience. Your selflessness and your sense of humor. I think about how forever with you doesn't sound long enough. I wonder how in the world today is going to be better than yesterday, because yesterday was the best day of my life. And it always is. You are my greatest joy, and there's not a single thing I'd change about you. You are perfect. You are perfect for me. You are..." he dips his chin and takes my hand in his. "You are the sun and you're the stars, and even on the worst days, when we're mad at each other or tired or frustrated, it's still going to be a good day, because you'll be by my side."

I love you.

I love you, I love you, I love you.

It thrums in my heart. It sparks behind my eyes. It runs through my veins, a loud, boisterous thing that won't quiet down.

I should tell him. I really should. But I kiss him first. I bring his mouth to mine and tell him behind the press of our lips. The glide of my hand from his shoulders to his stomach. The way my legs wrap around his middle and my hips lift up, conveying what I want to do with him.

He tastes like forever. Like every dream I've ever had and every wish I've made on a shooting star.

Dallas lifts me from the couch and walks us to our room. He never stops touching me—not even to open the door. His palms roam down my body. They tangle in my hair then touch my breasts. They rub my back, and when he sets me down on my feet, I feel a little drunk and dizzy.

"I think about this, too," he says hoarsely. "Your body. How you really feel like you were made for me. How badly I want you —all the time."

"So have me," I say, and I pull my dress over my head. He inhales sharply, and his eyes turn dark. "In whatever way you want." I unclasp my bra and let my breasts spill free. "Because I'm yours." I hook my thumbs in the waistband of my underwear and shimmy them down my legs. When I start to take off my stockings, his fingers curl around my wrist.

"No." He shakes his head and his Adam's apple bobs. His eyes move down my body, and he adjusts the front of his sweat-pants. "Leave those on. Please."

"Okay." I smile. "Anything else?"

Dallas dips his head and brings his mouth to my ear. His breath is hot on my skin, and I arch my back. "Get on the bed and get on your knees. I want to decide which hole of yours I'm going to fill first. Maybe I'll take two at the same time."

Oh.

It takes a second for my brain to catch up. To pull itself out of the lust-filled cave it's tumbled into, but then I'm there. Warm all over and desperate for him.

I walk to the bed and perch on my knees. I lean forward on my hands and look at him over my shoulder as I crawl across the sheets. He shoves his hand down the front of his sweatpants and tilts his head back, like he's trying to hold on to the last bit of his sanity.

"Come here," I say, and he walks toward me.

He stops at the edge of the mattress and takes off his sweatpants. He's not wearing any underwear, and his cock is thick and hard in his hand. I smile as he gives himself a couple of tugs and watch as bursts of delight dance across his face.

"Save some for me," I add, and his hand falls away.

"Spread your legs," he tells me, and I do.

Dallas runs his fingers down my back, and I shudder beneath him. When he gets to my hip, he reaches around me and touches my clit with his thumb. I gasp and lurch forward. A moan escapes me when he rubs in a slow, torturous circle. It gets louder when he kisses my shoulder and sucks on my skin, undoubtedly leaving another mark behind.

"So wet," he murmurs. "How many fingers do you want, Maven?"

"Three," I say. "All three."

My eyes roll to the back of my head when he pushes all three in at once. I cry out, the stretch just on the brink of painful, but then I see flashes of colors as Dallas kisses my neck and whispers in my ear.

"Take your time," he says, and he brushes his nose against my cheek. "I love feeling you clench around my fingers." I blow out a breath and relax into him. "That's it, baby."

His body curls over mine, a pressure that only intensifies the pleasure rippling through me. I have nowhere to go. No escape. He's in total control of me, and when he takes my nipple between his thumb and pointer finger, I whine.

"Too much," I rasp, but I grind into his hand. I circle my hips and ask for more.

"You sure about that?" Dallas laughs and bites my throat. "That's one hole. Open your mouth, Maven. Let's fill the second."

My lips part and he puts three fingers on my tongue. I moan as I taste myself on him, and my tongue runs up the length of his digits, wanting to take every drop he'll give me. I suck on his fingers like I suck on his cock, and his length presses into my ass, harder than before.

He pulls his hand away from my mouth and shoves my legs wide open. "That might be my favorite thing about you. How fucking desperate you are for me."

"You're desperate for me, too, aren't you Dallas?" I reach behind me and take his shaft in my hand. I stroke him up and down and grin when his grip on me falters. My thumb rubs over the pre-cum on his head, and I hum my approval. "Look at you. Where do you want to fuck me first?"

Dallas doesn't answer. He flips me over and my back lands on the pile of pillows. He grabs my thighs and scoots toward me with red cheeks and swollen lips. "Here," he says, and he slides the tip of his cock inside me. I groan and close my eyes, but his thumb presses on my clit. "No, Maven. Eyes open. I want to watch you when you come."

It takes effort to listen to him. To not succumb to the high I'm chasing because it's *so close*, but I finally look at him. Our gazes lock, and my breath catches.

His thrusts are rough and bruising and hard enough to leave me sore tomorrow, but his face is nothing short of tender. He watches me like I'm a precious gift. His eyes sparkle and there's the smallest smile on his face, like he's in awe. *Grateful* that he gets to do this with me.

"That feels good, Dallas," I say, and my hands grip the sheets when he matches the rhythm between his thumb and cock.

"Bring your knees to your chest. Let me get deeper," he says, and I nod. "*Fuck.* There we go. Do you feel that, Mae?"

"It's so good. *So good.*" I moan, and I let go.

I hand myself over to him and let him take full control, using me however he sees fit.

It's chaotic. It's exquisite. It's messy and loud. It's the brink of ecstasy.

When Dallas wraps his hand around my neck and squeezes, fire licks up my spine. When he tells me how good I am, I step one foot off the ledge. And when he pulls his cock out and replaces it with his fingers, adding a curl and a flick of his wrist I fall.

"So pretty when you come, Maven. You're such a good girl for me."

The orgasm takes over my body. I moan and squirm and fuck his fingers. I chase every ounce of bliss he can give me. Dallas doesn't stop until I'm begging him to, and even then, he doesn't give me a reprieve.

"Don't move," he says, his voice deeper than I've ever heard it. "I told you I'm going to fill you up. You didn't listen to me the last time I gave you a warning, so this is your chance to say no, Maven."

I give him a lazy grin. I feel weightless and invincible, like I could lift off the mattress and fly away. "We both know I want your cum inside me. Is that going to happen? Or are you all talk?"

"Such a brat," he murmurs, and he slams back into me. I gasp and reach for the headboard behind me, and his grin is sinister. "A brat who takes my cock so well, doesn't she?"

"Dallas." My fingers dig into the mahogany, and I moan. "I'm not sure I—"

His knee moves next to my hip. He leans forward and takes my breast in his mouth, sucking and biting on the nipple. "You can," he says against my skin. "I've got you, Mae."

I don't know what power he has, but he does something with his tongue and his teeth right as he rolls his hips and gets an inch deeper inside me, and I lose it again. My legs shake and my eyes sting with tears. A sob leaves my body, and as the intensity shifts to delirious perfection, I feel him pulse inside me.

Dallas groans into my neck and bucks his hips. He says my

name over and over again, like a prayer, until he pulls out and collapses next to me. I reach for him blindly, my eyes closed and my forehead prickled with sweat, and he drags me to his side.

"We're good at that," I say after a long stretch of time where we both calm down. "*You're* good at that."

"You're incredible." He runs his hand over my stomach and outlines my hip bone with his thumb. "Thank you."

"For letting you fuck me?" I ask, and I turn my head to look at him.

"For being perfect," he says, and he opens one eye to smile at me. "For being mine."

"Look who's talking. Two orgasms in a matter of minutes. You might be God's gift to women."

Dallas laughs. "Says the woman with a pussy so tight I forget my name when I'm inside her."

"You don't forget mine, though."

"No. You're a goddess." He pauses, and his eyes bounce down my body. "Can I—"

"Can you what?"

"Never mind. It's embarrassing," he says, and I curl my fingers around his chin.

"Don't hide from me. We're honest with each other about everything else."

"Can I see what you look like full of my cum?" Dallas asks.

"*Oh.*" I smile and sit up on one elbow. "You said you'd do anything for me, didn't you?"

"Yeah." His throat bobs, and he can't stop staring at me. "Anything at all."

"Get on your knees, Dallas. Get on your knees like a good boy, and I'll show you."

I don't think he'll do it.

He's the captain of an NFL team. An elite athlete who thrives off of having authority and people listening to *him,* not the other way around.

So when he licks his lips and moves off the bed, dropping to the floor and watching me, I almost combust.

"Please, Maven," he whispers, and he strokes my ankle. "Can I see? Can I see what it looks like after you make me lose my mind?"

I nod, at a loss for words. The power he gives me melts when he gently tugs me toward him and puts my feet on his shoulders.

"Can you hold yourself open for me?" he rasps. "I've been good, right?"

"So good, Dallas." I blow out a breath and bring my hands between my legs. "Do you like what you see?"

He nods and runs his fingers through his cum. He spreads it over my clit then pushes the remnants inside me. "*Fuck.* I've made a mess out of you, haven't I?"

"I like the mess," I say softly. "The before, during and after too."

"I wonder what you'd look like if I made you lie there until I was ready for round two. That cum would barely be dry before I filled you up with some more. You'd take all of that, too, wouldn't you?"

"Yes," I whisper. "I wouldn't waste a drop."

"Fuck, Maven." Dallas touches his release again and spreads it down the inside of my thigh. He lifts my hips and drags some of the leftovers to my ass, too, and I moan. "I don't want to, but I should probably clean you up."

"I can think of a few ways you could do that," I say, and I thread my fingers through his hair. "A shower. Your tongue. Your tongue in the shower."

He smiles against my leg. "You like me on my knees, don't you?"

"You do it so well, and you like being there, don't you?"

"Yeah." He hides his blush with a kiss to my hip. "I like when you tell me what to do."

"Then what are you waiting for?" I challenge, and he yanks me off the bed.

I laugh as I land on the floor next to him, and he kisses me with the glide of his tongue and the sting of his teeth. I climb into his lap and he lifts us, walking to the bathroom while his mouth never leaves mine.

Dallas draws a bath for us instead of turning on the shower. He holds me to his chest until the water goes cold, and all the while I come closer and closer to telling him *I love you, I love you, I love you,* once and for all.

FORTY-SEVEN

DALLAS

"GREAT WIN, BOYS," I shout. "We're going to the fucking Super Bowl."

The locker room descends into chaos. Someone pops open a bottle of champagne. I pull my dirty jersey over my head and spin it around like a helicopter before I launch it in the air.

Fuck, it feels good to celebrate.

It feels good to get past the roadblocks we faced this season and see our hard work pay off. All of those days practicing in the heat and the cold. The long hours in the weight room when I thought my legs were going to fall off if I did one more squat. The nights after our first, second, third and fourth losses when we reviewed film until my eyes hurt.

We fucking did it.

It's not the first time we've made the Super Bowl, but it's special, because this group of guys hasn't been there together. We've had our backs against the wall, and we came out on the other side stronger than before.

"Dal. Media wants you," Jett calls out, and he snaps a picture of himself with the George Halas trophy. "She's out in the hall."

"Thanks. Proud of you, man. Proud of you for not letting the adversity get to you. There's no better QB in the league, and I'm weirdly attracted to your right arm."

"That's how I feel about your right foot. We've still got work to do, though."

"The grind never stops. Let me do this interview so I can see my girl." I pull off my pads and drop them to the side, nudging them out of the way with my foot. "I miss the hell out of her."

"You have a *girl?*" he asks. He puts his phone away, and I have his undivided attention. "Since when?"

"It's been a few months." I give him a sheepish grin I don't bother to hide. "I'm obsessed with her."

"No shit." He mirrors my grin. "She must be pretty great—you haven't been this giddy in years. I'm happy for you, Lansfield. Behave yourself tonight."

I laugh and head out into the hallway, walking with a lightness to my step.

"Dallas."

Julie, our in-house sideline reporter, waves me over. I work my way through the throngs of people in the tunnel. It's nearly impossible to squeeze by as I get stopped for autographs and pictures.

"Hi," I say, out of breath. "Sorry for the insanity."

"That's okay. I'm sorry for taking up some of your time. I'm sure you would rather be celebrating."

"Nah. This is part of the job, and I'm happy to chat. What do you have for me?"

"Tonight you kicked the fifteenth game-winning field goal of your career, Dallas, which is a new NFL record. Does the pressure get easier to handle the more years you spend in the league?" she asks, and she holds the microphone out to me.

"I think it only amps up," I answer. "You get older. You start to wonder if someone is vying for your job. I learned that when I stopped focusing on everything that could go wrong and the mistakes I could make and instead put my energy into what I *can* control—kicking the ball as far as it will go—I performed better."

"You all are heading into the Super Bowl as the underdogs, which is rare for you. What are you going to do with your two weeks off to prepare?"

"Stay sharp and study film. It's easy to get lazy and sloppy, but this next week is going to be important for us. We have a lot of work to do."

"Thanks for your time, Dallas. Enjoy your night," she says.

"Thanks, Julie. Watch your back; I think some doofuses are bringing the champagne into the hall," I say.

I move away from the camera. I love the celebration and being here with my brothers, but I'm ready to find June and Maven and head back to the apartment. They were sneaking around before we left for the stadium, and I think there might be a chocolate cake waiting for me when we get home.

God, I really want to fucking hug them and enjoy this moment with them, too.

They helped me get here, and it doesn't feel right that they aren't with me right now.

I saw Maven on the sidelines a few times during the game. My eyes found hers right after I kicked the game winner. She was grinning from ear to ear as I got hoisted on my teammates' shoulders and held up a heart she made with her hands.

I held one up too.

"Dal," Shawn says, stopping me. He's wearing an NFC CHAMPIONS hat backwards on his head, and there's confetti stuck to his face. "Helluva game tonight, kid."

"Shucks, Coach. Thanks for trusting me."

"There's no one I'd rather have kicking the ball with only two seconds left on the clock. How are you going to—" He stops talking. His eyes bounce to my neck, and his smile disappears. "What are you wearing?"

"What?" I glance down and see the chain around my neck. It's usually hidden by my jersey, but now it's in plain sight. My hand covers the gold M resting in the hollow of my throat. I take a step back, and Shawn fixes me with a look so murderous, I'm surprised I'm not already dead. "It's nothing."

Shit.

Shit.

I try to put distance between us while I search for an escape. A way to get out of here before he starts asking question, but he's too fast.

My feet leave the ground and my shoulders slam against the wall behind me. I wince in pain, and the back of my head throbs with a dull ache.

"Why the *hell* are you wearing Maven's necklace?" he hisses.

"It's not hers. My mom got it for me," I blurt out. I'm grasping for straws at this point. Pulling something out of my ass that will keep him happy and keep me alive. "Like I said, it's nothing."

Shawn's eyes narrow into tiny slits. "That's funny," he says, and there's no humor in his voice. "It looks a lot like the necklace I got Maven for her sixteenth birthday. I'm going to ask you this one time, Lansfield. Are you sleeping with my goddaughter?"

I swallow.

There's a moment where I consider lying.

Consider laughing it off and acting like it's no big deal.

Turning it into locker room talk and claiming it belongs to someone I hooked up with one time, the jewelry a trophy of an excellent fuck.

But I'm so fucking sick of being secretive.

I want to hold her hand out in public. I want to kiss her on the sidewalk while people stare at us. I want the entire stadium to know who I belong to.

I care about her so much, and her needs have started to go above mine.

I feed her. I make sure she's getting enough sleep. When she's tired and frustrated after trying on the soccer field again and again and again, I'm waiting for her at home with a warm bath and a glass of wine.

Home.

That's what the apartment has become since she moved in.

It's bright, with pictures on the wall and a full calendar on the fridge.

It's her clothes in my dresser and my toothbrush next to hers in the bathroom.

It's stupid coffee mugs she picked up at a general store in Virginia when she went hiking with Isabella last month, cackling when she handed me the cup with porcelain antlers that says *I moose you so much.*

It's the fuzzy pink blanket she keeps draped over the left side of the couch—the side she and June sit on and cuddle when we watch *Frozen* for the sixteenth time that week.

It wouldn't matter where we lived; in a different penthouse apartment on the other side of town. A house outside the city. A ranch in North Carolina with nothing but open fields and mountain views.

Wherever she is, that's where I want to be.

Home isn't a place.

It's her.

And I'm done hiding it from the world.

"Yes," I say. I lift my chin and keep my gaze on Shawn. "Yes, it's her necklace, and yes, I'm sleeping with her."

I don't know what I expected to happen when I told him the truth, but it's not his fingers tightening around my neck. There's anger in his eyes. The admiration he used to have for me is replaced with loathing.

I should hate myself for breaking his trust. For going against his word and doing something I shouldn't have, but I don't.

I don't give a damn.

"What's your plan here, Dallas? Are you going to fuck her for a month then throw her out when you get bored?" he seethes. "Get rid of her after you're done using her to watch your kid?"

I've never been a violent guy.

My parents taught me to use my words, not my fists, but I don't care that Shawn is my coach. I don't care that he could pummel my face in with one punch. Hearing him talk about Maven like that makes me want to kill him.

"Fuck you," I snarl, and I try to lunge for him. "Don't fucking talk about her like that."

"Shawn? *Dallas?* What the hell is going on?" Maven asks.

I turn my head to the left and see her rushing down the hall. Her camera bounces around her neck, and she looks panicked.

"Go away," Shawn says as she gets closer.

"Stop it. You're going to hurt him," she says, and there's a tremor in her voice. Her hand folds over his bicep and she tugs on his arm. "Put him down."

"He deserves to get hurt," Shawn says, and he shrugs Maven off with one lift of his shoulder.

I take advantage of him being distracted and shove the center of his chest. "I'm not just fucking her."

"You were supposed to stay away from her," he yells, and my ears ring.

"I fucking love her," I yell back, and the tunnel turns silent.

Everyone stares at me—my teammates and their families celebrating the wins. The reporter waiting to interview Shawn. Reid, who is live streaming our celebrations to god knows how many social media channels. Paul, the locker room security guard, who grins at me.

"What?" Shawn growls, and I take as deep of a breath as I can.

"I said, I love her." My eyes move from his face to Maven. Her mouth hangs open, and she's gaping at me. "I love you," I say, softer this time. We might have an audience, but the declaration is just for her.

The pressure around my neck loosens. I blink, and my feet are back on the ground. Shawn watches me, and an ounce of his anger is gone.

"How long?" he asks.

I touch the necklace hanging from my neck. Checking to make sure it's still there has become a nervous habit. When my fingers graze over the gold M, my shoulders relax.

"Months. But I think I knew the minute I ran into her in the stadium, her first day on the job."

I turn my attention back to Maven. There are tears on her cheeks, and I so badly want to pull her into my arms and hold her close. To whisper that it's okay. That I'm still here and we'll figure it out. She gives me a small smile, and my heart lurches up to my throat.

"I just fell," I continue. "And I'd do it again without thinking twice."

Shawn takes two steps back. "Get back to the locker room," he says to my teammates, and they scatter like flies. Reid disappears, too, and I hope he took the video with him.

"I'm sorry," I say.

"I'm not happy with you. I'm really fucking pissed. There are plenty of women out there. Nice ones, who aren't eight years younger than you and my goddamn goddaughter."

"There are." I touch her necklace again and smile. "But none of them are her. It wouldn't be worth it."

He watches me for a beat then sighs. "Now that I know this is going on, I have to handle it like I would any other player having a relationship with someone on the team."

Shit.

I think a knife gets stabbed through my chest.

We knew the repercussions of what could happen if anyone found out about us but we—I—decided to be bold and reckless anyway.

I decided to be a smug asshole and walk around with her necklace hanging from my throat, as if no one would notice or put two and two together.

Now one of us is going to be in trouble, and I have a feeling they're not going to choose the guy who just hit the game-winning field goal to take the Titans back to the Super Bowl.

I turn to Maven. She's still watching me, and I'm desperate to know what she's thinking.

"Hey, sunshine," I say softly, and I reach out to cup her cheek. "Could you grab June? I'll meet y'all at the car."

"Oh." She swallows and bobs her head. "Yeah. I can do that."

I grab her hand before she can run off. "We're going home together, okay?"

"I'm afraid to leave you alone. I don't want you to get hurt, and I think Shawn might actually kill you."

I press a kiss to her forehead and she melts against me. "I'll be alright, baby. I'll see you soon."

Maven lets go of me and shuffles backward. Her eyes dip to my bare chest and to the necklace I'm not sure I'll ever take off. Her lips pull into a smile, and I know we're going to be okay.

"Dallas," Shawn says, and for a few blissful seconds, I forgot he was here. I forgot anyone was here but her. "We need to talk."

"I know we do." I watch Maven walk away, and I rub my hand across my chest. "But not yet. Can you give me a few days to try and figure some things out?"

"Figure *what* out, exactly?" he asks. "You broke the rules, and so did she. The last thing I need is the NFL complaining to me about workplace misconduct and inappropriate relationships happening under my nose. Again. Jesus Christ. Right before the fucking Super Bowl. I swear to God. If I have to bench you because you can't keep your dick in your pants, I will actually murder you."

I huff out a laugh. "Look. I have an idea. A few, actually. But I need a a couple days to make them happen. I know my whole outburst is probably trending on social media, but I promise to lay low. I won't make any comments or confirm anything to anyone who asks. Give me some time. Please, Coach. She and June are the best things to ever happen to me, and I want to make sure this is handled right."

Shawn drags his hand over his jaw and sighs. He stares at the bracelet around my wrist and shakes his head. "How did I miss the signs? Those bracelets. Thanksgiving. It's so obvious. You have until Thursday to figure your shit out. We fly out for the Super Bowl on Monday, and I cannot be dealing with this out there. Neither can you."

"You have my word."

"A lot of good that's done so far."

I grin. "Did you just make a joke, Coach?"

"Fuck off, Lansfield, before I change my mind."

"Yes, sir." I give him a salute and head for the locker room.

Four days.

I only have four days to come up with a plan.

But first I need to see my girls.

FORTY-EIGHT
MAVEN

I PACE around the living room.

Dallas is putting June to bed, and I hear his voice drift down the hall. It settles around my shoulders like a warm hug, and I smile.

He's reading her favorite book, the one with a princess and a dragon and an evil king. I know he's using his different voices. There are probably props too. It's a full theatrical production just to get his daughter to smile.

God, I love him.

And he loves me, too.

The thought hits me square in the chest, and I almost can't breathe.

When he yelled it to the entire team, to the entire *world,* I went weak in the knees. An arrow hit my heart and lodged itself there. I didn't have a chance to say it back during all the chaos, but I do.

I love him more than I've loved anything in my entire life, and I can't hide it from him any longer.

"Hey."

I glance up and find Dallas leaning against the wall. His

arms are folded across his chest and his ankles are crossed. His favorite pair of gray sweatpants hide his long legs, and there's a bruise forming on his cheek from where he got hit with a helmet during the victory celebrations.

He's so beautiful, it almost hurts to look at him.

And he's *mine*.

"Hi," I say, and the right side of his mouth hitches up in a smile.

"You do this thing when you're thinking really hard," he says, and he walks toward me. "You stick out your tongue."

"No, I don't."

He stops right in front of me. I tilt my chin back to look up at him, and his smile has melted to a full-on grin.

"I'm dead serious. You wrinkle your eyebrows, too, and it's really cute." He laughs and runs his thumb down the line of my throat. "It's one of the many things I like about you."

"Are there more?"

"Tons. Hundreds, in fact. Like when you're really happy, your nose scrunches up. When you're sad, your bottom lip does this pouty thing." His thumb moves across my mouth, and I sigh. "It's incredibly sexy."

"You think my sadness is sexy?"

"Everything about you is sexy."

I turn my head and kiss the center of his palm. "Should I leave? I can go and stay with my dad. Or Isabella."

"Leave?" Dallas frowns, and he hooks his fingers around my chin. "Why?"

"I don't know. I thought you might want some space after... that. Maybe you need some time to clear your head."

"My head has never been clearer, and I don't want to be away from you for a single second. Unless you want to go?" he asks, and I hear the hesitation in his question.

"I don't want to go," I whisper. Before a tear can fall, he's wrapping me in his arms. I'm enveloped by the warmth of his chest. The scent of his soap from his shower. The firm press of his muscles and how gently he holds me. "I want to stay here with you."

"Good," he says into the top of my head. The word gets lost somewhere in my hair, and he doesn't let me go. It makes me think he's afraid I might slip away. "I'm glad."

"But we should talk," I say to the cotton of his threadbare shirt. "About what happened."

"Yeah." Dallas untangles our limbs and laces our fingers together. "Let's go to our room."

It feels like someone takes an ax to my heart.

He pulls me down the hall, a steady rock against strong waves. We pass the same photos I admired when he gave me a tour of the apartment for the first time. He's added some new ones in the months that have passed.

The three of us at the zoo and our sunburned noses.

The cake June and I made for Dallas's birthday and the chocolate on our faces.

Me and June at the playground, her in my lap as we come down a metal slide.

Dallas with JB on his shoulders, a snapshot I took from behind when we went and saw *Sesame Street Live!*

All three of us at Six Flags with balloon hats on our heads and hotdogs in our hands.

It's a timeline of us falling in love.

If I arranged them chronologically, I wonder if I'd find the moment on our faces when we knew how we felt about the other.

Dallas opens the bedroom door, and I walk inside.

"Shawn knows," I say. "Shawn knows, and he's pissed."

"Does that bother you?"

"Bother me? No." I take a deep breath and smooth my hands

over my thighs. "But what about my job? I know we understood the risks that came with seeing each other. Now that the moment is here, it's terrifying. I'm sure Shawn is printing out my termination papers now. It's going to be hard to say goodbye to something I love."

"I'm not going to let you get fired," Dallas says. There's ferocity in his tone, but when he cups my cheeks, it's soft and tender.

"How?" I laugh, and it's bitter. "You're you and I'm me. Who do you think they're going to let go? The Super Bowl champion? Or the lowly photographer who snaps a couple of photos once a week? I'm replaceable, Dallas, and you're not."

"Hey." His thumb wipes away a tear that escapes from my eyes. "You do so much more than snap a couple photos. You've built a brand and a following. People adore your work because it's *good*, Maven. If anyone's going to go, it's going to be me. I've played enough football to last me twenty lifetimes. I'm not going to let you give up your dream just so I can keep kicking a ball around."

"What?" I whisper, and I go still. "What are you talking about?"

"If it comes down to it, I'll retire. I'll walk away from the game. I've accomplished everything I set out to do when I entered the league, and then some. I have two rings—and maybe a third soon. I've broken records. It's all been fine and good, but I don't care about them anymore. The thought of spending every day and every night with my daughter and the woman I love beats the hell out of getting knocked around on the field."

"You can't give up *your* dream." I grip his collar and my fingers tangle with his—*my*—necklace. "That's not fair."

"Don't you get it?" Dallas brushes his nose against mine, and I let out a breath. My heart races in my chest, and somehow, even with his hands on me, he's still too far away. "Dreams change. You're what I want now. You and June and the family we've created. I don't care about the rest. I've done my time, and I'm ready to settle down. I'm ready to not be away from the best things in my life day after day. Because, *fuck*, Mae. I miss you when I'm gone. I miss you so fucking much my heart hurts. I can't—I don't know how long I can do this schedule when all I want is to be with you. Everything else is just extra shit I can live without. I can't live without you."

A sob racks my body.

I bury my face in the crook of his shoulder and his arms wrap around me again, holding me close.

"I love you," I whisper, and it sounds so permanent in the home we've built together. So real and so full of promise. "I love you so much. I love June too. I know I'm not her mom, but god, I wish I was. You two have become my entire world, and I don't want there to ever be a day when you're not in my life. I'm a better person because of you, Dallas. And if you want to walk away from football, I won't stop you. I want you to do what makes you happy, because you've made me happy for months now, and all I ever want is the same for you. Just please don't do it for me. This is my problem to solve, and if I have to pick between you and photography, I'm going to pick you every time. I'll find a new dream, but I'll never find another you."

"We're going to figure this out, baby," he says, and I look up to find him crying too. "I promise we will."

His cheeks are wet, and there's a tear hanging in the corner of his eye. He brings his mouth to mine and kisses me, slow and sweet. I kiss him back, and there's so much behind the press of my lips.

Thank you.

I'm sorry.

I love you. I love you. I love you.

Forever.

I don't know how much time passes. I don't know how long we stay like that, the two of us hidden away from the rest of the world, just that it's not enough.

"What do we do now?" I ask, and I kiss his bruise. "You have to be at the stadium tomorrow for practice."

"I have a plan, but I need to talk to—" His phone rings, and he glances at it on the bedside table. "Let me grab that. Just in case."

"Okay. Yeah." I sit on the bed and watch him pick it up. "Who is it?"

"Maverick. The exact person I wanted to talk to. Can I—"

"Answer it," I say, and I pat the spot next to me. "And put it on speakerphone."

"Hello?" Dallas answers, and his knee nudges mine as he sits beside me.

"You're out of your damn mind," Maverick says, and he follows it up with a laugh. "How come you saved the grand gesture for when I'm on a five-game road trip, you asshole?"

"How do you know what happened?"

"Are you kidding me? It's all over the internet. You're trending on social media. Someone captioned the video and said: 'if our love isn't like this, I don't want it.' I'm not going to lie, I teared up a little."

"Jesus." Dallas wipes his eyes and sighs. "I thought Reid would delete the video."

"Yeah, right. The Titans' social media accounts have gained over five hundred thousand followers in an hour. You both have gained a lot too. Hi, Maven."

"Hi, Maverick." I rest my cheek on Dallas's shoulder and smile. "Where are you?"

"Fucking Toronto where it's fucking freezing. I can't wait to get to the west coast."

"Says the guy who skates on frozen water for a living," I whisper, and Dallas grins down at me.

"I heard that."

"I have to go, Miller, but there's something I want to talk to you about. Can I call you tomorrow?" Dallas asks.

"Listen, Dal. Maven was going to find out about our feelings for each other eventually. Might as well come clean now," he says, and he follows it up with a string of curses. "Jesus Christ. I think my balls are going to freeze off."

"Women everywhere are going to mourn," I say. "And that's perfectly fine if you two are in love—as long as we can share custody."

"Fifty-fifty. You can have him on the weekends. It's when he does his best work. I'm happy for you two. You know I have your backs, and I'm here if you need anything. I'm sure the timing isn't ideal, but now you don't have to hide anymore. You can just be with each other, and that's pretty fucking cool."

"Yeah." Dallas leans in and kisses me. He threads his hand through my hair, and I smile against his mouth. "It is."

"Okay, gross. Keep the make out session to yourself," Maverick says. "Dal, call me whenever. Maven, you know I love you. Take care of my boy. He's fragile."

"I will," I say, and take the phone from Dallas's hand. "Bye, Maverick."

"We have a couple days to figure this out. Shawn said he'd give me to Thursday to see if my idea can pan out," Dallas says when I end the call.

"Are you going to tell me what it is?"

"No." He rests his forehead against mine. "Not yet. I don't want to get our hopes up."

It's my turn for my phone to chime with a notification, and dread settles in my stomach.

"Can you get it?" I whisper.

"Sit up," he says, and pulls my phone from the back pocket of my jeans. His hand lingers for a second, and he hums when I arch my back into him. "I just wanted an excuse to touch your ass. I'm glad the universe gave me one."

I laugh despite the tension I'm feeling. "Will you read it for me?"

"It's from Shawn. 'Maven, attached you'll find a meeting request to discuss the disciplinary action for your violation of team and league rules. Next steps will be discussed, which, upon review of evidence, could lead to termination. Please be in my office by 9 a.m. sharp tomorrow morning. Thank you for your time. Shawn Holmes.'"

"He couldn't have made that more formal if he tried. The man has seen me in diapers and he's acting like I'm some nameless employee he's never met." I groan, frustrated. "So much for your plan. Guess my fate has been decided."

"Fuck. *Fuck.*" Dallas stands up and walks around the room. "Maven. Please, baby. Don't go there tomorrow. I can't live with the thought of you giving up your job for me."

"I'm not giving it up." I stand and join him in the middle of the room. "It's just a pause until the league can get their shit together with these outdated rules. But now that I know I'm *good* at photography, I can do other things with it, too. It doesn't have to be sports."

"This is my fault." He hugs me and rubs his hand down my back. "I should've stayed away from you. I should've behaved."

I hold my breath, afraid of what he might say next. "Do you regret it?"

"No," he whispers, and I melt into him. "And I feel like an asshole because of it."

"The only way for me to keep my job is if we break up." I pull back to look at him. "Do you—is that—"

"*Never.* Fuck, no, Maven. I told you I'm all in, and that

includes right now, when things get hard. What if we both quit? Maybe that will get the league to listen to how fucking stupid it is that we can't be together and both keep our jobs."

"Your contract isn't guaranteed. You'd lose out on *millions*, Dallas."

"So? I can have ten bucks to my name, but as long as I have you, I'll be happy."

I laugh and my eyes sting with tears again. "You've been reading too many books."

"Never enough romance books," I say.

"I love you. I love how willing you are to help, but this is something I need to do on my own. Maybe I can get Shawn to see it from a different side. Maybe it doesn't have to end in termination."

"Maybe," Dallas agrees. "Maybe it doesn't. But we can't control that anymore. Tell me again how much you love me instead, sunshine."

And I do. For a minute, we pretend. We slip into a fantasy world where no one gets in trouble. Where we get to keep being coworkers and partners and everything is *perfect*.

FORTY-NINE

MAVEN

I DON'T SLEEP.

Dallas doesn't either. I felt him tossing and turning next to me all night. Every time we drifted too far away from each other, he'd reach across the mattress and pull me back to him, like the tide to the sand.

It feels like a cloud of dread has been hovering over my head since I got Shawn's message last night, but the second I'm in Dallas's arms, I'm calm.

"Morning," I whisper. I touch his face and he smiles slowly under the morning light. "How did you sleep?"

"Morning, pretty girl." He kisses my forehead and rubs his hand down my arm. "Not well, but I love waking up to you."

"Me too." I roll onto my side and look up at him. The bruise on his cheek seems to have dulled overnight, and there's a twinkle in his eye. "What time do you need to be at the stadium?"

"One. I figured I'd stay here with June until..." he trails off and clears his throat. "Reid is on standby for babysitting duties if today goes to shit and you want the afternoon off to clear your head."

"I think it's a matter of *when* things go to shit, not if." I bury my face in his bare chest and sigh. "June is the highlight of my day, and after my morning with Shawn, I'm probably going to need some cheering up. I thought about it all night, and I don't even know what I'm going to say to him. There's no way to defend our actions, and I think the easiest thing to do is just take the punishment and move on."

"There might not be a punishment."

"Come on, Dallas. We both know there's going to be a punishment. He held you against a wall and tried to choke you."

"I think that was less because we work together and more because of who you are to him." Dallas brushes the hair out of my face and traces the shell of my ear. "He's going to be fair. He loves you, and he's not going to hurt you. He knows how much this job means to you. It'll probably be a suspension at most. You and I don't have any direct interaction on the field. It's totally different from our old assistant coach; she was with the guys every day."

"You're right," I agree, but it brings me little comfort. A huge unknown is looming on the horizon, and I hate that I can't skip ahead to the ending. "I should go get ready."

He kisses my shoulder and smiles. "Whatever happens, you're going to come home and June and I will be waiting for you. We're going to love you more this afternoon than we do right now. And that's how it's going to be every day, Maven. It doesn't matter if you're a sports photographer or temporarily unemployed. We're still so proud of you, and we're still going to cheer you on, no matter what."

"Thank you." I squeeze his hand and throw back the sheets. My heart thumps in my chest, but the longer I'm next to him, the more relaxed I feel. "How lucky am I to not have one love of my life, but two?"

"We're the lucky ones, honey. Call me as soon as you talk to him."

"I will." I give him the best smile I can muster and head for the closet, all the while feeling a lot like I'm heading to my own funeral.

UPS FIELD IS EMPTY.

Twelve hours ago, this place was alive with confetti and screaming fans. Reporters were asking for interviews and the players were celebrating. Now it's eerily quiet. There's no music or cheering. There's no applause from the crowd. The only sound is my shoes echoing down the hall as I make my way to Shawn's office.

I try to walk slowly and delay the inevitable, but my feet move on their own accord. It's like they know what's coming and they're ready to get it over with.

I wait outside Shawn's door and try to take a deep breath. I roll my shoulders back, and when the clock on my phone turns to nine, I walk inside.

"Hi." I close the door behind me and lean against it. "You wanted to see me?"

"Sit," Shawn says, gesturing to the seats in front of his desk, and nothing about his tone is friendly.

I take the one on the left and familiarity hits me. It's the same one I took the day I interrupted his meeting with Dallas. The meeting that kickstarted what got us to *this point,* all those months ago.

It's a full circle moment, and as I get comfortable on the leather and brace myself for the news I don't want to hear, I can't help but remember how different Dallas looked back then.

His hunched shoulders and the exhaustion on his face. The

defeated look in his eye and the sadness that exuded from him, like all he wanted was for someone to tell him how *good* of a dad he is and ask how they could help.

"How are you?" I ask, trying to make casual conversation. Shawn narrows his eyes, and I know he doesn't want any of my pleasantries.

"What were you thinking, Maven?" he asks, and I guess we're diving right into this. "You *knew* you weren't allowed to get involved with anyone on the team. You signed a contract stating you understood the team and league rules, didn't you?"

I swallow. "Yes."

"But you violated them anyway. *Why*?"

"I don't know," I admit. "I guess I wasn't thinking about those things when I was with Dallas off the field. He's not the football player everyone loves when he's around me. He's just himself. A dad. A good friend. That's all it was at the start—*friends*. One thing led to another and we started to fall for each other. If I matched with him on a dating app or met him at a bar, it would've been the same thing."

"Except, in this version, he's the coworker you were supposed to stay away from. Goddammit. I'm really fucking pissed off by this. By the lying. By the secrecy. By the blatant disregard for the rules. I'm the one who went to bat for you and recommended you to the media staff. And don't even get me started on him. I want to fucking kill him."

"Don't," I say sharply. "He didn't do anything wrong."

"He sure as hell did. This is after watching me deal with the fallout of an assistant coach doing the same fucking thing years ago. Dallas does it, and, what? Thinks he can get away with it because he's the best kicker in the league? Like the rules don't apply to you two because of who you are to me? There's no special pass for being two idiots, no matter how we might know each other."

Anger boils inside me. I've tried *so hard* to stay level-headed about this, but I'm allowed to be pissed about shitty rules even though I broke them.

"Instead of being an asshole, why don't you start to fight the league on these horribly restrictive rules they have in place? You put anyone together in the same space and attraction is *bound* to develop. We're not the first couple who worked together on a team and fell in love, and we're not going to be the last, either. The only reason this is an issue is because we got caught. Guess what? We've been living together for *months*, and it hasn't jeopardized anything. In fact, Dallas is playing some of the best football of his career. I guess I'm not too much of a distraction."

Shawn blinks and goes very still. "You're living together?" he repeats. "Christ. You're really fucking trying me, aren't you? You're an adult now, not some college kid who overslept and missed a class. This is the real world with real consequences."

"Why are you acting like this is illegal?" I ask, and I raise my voice. "You're not my father, and you don't get a say in my love life just because you've known me for years. If you're this strict when you and Lacey have kids, I'm going to feel sorry for them. I wish you'd stop treating us like we're goddamn criminals and start treating us like people. Being in love isn't a crime."

He flinches, and I cover my mouth. "I'm sorry you feel that way," he says, and I can hear the hurt in his voice.

"I'm sorry," I whisper. "I'm so sorry. That was a horrible thing to say. I didn't mean it like that. I'm pissed off and—"

"You're right." Shawn doesn't look at me. He stares past my shoulder, and my eyes sting with tears. "I'm not your father. I'm just the guy who watched you grow up and spent night after night with you while your parents were working. I'm just the guy who saw you take your first steps and picked you up from prom after your date started making out with someone else. I have no jurisdiction over who you may or may not love."

"Stop. You know you're more than that to me." I knock over a pencil holder when I reach across the desk and find his hand. "I'm just... I'm so mad at you."

"I'm mad at you, too. This is my job, and *that's* why I care about your love life. I can't be in favor of your relationship when I have to face the league's ethics office—again, for fuck's sake—and reprimand you on something you knowingly did wrong."

"Okay." I sit back and put my hands in my lap.

"I really hate that I have to do this," Shawn says, and his voice cracks. "I know this job makes you happy, and I wish I didn't have eighteen people breathing down my neck about how it's handled, but I do. I do, and I'm sorry."

He drops a stack of papers in front of me, but my vision is too watery to read it.

"Your job with the Titans will be terminated immediately." He pauses, and I squeeze my eyes shut. "An investigation will be conducted to verify the means in which your relationship started and to make sure there was no exertion of power by Dallas or any other members of the Titans team."

"*What*?" I blurt out. "Are you serious? Shawn, we're two adults who—"

"You'll turn in your badge, and all on-field access will be revoked immediately. You can keep the licensing rights for the photos you took, but you cannot credit the team anymore."

"Fuck," I whisper, and I wipe away tears. "Termination?"

"It was preventable."

"Did you try to stop yourself from falling in love with Lacey?"

He tilts his head to the side and frowns. "Why do you ask?"

"Did you?" I challenge, and he nods.

"Yes," he admits. "I thought it might ruin our friendship if we got together. And I valued her as my best friend so damn much."

"And what happened?"

"I fell in love with her anyway." Shawn smiles and plays with his wedding band. "I'm glad I did."

"That's exactly what happened with me and Dallas. I knew the rules, Shawn, but I couldn't help it. I know I can't keep both, and I want to keep him because he's the best thing to ever happen to me. But it still really fucking hurts to have your dream taken away from you."

"It's that serious?"

"Forever kind of serious."

His face softens. "It doesn't change the outcome of this, but I'm glad you're happy."

"Let's just get it over with." I grab one of the pens off his desk and uncap it. "Where do I—"

The door swings open and Dallas comes storming inside.

"Dallas?"

"Get the hell out of here, Lansfield. This is a private meeting. I'm dealing with you later."

"Don't sign anything," Dallas pants. He braces himself against the door and sucks down a breath. "Don't sign it, Mae."

"I don't have a choice," I say. "We talked about this, and you better not be doing anything stupid."

"Maverick," he says, and I narrow my eyes.

"Do you have another concussion?"

"No." He walks over and collapses in the seat next to me. "The D.C. Stars need an in-game photographer. Their lead woman is going out on maternity leave, and she's going to miss all next season. He mentioned your name, and with how good your photographs are, the media team wants to meet you for an interview."

"Are you serious?" I turn and face him. "When did this happen?"

"Ten minutes after you left. That's what I wanted to talk to him about. It's not guaranteed, but it's a maybe."

"A maybe? A maybe is better than a no." I lean forward and hug him tight. "Thank you. Thank you so much, Dallas."

"You cannot sign that termination contract," he repeats when he pulls away from me. "There's probably some bullshit clause in there about not working for another professional sports team for a certain number of years. That was the case with our old assistant coach. She was basically blacklisted and never coached again." He looks at Shawn. "Is there?"

"Oh, you do remember that. I was thinking you didn't," he says flatly, and he flips through his copy of the contract. "It does. On page seven."

"Don't sign it, baby. Quit instead."

"*Quit*? I've never quit anything in life willingly," I say.

"I know you haven't." Dallas smiles and cups my cheeks. His palms are warm and soft, and I relax for the first time since I stepped foot in this office. "That's one of the reasons why I love you so much. You're so fucking headstrong. But there's a first time for everything, and I'm right here by your side."

I glance at Shawn. His murderous look has eased into hesitant acceptance, and that gives me hope.

"I quit," I whisper, and Dallas squeezes my knee.

"I accept your resignation, but I'm still pissed as shit." Shawn turns to Dallas. "You broke my trust, and there will be consequences. Losing your captain title is a possibility, and I'm not above benching you for the first half of the Super Bowl. I hate to make an example out of you, but I might fucking have to. It clearly didn't stick the first time."

"Yes, Coach," Dallas says, and he hangs his head. "I get it. I do. I just—I love her, you know? And I've never loved anyone like her, so I've been an idiot. I've been a little daring and a little stupid. I get caught up in her sometimes—okay, all the time, if we're being honest. Maven is the most wonderful thing to ever happen to me, and I'm a better man because of her. I know I messed up, and I know it's going to take some time to earn your trust back. You have every right to punish me, but I'm going to be honest with you, Coach. I'd do it again. I'd do it again in a heartbeat. I'm not learning from my mistakes because loving her isn't a mistake. It's the easiest, surest thing."

Shawn rubs his forehead and stares at us. "You make it really fucking difficult to stay mad at you when you're acting like a modern-day Romeo."

"It's working," Dallas whispers to me, and I laugh and sniff at the same time.

"You love her?" Shawn asks. "You really, truly love her?"

"I do. Enough to get choked by you and make a fool of myself on television."

His eyes move to me. "And you love him?"

"Yes." I nod and glance at Dallas. "I love him very much."

Shawn is quiet for a moment, but then he sighs. "I'll have the PR people put out a press release confirming your relationship and that it happened off of team premises. I'll let the league office know you handed in your resignation, and no investigation is needed."

"Investigation?" Dallas asks. "Who's being investigated?"

"You were going to be," Shawn says. "To make sure you didn't coerce her into anything or use your power to persuade her into a relationship she didn't consent to."

"Are you serious? She's the one with the power. When she walks around in those—"

"Shut the fuck up, Lansfield, or I will pin you to the wall again," Shawn says, and I turn bright red. "Both of you get out of here so I can deal with this."

I walk around the desk and hug him. "I know you're not my dad, but I love you like one. I'm sorry for putting you in this position and I'm sorry for the things I said."

"I love you, Mae. I've always loved you, and I only want the best for you." He looks over at Dallas and sighs. "And if Lansfield is the best, then I'll have to accept that."

"You'll be seeing me at Thanksgiving every year, Coach. How does that make you feel?" Dallas asks, and I laugh when Shawn groans.

"Let's get through the Super Bowl first," he says. "Then we'll talk about Thanksgivings."

I kiss his cheek and walk to Dallas. I rest my head on his chest and smile. "Thank you, Shawn."

"Love you kid," he says.

"Love you more," I tell him.

"I love you the most, Coach," Dallas adds, and I drag him toward the door.

"We're leaving now. See you soon!" I wave and lead him to the hallway.

"That went well," Dallas says. "Right?"

"Yeah." I nod and lace our hands together. "As well as it could. I know it's going to take some time for him to come around, but he'll get there."

"I hope so. I wasn't kidding about the Thanksgivings, and he looked *pissed*."

"One day at a time."

"Ready to head home?" he asks, and he kisses the top of my head. "Reid is with June, and when I left them, she was putting beads in his hair. He might need some rescuing."

"Home," I repeat with the biggest grin on my face. "There's no place I'd rather be."

FIFTY

DALLAS

"DO I HAVE TO GO INSIDE?" I ask. I stop outside the door to Maven's dad's apartment and clutch the wine bottle to my chest like it's somehow going to protect me. "Maybe I should head home. Maverick might need help with June and—"

"Dallas." Maven tugs on my sleeve and gently guides me forward. "You've met these people before. Tons of times. You spent Thanksgiving here two months ago, and you gave Shawn shit about spending every Thanksgiving with him going forward. What's going on?"

"They didn't know about us then. Now there's an opportunity for someone to use those knives you mentioned, and I think I'm going to be sick. This is a lot of pressure."

"You play football in front of millions of people every week, and *now* you're worried about pressure?" She loops her arm through mine and keeps us moving. "You're the king of being cool."

"That's football, not the family of the woman I love. I want to make a good impression not only because they're important to you, but because they're going to be in our lives for a long time. I want them to know I'm serious about you. That my intentions are good. I'm going to marry you one day, Mae, and I don't want there to be any resentment toward me."

"Hey." She stands on her toes and touches my neck. "I love you. And *they* are going to love Dallas, my boyfriend, even more than they love Dallas, the football player. Do you know why?"

"Why?" I ask, and I run my fingers through her hair. I feel grounded when I'm touching her, and if I had it my way, I'd sew myself to her so we'd never have to be apart. "Tell me."

"Because you make me happy. All anyone wants for someone they love is for them to be happy. I haven't felt this way before, and it's because of *you*, sweetheart." She kisses my cheek, and I melt at the endearment. "I found a job I'm good at. I'm slowly getting back into the sport I adore. I have a little family who is so special to me, and sometimes I have to pinch myself because it feels like I'm dreaming. You are worth every risk, Dallas, and I'd choose you and June every single time."

"Fuck, I love you." I move my hand to her chin and tilt her head back so I can look in her eyes. "I love you so very much, Maven."

Her palm drops to my chest and her thumb rubs across my shirt before settling over my heart. "We're one of those obnoxious couples, aren't we? We're going to end up being the psychopaths who sit on the same side of the booth and hold hands everywhere."

"God, I fucking hate those people. But I think you might be right."

The door flies open and we spring apart like we've been caught doing something we shouldn't.

"Are you two going to keep doing this whole cheesy love confession thing, or are you going to come inside?" Lacey asks. She leans against the doorframe with a sly grin, and I've never blushed so hard in my life. "You know, Dal, if you were going to replace me as the number two woman in your life behind June, Maven is the only one I'd concede to."

I bark out a laugh and release a breath. I feel the tension unravel from my spine as Maven slips her hand in mine and tugs me toward the door.

"Hi, Lacey." I bend down and kiss her cheek. "It's good to see you."

"It's good to see you, too, lovebirds." She squeezes Maven's shoulder and her eyes bounce between us. "Are we ready to get this party started?"

"What's the vibe in there?" Maven asks, and her fingers tighten around mine. "Are there any weapons?"

"Just a crowbar and an ax. A shotgun, too."

"I can handle a crowbar," I say, and her eyes crinkle with glee.

"If you're asking whether your father and godfather are plotting ways to knock your boyfriend off the map, the answer is no. I had a nice long talk with Shawn earlier this afternoon, and he's going to behave himself." Lacey looks at me, and her face hardens. "If you try and hurt Maven, I will hunt you down, though, and I'll use something much worse than a crowbar."

"Noted." I pull Maven to me and drop a kiss on the top of her head. "I have no plans to go anywhere. And especially not without her."

"Good." Lacey brightens and waves us inside. "Let's do it."

I hang my jacket with hers on the rack next to the door, and I smile when I see the fuzzy socks I got her when the weather turned cold.

"Doing okay?" Maven whispers, and her finger slips into my belt loop.

"I'm better now." I run my thumb along the inside of her wrist, and she sighs. "I'm happy I'm here with you."

She leads me into the living room and Maggie looks up from the couch.

"There you are. It's good to see you," she says, and she smiles.

"Mags." Maven hugs her, and I watch the women embrace. "How's the hospital?"

"Busy, as always. Your father is trying to get me to retire early." She rolls her eyes and sits back down, gesturing to the two seats next to her. "The joke is on him, though. I'm not going anywhere until they name a wing after me for all the work I do."

"You and Lacey are the most badass women I've ever met." Maven plops down and stretches out her legs. "How's Dad?"

"Good. He's waiting to pull the lasagna out of the oven, so he'll be here in a minute." She smiles up at me. "Sit down, Dallas. This isn't an interrogation."

"I know." I lower myself onto the couch and perch on the edge of the cushions. I tap my foot and wring my hands together. "I'm just nervous."

"Don't be. Aiden was disappointed that you all hid your relationship from us, but he loves you. Shawn finally got his head out of his ass thanks to Lacey talking some sense into him. You're going to be fine," Maggie assures me.

"Remember when I met you for the first time?" Maven laughs. "You tried to pretend you and Dad were just friends, but it was so obvious how much you meant to him by the way he looked at you."

"I sweated through three shirts before that dinner. You wouldn't stop asking me questions, and I was convinced you hated me at the end of the night." Maggie smiles and plays with the ends of Maven's hair. "Turns out I was wrong. I couldn't have asked for a better bonus kid."

Footsteps echo from somewhere deeper in the apartment, and I brace myself. Aiden comes around the corner and walks toward us. His arms are behind his back and there's a frown on his mouth. I suck in a breath and hold it, fearful of what he's going to say.

"Mae," he says, and he nods to his daughter. His gaze cuts over to me. "Dallas."

"Hey, Mr. Wood. Er, Aiden. Sir," I say, and I stand. I tower over him but he still intimidates me. "It's good to see you again."

"Wish I could say the same for you." He sighs. "And under such shitty circumstances."

"Dad—" Maven interjects, and he holds up his hand.

"Not now, kid. What do you have to say for yourself, Dallas?"

Shit. I thought I'd have more time to prepare for this.

"I—I love your daughter. Very much. And I know this is all kind of convoluted, but it's going to be alright," I blurt out.

"My daughter?" Aiden asks, and his eyebrows wrinkle. "I'm talking about my fantasy football team. What are *you* talking about?"

"You don't—I thought—she told me—oh, fuck. Shoot, I mean. I'm sorry, but I—"

"Gotcha, sucker." Aiden pulls out a NERF gun from behind his back. He shoots me square in the chest five times and grins as I stare at him, flabbergasted. "That's what you get for not having field goals in the final game of the regular season and making me lose the championship."

"I'm glad we're all being so mature about this." Maven stands next to me and puts her hands on her hips. "Where the hell did you get a NERF gun, Dad?"

"Maggie bought it for me," he says sheepishly. "She says I work too hard, and this is my way to let off some steam. Shawn and I have this game where we randomly attack each other; in the hallway. In the parking lot. I tried to bring it to UPS Field once, and spent an hour with Titans security. We have a running tally of who's hit the other the most times."

"You are a literal cancer doctor and this is how you use your free time?" Maven shakes her head, and I have to bite back a laugh. "Good grief."

Aiden holds out his hand, and I shake it. "I don't give a shit about how you two started your relationship or what rules you did or didn't break. I only have three questions for you. Do you make my daughter happy?"

I glance down at Maven, and she looks up at me. She bobs her head, encouraging me along, and I swallow.

"Yes sir. I think I do."

"Do you love her?" Aiden asks.

"More than anything in this world," I say easily.

"Do you promise to always communicate with her? Even if it gets hard and that love starts to fade, will you be man enough to not string her along when you both know things are beyond repair?"

I consider his question.

I haven't thought about a world where Maven and I aren't together, but it's possible. As much as we want to say it's a sure thing, life happens. Shit can hit the fan. People fall out of love every single day. While I hope it's never us, it could be, and I fucking hate the idea of us not being together.

I know he's also asking because he's divorced. I'm a single dad, and I don't speak to my daughter's mother. There's broken trust all over the place in this room, and he doesn't want to see his own daughter put through the gauntlet like that.

I wouldn't either.

"Yes," I say, even though it's difficult. "If letting her go is what would make her happy, I'd do it in a heartbeat."

"Good man. Welcome to the family."

"That's it?" I look around, and my shoulders relax. "I thought there would be more of an initiation."

"Nope. Not on my end. You can deal with your coach, though. He's still got a stick up his ass."

"What was that about a stick up my ass?" Shawn asks. He walks into the room and crosses his arms over his chest when his gaze meets mine. "Lansfield."

"Coach. Er. Shawn. Uh. I don't know what the protocol is in this situation. Are we bros or..."

"This is going to be fun." Lacey pats Shawn's shoulder and sits next to Maggie. "Can you make it quick, sweetie? Dinner is ready, and I'm starving."

Shawn turns his attention to her, and his smile is so different from anything I've seen from him before. It's private, like they can communicate just through the twitch of their lips, because Lacey returns it. An entire conversation passes between them, and I wonder if Maven and I do that, too.

As if she's reading my mind, Maven pokes my side. She tilts her head to the left, a question there.

You okay? she asks.

Perfect, I say back with a smile, and she smiles, too.

"You're part of this family, and I'm going to be nice to you," Shawn says. "I can still be pissed at you on the field, but off of it, when we're here with the people we love, we're friends."

"Wow." I clutch my chest. "That was so sweet of you, Coach."

"Don't get used to it. Where's June? I thought you'd bring her with you."

"Ah." I shrug, not liking all this attention on me. "She's with my friend, Maverick. I didn't want to impose, and she—"

"Bring her next time," Aiden says. "We have a spare bedroom. You can set up shop for her there when it's time for her to go to sleep."

"We'd love it if she were here," Maggie agrees. "She's your family which means she's our family now, too."

I don't know why those words feel so important, but they do.

They make me squeeze Maven's hip and take a step back from everyone.

"Do you have a restroom I can use?" I ask.

"I'll show you," Maven says, and I think she understands I need a minute. She leads me down the hall to a door on the left and pauses. "Do you want to be alone?"

"No. I want to be with you. That just made me kind of emotional."

"Why?" she asks, and she rests her head on my chest. "Is it a good kind of emotional?"

"Yeah. For so long, I thought I was doing this parenting thing alone. And I thought I was doing it really poorly, too. I thought people would call me a burden because I have to bring my daughter places, but then your family tells me she's welcome here—my kid with another woman who will never biologically be yours—and it's a reminder that good people exist and I have an army of friends to help me when I need it."

"You do." Maven kisses my shirt, and I sigh at the feel of her lips through the thin cotton. "And I hope you know June might not be mine, but she *is* mine. I've never had the experience of holding a kid of my own, maybe I will one day, who knows, but I imagine it's a lot like how I feel when I look at her."

"Like the most magical and terrifying thing in the world?" I ask, and her laugh settles me.

"Exactly." She hums and wraps her arms around my waist. "I'm so glad you're here, Dallas. And they're glad you're here, too. My people are your people, and I hope I can meet your family one day soon."

"The Super Bowl. My sister, January, and her daughter Lilah are coming. My parents will try to be there, but they're halfway across the world right now, so I'm not sure it's going to work out. They're all going to love you."

"Hang on. Your sister's name is January?"

"Have I not told you that? Yeah. She's older than me and lives in Georgia."

"Do your parents have an infatuation with calendars and cities in Texas?"

"If you think that now, you really don't want to know our middle names."

"You have to tell me." Maven pinches my side, and I laugh. "Please?"

"Fine. But only because you're so cute," I say, and drag my thumb across her bottom lip. "Her middle name is Austin. Mine is August."

"Forget infatuation. It's a whole ass kink."

"Stop." I groan and try to cover my ears. "Please don't ever mention my parents and *kink* in the same sentence ever again."

"I can't wait to meet them." She kisses the hollow of my throat and plays with the necklace sitting there. "I love you, Dallas. I'm so lucky you're mine."

"I love you, too, sunshine." I pause, and an idea comes to me. "Do you think your dad would be happy if I got a NERF gun and surprised him with some sort of NERF war in a warehouse or something? Like paintball, but less painful."

"God. You're going to replace me as favorite kid, aren't you?"

"Hey, you can play too, Mae. It would give you a chance to redeem yourself after losing at the art room."

"I did *not* lose at the art room. I reached the table first. You're the one who decided to knock it over," she says, and she twists out of my grip. The fiery look she gives me is one of my favorites, and I grin. "Maybe you really did lose some of your memory with that concussion."

We argue all the way to the kitchen, and as we settle around with the people she loves, I feel it in my heart how much I already love them, too.

FIFTY-ONE

DALLAS

"CAN you believe we're back here?" Jett asks. He props his foot on the wood bench between us and adjusts his socks. "Third Super Bowl in four years. We're a fucking dynasty, man."

I pull my jersey over my head and fix my shoulder pads. "Feels just like yesterday we had a losing record."

"Now we're back on top." He grabs his mouthguard and spins it around. "How are you and Maven doing? Is Shawn still pissed?"

"Less so, now. I get why he's mad about it. I didn't just break the rules—I broke his trust too. He's coming around, though. We're going to be just fine."

"I'm glad. You're a good guy, Lansfield. If I had a sister, you're the only one on the team I'd let date her. Is Maven going to be here tonight?"

"Yeah. She's out in the stands with our families. June is with her." I laugh and run my hand through my hair. "If you had asked me at the start of the season what I imagined my cheering section at the Super Bowl would look like, it definitely wouldn't have included them."

"Funny how things work out," Jett says. "You're happy, man, and it's about damn time."

"It doesn't seem real. It feels like I'm in some alternate reality where the girl of my dreams somehow falls for me and we live happily ever after. I want to win tonight for her."

"Course you do. Just don't show off too much, okay? Save some glory for the rest of us," he teases.

"Yeah, because the one hundred million people watching tonight are really going to look at *me* and say, gosh, I want to be just like him when I grow up. No way, man. Not when they see you play," I say.

"Are you two done flirting with each other?" Odell throws an arm over both of our shoulders. "It's time to head to the field."

"You're just jealous no one wants to flirt with you," Jett says, and he shrugs off the defensive lineman's embrace. "Let's do this, boys."

"Y'all go ahead," I tell them, and I grab my phone. "I'll be there in a second."

I pull up my text thread with Maven and type out a quick message.

ME

About to take the field.

Her response comes right away.

MAVEN

Are you allowed to be texting me right now?

ME

When it comes to you, I've never really given a fuck about the rules.

MAVEN

I like when you get possessive.

ME

How are the seats?

MAVEN

Incredible. We're right in the front row. You'll be able to see us when you're on the field.

ME

I don't know if that's a good thing or a bad thing. You're going to distract me all night.

MAVEN

Is now the time to tell you I'm wearing Justin's jersey instead of yours?

ME

I'll have no problem ripping it off of you.

MAVEN

Don't tempt me with a good time.

ME

I love you.

MAVEN

I love you too. We're so proud of you.

I shove my phone in my bag. Before I head for the tunnel, I check my reflection in the mirror hanging from my locker. My eyes flick to the photo I taped up, and I smile.

It's one of me, Maven and June during a blizzard three weeks ago. We're hardly noticeable through the sheet of snow, but I can make out three smiles. Crinkled eyes from laughing our asses off and Maven's hair blowing everywhere.

I pull it off the wood and fold it up, small enough so it'll fit in the waistband of my pants. I want to take them out there with me today.

New Orleans is buzzing with energy when I run onto the field. Fans from both Kansas City and D.C. made the trek to the Big Easy for the game, and it's electric in here. I scan the crowd and try to find the section Maven and June are in before I give up and ask one of the security guards for help.

"Hey, man," I say. "I'm looking for section 110."

"Right behind your bench," he answers, and he points to a line of seats. "Best view in the house."

I start heading over but only make it a few feet before I'm stopped for a picture then an interview. It takes me fifteen minutes to get ten yards. When I finally break free from the chaos, blonde hair and a smile that makes me weak in the knees is waiting for me on the other side.

I light up when I see her. My walk turns into a run, and the next thing I know I'm in an all-out sprint, desperate to see her.

"Hey," she calls out as I get close, and she picks up June so she can see me. "Look who it is."

"There are my girls. Come here, JB," I say, and Maven passes her carefully over the railing to me.

"Daddy!" she squeals and kisses my cheek. "Time for football?"

"Almost, Bug. How are y'all doing?"

"Good. Mae Mae got me ice cream!"

My eyes meet Maven's, and she's giving me a guilty smile. "Of course she did. Hi, baby."

"Hi, sweetheart." Maven leans over the metal ledge and I hold the back of her head so I can kiss her. "How are you feeling?"

"Good. I'm about to play some football. I have all my favorite people here." I look down the line of folks and wave to Maggie, Aiden and Lacey. "I'm really freaking happy."

"Your sister and Lilah went to get food, but they'll be back soon. Hopefully you can see them before kickoff," she says.

"I really wish y'all let me buy you a suite. You'd be so much more comfortable."

"It's not about being comfortable. Down here with the fans is where all the fun is. No way I'm going to miss that."

My eyes catch on her white top. "Is that a new Titans jersey, Mae?"

"It is. Want to see the best part? It's custom-made." She turns around, and I see **Daddy Dallas** across the back. "June's says Daddy, so I thought I should match."

I burst out laughing and stand as tall as I can, tracing the stitching with my thumb. "You're such trouble."

"You like it." Maven turns back around and takes my hand in hers. "I'm so proud of you."

"Hey, Dallas. Can we not take this game to another last second touchdown like a couple years ago?" Maggie calls out. "It would be great if my blood pressure didn't go up."

"I'll do my best. Just for y'all." I give June a kiss and snuggle her to my chest before handing her back to Maven. "I should go before Shawn starts yelling at me about fraternization."

"The audacity." Maven grins. "We'll be cheering loud for you."

"I know you will be. Oh. I have this for you." I pull out the postcard I wrote to her on the drive over from the hotel and hand it to her. "For the pile."

"What does this one say?"

"Probably something stupid about how much I love you and how I can't wait to spend the rest of our lives together."

"Yuck." Maven sticks out her tongue. "Disgusting."

"Seriously. It makes me sick," I agree.

She lifts her chin toward the field. "Go on. You know where we'll be."

"I'm so glad you're here," I say. "Eighty thousand people are going to be cheering tonight, but I only care about the two in front of me."

"Well." She makes a heart with her hands and I smile like a maniac. "Be careful, please. We want to take you home in one piece."

"But what about the nurse costume idea?"

"Go away," she laughs, and I blow her a kiss. "I love you," she adds as I jog away.

We could lose by thirty, and I know I'd walk out of this stadium the happiest motherfucker in the world.

"WHAT THE FUCK is going on with this field?" Shawn yells, and he throws his headset on the ground. "How do we have another player injured? Is this fucking grass cursed? Does someone have a goddamn voodoo doll?"

"I can't see. Who is it?" I hop off the bench and stand next to him. "It's not Jett, is it?"

"Another running back, which makes four down tonight. This is impossible to watch."

I check the scoreboard. We're losing by five with just under ninety seconds to go, and it's so similar to the position we found ourselves in a few years ago.

Our backs are against the wall. The clock is not on our side and guys are dropping like flies. Hope is slowly slipping out of our fingers, and everyone knows it. We have to score a touchdown, or the game is over.

Kansas City has been brutal to our offense, and points have been nearly impossible to come by. The only reason we're still in this is because our defense has been just as tough, limiting their offense to fourteen points against our nine.

"What's the plan?" I ask, and I put my hands on my hips.

"There is no plan," Shawn says. "I'm out of options. We're already on our back up's back up."

I stare at my teammates. They look battered and bruised, and I've been sitting here doing jack shit when I could be helping. I can't stay on the sidelines while they give their heart and soul. It's not fair.

"I have an idea," I say slowly, and Shawn looks at me. "I'll go in."

"What do you mean you'll go in? We're seventy yards away. Not even your foot is that good, Lansfield, and it won't win us the game."

"I'll go in at RB. I'll take Kenny's spot."

He stares at me. "You're fucking joking."

"Dead fucking serious. You know I used to play that position, and I was *good*. I've seen the routes. I've studied them a hundred times. Jett and I have been through them after practice when he feels like he hasn't been throwing well."

"Do I need to remind you what happened earlier this season when you got tackled?" Shawn asks. "You lost consciousness. Got taken to the hospital in an ambulance and entered concussion protocol."

"Yeah, because of a cheap shot," I say fiercely. "I was caught off guard. That's not going to happen today."

He rubs his jaw and his eyes flick back to the field. The training staff is still attending Kenny's injury, and it doesn't look good.

"What about your leg?"

"What about it?" I ask.

"If you tear your ACL again, you're done. Next year is gone."

"Fuck next year, man. I care about right here, right now. And if this is it for me, then so be it. I have everything I want, but I'm not letting my teammates go down without helping to at least give them a shot."

"You're out of your mind." Shawn laughs and scoops up his headset. "Out of your goddamn mind."

"Maybe." I shrug and start stretching my hips. "But what other choice do you have? Donny Deluca who hasn't played a single game all year?"

"Christ. Okay. I need to talk to the folks upstairs."

"Talk away. You know where I'll be."

"You aren't doing this hero shit to impress anyone, are you?"

I snort. "You mean Maven? She doesn't care if I play or not. Come on, Coach. Let me be useful."

He speaks into his microphone and nods along to whatever is being said in his ear. "Bill gave me the okay. Don't try anything stupid, Lansfield."

"No promises." I grin and grab my helmet, taking off for the huddle.

"What are you doing here?" Jett asks when I squeeze in next to him.

"RB," I say, and his eyes widen.

"Really?"

"Yeah. Might as well spice things up. It can't get worse, can it?"

"Holy hell." He clasps my shoulder. "I've got your back, Cap."

"I've got yours too, QB. Let's win this fucking thing."

FIFTY-TWO
MAVEN

I WATCH Kenny Jenkins hobble off the field, and I groan.

"That's like our fifth guy to be injured tonight," I say to Dallas's sister, January. "Is there even anyone left on the bench who can play?"

"I think at this point, anybody that can just stand on the field long enough to knock out a defender is best." She sighs and kicks her feet up on the railing. "Oh well. It was a good game. It sucks the only thing people are going to remember about it are the—what the *hell* is he doing?"

"Who?" I ask. I lean around June to see what's going on and my heart sinks to my stomach. "Is that—"

"Dallas? It sure as shit is." January jumps up, and everyone around us begins to stand. They can sense something is happening, and my pulse quickens.

"He's not kicking, is he? They're on the opposite end of the field." I stand, too, and hold June on my hip. "That would be impossible, and it wouldn't win them the game."

"He's not kicking. He's going in as a running back."

"*What*? Is he out of his goddamn mind? Sorry, June Bug, don't listen to me right now, I'm mad. He had a concussion earlier this season. He ended up in the hospital, for god's sake, and I thought he was *dead*," I say.

He's lucky he's so far away from me, because if he was close enough to hear, I'd be giving him a fucking earful right now. All the excitement I was holding onto washes away, and now I just feel nauseous as hell.

"That's Dallas for you." January takes my free hand and squeezes. It does little to calm my nerves, and my palm gets clammy around her fingers. "You know he wouldn't let his team-mates go down without trying to help."

"Yeah, but how much is he helping if he gets hurt again?"

"Is Daddy okay?" June asks, and she looks up at me, worried.

I forgot that kids feed off of an adult's emotions, and I take a deep breath, trying to steady myself for her sake. If something happens to him and she's here to see it, I need to be brave.

"He's just fine, sweetie," I say, and I kiss her forehead. "I promise."

The refs blow the whistle to end the injury timeout, and I'm tempted to cover my eyes. Dallas is like a magnet, though. I can't look away, even if I try.

I'm drawn to him as I watch him and Jett exchange some words and a quick hug before they confer with the rest of the offense and get on the line of scrimmage.

Dallas marches to the right side of the field like he knows exactly what he's doing. I guess he does; sometimes I'll catch him watching video after video of old game footage. He jots down notes about play calls that will never affect him, and I can see his dedication to the game in the thoroughness of his research.

The ball gets snapped, and Jett steps out of the pocket. He looks left and spots Sam down field. He throws the ball for a completion that's good for twenty yards.

The clock stops and the play moves forward as hope creeps

back into Titans fans. For half a second, I think the game can go on without Dallas having to touch the ball at all. He's there as an eleventh man, a diversion, not an actual offensive piece to use.

Except when the ball gets snapped on the next first down and Jett looks right, I hold my breath.

He finds Dallas open on the forty-yard line and throws a perfect spiral his way. Dallas catches it—awkwardly, but it's still a catch—and steps out of bounds to stop the clock before he can get tackled.

"He looks like a giraffe learning to walk," January says, and a laugh bursts out of me.

"If I wasn't so worried, I'd give him crap about how he's acting like he's never been on a field before. He was that good before he got hurt?" I ask.

"Oh, yeah. Scouts lined up at the start of his freshman year in high school, and they kept coming. He was approached by some of the biggest names in college football, but he decided on a smaller school because it was closer to home. On a full ride, too. He was—is—incredible, but that was twelve years ago. His body has changed, and I have no idea how he's going to handle this kind of intensity."

I hold June close to my chest—as if the nearer she is to me, the smoother the next play will go. The Titans snap it again, and the clock dips under one minute left in regulation.

The roar of the crowd only grows as our boys charge down the field and take it play by play. There's no rushing, and Jett doesn't look the least bit frantic even as precious seconds tick by. He's totally in his element.

At third and eight with forty seconds left, Jett throws the ball fifteen yards down the field to a waiting Dallas.

He catches it and takes off, using speed I've never seen from him before.

It's beautiful, like poetry in motion. His movements are fluid.

His body anticipates the defense before they can react. It's effortless, and he makes it to the ten-yard line to earn a first and goal before being taken down by a Kansas City lineman.

I wait for him to get up, and when he springs to his feet and shrugs off the attention from medical staff, I finally relax and let myself enjoy.

"Go, Daddy!" June screams, and I bounce her up and down.

"There's no way they're doing this, is there?" I shout to January.

"I think they are," she shouts back.

The next two plays get them nowhere. There's a loss of two yards then a gain of one. On third and long with ten seconds to go, the hope that worked its way into the dome seems like it's slipping away for good.

Dallas, Jett and Sam Wagner stand off to the side, away from the huddle. Dallas is using his hands to explain something to the other two, and they nod along. They knock their helmets together and rejoin the line of scrimmage, and it all comes down to this.

The whistle blows for the final time and the Titans wait to snap the ball. When they do, Jett catches it and immediately throws a lateral pass to Dallas. Dallas moves forward two yards before tossing a lateral to Sam.

Everyone on the Kansas City defense is confused and thrown off by the trick play. They get to Jett then Dallas a beat too late, and Sam uses it to his advantage.

He takes off. His long legs get him past the five-yard line, then the four and three. He crosses the goal line just as the clock expires, and he spikes the ball in the end zone.

Everyone around us screams and the Titans players rush the field. Confetti falls from the ceiling, and it's so loud, I can't hear myself think.

"Holy shit!" January screams, and she jumps up and down. "They did it!"

"Did Daddy win?" June asks, and she screams, too.

"Daddy won," I say, and I bury my face in her hair. "Daddy did it."

Reporters try to shove their way past security, and I've never seen so many cameras in my life. Around me, the fans celebrate with hugs. My ears ring and I grin, watching the elation play out.

"Maven," someone yells from below me, and I look down to find Dallas under the railing. "Get down here, baby."

"I have June!" I yell back.

"Give her to me," he says, and he lifts his arms. I hand her over, and he spins her around like an airplane when he has her safely in his hold. "Climb over and jump."

"These pants are not made for jumping." I laugh and point to the leather that feels like it's painted on my body. "If they rip and I show off my ass to the world, I'm blaming you, Lansfield."

"A risk I'm willing to take. Aiden—" he yells, and my dad looks our way. "Can you help her over?"

My dad goes into protective dad mode. He helps me navigate the ledge, not letting go of my arm until I'm on the other side. As soon as my feet hit the ground, Dallas is kissing me everywhere his lips can reach. I'm crying—I don't know when I started to cry, just that I am—and his sweat-soaked jersey sticks to my skin.

"You did it," I say into his neck. "Holy shit, Dallas. You did it."

"Champions!" June yells, and I laugh.

"I couldn't have done it without you," Dallas says, and when I pull away to look down at him, his eyes are watery, too. "God, Maven. You've made this whole thing possible. This season. This win. This ring is yours, not mine, baby."

"No. No way. You—Dallas. You played running back."

"I know." He grins. "It felt so good to be out there again on offense. I haven't had that much fun in a game since college."

"Does anything hurt? How's your leg? And your head?"

"Fine and fine. I can't believe y'all were here to see that."

He holds my hand. We walk toward the celebrations, and he accepts a hat from someone. He puts it on backwards and I almost moan at how delicious he looks with his smudged eye paint and the red on his cheeks.

"As if we'd be anywhere else." I kiss him again, and June squeals. "That was insane in the best possible way. You almost gave me a heart attack when you took the field, but look how it ended up."

"I know. I couldn't let my boys go through this alone. I knew there was no way I'd make it worse, and if I got hurt, then so be it." He grins down at me. "Shawn told me to knock off the hero shit."

"You *do* need to knock off the hero shit," I agree.

"Shit!" June says, and Dallas and I sigh in unison

"We really need to be better about that," he says, and I nod. "She's going to be expelled from kindergarten with that mouth."

He gets swept into interviews and media coverage but keeps me by his side like he's showing me off. When a reporter asks who I am, he turns to look at me, and with the dopiest grin on his face he tells her, "This is Maven. A phenomenal photographer, my best friend, and the love of my life."

It makes me cry again.

We watch Jett win MVP, and he pulls Dallas on stage with him after he accepts the trophy. The whole time they speak and congratulate their team, I'm hit with the overwhelming sensation of how much I love that man.

I know we've said it dozens of times now, and millions more have yet to come, but I still feel that swoop in my stomach when he looks at me. I feel it in the way his eyes find mine over the throngs of people who want to celebrate him.

It's especially noticeable when he politely bows out of a conversation with someone important the second June falls asleep against me. He takes my hand in his and leads us toward the locker room.

"Don't you want to stay?" I ask. "I'm sure all the guys are going out, aren't they?"

"Why would I want to go out when I have everything I need right here?" He reaches into the waistband of his pants, and I lift an eyebrow.

"I don't think this is the time or place to take your dick out, Lansfield."

"Shut up, you menace." He laughs and pulls out a small folded piece of paper. It's wrinkled, and the corners are ripping. "If someone asked why I played, or why I wanted to get out of here early, or why I'm so goddamn happy, I'd show them this."

"What is it?" I ask, and he opens it so I can see the picture. "*Oh.*"

"That's why I hung that picture of us in my locker. That's why I had this with me all night. Whenever I thought about my why, I thought about you and June. Who knows when I'll retire. Maybe it'll be next year. Maybe it will be in five years from now. Until then, you are what keeps the fire going, Maven, and I have a feeling we're just getting started."

I bite my bottom lip and tug on his arm. I stand on my toes and kiss him long and slow. He hums against my mouth, and I laugh when he traces the letters on the back of my jersey.

"I love you," I say when I pull away, needing to come up for air. "I will always love you."

"And I'll love you right back." Dallas breaks out into a smile, and he lifts his chin. "You feel like celebrating with me tonight, Mae?"

"That depends. What's on the agenda, Lansfield?"

"You. Me. June. A hotel bed and a massive fucking pizza until our stomachs hurt."

"And then?" I ask.

"Ice cream, probably, if you two have anything to say about it. But after that?" He shrugs and brings his hand to his mouth. He kisses my knuckles and his eyes meet mine. "I was thinking we lose our minds a little bit. Maybe for the next sixty years. We could buy a house. Have a couple kids. Throw a wedding in there, eventually. What do you think?"

"I think that sounds like the stupidest idea in the world." I grin. "Let's do it."

EPILOGUE

Maven

Nineteen months later

"ARE YOU NERVOUS?"

I look up from tying my cleats and find Isabella smiling at me.

"Terrified," I admit. "But that's part of the fun, right?"

"It's all of the fun." She flings her arm around my shoulder and squeezes tight. The hug centers me. It helps me relax and take my first deep breath of the day. "You look good, Mae. I forgot how well you rock a pair of shin guards."

I beam and adjust my athletic shorts, pulling the drawstrings tight. "Thank you for being here. I need all the emotional support I can get."

"I'm so proud of you, but we should get going."

"The game doesn't start for almost an hour," I say, and I level her with a suspicious look. "What's the hurry?"

"Can you stop asking questions for six seconds and just head to the field, please?"

I give the soccer ball at my feet a soft kick and follow behind it. "What are you hiding?"

"I'm not hiding a damn thing." She opens the door and nudges me forward. "I just want to make sure you have plenty of time to warm up."

I laugh and step outside. The temperature is still warm and humidity hangs in the air. I savor it for a second. I relish in how good it feels to be stretching my legs and heading toward something I'm excited about.

"You're so bad at keeping secrets," I say. "But so am I, which is why I should tell you I have a ticket saved under your name for the Stars preseason game tomorrow night. I hope you'll come. It's a sellout, and I had to pawn off my kidney to get you a seat."

"You bet your ass I'll come." Isabella sighs dreamily and falls in step beside me. "I still can't believe you get to photograph the hockey boys."

"And hockey girl. She's incredible, but I prefer kickers." I bite my bottom lip and sigh. "I wish Dallas was here. I wish the weather in Phoenix wasn't shitty so they could've taken off last night, not late this morning."

"I know you do," she says gently. "I told him I'd record the whole thing. So he didn't miss out."

"Thank you." I take her hand in mine. "You aren't allowed to laugh when I'm slower on the field than I used to be, okay?"

"Who am I to judge? The best part about being a coach is not having to participate in workouts."

A smile tugs at my lips as I stare out at the field a hundred yards away. There's a soft pull, a yank that draws me closer to the center circle and corner mark.

So much has changed since the last time I dressed for a game, but it feels like so much has stayed the same.

I nailed the interview with the D.C. Stars hockey team as their new in-game photographer. They might have a losing record and play four times as many home games as the Titans do, but I still get to do what I love: take photos of incredible athletes doing incredible physical feats.

The friend of a friend of one of the players said they were looking for people to join their recreational soccer league, a coed team with games once a week until winter.

The stakes were low—no pressure. No extra training. A fun, laidback environment with a group of people who just want ninety minutes of exercise and some fresh air.

I felt comfortable enough with my mobility to agree to be their eleventh player, and now I'm about to take the field for the first time in years.

I'm so fucking happy.

I just wish Dallas and June were here so I could share my excitement with them.

He took her to Denver for their preseason game. She's older and travels like a pro, so she gets to go with her dad more often these days. If I can't join them because of work, Lacey takes my spot, playing babysitter while Dallas is on the field.

I miss them when they're gone, but they always come home with stories and a postcard for me. It's a scribbled mess of words, a letter he writes on the plane or when he slips into his car.

They're all in a box in our closet, a pile of love notes where he tells me how much he cares about me. How much I mean to him, and how lucky he is to be mine.

I wonder how many there will be in five, ten years. When he hangs up his cleats and comes home for good, done with the game and ready to move to the next stage of life.

I love him, too, and every day I see him, I love him a little more.

I still get that giddy feeling when I'm with him. When he pulls me close and kisses me like we might die tomorrow, a swarm of butterflies flutter in my stomach. It's like my feet are off the ground and I'm swept away, caught up in him.

He pushes me to work harder and to never give up. It's why I'm standing here, the familiar itch of the shin guards on my legs and the breeze in my hair. If it weren't for his gentle encouragement, I never would've tried.

"I'm doing this," I say.

The wind scoops it up and releases it out into the universe, and I stand taller.

Dallas was right.

Dreams do change. It might not be the Olympics. It might not be the World Cup. There might not be twenty thousand spectators, but it's exactly where I need to be.

"Ready?" Isabella asks, and I nod.

"Ready," I say.

Elation practically bursts out of me as I jog onto the field. One of my teammates, Avery, looks up from her phone and waves.

She's the most badass woman I've ever met. The head of the Thunderhawks' social media, she's taken the sports world by storm. The only time I've seen her put her phone down is the one-hour practice we have during the week. Otherwise, it's practically glued to her body.

I haven't told Reid I've met his archnemesis yet. I think he might kill me when he finds out.

"Hey, Mae," she says when I approach her. "How're you feeling?"

"Good." I smile because it's the truth. The air tastes sweet in my lungs. My legs feel light. Everything about the moment feels almost perfect. "I'm really good."

"That makes me so happy. Where's your cheer squad? I'm excited to meet Dallas."

"Their flight canceled in Phoenix last night because of the bad weather. They're on their way to D.C. now, but they won't land in time to spectate."

"I'm sorry. I know how much you were looking forward to today."

"Flexibility is required when you're dating a professional athlete. Hopefully there will be plenty more games for him to see."

"There definitely will be." Avery smiles. "Want to warm up? I'm afraid I'm going to forget everything you taught me about playing defense."

"Stop." I laugh and kick the ball to her. "You're going to be just fine."

"I hope so. I can't make a fool of myself in front of the Big East player of the year," she says, and I blush. "I watched your highlights, Maven. You're so good."

"Was. I was good," I say, correcting her.

"That badass woman is still in there. I can tell."

"Thanks, Ave. If you want to practice defense, I'll come up the field and—"

The sound of a helicopter drowns me out. It gets progressively louder, and I look over my shoulder, shocked to find the chopper descending on the adjacent field.

Grass goes everywhere. The corner flags whip around. The ground vibrates under my feet. Both teams crowd together and try to figure out what's going on.

The glare of the sun makes it almost impossible to see. I can make out the door opening and a figure jumping out, but I have no clue who it might be.

"This is weird, right?" Avery yells, and I nod.

"Yeah. I wonder if it's a training exercise or something," I yell back, and I shield my eyes.

A man jogs toward us. His long legs cover the distance between the two fields in a matter of seconds. My breath catches in my throat when I realize who it is.

I know that body.

I know how those arms feel when they wrap me in a tight hug.

I know how those hands feel when they run up my thigh.

Seconds pass, and then he's right in front of me, inches away. His hair is a mess and his shirt is wrinkled, but his smile is dazzling.

Dallas.

"Hey, sunshine," he yells, and I stare at him, bewildered.

"What are—aren't you supposed to be on a plane?" I sputter, and his smile stretches wider. It crinkles the corners of his eyes and scrunches his nose, and I've never seen a more beautiful sight. "How—why—"

"I was on a plane. Until fifteen minutes ago. I bought tickets on an earlier flight then arranged a helicopter to bring me to the field because I knew traffic on a Monday afternoon was going to be fucking horrific."

"*What?* Why would you do that?"

"Because, Maven." Dallas steps closer. Our toes touch, and he cups my cheeks with both of his hands. "There's no way in hell I was going to miss my girl's first game."

My throat feels like it's closing up. I can't get a good breath to stop my lungs from seizing. My eyes sting and my bottom lip quivers. I think I'm dangerously close to falling apart.

"You did this for me?" I whisper.

He tips my chin back. His thumb drags across my bottom lip. "I would move mountains for you, honey. I told you I'd be here, and I am."

My heart splits in two. Cracks straight down the center because I love this man so much, it hurts.

"I didn't mean you had to pay for a helicopter ride just to be here," I say, and I grab a fistful of his shirt. "How expensive was that?"

"Who cares? What's the point of having a shit ton of money if I don't use it on a worthy cause? You know I'd spend more than that just to be by your side."

"Aren't you exhausted? Where's June? Shawn let you ditch the team?"

"Who do you think suggested the helicopter?" Dallas asks, and he steps to the side so I can see the other people heading toward me.

There's Shawn, holding June in his arms and nodding along to the story she's telling.

Lacey is next, one hand in Maggie's and the other holding a big poster board that looks like it has a hundred signatures on it.

My dad follows them, wiping his eyes and getting teased by my mom, who walks beside him with her partner.

Maverick and Reid bring up the rear, talking animatedly about something.

"Everyone showed up," I say. "Everyone's here."

"Of course they are." He wipes a tear away from my cheek and kisses my forehead. His lips are warm on my skin, and I melt into him. "We're always going to show up for you, Mae. The rest of the boys wanted to be here, but it didn't work out logistically. They all signed the poster to celebrate your big day, though. I figured we could frame it and put it next to the ticket from June's first football game."

"I love you a ridiculous amount." I drape my arms around his neck. My thumb runs along the gold necklace he still wears. He added a J to the chain too. The two letters sit in the column of his throat, not far from his heart. "I'm so glad you're here."

"There's nowhere I'd rather be."

"Mommy!" June yells. Shawn sets her down, and she runs toward us. "Were you surprised?"

There was a moment of panic when June started calling me Mom.

It felt like I was stealing the role from someone else, earning a rank I didn't deserve. Then Dallas told me there's no one else he'd ever let have that title.

It was always meant for me.

We haven't looked back.

"I was so surprised, June Bug. Was the helicopter fun?"

"I want to ride in it again," she exclaims, and I laugh.

"I think you might have created a monster, Dal," I say.

"The price I'll pay to make my girls happy." He lifts June and holds her against his hip. His arm loops around my waist and his palm settles on the small of my back. "Have I told you how proud I am of you today?"

"You did. Several times from thirty six thousand feet in the air."

"Doesn't count. I have to say it again. I'm so proud of you, Mae. For getting back on the soccer field. For succeeding in your career. For building a brand and finding yourself. I love you so much, and I'm honored to stand by your side."

"Hey. Keep the PDA down over there, Lansfield," Shawn says, and he runs a hand through his graying hair. "No one wants to see that."

I move toward the rest of the group. I hug my mom and dad and let them squeeze me tight. They tell me they're proud of me, too, and I cry again.

The waterworks start to flood as the hug turns into a group piling of Maggie, then Lacey and Shawn. Soon, Maverick, Reid and Isabella join the mix, and I'm surrounded by all of my favorite people.

"Thank you all for being here," I say, and my voice is muffled in someone's shirt. "It's such a silly thing to be excited about when you've been to so many other important events, but—"

"It's something you love, Mae," my dad says. "It's never silly."

"Right." I laugh and wiggle free from their embraces. "I should probably get back to my teammates. I don't want to be kicked off the squad before I even play. Can we all get together after?"

"Lacey made a cake," Maggie says, and she rests her head on my dad's shoulder. "If you want to come back to our place."

"I'd love to." I put my hand over my chest and head toward my team. "I love you all so much."

"We love you too, hot stuff," Lacey calls out, and Shawn shakes his head.

"Hey." Dallas grabs my wrist, and he tugs me to his chest. "I have something for you."

"Is it my postcard?" I ask, and I grin up at him. "They're the only reason why I don't mind you being gone."

He shifts June around and reaches into the back pocket of his jeans. He hands me the paper and bends down to kiss me. "I hope you like it. It's probably my favorite one yet."

"I have no doubt I will, lone star," I say against his mouth. "I love you."

"I love you too, sunshine. Go kick some ass out there."

"Daddy said ass," June repeats, and Dallas sighs, defeated.

I laugh and almost skip back to the field as happiness surges through me. I glance down at the note from Dallas, and time stops.

M-

Remember that time I said I was going to give you

my last name and put a shiny ring on your finger? And you told me I'd never?

I always follow through.

Turn around.

-D

COMING SOON

Looking for more of my books?

Stay tuned for the rest of the books in the **Love Through a Lens** series, coming later this year!
Off Camera (Reid's book) — July 27
Camera Shy — October 19

Also coming soon is book one in the **D.C. Stars** series, a hockey romance!
Face Off (Maverick's book) — May 30

ACKNOWLEDGMENTS

Acknowledgements are such a weird part of the book writing process. I can churn out 124,000 words about people kissing, but this part is difficult.

First, my appreciation for you, dear reader. Thank you for taking the time out of your life to read Maven and Dallas's story. I hope you loved them like I love them. If you did, I'd be grateful if you left a review on Amazon or Goodreads. Positive reviews do wonders for indie authors like myself.

Thank you, Kristen, for working with my insane timeline (again). Thank you for helping me come up with a schedule going forward.

Thank you to my beta readers: Shay, Megan, Linna, Amanda, Katelin, Katie, Sammie, Kae, Dani, Addy, Kristen and Megan. Your feedback was truly instrumental in making this book what it is.

To my MFers, Amanda, Katelin, Haley and baby Andi: I love y'all. None of these stories exist with you. Thank you for believing in me, and thank you for being here from day one. I love you so much.

Thank you, Sam (@inkandlaurel) for another wonderful cover!

Thank you, Ellie (@lovenotespr) for your magical powers. You work so hard, and I so appreciate all you do.

To my Mikey and Riley: I love you. Thank you for being my happily ever after.

And, finally, to the book community. This is book number

seven for me, and the more I write, the more fun I have. This is possible because of you, though. Thank you for every review, every post, every tag and every comment. All of your kindness and enthusiasm for my work fuels me forward, and I know the best is yet to come.

ABOUT THE AUTHOR

Chelsea Curto is a flight attendant who lives in the Northeast with her partner and their dog. When she's not busy writing, she loves to read, travel, go to theme parks, run, eat tacos and hang out with friends.

Come say hi on social media!

instagram.com/authorchelseacurto

tiktok.com/@chelseareadsandwrites

amazon.com/author/chelseacurto

ALSO BY CHELSEA CURTO

Love Through a Lens series

Camera Chemistry

Caught on Camera

Behind the Camera

Off Camera

Camera Shy

D.C. Stars series

Face Off

Boston series

An Unexpected Paradise

The Companion Project

Road Trip to Forever

Park Cove series

Booked for the Holidays

Made in the USA
Columbia, SC
02 June 2024

36533264R00251